Rebel Bitten

D1727229

USA Today Bestselling Author
Lexi C. Foss

This is a work of fiction. Names, characters, places, and incidents are either the product of the author's imagination or are used fictitiously, and any resemblance to actual persons, living or dead, business establishments, events, or locales is entirely coincidental.

Rebel Bitten

Copyright © 2020 Lexi C. Foss

All rights reserved.

No part of this book may be reproduced in any form or by any electronic or mechanical means, including information storage and retrieval systems, without written permission from the author, except for the use of brief quotations in a book review. This book may not be redistributed to others for commercial or noncommercial purposes.

Editing by: Outthink Editing, LLC

Proofreading by: Katie Schmahl, Jean Bachen, & Julie Robertson

Cover Design: Covers by Julie

Cover Photography: Eric Battershell Photography

Cover Model: Johnny Kane

Published by: Ninja Newt Publishing, LLC

Print Edition

ISBN: 978-1-950694-71-6

"ARE YOU FLIRTING WITH DEATH, SWEETHEART?" Ryder asked me, his eyebrow arching.

His dark eyes held a note of amusement in them that didn't match the threat of his hand around my throat. Perhaps this entertained him—my weakness and impending death. Typical vampire.

It made me want to defy him, not by withholding my name but by giving one, to show him I'd been living in a world of defiance for years. That his oppression meant shit to me. That I would overcome this, even if it required my death.

"Willow," I mouthed at him, the lack of air making it impossible to add sound.

His gaze dropped to my lips. "Say that again."

"Willow," I repeated, then gasped violently as he loosened his grip on my throat.

"One more time," he demanded.

"Willow." It came out on a rasp, my lungs burning as much-needed oxygen poured down my abused airway.

"Willow," he said as if tasting the name. "Yes, I like that."

He drew his thumb across the pulse point of my neck, his body solid and hard against mine.

"What will I do with you?" he mused, his gaze dropping to where my breasts met his chest. His pupils flared, as did his nostrils as he inhaled my scent.

I swallowed, my throat raw.

"You intrigue me, pet," he finally said after a beat. "I suggest you continue to do so. It's the only reason you're still alive."

I didn't know what to say. How to react. Where to even look. So I just continued to stare into his fathomless eyes, those dark, hypnotic orbs giving nothing away.

Age and experience poured off him in waves.

This vampire was old. Lethal. A royal. And he claimed that I intrigued him. What the hell was I supposed to do with that information?

Blood Alliance Series

Chastely Bitten

Royally Bitten

Regally Bitten

Rebel Bitten

To Tracey, for your friendship and for always making me smile.
Your Jace is next. <3
And to Wendy, I hope I did your Ryder justice. ;)

REBEL BITTEN

Book Four

A NOTE FROM THE AUTHOR

Dear Reader,

Thank you for joining me on this journey through the future. It's dark and depraved and so much fun to play in. Willow and Ryder's story was actually the first one in my mind when I started the Blood Alliance world, but as I learned more about them, I realized they couldn't lead the series.

Why?

Because Ryder is terrifying. He's unapologetically sadistic, lacks all semblance of humanity, and is not a man I'd ever want to piss off. He's the epitome of vampire, a monster of the night who sees humans more as food than beings. And that carries in his voice.

Yet somehow, he's exactly what Willow needs. He even makes me swoon at points.

I hope you enjoy their story. I would also love to hear what you think about Ryder and Willow when you're done, either in a review or via comments in my Facebook reader group!

Happy Reading! <3

Hugs,
Lexi

Ps. Join my newsletter for exclusive excerpts, release news, and more!

*O*nce upon a time,
humankind ruled the world while lycans and vampires
lived in secret.

*T*his is no longer that time.

*W*elcome to the future where the superior bloodlines
make the rules.

*P*ROCEED AT YOUR OWN RISK.

THE BLOOD ALLIANCE

International law supersedes all national governance and will be maintained by the Blood Alliance—a global council of equal parts lycan and vampire.

All resources are to be distributed evenly between lycan and vampire, including territory and blood slaves. Societal standing and wealth, however, will be at the discretion of the individual packs and houses.

To kill, harm, or provoke a superior being is punishable by immediate death. All disputes must be presented to the Blood Alliance for final judgment.

Sexual relationships between lycans and vampires are strictly prohibited. However, business partnerships, where fruitful and appropriate, are permitted.

Humans are hereby classified as property and do not carry any legal rights. Each will be tagged through a sorting system based on merit, intelligence, bloodline, ability, and beauty. Prioritization to be established at birth and finalized on Blood Day.

Twelve mortals per year will be selected to compete for immortal blood status at the discretion of the Blood Alliance. From this twelve, two will be bitten by immortality. The others will die. To create a lycan or vampire outside of this process is unlawful and punishable by immediate death.

All other laws are at the discretion of the packs and royals but must not defy the Blood Alliance.

A Warning From

Ryder

All right, here's the deal. I'm not a hero. I'm not a good guy. I'm not a prince. Well, technically, that last bit is a lie considering I'm sitting in as the temporary Royal of Silvano Region—soon to be renamed Ryder Region because, let's face it, that has a better ring to it.

Anyway, as I was saying, I'm not a knight in shining armor. If you want a pretentious hero type, go talk to Jace. I hear he's good at saving people.

I'm more practical. If someone stands in my way, I remove them. Permanently. If something amuses me, I play with it. Which brings me to the point of my story.

Willow.

Ah, Willow.

She's a gorgeous little thing. Sort of broken from her

time with the wolves, but I see the beauty in her fractured state. And I have no desire in improving on her imperfections. If anything, I wish to exploit them. Use them. Craft her into a shattered toy designed for my pleasure alone.

So if you're looking for a story with happiness and flowers, this isn't that book.

I'm a brutal man.

I've lived alone for over a century for a reason.

And I'm not a fan of the political bullshit plaguing immortal kind.

This world is dark. Humans are slaves. Vampires and lycans make the rules (because we're the superior species). It's been that way since the revolution a hundred and seventeen years ago, and there doesn't appear to be an end in sight.

Unless someone stands up and fights.

I doubt I'll be that man. But hey, the Blood Alliance is full of surprises. So let's dance, shall we?

Welcome to my mind.

It's a dangerous fucking place.

Don't say I didn't warn you. I did. And the proof of it is on this page.

Enjoy.

Chapter One

Willow

Pain.

So. Much. Pain.

I tried to move, to scream, to beg them to stop, but nothing worked. Not my lips. Not my throat. Not even my lungs. I was a prisoner in my own body, feeling every torturous assault as they ripped me in half.

The drugs numbed me enough to keep the concept of reality from fracturing my mind. Yet I felt every prod. Every dig of their claws. Each swipe of a tongue.

Something was very wrong.

They usually came at me one at a time, reeking of liquor and smoke.

But the stench of alcohol was different this time, the poking sharper and drawing blood.

"She's crashing," one of them said.

"No shit, asshole," another hissed.

"Fuck off," a third snapped. "Out. Now."

I tried to open my eyes, to see my aggressors, to figure out what had changed. They always kept me lucid enough to *feel* them, to force my unwilling participation through this wretched dance with fate.

Yet I was floating now.

High, high, high above the ground.

Mmm, that's good. A cloud of bliss and nothingness. So dark. So bleak. So *me*.

Electricity sizzled through my veins, forcing me back into awareness, my fate a dark blip on the horizon.

No. No. No.

I don't want to be here.

I don't want to see.

Please don't make me. Please!

Growls penetrated my ears, excruciating agony ripping through my insides. It was too much. My eyes flashed open, the startling light of the room flipping on a switch inside my mind. Blazing green irises grinned down at me, his feral enjoyment palpable and consuming.

Then silence fell, the only sound the beating of my own heart.

I glanced around, searching for the perpetrators and finding myself alone in a sea of blood-red and white.

The door hung open, illuminating a hallway of dusky stone.

Where am I? I wondered, swallowing and flinching at the sandpaper feel of my throat. *This isn't my cage.*

It reminded me of a physician's examination room, similar to the ones I'd visited monthly at the university. Had they just taken samples again?

No. I frowned. *I'm not at the university anymore. But where am I?*

Then my gaze fell to my abdomen, and a scream threatened to escape my mouth. I clamped a hand over my lips before I could release it, black dots dancing before my eyes at the gruesome display below.

Claw marks.

Bites.

Blood.

Oh, Goddess… They'd tried to *eat* me. *Fucking lycans!*

I wanted to slaughter them all.

Burn this entire world to the damn ground.

I should have been a Vigil. No, I should have gone to the Immortal Cup. Not to the breeding camps.

My stomach heaved as I leaned over to expel the contents onto the linoleum floor. Nothing came out, just acidic burn.

This place resembled the worst kind of nightmare, one I'd barely acknowledged for however long I'd been here because of the drugs.

But I was fully lucid now.

Why?

Had they left me here in this pool of gore to die?

Fuck. That. I hadn't survived this horrible existence just to meet my end on a table in some stark white lab.

The door, I thought, finding it again. *It's still open.*

Some part of me had expected it to close, for my mind to play an evil trick on me regarding a potential escape. Because there was no avoiding this life.

Humans were cattle.

Prey.

The bottom of the food chain.

Lycans and vampires ruled. They made the edicts. They chose our fates. They sent me *here*.

I hated them. Wanted to slaughter them all. A false fantasy, one I knew couldn't be done. They were too strong. Supernatural. *Immortal.* But a girl could dream, and dream I did.

That door, I thought again, stirring from the table. *Still. Open.*

It had to be a trick. A game. Perhaps the lycans had

decided to invite me into an infamous moon chase.

I shivered at the notion. *No, thank you.*

But what if I outran them?

My legs were okay.

Wouldn't dying with dignity be better than succumbing to fate on this table? I wondered, slightly delirious from the idea of running. It would exhaust me. Probably kill me. But that had to be better than being fucked to death.

Which was exactly what would happen if I remained here, in the custody of these lycans.

Breeding was the last thing I wanted.

They could create their own fucking wolves. My body was mine. Now and always.

Prove it, a dark voice in my mind whispered. *Run.*

And go where? I asked myself.

Anywhere is better than here.

I groaned, my stomach churning with a fresh wave of torment. I curled into a ball and immediately regretted it, my insides pulsating with wrongness.

I'm going to die, I realized, my blood suddenly on fire from the mental proclamation. *I'm going to die on this fucking table. In this fucking room. By my fucking self.*

A growl threatened my raw throat at the injustice of it all.

I had worked so hard for my position in this world. To be relegated to the breeding camp was a big slap in the face. That these animals had pummeled me into a pile of raw meat only grated on my nerves more.

No.

I was not going to die like this.

Not here.

I would at least see the sun one more time. Because screw the lycans. Screw all of this.

A scream caught in my throat as I forced myself to roll off the table onto my feet, but my knees locked, holding me up.

The bruises on my thighs throbbed with each step

toward the door, just as a sticky substance ran down my legs. *Blood. My blood.*

"Move," I breathed to myself. "Don't think. Just run." I barely recognized my voice. It was a rasp of sound, one the lycans probably heard. Only, the hallway was empty.

I didn't recognize this part of the compound. It had bare walls, more exam rooms, and very little else.

It reminded me of a hospital ward.

However, the one I'd visited at the university after an accident had a lot more movement. Silas had prodded me during a sparring exercise, his knife swiping too close to my ribs and creating a harsh gash. He'd felt horrible afterward, but I'd healed.

I glanced down. *Not sure I'll be healing from this.*

My palm was red, my fingers more inside me than out. The claw marks across my skin resembled grooves of hideous intent. I couldn't remember how they appeared, and I wasn't sure I wanted to.

No one stopped me as I reached the exit.

Alarms didn't sound as I pushed outside, where I was met by the moon and not the sun. I shivered, taking in the size. *Please don't be full.* If they'd released me just to chase me… *Oh, Goddess, no.* I'd fight them. I'd go down screaming. I no longer cared. I refused to be raped and used again. To be *bred.*

Fuck!

I started to move, adrenaline coursing through my system and sending me tumbling—

Down, down, down to the riverbank.

The world shifted as I rolled violently into the chilly water below. I wasn't even sure how I'd gotten this far, my memory of the last few minutes skipping through my mind.

This is death.

The final moments.

No. Keep. Running.

The stench reminded me of hell. Murky. Gross. Thick.

I cradled my stomach, the mud mingling with my

wounds.

Maybe it would deter the lycans from eating me later.

Run. Run. Run.

Everything was spinning. The world. My life. So much blood. I whirled around, startled by the light above, only to realize it was still the moon. Hysteria blinked into my mind, fracturing my thoughts for too brief a moment.

And still I ran.

Unsure of where to go.

Just run, run, run.

The warm air kept me alive, the water and mud a cocoon of disgrace coating my skin. This world was a nightmare. What had I done to deserve this fate? I'd studied hard. "I shouldn't be here," I mumbled to myself, again glancing around and finding nothing but trees, endless sky, and river.

My feet were numb.

Cut up.

Bruised.

All of me a twisted mess of tormented fate.

But the chant repeated. *Run. Run. Run.*

I couldn't give up. I just had no idea what I was running toward.

Until a voice echoed from above. I froze, the darkness in that tone sending a chill of foreboding down my spine. *The lycans. The moon chase. They're here. They've found me. They're going to eat me!*

I started to run, only to have my arm caught by an assailant. I swung with all my might, my training kicking in as a last resort.

Run, run, run, became, *Fight, fight, fight.*

I slammed my knee into his groin, his "Oomph" of surprise music to my ears. Then another tried to grab me from behind. I reacted, doubling down on my instincts, kicking, biting, snarling, screaming, and making myself the most unattractive prey imaginable. I'd make them kill me before I subjected myself to any more of this delirious torment.

Only, an elbow to the side of my head had me stumbling backward.

A masculine curse graced the air.

Followed by a series of stars dancing before my eyes.

As down, down, down I went.

This time into the muddy bank, not the water.

I hope they just let me drown, I thought as my world began to spin. *Just let me drown.*

Chapter Two

Ryder

I gaped at the tattered human drinking in mud as if it were oxygen at my feet. "What the fuck just happened?"

"Seems someone just lost a plaything," Damien drawled, folding his arms and narrowing his caramel-brown eyes.

Yeah, a plaything that nearly damaged my pride and joy with that cruel jerk to the groin. Had I not shifted my thigh at the right second, I'd have been knocked down to my knees—a feat no one had accomplished in centuries. Not even Damien.

The female sputtered, her consciousness wavering between life and death. Another minute in that position and she'd drown herself. Maybe even less. She wasn't in the best shape but had put up one hell of a fight. Not that Damien and I had been trying to harm her—we'd been too startled by her sudden appearance to muster up a reaction.

Yet she'd come at us like a damn hellcat, which I found oddly admirable. *Hmm.*

I glanced at Damien. "Anyway, as I was saying, Lilith has promoted me to temporary Royal of Silvano Region."

My best friend arched a dark brow at me. "Is that supposed to be a punishment?"

"I'm pretty sure it's more of a punishment for her than for me," I replied, amused. "What do you think? Should I keep Silvano Region as my own?"

"I suspect there will be a few who will be displeased by that decision."

"Which only makes it more appealing," I admitted as the mortal began to choke in earnest on the ground. "That's not a very attractive noise," I informed her.

"Should we just put it out of its misery?" Damien asked, following my gaze. "Seems a bit pitiful."

I cocked my head to the side, studying her. "She had a reasonable fight in her. I hear that's rare these days."

"It is," he replied. As Damien spent more time with current society than I did, I took his words to heart and squatted down beside the fragile female. Her gaze locked on mine, blue flames dancing in her irises.

So much anger.

Pain.

Retribution.

All emotions I understood far too well.

Her pupils flared as I reached for her, pushing her just enough to draw her mouth and nose away from the mud.

"Seems cruel to torture it," Damien pointed out.

"Yes, but I'm curious to see how long her fight survives." Something about her intrigued me. And it'd been a long time since I had found anything remotely interesting in this life. "Did I tell you Kylan took Silvano's head?" I asked Damien, my focus still on the sputtering female.

"That would have been a fascinating sight to witness."

"It was," I admitted. And yet, this human captivated me

more. Particularly as she scowled at me with adorable menace. "You really are a little warrior, aren't you?" I pushed her fully onto her back, then looked at Damien. "There's something strange going on with Kylan and Jace, by the way. I want to know what it is."

"Strange how?"

"They were getting along." I swiped a lock of muddied hair out of the woman's face, wanting to study her features. "And Kylan doesn't get along with anyone."

"I'll look into it."

"I'm going to need a survey of the region as well. A list of those who might oppose my leadership." I wasn't sure if I intended to remain as the royal or not, but having those details would certainly help me formulate an appropriate decision.

"Anything else?" Damien asked.

The female began to cough, her eyes losing their flare with each hacking vibration. "No," I told him. "I think that's all for now." My brow furrowed as I watched her life flicker in and out of existence.

Humans were so pitiful.

Broken.

Weak.

However, she'd tried to fight me. It'd be laughable if it weren't so sad. I ran my fingers through her matted blonde hair. *What would she have looked like in another reality?* I wondered idly, running the back of my knuckles down her cheek. "Dying beside the Sabine River," I said, shaking my head. "Not the burial place I'd choose."

Damien grunted. "Her body will be gone by morning. If it's not a wolf, a gator will take care of it."

"Hmm." I started to stand, when I saw a flicker of something in her gaze that held me still once more. *A golden shine. Like a wolf.* There and gone in a flash, but the warrior remained once more. Murder stared up at me. The promise of death. A seduction I couldn't ignore. "All right, little human." I slipped my arms beneath her, lifting her slight form with ease.

"What are you doing?" Damien asked, his nose curling at the stench wafting off the girl. "Do you plan to return her?"

"Why would I do that?" Seemed wasteful to give her back to the wolves. "I'm going to keep her."

"What? Why?"

I lifted a shoulder. "She's amusing."

"She's fucking dying."

"Yes," I agreed, staring down at her again. "Seems like a waste of blood, if you ask me."

Damien looked like he'd swallowed a toad. "You're a sick fuck, Ryder."

I'd never denied that. Actually, I rather owned up to the reputation. There was a reason I didn't play well with others. "Call me when you have the information I need," I told him as I started down the road near the riverbank.

"Try not to catch anything," he tossed back at me.

"She's a human, not a raccoon," I returned. Not that vampires could catch zoonotic diseases, or any others for that matter.

"Seems more like a rat," I heard him mutter before opening the door to his vehicle. He'd driven one of those four-by-fours out here, the kind that revved loudly. I had a few in my garage, most over a century old.

One of the perks of country living was having adequate storage space. I had more than enough resources to live out here for a few more centuries alone. The world had gone to shit a hundred and seventeen years ago when vampires and lycans took charge and demoted humans to the position of cattle.

I wanted none of it.

Did I agree that vampires and lycans were the superior species? Hell yes. We sat at the top of the food chain. But that didn't mean I fancied turning my prey into meek little rabbits. What fun was it to hunt a rodent when we used to chase tigers?

Seducing women into bed had been a fun pastime.

Now they just knelt like good little girls and sucked cock on autopilot.

Fuck. That.

I wanted to work for it. Make my conquest cry out for more, not just cry because it hurt. Well, I wasn't opposed to the latter, but I preferred it in combination with the former.

"What about you, little warrior?" I asked the female in my arms as I reached the edge of my driveway. "How do you take cock?"

Her eyes had rolled into the back of her head, making a reply impossible.

She was barely even breathing now.

I sighed. "It's just not fun anymore," I told her. "You mortals are all conditioned to bend over and take it. Which has its rewards and benefits, but it takes the excitement out of things."

I took the stairs up my porch two at a time, then kicked my door open with the heel of my boot.

The alarms I had rigged up didn't flare, my technology recognizing my body scan upon approach. I paused, listening for anything out of the ordinary, and found it all peaceful and quiet. Just the way I liked it.

I nearly smiled until I recalled the reason I'd left my sanctuary almost a week ago.

Fucking Silvano.

He'd waltzed through my backyard like a king, setting off every damn alarm along the way. I'd been so pissed that I'd followed him to Clemente Clan, just to see what he was up to.

When all hell broke loose, I'd stayed, somewhat amused by the fight.

A huge mistake—something I'd learned the second Lilith arrived. That bitch fancied herself a Goddess. "The only thing regal about Lilith is her ostentatious tower in Chicago," I muttered, heading down the stairs to my basement. "And that would look better as a pile of rubble."

The hierarchy of this world made no sense.

And now I was part of it.

Maybe Damien was right about the punishment being mine.

Well, I'd certainly make Lilith's life hell, too, just for fun.

It'd also been my idea to step up, mostly because I didn't want that bitch anywhere near my property.

Why did everyone worship her? She was just an ordinary vampire, and a younger one at that. At least when compared to me and Kylan. And Cam.

Where the hell is Cam?

I didn't believe for a second he was dead.

That asshole was at the bottom of a pit somewhere, just waiting to be found. His *Erosita* was living and breathing up in Majestic Clan, something no one else seemed to notice. But I did. Just as I recognized a plot brewing between Jace and Kylan. Hopefully, it would involve Lilith's demise.

The female in my arms gasped, not in surprise but in a last-ditch effort to save herself.

"Right." I knelt and laid her across the concrete floor. "Now what am I going to do with you?"

I ran my finger along her neck, then down her sternum to the jagged marks across her stomach. It seemed someone had done surgery on her with teeth and claws rather than proper surgical equipment.

"You came from the breeding camp," I guessed. My property unfortunately bordered the farm of homes used to create more Clemente Clan lycans. *Would Edon continue the practice?* I wondered. Something about the new alpha struck me as different from the others of his kind. He seemed almost humanized.

Watching his leadership might prove interesting.

Not that I cared enough to truly engage.

Of course, if I remained a royal, I wouldn't have a choice.

"So many decisions," I mused out loud, taking stock of the little warrior's injuries once more. I could see why the lycans chose her for breeding. She had nice hips. Toned legs. Her breasts were a bit small, but some calories would fix that right up. Same with her protruding ribs.

"Hmm." I brought my wrist to my mouth and bit down. "Let's see what a little bit of my blood does for you, shall we?" I pressed the open wound to her lips, allowing my life essence to seep into her. "You're going to need to swallow, little one."

She didn't comply right away, which only made her gurgle as she began to choke.

With a dramatic exhale, I repositioned myself on the ground and used my opposite hand to guide her head onto my thigh to a better angle for drinking. Her throat began to work automatically, as if her spirit had taken over and recognized the gift I offered her.

I stroked my fingers through her hair while she fed, whispering encouragement under my breath. If Damien saw me, he'd gape. Because this wasn't me at all. It just seemed like the right thing to do for my new pet.

"When you're more coherent, we'll pick a name," I told her softly. "Or perhaps you already have one. I'm good with that, too." Unless it was something like Veronica or Whitney. I didn't much care for those.

Actually, there were a lot of names I didn't like.

So maybe I would have to pick one for her.

My wound began to close, so I reopened it and pressed it to her lips again. "Keep drinking," I ordered. "When you're done, I'll bathe you."

Then I'd end up either eating her or playing for a while.

It depended on how entertaining she proved to be.

For her sake, I hoped she showed more than a little fire. Otherwise, I'd just wind up dousing her flames and extinguishing her life. For good.

Chapter Three

Willow

Cold.

Hard.

Cement.

I nearly groaned at the feel of it pressing into every inch of my body, the unforgiving substance the bane of my existence. There were so many times I just wanted to crawl into the concrete and hide, but I couldn't. It left me exposed. Vulnerable. *Pained.*

Except, I didn't feel all that agonized right now, which was strange because I could tell I'd slept for some time on the ground. Usually, I awoke achy and sore after my naps, but my limbs felt alive today. Energized.

I stretched, my muscles loosening and warming in response. *Odd.* I couldn't remember the last time I felt this alive.

My lips curled down.

Actually, I couldn't remember much at all. Everything felt foggy, as if I'd existed in a haze all my life and I was just now coming out of it.

It must be the drugs, I thought, rolling onto my back to stare up at the iron bars over my head. My eyes widened. *Those are new.*

I glanced left—more bars. Same to my right.

I'm in a cage.

Not a small one, maybe ten feet by ten feet, all sides exposed to open air. And below me was a slab of cold concrete. No windows decorated the walls beyond my prison, and the room held a slight musky odor. And dust particles floated in the air.

Oh, those are interesting. I narrowed my gaze at them, watching as they caught in the dim lighting, their colors a flash of intrigue. It was as if I'd never really seen dust before. Was it always this hypnotizing?

And has my skin always been this soft? I wondered as my fingers grazed my bare thigh. I drew my nails over my hips to my abdomen, tracing across my skin in a hypnotic wave of heat. *So smooth and perfect.*

I was naked—no surprise there. But I was also clean, and that struck me as odd. Although, I couldn't really remember why. The reason was lost somewhere in my memories, the thick fog preventing me from latching onto any specific one.

Did it really matter?

I felt good. Like, *really* good.

I rolled onto my stomach, then pushed myself off the ground and easily onto my feet. The cage provided a little more than a foot of clearance over my head. I reached up to wrap my fingers around the cold steel and marveled at the silky texture. *Sturdy. Heavy. Perfect.*

My knees buckled as I tested my grip. I hung with ease and even lifted myself up a little in a version of a pull-up. *Nice.* I couldn't remember the last time I'd been able to do this. At the university? In a class with Silas?

I canted my head, trying to recall the course, but it hovered just out of range of my mind.

The lack of focus probably should have concerned me, but after months or years of drug abuse, I couldn't really think beyond the peace of having a clear mind.

No nightmares.

No lycans.

No classwork.

Just existence.

I released the bars to spin in a circle, feeling lighter than air. Then I fell into a fighting stance, my legs moving with a fluidity that just felt right. Perfect. I jumped, careful of my head, then started a routine my body seemed to grasp more than my mind.

Silas taught me this, I recognized, uncertain of when that was. Yesterday? A month ago? Years, maybe? Time seemed irrelevant. Particularly with how fast my hands were flying in front of me. I went through each kata with a precision I could feel in my very soul.

By the time I finished, sweat dotted my brow and my chest was heaving from the effort. But I also felt invigorated. Powerful. Complete.

More of those dust particles flickered, drawing my focus to the darker shadows of the room. *Where am I?* My mind refused to answer. Something about the breeding camps— which I immediately locked a door on. Had they moved me to a new dungeon cell? When would they return? Would they drug me again?

I shivered. That had to be the cause of my bizarre state. Maybe they'd increased my dose and this was all a dream.

No. Impossible. My mind didn't allow for a positive imagination. I lived in a nightmare. Trapped. Forever considered—

What is that? I narrowed my gaze on the glint in the dark, some gleam of silver shining in the shadows.

Then it began to move.

I jumped backward into the bars behind me, my hands going around the metal columns beside my hips.

The being appeared to grow, as if lifting from a seated position on the ground. And then he stepped into the dim light.

My heart stopped. *Oh, shit…* He was too perfect to be human, his features flawless and sharp as if etched from marble.

Square jaw.

Straight nose.

Harshly cut cheekbones.

Eyes that glittered like black diamonds.

Dark, tousled hair that matched the light dusting of a shadow across his chiseled jaw.

I swallowed. *Vampire.* Yet he held an animalistic edge as he prowled toward me, a distinct intrigue playing through his gaze that appeared to be underlined in cruelty.

Where am I? I wondered again, caring much more about the answer now. How had I ended up in a vampire's lair?

Potent didn't even begin to describe the male coming to a stop just outside my cage door. He oozed power and sex. Domination. Superiority. Arrogance.

I nearly suffocated on his presence, his hypnotic gaze holding me captive before him.

My vampire professors had nothing on him. They could command a room, but this male seemed like he could command an entire army with a single look.

"Where did you learn how to do that?" he asked, his voice so deep and sensual that it scattered goose bumps down my arms.

I swallowed, my throat suddenly dry. "Th-the university." My palms clamped tightly around the bars as my knees threatened to buckle beneath his penetrating stare, his irises roaming over every inch of me.

"You took warrior classes?"

"Yes," I whispered.

"Why?" His midnight eyes met mine once more. "What

was your goal?"

My heart went from stuttering to racing in my chest, answers populating my mind before I could think them through. "I wanted to be a Vigil." Although, I couldn't quite remember why at the moment. *So foggy. So strange.*

What silver glimmer had I caught in the dark? I wondered then, glancing over his T-shirt and jeans, only to spy a watch on his right wrist. *That. How had I missed that?*

"And they sent you to the breeding farm instead," he replied, his sinful gaze dropping to my chest before lowering to the apex between my thighs.

A shiver skittered down my spine.

I'd stood naked in front of countless supernaturals before—humans, too—but something about this vampire had my nerves climbing into my throat.

"I think you would have served better in a harem," he mused. "But your genetics must have marked you for breeding."

I wasn't sure how to answer that, so I said nothing.

He continued to study me as if I were a present, appreciation evident in his gaze.

"How did I get here?" I blurted out, then immediately froze as his eyes snapped up to mine.

"You don't remember?"

"N-no," I admitted.

"Fascinating." He tilted his head in an eerie manner, another wave of intrigue overtaking his features. "I suppose you did imbibe a lot of my essence."

My eyebrows shot up. "I what?"

"My blood, pet. You drank my blood."

"Why?"

"To live," he answered as if that explained everything. "Your memories will return shortly. I suspect nightmares will accompany them."

He spoke the words nonchalantly, which only seemed to heighten the chill sweeping over me.

I don't want to remember.

19

But I did want to know a few things. Such as… "Who are you?" I realized the faux pas of my question the moment his eyes widened.

A series of edicts from my life began to chant through my mind, some course I took as a child ingrained forever in my head, even beneath my apparent memory loss.

Humans do not address their superiors.
Humans do not look at their superiors.
Humans do not engage their superiors.
Humans bow to their superiors.
Humans are here to please their superiors.
Humans are food.
Humans are meant for pleasure at the hands of their superiors.
Humans do not—

"I thought society broke humans of the penchant for speaking out of turn," the vampire mused, dragging me out of my inner chant.

I needed to apologize, to beg forgiveness, to bow at his feet. And yet, my body refused to do all those things, as if I were being held up by invisible puppet strings that forced me to disobey.

Some part of me was fundamentally broken.

I'd given up on the idea of perfect acquiescence. I no longer wished to be an obedient human. But I couldn't figure out when or how that had happened, the deciding memory a loose strand in my mind without a proper end.

However, defiance felt right.

Powerful.

Freeing.

"I'm Ryder," he murmured after several long beats of silence. He didn't so much sound displeased as he did amused. "As to your earlier inquiry about how you got here—you stumbled onto my property and attacked me and my lieutenant. Well, I suppose he's a sovereign now."

"Your sovereign?" I repeated, the title meaning something deadly inside my brain. *Only royal vampires have sovereigns.*

"Yes. A recent change that occurred while you napped on the floor." He lifted a shoulder. "I needed someone I could rely on to handle a few affairs down in San José, and he's the only one I could trust."

"San José?" I felt like a parrot repeating words, but this location was one I didn't recognize. *Where am I?* I wondered, not for the first time since waking up. However, now I no longer wanted to know so much as *needed* to know.

"Ah, yes, you wouldn't know it, would you?" He sighed, the sound distinctly underlined in annoyance. "I've never enjoyed the whole region renaming, but I suppose I'll need to remove the current title, won't I? Can't have the vampires of this region thinking Silvano is still in charge since Kylan killed him and all."

Kylan.

Silvano.

Two vampire royals.

And if Kylan killed Silvano, that meant there'd been a change in the regime. And if this male was talking about sovereigns and renaming regions… then… "You're a royal vampire," I breathed. Which I'd already deduced a few minutes ago, only his name hadn't registered as familiar, so the full thought hadn't connected.

Until now.

"Apparently," he muttered. "It's not a job I ever desired to obtain, but here we are." His gaze returned to mine, a calculating gleam radiating from his depths. "Which means, sweet pet, that I need to decide what to do with you."

I shivered, the bars at my back suddenly colder than before.

Twenty-two years of training just to become a breeding doll. And now this.

No, thanks.

I was done with this bullshit life. If he didn't kill me outright, then I'd just have to fight—

"Are you hungry?" he asked, interrupting my thoughts.

Am I hungry? Is that some sort of vampire joke?

Rather than reply, I just stared at him.

He studied me back in kind, his inquisitive gaze unnerving. It was the kind of look a monster gave his food before playing with it.

"You're still hopped up on my blood, so perhaps you don't feel it yet. But with all that physical activity, in addition to healing several fatal wounds over the last three days, you should be famished." He slid his hand into his pocket to pull out a key. "So how about we discuss your fate over a meal?"

This had to be a trick.

Some cruel game.

What royal vampire asked to dine with his food unless he intended to make her the meal?

The door clinked as he swung it open. "Come, pet. Let's find you something to eat." He turned as if he didn't have a care in the world, which, I supposed, he didn't. I was a human. A mortal. The bottom of the food chain in his eyes.

But what he misunderstood was the fact that I had nothing to lose.

If he didn't plan to return me to that breeding prison, then he intended to dine on my blood. Neither option appealed to me.

However, I wasn't going to turn down his invitation to leave my cell. I just had no intention of following him to the dining room.

The cement floor was cold beneath my feet as I trailed after him, my eyes scanning for anything I could use to incapacitate him. It all depended on my ability to catch him off guard, which wouldn't be hard since he'd given me his back.

He thought I was a meek little human.

A broken doll to fuck with.

Oh, he couldn't be more wrong.

I was fueled by hate and vengeance. A will to kill. To slaughter. To *survive*. I would take him down and escape, or die trying.

There, my brain supplied as we turned a corner toward a staircase. Just along the wall before it was a table littered with various tools, the metal glimmering enticingly in the low light.

Take me.

Use me.

Hurt him.

That was what those items told me. I grabbed one as we passed, my fingers wrapping around the wooden handle that led to a blunt top. *A hammer. Perfect.*

I raised the item in the air, angled it right for his head, and swung downward.

Only to have him spin around in a flash, his hand catching my wrist and halting my movement midway. His opposite hand snagged my hip, forcing me to turn with him as he slammed me up against the wall across from the table.

"Drop it." Two words uttered like a command one might give a dog.

I didn't have a choice, his strength superior to mine in every way. I released the hammer, and it fell to the floor with a loud clatter.

"Good girl," he said, pressing me into the wall with his thighs against mine. He released my wrist and grabbed my throat, giving it a squeeze. "Hmm, tell me your name." His irises captured and held mine, daring me to lie to him.

I knew better than to try.

Mortal identities were all meticulously cataloged, and I'd undergone countless classifications at the university, each one requiring blood donations and fingerprinting for identification purposes.

"Seven hundred and one of year one hundred and seventeen," I replied formally, my hands lying limply at my sides. During my university days, the term *prospect* would have been added to the beginning. But I was no longer a prospect. I was *assigned*.

He blinked at me. "I asked for a name, not a bunch of fucking numbers. What do people call you?"

"Seven hundred and one of year—"

His palm tightened around my throat, restricting my airway and effectively silencing my voice. "No. What did the other humans call you at the university?" He didn't release me, his gaze narrowing. "If you give me another damn number, I may not allow you to breathe again. Nod so I know you understand."

I tried to swallow but couldn't, his grip so tight I was starting to see spots.

So I bobbed my head, hoping that would convince him to release my throat.

He didn't.

Instead, he said, "Mouth a name for me."

Tears stung my eyes, my inner fight battling the urge to just succumb to his strangulation. I was so conflicted that I couldn't even seem to lift my hands to claw at his grip. It wouldn't change anything. He'd just hold on, perhaps even tighten his grasp and snap my neck.

Wouldn't it be so much easier if I just ceased to exist? But then I would have fought all these years for nothing.

Which was exactly how I felt when they put me in that breeding camp.

Yet my abhorrence still felt fuzzy, as if it had all been from a nightmare, not reality. However, I knew the world didn't work that way. Everything was real. Including the hand squeezing my throat, threatening to kill me if I didn't give this royal vampire a name.

How incredibly bizarre. Names were for supernaturals, not humans.

That wasn't to say I didn't have a secret one.

Because I did.

I just wasn't supposed to go by anything other than my number.

My university roommate, Rae, had given me the nickname over a decade ago, telling me we needed a way to communicate. It served as a defiance. I couldn't remember now why that was important, the memory fading before I could grasp it. That disappointed me because somehow I knew that was a day I didn't want to forget.

"Are you flirting with death, sweetheart?" Ryder asked me, his eyebrow arching.

His dark eyes held a note of amusement in them that didn't match the threat of his hand around my throat. Perhaps this entertained him—my weakness and impending death. Typical vampire.

It made me want to defy him, not by withholding my name but by giving one, to show him I'd been living in a world of defiance for years. That his oppression meant shit to me. That I would overcome this, even if it required my death.

"Willow," I mouthed at him, the lack of air making it impossible to add sound.

His gaze dropped to my lips. "Say that again."

"Willow," I repeated, then gasped violently as he loosened his grip on my throat.

"One more time," he demanded.

"Willow." It came out on a rasp, my lungs burning as much-needed oxygen poured down my abused airway.

"Willow," he said as if tasting the name. "Yes, I like that."

He drew his thumb across the pulse point of my neck, his body solid and hard against mine.

"What will I do with you?" he mused, his gaze dropping to where my breasts met his chest. His pupils flared, as did his nostrils as he inhaled my scent.

I swallowed, my throat raw. It had seemed like a rhetorical question, so I remained silent while he considered me.

"You intrigue me, pet," he finally said after a beat. "I suggest you continue to do so. It's the only reason you're still alive." His dark eyes met mine once more, holding for a long second. Then he took a slow step backward, his hands falling to his sides.

I didn't know what to say. How to react. Where to even

look. So I just continued to stare into his fathomless eyes, those dark, hypnotic orbs giving nothing away.

Age and experience poured off him in waves.

This vampire was old.

Lethal.

A royal.

And he claimed that I intrigued him.

What the hell was I supposed to do with that information?

He didn't break my stare, his lips curling into a cruel grin. "Try to attack me again and you won't enjoy the consequences."

With a final look that promised punishment should I disobey, he turned for the stairs once more.

"Come, little Willow," he called back to me when I didn't immediately follow. "And leave the hammer. I have much more efficient weapons upstairs."

I gaped after him. Was that a threat or an invitation?

Only one way to find out…

Chapter Four

Ryder

A hammer. My lips twitched. Not the most inventive solution. However, it was nice to know that my new pet had a fighting spirit. We'd explore more of that side of her later.

Her footsteps were quiet behind me. Hesitant.

She probably thought I intended to bite her.

A fair expectation, one I would absolutely be taking her up on at some point, but not today. She was only recently recovered, and I wanted to ensure she had her strength before we truly played.

I led her to the kitchen, then pointed to a pair of stools framing my kitchen island. "Sit."

She didn't argue, just slid up onto the leather seat and folded her arms across her bare stomach. Nudity didn't seem to bother her at all, something I suspected was a result of her upbringing.

A gentleman would probably offer her a shirt.

As I skipped etiquette school, I didn't see the point. If she wanted to prance around my house naked, I wasn't about to stop her. Plus, she had nice tits, which I could see now over the island.

Beautiful sight.

She could sit there all day like that, and I'd be a very happy man.

Besides, it'd been a while since I entertained a woman in my home. Let alone one as stunning as Willow. It shocked the hell out of me that society had wasted her looks on the breeding camp. She had "harem" written all over her with those long legs and fuck-me eyes.

But I imagined many humans were built like her nowadays with all the specialized breeding Lilith had put into place.

So robotic and boring. Although, I supposed it was efficient. They created Willow, and for that, I could be temporarily pleased with the system.

I went to my fridge to find some bread, deli meat, and cheese. With Damien's recent visit, I had some fresh groceries from Silvano Region. He lived just inside the nearest city, making him a decent connection to current society when I wanted an indulgence.

While I had pretty much everything I needed in storage, I sometimes craved something a little different. And Damien knew my appetite well.

Willow watched while I assembled two sandwiches—one for her, one for me. Her eyes grew round as I moved, her shock coming to a head as I slid a plate across the island to her.

"You don't like turkey?" I guessed.

"Wh-what?" She shook herself. "I… I mean, I think, yes." She frowned at the food as if it were foreign to her.

"Do they not give you sandwiches at the university?" I wondered out loud, unclear of what was customary for the human diet these days.

"Um, no," she said, lifting the bread to examine the contents.

I picked up my sandwich and took a bite while she watched. Then I asked, "What do they feed you?"

"Vegetables. Protein." She set the bread back on top, then picked up the food like I did, and brought it to her nose for a sniff test.

I smirked. "Worried?"

"N-no," she stammered softly before taking a nibble out of the crust. Her brow furrowed while she chewed. "What nutrient is this?"

"Bread."

"Bread," she repeated. "Like a carb?"

"Yup." I enjoyed another mouthful of my creation while she set hers down on the plate.

"We're not allowed to eat carbs," she said, confusion evident in her voice. "They're not nutritional for our body chemistry."

I just stared at her. "Seriously? You're going to argue with me over a sandwich?"

"I, no, I'm just… I don't understand. Is this a test?"

"Yes," I drawled. "It's a test of my patience. Now eat the fucking sandwich, Willow." *Not nutritional for our body chemistry"? What kind of bullshit is that?*

No wonder she was so thin. Society had fucking starved her.

She tentatively ate another bite, her eyes on me the whole time as if she were afraid I might punish her for disobeying.

Where the hell did my fighter go? I preferred the chick with the hammer, not this breakable little doe. Had I choked it out of her? Because that would be disappointing.

Her nose scrunched as she continued to eat, her distaste showing.

What was there not to like about a damn sandwich?

"Do you need mayonnaise or something?" I asked her.

"Mayonnaise?" she repeated. "I don't know. What is it?"

I waited for the punch line, yet it didn't come. Because she was one hundred percent serious.

Wow. I knew Lilith was a bitch, but this took it to a whole new level.

"You're probably not familiar with chocolate either, are you?"

Her blank stare gave me the answer before she whispered, "No."

I shook my head and focused on my sandwich. She did the same, the two of us falling into a comfortable silence with her on the stool and me standing across from her. Having company was a little weird, but not entirely deplorable. Although, we definitely had to work on her exposure to old-world things.

No mayonnaise.

No bread.

No carbs.

"This is exactly why I wanted nothing to do with the new world order," I told her conversationally. "While some part of it makes sense from a regulation standpoint, it's a bit overstated and, frankly, boring as fuck. There's no chase anymore. No excitement." I sighed and set my empty plate in the sink just as my watch buzzed.

Frowning, I glanced down at the notification, then went to the monitor hooked into the wall beside my fridge to pull up the display.

Screen number one fourteen showed me the reason for the alert.

Damien.

He gave me a wave, knowing I'd see him on the camera, then he jogged up the walkway to my front door. I hit a button on the panel next to my screen, unlocking it for him.

When I turned toward Willow again, I found her gaping at my security system. "You should see the one in my office," I told her. "This is just the baby version." I had one of these in every room of the house for easy access.

Most vampires invested in a security team.

I preferred technology.

"Now that you're aware of my penchant for security, you'll hopefully adhere to my suggestion that you not venture anywhere without my permission. Those cameras are just the tip of the iceberg, little pet. You don't want to know what I have rigged outside."

Damien stepped into the kitchen as I finished the last sentence, his golden-brown eyes immediately going to the blonde beauty at my counter and her half-eaten sandwich. "She cleaned up nicely," he mused.

"She did," I agreed, not bothering to introduce them. He knew where I found her. Until I decided what I wanted to do with her, there was no point in providing additional details. "I assume you have news for me?"

I phrased it as a question because there really was no other reason for Damien to stop by again so soon after our last meeting. And we'd just chatted on the phone yesterday when I informed him of his new Sovereign title.

"Yes." His attention remained on Willow, his pupils flaring with interest as he took in her nude state. "It seems there are those who are not taking your candidacy seriously. I've received word from Silvano City of several potentials stepping forward to take over in the interim."

"Oh?"

He hummed a confirmation before adding, "I think a show of force may be required."

"Did Jolkin not accept your newly appointed title?" I questioned.

"He did not," my best friend confirmed. "I considered killing him to make a point but thought you might want to do the honors."

I considered the old sovereign of former-day Houston. "You have, what, five, six hundred years on him?"

"Seven, actually," Damien drawled, finally taking his gaze away from my pet and shifting his focus to me. "But the pup still fancies himself king."

31

I grunted. "King of Houston." What an unfortunate title. "Do you want to remain in Houston as sovereign or take another area?" Offering a switch was the least I could do for Damien. He was the only being I trusted in this world.

Well, that wasn't true.

I trusted one other person, but I hadn't spoken to her in over a hundred years. Most considered her to be dead. However, she was very much alive. Just hiding and biding her time.

Similar to me.

Only I chose to hide alone.

"I would like to accompany you to Silvano City," Damien said. "That's where all the fireworks are going to occur, and you know how much I enjoy a good show."

My lips twitched. "You're just as sadistic as I am."

"Perhaps slightly less," he replied, moving to stand right beside Willow. "Have you tasted her yet?" He reached for her hair, pulling the strands back to expose her throat.

I approached her opposite side, repeating the action to arrange all of her blonde hair at her back.

She didn't move.

She barely even breathed.

But I caught the flicker of fire in her gaze, even while her body openly submitted.

I leaned in to inhale her scent, my nose grazing the pulse point of her neck. "Not yet," I admitted softly against her tender skin. "She's still recovering."

She swallowed, her nerves spiking just enough to tell me we were making her uncomfortable. Yet she remained obediently still, ever the trained human.

I sighed against her throat. "She needs some work." Because I didn't really care for subservience.

"Seems pretty perfect to me," Damien countered.

"Because you're into the mind manipulation Lilith has orchestrated." Which I couldn't fathom at all. It was a fucking travesty that defied nature.

Damien brushed his knuckles over her erect nipple. "Nothing wrong with teaching humans their place."

I couldn't fault the logic; I just felt there had to be a better way to go about it.

"What do you plan to do with her?" he asked.

Pulling away from her neck, I stared at her profile. "I don't know yet." I drew my finger down her arm, then refocused on him. "I need you to make me a list."

"Of ideas?"

I snorted. "No. I have plenty of those. I need a list of who needs to be brought to heel in Silvano Region."

"Hmm." He shifted his attention away from her tits to meet my gaze. "I can do that."

"Excellent." I pressed my palm to Willow's lower back. "Do you have anything else to report on, Damien?"

"No." He glanced at my proprietary touch and took a step away from my pet. "I'll work on a list for you."

"Good." I drew my thumb along Willow's spine and admired the goose bumps pebbling down her arms. "Also, evaluate the sovereign territories. Let me know which one you fancy, and I'll make the appropriate arrangements. After we're done with Silvano City, I mean." Because I wouldn't turn down his offer of help. I'd need his alliance.

Vampires valued loyalty.

Alas, I'd turned my back on this new society, opting to live within the borderlines of two conflicting regions. No one fucked with me because I kept to myself. However, claiming temporary royalty had changed that.

I wasn't naive. I knew I would have enemies as a result of my decision. And I welcomed those assholes to step forward and try to dance with me.

Lilith accepted my self-nomination for a reason.

I just needed to make sure everyone else in Silvano Region understood that.

Damien nodded. "I'll let you know which territory I desire, but I'll focus first on your list of contenders. It's going to be long."

"I know." My kind adored hierarchy and respected age. All they required was a stern reminder of why they should bow to me. I'd use Damien's list as a starting point, publicly put those opposing me in their place, and go from there. "Are you done with your sandwich, pet?"

I ran my thumb up and down Willow's spine once more and listened as her pulse sped up.

"Yes, My Prince," she said, addressing me formally.

I glanced at Damien. "Is that a thing I should get used to?"

"Yes, My Prince," he repeated, his lips hiking upward in a taunting grin. "You're a royal now."

"Indeed, I am," I replied. "In a society I don't fully comprehend." I'd witnessed enough to grasp the ins and outs, but I wasn't as well versed in the human norms and rules.

Which actually gave me an idea.

I grabbed Willow's hip and spun her on the stool, forcing her to face me and give Damien her back. "I now have a use for you."

She didn't meet my gaze, her submission resolute.

It irritated the shit out of me.

"Look at me when I talk to you, Willow," I demanded.

"She's trained not to," Damien put in.

I muttered a curse. "When in private or around just me and Damien, I want you always to look at us. Fuck the rules." I caught her chin between my thumb and forefinger to draw her gaze upward in demonstration. "All right?"

"Yes, My Prince."

"Yeah, cut that shit out, too. Call me Ryder."

"Another thing she's taught not to call you," Damien unhelpfully informed me. Well, technically, it was helpful. I just didn't care for the inane edict.

"You can go now, Damien," I told him.

He lifted a shoulder. "I have work to do anyway."

"Yes, you do."

"I'll see myself out, then." He flashed me a shit-eating

grin before leaving. I waited until I heard the alarm engage again—something Damien did by pressing a button for me outside at the gate—before I locked gazes with Willow once more.

"You're going to help me learn more about society's current rules for humans," I advised her. "I assume you've also taken classes in the current political structure?"

She blinked at me. "I… yes."

"You know the names of all the royals and clan alphas?" I pressed. Most of them I knew as well. This was more valuable in terms of her being able to keep up with me when required.

"Yes. At least those who were in leadership roles while I was in university."

"You're year one hundred and what again?"

"Seventeen."

"Which is the current year," I said. "So you were only in the camps for a few months since the Blood Day ceremony wasn't too long ago." Something I only knew because of my recent stay with the Clemente Clan. The new alpha's male playmate had been a recent addition to his territory from the Immortal Cup.

Her eyes flashed. "Only a few months?"

"Yes, pet. Maybe one or two. I'm not sure because I've never attended."

"But you're a royal," she protested. "All royals attend."

"Which, I suppose, means I'll be at the next one. How fortunate for me," I deadpanned.

Her lips parted, but no words escaped, as if I'd stolen her ability to reply. Good. This wasn't the point of our discussion.

"You will teach me more about current customs," I said. Not because I intended to adhere to any of the ridiculous ordinances, but because I just wanted to be aware of them. "And in private, you will always address me as Ryder. You will also look at me when I speak to you. Actually, none of the rules apply when we're together. I'd rather you be whoever you are, not some mindless puppet."

Now her mouth reminded me of a fish, her eyes wide with confusion.

"That's not an attractive look, Willow," I told her. "You're supposed to be intriguing me, remember? Or did you lose your will to survive when Damien appeared?"

Her nostrils flared in response, but she said nothing.

"Wrong answer, pet." I curled my fingers around her hip and yanked her into me, my opposite hand going to her throat.

Flames flourished in her blue depths. "What do you want me to say?"

"Words."

"Words," she repeated.

I narrowed my gaze. "Creative words."

"Creative words."

I started to squeeze, just enough to inform her that this little game of hers was not working for me. "Careful, Willow. Your disobedience will lead us to a place you might not enjoy."

"But isn't my disobedience exactly what you want from me?" she countered.

My annoyance melted marginally. "Are you being clever, little pet?"

"I don't understand you," she said as I wrapped an arm around her lower back, holding her to me while my opposite hand remained around her throat.

So delicate and pretty.

Fragile yet strong.

"Mmm, you really do interest me, pet," I praised her, deciding to allow her earlier slip into her society programming. Because I could see the fighter beneath the demure exterior. I just had to work on coaxing her out to play. "This world is designed to break humans, which makes your resilience that much more alluring."

"Are you applauding me for having a will to live?"

"I am."

"Maybe I don't," she suggested, all signs of her submission disappearing beneath a wave of defiance.

"I think you do, Willow." I slowly released her and took a step backward. "I think you haven't survived this long just to give up now. Which is why you're going to follow me upstairs like an obedient pet and let me show you to your new room."

I could keep her in the basement, but I had a much more comfortable guest area attached to my suite. So long as she didn't try to attack me with another hammer, I'd allow her to stay there.

"Are you done with this?" I asked, lifting her plate.

"Yes," she replied, glancing at her half-eaten sandwich. "I'm... not used to large meals."

Another issue with societal programming. Rather than comment on it, I discarded the rest of her food and set her plate in the sink. "Follow me."

She didn't argue.

She didn't try to grab a knife from the block on my counter as we walked by it.

She merely trailed after me, up the stairs, down the long hall, and to the door at the end. I opened it to reveal a seating area that joined two bedrooms together. Pointing to the one on the left, I said, "That's where I sleep. I don't recommend entering it unless you want to fuck." I led her to the other room, walked through the threshold, and added, "You'll be staying in here."

It had a queen bed, two dressers, a nightstand, a connected bathroom, and a walk-in closet. The room also opened to the wraparound balcony that spanned my entire suite. Her doors had sensors on them, though, so I would know if she stepped outside. Being on the second floor should deter her from trying to escape, but something told me this female might try it anyway.

If she did, I'd catch her.

Then I'd punish her.

My lips threatened to curl at the notion. *I may actually enjoy that.*

I flipped on a light to allow her to take it all in. She didn't seem nearly as thrilled as I'd anticipated. If anything, she looked nervous with the way her eyes flicked around the space.

"Unless you prefer the basement?" I offered, turning toward her. "Personally, I think this is a little more convenient."

"I, yes, this is… nice." She didn't sound very sure.

"Nice?"

"It's…" She pinched her lips to the side as though searching for the words. I waited, giving her time to formulate whatever she wanted to say. But rather than speak, she wandered into the bathroom.

Curious, I followed.

The lights came on automatically with our movement, the switch by her door turning on the sensors in the room. She jumped and glanced upward, then searched for the source before spying the walk-in shower in the corner. It was a reasonable size meant for at least two people, with dual showerheads, a heated floor, and a few different water settings.

Just because I lived alone didn't mean I skimped on life's luxuries.

Willow nibbled her lip before turning toward me. "I… I don't know how any of this works. The university had dorms. We shared showers. And I don't… my memories…" She flinched, her gaze sliding to the ground.

I stepped toward. "What about your memories?"

"They're fuzzy," she admitted softly. "I'm having a hard time remembering the breeding camp and certain things about my past."

"I see." That usually happened when a human transitioned into a supernatural state. I could hardly recall my mortal days. Of course, I was fucking old. So that was to be expected. "It's probably related to drinking my blood."

Her eyes flashed up to mine. "It takes a human's

memories?"

I chuckled. "No, pet. It gives a human temporary immortality, which is why you were able to heal. But part of the immortal transition is to forget your mortal past." I reached out to play with a light strand of her hair, the end curling near her breast. "It'll pass. You just required a lot of my essence to heal."

"Vampire blood gives humans immortality?"

"I'm guessing they didn't teach you that at the university," I murmured, smirking. "Wouldn't want anyone to know such things, would we?"

This was exactly why Willow could be of use to me. As long as she continued to speak freely, I'd be able to use her knowledge and experience to craft my approach to this new world. As a twisted happenstance of fate, the young female knew more about society than I did. At least to an extent. Working as a team, we could put all the pieces together.

"Come on," I said, tugging on her hair playfully before releasing the strand. "I'll show you how to use the shower and the other amenities in the room. Then I'll leave you to acclimate yourself." I had some files to review that Damien sent over yesterday.

Playing the role of a royal vampire was going to be so much work.

Maybe I would end up serving a temporary term after all.

Only time would tell.

Chapter Five

Willow

Acclimate yourself.

I wasn't even sure what to do with that term. Nor was I sure how to handle him actually leaving me alone in the room.

He walked out.

Didn't lock the door.

And just... left me by myself.

It took me nearly an hour before I forced myself to move around the room. I kept expecting him to appear, to tell me this was all some sort of cruel joke, but he never came back. Not even when I decided to shower. Not when I wrapped a towel around myself. Nor when I stepped outside onto the balcony to take in the scenery of his estate, bathed by the night sky.

Endless stars danced overhead, as well as a bright moon that wasn't quite full.

I stared up at it for countless minutes, the fresh air a foreign concept that rendered me frozen. Had I ever experienced such a moment? One where I wasn't expected to be somewhere right away, didn't have a monster looming over my shoulder to dictate orders, or wasn't outside just for a field exercise?

I searched my foggy mind and came up blank.

Then I gazed upward once more, inhaled slowly, and exhaled in a similar fashion.

It wasn't until I scented a minty aftershave on the wind that I realized I wasn't alone.

The hairs along my arms stood on end, my throat constricting. "I… I'm sorry. I just… I was…"

"Admiring the night?" Ryder finished for me, stepping out of the shadows and into the moonlight shining down on the balcony. "You're allowed to stand outside, Willow." He trailed a finger down my arm, his touch oddly soothing while simultaneously terrifying.

He's a royal vampire.

That made him old. Powerful. Dangerous.

I swallowed and forced myself to face him, needing to see his eyes. They served as a stark reminder of his lethality, the coldness of his dark orbs sending a chill through my spirit. This was not a male I wanted to trust, even if he had offered me something no one else ever had—a moment of peace.

"I'm getting ready to retire for the evening," he informed me softly. "I just wanted to make sure you didn't need anything else. More food, perhaps?"

My stomach churned at the notion, his sandwich sitting heavy inside me still. "No, thank you." It came out so polite. So quiet. So… strange.

I'm talking to a royal vampire.
Why the hell am I talking to a royal vampire?

As the hours had spun onward, my memories had begun

to trickle in. Not all at once, just pieces and splashes of my history, including startling moments from my past and punishments I longed to forget. Courses I never wanted to take again. Exams that haunted my nightmares.

Part of me wanted to bow at his feet. That was the obedient servant part of my mind that had been trained over countless years to always submit.

Never look a superior in the eye.

Bow.

Beg.

Please.

I shivered at the latter, my experience with *pleasing* lycans not one I wanted to revisit anytime soon. Thankfully, the breeding camp still resembled a haze in my mind. Perhaps because of the drugs. Or maybe it was just his blood. In which case, I'd likely wake up screaming later when the night terrors came.

"I don't suggest running," Ryder said quietly. "Because if the wolves don't catch you, I will. Neither outcome will end well for you." He brushed his knuckles down my cheek, pausing at my neck. "I put some clothes on your bed. Feel free to do whatever you want with them."

With that, he turned away from me and disappeared through a set of glass doors that I suspected led to his own room. He didn't slide them closed, leaving me to wonder if they had been open this entire time. Or had he come out here through my room?

My room, I repeated to myself, frowning. What a strange concept. Rae and I had shared a room once, or what the university called a room, anyway. It was more like a space with wall dividers within one giant hall. Our beds were pushed together. We had two little chests for our uniforms. And nothing else. The bathroom was shared and open, as were the showers. They were gender-neutral as well, something that started to cause discomfort around puberty, but I quickly learned not to care about nudity.

Yet Ryder had gifted me clothes.

Curiosity caused my feet to move into my room, my hands immediately seeking out the outfit he'd left for me on the bed.

A white T-shirt that smelled like him.

And a pair of too-big gym shorts.

They were probably the thickest materials I'd ever been allowed to own. Not worn or translucent, but actual clothes.

Who are you? I wondered at him, disturbed by his behavior. *Why are you doing this?* I'd never met a royal before, but I knew their reputations well. They enjoyed playing with their food, their games notoriously cruel.

Was he doing this to placate me? To give me a false sense of hope?

If that were the case, he'd have to try a heck of a lot harder.

I didn't buy the whole chivalrous act.

All vampires had ulterior motives. He claimed he wanted me to teach him about society, but as a royal, he already knew the rules. Except he wasn't acting the part of a royal. Starting with his home. *Where are all the Vigils? His harem? His mortal staff?*

The only being I'd seen so far was Damien, who had acted more on par with my expectations than Ryder. Yet their easy candor had been unique, too.

Oh, but when they touched me together, I thought I'd just become dinner. And rather than feel terrified, I'd felt… *hungry*. Interested. *Intrigued*, as Ryder would say.

Which was so damn wrong.

Yet, also expected.

Vampires were alluring creatures of the night, their flawless looks and hypnotic appeal two lethal traits that aided in their ability to captivate their prey.

And I'd fallen victim to their allure.

I'd almost leaned into Ryder, to entice him to bite me.

Only, he said I wasn't ready, thus implying he intended to make a meal of me in the future. While also using me for information.

I shook my head, the entire experience morphing into a cataclysm of confusion.

What I needed to do was rest, take advantage of the amenities while I had access to them, and plot my next steps. Becoming Ryder's dinner wasn't going to work for me. But I couldn't escape until I had a better idea of where we were, as well as a notion of where to go.

I pulled on his shirt and shorts, then slid into the sheets on the too-soft bed. Sitting up, I frowned down at the plump mattress. Why was it so cushiony? Where were the lumps? The hard cement slab beneath? How could anyone sleep like this?

Rather than try, I pulled the blankets off the mattress and made myself a proper bed on the floor. No pillow.

It was much better. More solid. Reminding me of my previous home.

A life I no longer lived.

A world I left behind.

For a future I didn't understand.

Chapter Six

Willow

Three days later and I still didn't understand Ryder.

"You want me to attack you," I said slowly, eyeing his position on the mat.

We were in his training room, surrounded by a variety of weapons. He'd given me a knife to use for our sparring match—an activity that was his idea, not mine. Just like everything else we'd done over the last few days.

"I want you to try, yes," he replied. "Consider it a test of your abilities. Or do you prefer the term *exam*? You've referenced that a few times when discussing your courses."

The man was obsessed with my university experience. It made no sense. He should already know what courses I took, what marks I earned, and the paths they opened me up for in this world.

Yet he questioned me as if he knew nothing about the current world, something I found hard to believe since he was a royal vampire. Except, he didn't act like any of the ones I'd studied before. He lived alone. No security. No servants. And he asked me to do strange things like spar with him.

"All of my exams involved human opponents," I informed him. "I've never attacked a superior."

"Oh?" He cocked a brow. "So the hammer incident was meant to seduce me, not hurt me?"

I flinched. "That was different."

"How so?"

"I wanted to escape. It wasn't an exam."

"And do you want to escape now, pet?" he asked, stalking toward me, his dark eyes smoldering with malevolence. "Is that how I provoke you into a fight, by evoking fear?"

I swallowed and stumbled backward, only to find myself up against the wall with a shirtless vampire closing in. I tried to dart to the side, but his hand shot out, his arm blocking my path. Then he repeated the action on my other side, caging me between him and the wall.

"Is this the inspiration you require, Willow?" He leaned in, the heat of his body a luring prospect against mine.

He was lethal.

Gorgeous.

A predator cornering his prey.

A darkness I shouldn't admire.

And yet, my heart skipped a beat at his proximity, the minty quality of his breath an invitation between us.

Just three days ago, I'd wanted to fight for my life. Then he'd shown me a kindness I'd never experienced before, he spoke to me as if I mattered, and he fed me, clothed me, and gave me a bed.

Every move he made floored me.

I sensed the danger lying beneath the surface, but his actions were unbearably foreign. He called me his pet, yet it sounded more like an endearment than a classification.

He pressed his nose to my cheek and drew a line to my ear, the light caress stirring a swarm of butterflies inside. I didn't know how to process this. My body nearly leaned into him, but my mind held me back.

This was all a trick, his vampiric abilities overriding my sensibilities.

He's not a lover.
He's not a friend.
He's the enemy.

"You're supposed to be piquing my interest," he reminded me softly, the warmth of his breath tickling my neck. "Playing this mousy role isn't very appealing, Willow."

I shivered, my lips working without sound. What did he want me to say? Perhaps nothing. What he really wanted was for me to fight. I still had the knife in my hand, and my arms were free at my sides.

It would be easy to attack him.

To hurt him.

Then maybe I could run.

That'd been my original plan. I'd ignored it these last few days because I needed time to acclimate to my new situation. But I was just as confused today as I was when I woke up several days ago.

"I know you're struggling with your memories," he murmured. "Have you forgotten how to fight as well?"

It wasn't so much a struggle as it was a fog. I remembered everything, but there was this intangible gray film over every thought, shading my recollections with a dreamlike filter.

The only experiences I couldn't recall at all revolved around my time at the breeding camp. Something terrible had happened there. Something I didn't want to think about. Something that involved glowing green eyes.

Instead, I focused on my university background, the classes I'd taken, the friendships I'd made, and worked on pulling those into my mind. They weren't perfect, but they were there, lurking inside the bizarre mist I'd mentally contrived.

Ryder sighed. "If you don't want to spar, then I'll just eat you instead."

My focus flew upward to his smoldering irises once more, his expression severely serious. He'd bite me right here, right now, if I didn't do as he required. I could see the conviction in his stare.

I'd never been bitten by a vampire before.

I didn't want to start that habit now, either.

That eyebrow of his remained arched, his patience hanging on by a thin wire.

He wanted me to fight him? Fine. I was the one with a weapon, not him. And his hands were busy propping him up against the wall in his human-formed cage.

I lashed out with the blade, only to have him jump backward a beat ahead of me reaching my target. The end of my knife only grazed his bare abdomen, his lips pulling into a feral smile.

"Good choice," he praised. "More."

This man was insane.

Certifiably nuts.

Maybe the whole royal thing was a lie? Some fucked-up fantasy he'd created for himself in the middle of wherever the hell we were located. The geography I understood was region based; they didn't explain where the breeding camps or other destinations were. Just the regions and capitals.

Ryder fell into a crouch, his expression inviting me to play.

Rather than turn him down, I went for it. If I could injure him even a little, it'd provide me with an opportunity to escape. And if nothing else, it would tell me what I was up against.

I considered throwing my dagger at him—I'd taken an entire course on knife fighting—but I didn't want to lose my only weapon.

Instead, I darted around him, trying to reach his back,

but he spun with me, reached out, and snagged my wrist. I whirled in an attempt to escape him, my instincts taking over. Except his grasp caused me to twist in a way that forced me to drop my knife.

Fuck.

I should have thrown it.

Alas, there was no time to correct the error. Ryder was already coming for me, trying to find a way to subdue me.

He brought my arm up behind my back, but I used the momentum to my advantage to spin and tried to take out his knee. Ryder dodged me, his counterattack hitting me square in the sternum.

Shit, he's fast.

Silas had been my primary opponent at the university. Sometimes Rae. And neither of them had anything on Ryder.

He moved with a precision I would have admired had I not been the subject he sought to cut down.

I escaped his hold once more and ran toward the weapons rack. He chuckled behind me, then cursed when I found a pair of throwing stars. I aimed both at his torso, only to watch him avoid them with a crazy backbend that should not have been possible.

It shocked me so completely that I stopped moving, just to be yanked down onto the mat a second later by his much stronger body. I tried to dislodge him in the way I'd been trained, but he captured my wrists in one hand and pulled them over my head. Then he put his opposite palm at my throat, his gaze thoughtful as I squirmed beneath him.

"That was cheating," he informed me, his breathing far more even than my own. "I gave you one knife. You lost it."

I inhaled a gulp of air before replying, "You didn't say I couldn't grab more."

His lips curled. "I suppose I didn't." He cocked his head to the side, his thumb brushing the pulse on my neck. "That wasn't a horrible performance, Willow. Better than I anticipated, actually."

That didn't appear to be much of a compliment. Not that a compliment was warranted. How long had I lasted against him? One minute? Maybe two?

I nearly growled in frustration.

Then his hips settled between mine, and my frustration morphed into something else entirely. Heat spread through my veins from the point where our groins touched, my heart hammering an unsteady beat in my chest.

He has me pinned in a helpless state with no option but to comply. And he's turned on.

My throat went dry with the realization. *I'm completely at his mercy.*

"You need to eat more, Willow." His dark eyes radiated with a hunger that rivaled his growing arousal below. "It'll help with proper muscle growth and fill out your curves." His gaze dropped to my mouth, and then lower to the fabric covering my heaving chest.

I wore his clothes—a plain white shirt and a pair of boxer shorts. Neither left much to the imagination, especially as I felt myself dampening at the apex between my thighs.

He's a hunter, I thought, inhaling sharply. *A vampire. A predator encased in a mirage of perfection.*

And right now, all that perfection was pressed up against me, his muscles resembling a brick wall above me.

His dark eyes finally returned to mine, the knowledge in his depths stealing my ability to think. He could smell my reaction to him. He could feel it with his thumb against my pulse. He knew he had the upper hand in every way.

I was lost to his superiority.

No was a word I could never utter in his presence. Not without experiencing swift punishment.

Yet a part of me had to admit that I wouldn't refuse him for more than just societal reasons. His presence endangered my senses, making it difficult to think.

Which was why it took me a moment to register the

alarm sounding around us. The blaring siren barely penetrated my thoughts until Ryder leapt to his feet to stalk over to one of his security panels.

He had one in every room, including his guest suite upstairs. I'd tried to play with the one in my temporary room yesterday, but I couldn't activate it. Which told me they only responded to him.

"Hmm," he murmured, scanning the security images populating his wide screen. "We have company." He looked at me. "Do you know how to use a gun?"

"No." Humans weren't allowed to handle weapons of that nature, only combat-style tools like batons and swords. That seemed like something he should know, in addition to several other things.

"We'll rectify that later," he said, typing in a code on his panel that caused the wall to part beside it.

My eyes widened at the adjoining room Ryder had just revealed. It was a giant armory. His hammer paled in comparison to all this, telling me he hadn't been kidding when he'd said there were better weapons upstairs.

Because wow.

The large room boasted several rows of knives, guns, grenades, and a variety of other items. Ryder turned left out of my view.

I forced myself up onto my feet, my intention to follow him, except the panel caught my attention. Yellowish-orange silhouettes painted the purple-shaded background. It reminded me of the thermal scanners I'd studied in my university security course. The purpose of the class had been to demonstrate all the ways humans were observed and "protected." Really, it was a way to deter us from escaping. Or that was how Rae, Silas, and I had interpreted it, anyway.

"How many?" Ryder asked from the other room. When I glanced at him, I found him watching me from the threshold. He didn't seem to care that I'd checked out the footage. If anything, he appeared pleased by it.

"Nine," I replied, assuming he wanted me to tell him how many yellowish-orange blobs were on the screens he'd left up on the panel.

"Twelve," he corrected, disappearing back into his armory. "But you were close," he called back to me.

I frowned at the screen. "Where are the other three?"

"They're coming in from the west," he replied from the other room.

"The west?" I repeated, trying to figure out which monitor showed that. There were six up on the screen, all angled at different parts of his property.

"Upper right corner," he said as he returned with a gun in his hand. He used it to tap the image on the panel before securing it in his belt, where he had two others tucked away.

I squinted at the purple shading, my brow furrowing as I caught a slight shift in the color. "What is that?" They weren't yellowish orange like the others. "Why are they so faint?"

"Age," he replied. "Go pick out some knives. You're going to need them."

That didn't sound good. I wanted to ask him what was happening, but he disappeared into his armory again before I had a chance.

So I did as he requested and picked a few knives from the wall of weapons decorating his sparring area. They were combat-style tools meant for hand-to-hand training, very unlike the items in his secret room.

I also selected two throwing stars, one of which I carefully tucked into the back of my boxer shorts. The other stayed in my hand, while I held two knives in the other.

This isn't very efficient, I thought as Ryder returned in a dark vest that matched his black pants. He was still shirtless beneath, leaving his muscular arms on display. They bulged threateningly as he slipped a blade into his tool belt. It reminded me of one a Vigil would wear, only more high-tech.

I was about to ask for one, but my mouth forgot how to

function as I caught the dark glimmer in his eyes.

"If you ever go in there without my permission, you'll regret it," he informed me as he approached. Then he seized my chin between his finger and thumb and forced me to look at him. "And if you even think about using those daggers on me tonight, you'll find out how I prefer to use a knife. Got it?"

"You're the one who told me to attack you," I reminded him. This wasn't the time for a debate, but my exhausted mind couldn't help throwing words back at him. Everything he did went against the norm.

Shouldn't his Vigils be handling the attack outside? Wasn't that one of their key responsibilities—to ensure the safety of their royal vampire?

Is Ryder even who he says he is?

His eyes narrowed. "Now isn't the time for being clever, little pet."

"I'm just saying, you keep changing your rules." Making it impossible to know what to expect from him.

"Then learn to read me better," he replied, tightening his grip on my chin. "Those assholes want to kill me. That's why they're here. I strongly suggest you do what I say if you want to survive."

I held his gaze. "What do you want me to do?"

"Help me kill them."

"How?"

"By protecting my interior," he murmured, his grasp loosening just a little. "And try not to die. I'm not done with you yet."

That sounds promising, I thought with a mental snort.

"The power is going to go out in about sixty seconds as a result of my emergency protocols," he added. "Now go find a decent hiding spot before that happens. If anyone who isn't me touches you, stab them. Understand?"

Part of me wanted to deliver a snarky retort, but the moving blobs on the screen had me reevaluating my stance and nodding instead. "Okay."

"Good girl," he murmured, pressing a kiss to my lips that sent a tingle down my spine. "Happy killing."

Chapter Seven

Ryder

These assholes thought they could sneak up on me. I would have laughed if it weren't such a fucking insult.

I crept over the roof of my home, careful to stick to the shadows. My security had sprung to life about forty seconds ago, cloaking my property in darkness. But I couldn't do anything about the moon hanging overhead.

The idiots with death wishes were coming in on all sides, making it difficult for me to pick a position. So I went with the corner facing the three with minimal body heat. They would be the oldest. Vampires didn't grow colder over time; we just required less blood to survive. And my thermal scans picked up on that aspect of the body signature. It helped me know whom I was up against before they arrived.

None of them would compare to me in age unless Kylan

had decided to pay me an unexpected visit. But last I checked, he had a brain. So no way in hell would he be creeping over my yard now.

I rolled my neck, loosening my shoulders, and lowered myself into position near the sniper rifle I kept up here just for this purpose. I had seven, all in different areas and facing opposite directions.

One could never be too prepared in my position.

I'd pissed a few vampires off when I originally opted to remain here instead of taking a leadership role. Most had given up trying to punish me for it. So I suspected these bastards were here for an entirely different reason.

All right, Dick Number One, let's see where you are.

My scope had night vision equipment enabled, allowing me to easily spy my target about seven hundred yards out. This was precisely why I had my security equipment set up at my borders. It gave me time to prepare, and the alarms wouldn't be heard that far out, even by lycan ears.

I scanned the area for Dick Number Two and Dick Number Three.

They'd spaced out a little, making it difficult to take them all down in sequence. Which meant one or two might disappear after I fired off the first bullet.

I waited half a beat, measuring the distance of their varied trajectories, then fired one bullet directly into Dick Number Two's skull. He'd survive with a mild headache but wouldn't wake for at least an hour. That would give me enough time to take down some of the others permanently and leave him alive for questioning.

Dick Number One tried to fall to the ground, just like I expected him to. I pulled the trigger to ensure he stayed there permanently, then focused on Dick Number Three. He'd also collapsed to the ground, my lack of trees making hiding difficult.

Five.

Four.

Three.

Two.

I pulled the trigger, his angle of escape predictable.

And those were the oldest of the group, leaving nine young vampires left to play with.

My rifle compromised my position and cost me the element of surprise, but it was worth it to take down the larger threats.

Rolling up to the balls of my feet, I edged along the side of my roof to one of the makeshift ladders I'd built into the brick siding. Several quick steps later, my boots touched the gravel below.

I didn't waste time looking around. Even if the vampires had run, they wouldn't be here yet.

Moving a few feet to the right, I knelt and pulled open one of my trapdoors in the dirt, then dropped into the tunnel below. My entire property held a maze beneath the surface, all lined with hidden entrances that could only be accessed by my thumbprint.

Maybe I should have put Willow down here, I thought as I closed the door over my head. Then I frowned at the notion.

Since when did I try to protect others?

Shaking my head, I took off at a sprint toward the area where the largest cluster had been seen on the cameras. They'd probably already split up, but I could catch a few off guard with some of my presents lying in wait throughout the fields.

After a bit of a jog, I slowed my pace, then stopped beside one of my panels to bring up the footage of my property.

Two offenders had already reached the front door.

Three more were rounding the back of my house.

One stood near the outer perimeter, unmoving. Maybe he no longer wanted to play. That'd be the smart decision.

Another was less than ten feet from my position and frozen, likely because he could sense my presence.

I ignored him to hunt for Willow. I found her in the living area with her back pressed up against a wall, her body position alert and defensive. She'd chosen to hide in plain sight, giving her two avenues to escape, both of which were highlighted by the moon coming in through the windows.

Good girl, I thought at her, then searched for the final two intruders.

There. I smiled at their location about a hundred yards from my house. *Just a little closer,* I urged them as I called up an administration screen on the panel beside their image.

Come on. Take a few steps.

That's a good boy.

All right, you, too, buddy.

And... three... two... I hit the button and grinned as the explosion rocked the infrastructure around me. My tunnels would be safe—the blast radius was confined to the area they'd just entered and away from my underground haven—but those two vampires would be severely injured or dead, depending on how close they were to the detonation point.

All right, I had seven to go.

The one closest to me had started forward again, making it easy to catch him.

Using my security panel, I engaged a trap point within his trajectory and smirked as he stepped right into it. His resulting howls of pain were music to my ears. The only way out of that literal bear trap was to lose his limb. Oh, it'd grow back eventually, but not quickly enough to save him from me.

The trio behind my house started toward me, searching the field for my location because the idiot above me was shouting about me being nearby.

Yes, walk this way, I encouraged them, an old song popping into my head that I began to hum beneath my breath. No one made music like that anymore. Cinematic arts had died with the human population. A real pity because I rather enjoyed theatrical entertainment. Lycans were somewhat into it, creating their own on occasion, but it wasn't the same.

I started dancing around to the tune playing in my head

while watching the idiots on the monitors move exactly where I wanted. With a little spin, I engaged another explosive and chuckled when they stepped right into it.

"Thanks for playing," I murmured, not caring if the idiot above me heard it. "Who wants to dance next?"

Still singing the previously famous song, I pulled up the screens of the house and found the other two inside, walking right toward Willow. Smart Guy Number Twelve had retreated, his presence no longer on my property. I'd try to track him down later by scent.

First, I needed to take care of the final two jokers inside my house.

Willow's tense stance told me she heard them coming for her. Hopefully, she could hold them off until I arrived.

I really should have put her in a safer place.

Why do I care? I wondered as I started running toward her location via the tunnels. I barely knew the girl. However, some part of me had claimed her.

Willow fascinated me, in a refreshing way. She was obedient yet defiant. Beautifully broken where society was concerned—an attribute that made her perfect in my mind.

I also sensed her innate hatred for my kind and her desire to escape this life. All the while, a warrior lurked inside who was hell-bent on surviving. That she smelled edible and possessed alluring curves only added to the appeal.

And her eyes.

Mmm, yes, those beautiful blue orbs showcased a myriad of feelings she held back. I wanted to shatter her walls to release the volcano beneath, but I was biding my time with her. Playing our own little intimate game.

That had to be why I was sprinting toward her now.

We weren't done, and if those assholes took my new toy from me, I wouldn't just kill them. I'd annihilate their very souls before allowing them to fall into the clutches of death.

I reached my basement hatch in record time, then pulled up the panel beside the door to check on everyone inside.

The intruders had split up. I ignored the one on my

second floor and watched the one on the first level round the corner into the living area where Willow hid.

He found her immediately, her scent a beacon in the dark to a vampire.

But he didn't see her knives.

She threw one with a precision I admired, hitting him right in the chest. Then she aimed a star at his neck, lodging both instruments into him on impact.

Nice, I praised, impressed. But her actions drew the second predator's attention, his steps harsh on the stairs as he sprinted down to locate her and his buddy.

I opened the trapdoor in my basement, my blood heating in my veins at the thought of him reaching my Willow.

Her gasp pierced my ears, the sound of a male growl vibrating off the walls.

I entered to find her sparring with the vampire, her technique on point, but she was no match for his supernatural strength. One of her stars was lodged into the wall—a missed throw. Which meant she had only one knife left.

"Bitch!" the vampire shouted. The sound of a bone snapping followed and sent a chill down my spine, Willow's resulting shriek of pain forcing me to move.

I didn't think.

I acted.

My gun fell into my hand, the aim resolute, and a bullet sailed into his head, forcing him to release her.

But that wasn't good enough.

I walked up to him and fired three more rounds into his skull, then two more into his neck. Willow's knife glinted on the ground in the moonlight coming in through my back windows. I holstered my gun, retrieved the blade, and went to work on dislocating his head from his body.

The other guy received similar treatment, and it wasn't until I completed the task that I realized the harsh sound in my ears came from my chest.

I was panting.

Bloodthirsty.

Furious.

Willow cowered on the floor, cradling her arm to her chest as she bit her bottom lip, trying not to cry. *My strong little warrior.*

I set the knife down. Then I went to my quivering pet and knelt down beside her. She flinched away from my touch, her pain evident. "Shh, I'm not going to hurt you. Let me see it."

She trembled but did as I requested.

The bastard had snapped the bones in her forearm, likely by twisting her wrist while trying to dislodge the knife from her hand.

She'd heal eventually, and I needed to go ensure the vampires outside would never wake up. Yet I couldn't leave her.

Instead, I rearranged myself on the floor to sit beside her, then bit my wrist and brought it to her mouth. "Drink."

Her eyes flew to mine, the tears lurking in her depths a glisten I never wanted to see again from her.

"Now, Willow," I snapped, not willing to allow her to suffer.

She visibly swallowed, her nose scrunching up in distaste, but she complied and pressed her mouth to my open wound. Her first lap against my skin was tentative, the action not at all what I needed from her. I opened my mouth to instruct her, but she began to suck before I could tell her to.

A low groan vibrated my arm, her pleasure at drinking from me a euphoric hit to my senses. Using my free hand, I threaded my fingers in her hair and gently pulled her closer until she rested against my side.

She relaxed into me, her damaged limb still pressed against her chest while my forearm rested against her spine to keep her upright.

Holding her felt right. Warm. Intoxicatingly real.

What is happening to me? I wondered. I didn't cuddle.

Ignoring the oddity of our situation, I opted to embrace it and ensured she took more than her fill of my blood. It would expedite her healing, just like it had a week ago.

"Soon you'll feel a tingling sensation in your arm," I told her softly. "That's how you know the bone is mending. We'll need to set it properly and keep it at that angle through the process. Then it should return to normal in a few hours, if not sooner." My blood was ancient, my immortality resolute. A human drunk on my essence should heal faster as a result.

I combed my fingers through her hair, belatedly noticing the blood coating my skin.

Oh well. We'd both need a shower after this anyway.

After several minutes of allowing her to acquire her fill, I eased her away from my wrist. "That should be enough."

She didn't reply, just gazed up at me dreamily.

My lips curled at the contentment in her features. "Yeah, that was definitely enough."

She hummed something unintelligible in response.

"I think I like you in this state," I murmured, pulling her carefully into my lap. Her head fell to my chest on a sigh, her body completely relaxed against mine. "There's so much I could do, and something tells me you would approve so long as I just let you have a little more blood."

My words had no impact on her, confirming my statement.

"The healing may disturb your euphoric state," I warned her. "The bone-mending process is more painful than the original fracture."

At least it wasn't a gunshot wound. Those were a bitch to recover from, which the vampires outside would currently be experiencing. I really needed to take care of them before they woke up, and I needed to track down the final intruder—the one intelligent enough to run.

"I'm going to put you in a temporary dream state," I whispered to Willow. "You'll be safe, and you'll heal faster."

She hummed again, but it didn't sound like a protest.

I stood with her in my arms and walked over to the couch to arrange her in a comfortable position that protected her arm. Then I carefully repositioned her forearm to ensure her bones healed accurately.

Willow didn't cringe or complain, her mind lost to a dreamy state of euphoria brought on by my blood. It would change as the mending started, but for now, she just stared up at me with a sated appeal that I wanted to replicate in the bedroom.

Leaning down, I brushed a kiss against her temple and compelled her into a deep sleep to help soften the mending experience. My compulsion served as an apology of sorts, one I didn't really comprehend. Had I protected her better, she wouldn't have been injured. And yet, at the same time, I needed to know how she handled herself in dangerous situations.

"What am I going to do with you, pet?" I asked her for the thousandth time, bewildered by this odd little attachment building between us. It would pass, of course. But it temporarily intrigued me.

With a shake of my head, I left her to heal. I had a few bodies to decapitate.

Chapter Eight

Willow

Dark green orbs haunted my mind, smoldering and intense, reminding me of something I couldn't quite grasp.

Another dream?

A dark memory?

I couldn't say, the knowledge there and gone in a flash as something nudged me back to reality. My mind eagerly accepted the reprieve, not ready to indulge in the sadistic thoughts of my past.

Something about a—

"Willow." The voice intruded on my thought, drawing me into a state of awareness and away from the experience I longed to forget.

I opened my eyes. The lights were all on, and he stood before me with damp hair and a towel wrapped around his waist.

Nothing else.

All that perfection on display had my throat drying and my tongue eager for a different kind of taste of him.

This was why vampires were dangerous. They were alluring and beautiful and lethal. He could snap my neck as easily as that monster had my arm and drink the life from my veins. Yet he could effortlessly bring me to my knees, his very appearance a seduction to the senses. And he knew it, too.

"Feeling better?" he asked me, his gaze going to my forearm.

I glanced at it, frowning. It was completely healed.

"How long was I out?"

"About six hours." He helped me roll onto my side, then sat on the couch beside my hip and played his fingers over my arm. "Good as new."

What is with this vampire? His actions and words made my head spin. They weren't at all what the university had prepared me for.

Lycans and vampires broke human bones all the time at the university, and then they made the mortal suffer through the pain of healing. It served as a reminder of their power and their ability to injure those who stepped out of line.

From my experience, their cruelest punishments didn't always equal death.

Torture could do a lot more to hurt someone. And forcing that person to live with the memories of their torment was the ultimate castigation.

Yet Ryder had healed me. *Twice.*

It didn't make any sense. Royal vampires took what they wanted. They were savage creatures. And while Ryder exuded that same air of violence, he treated me as if I were something precious. Not just a snack.

His dark eyes captured mine as he drew his touch up to my neck, his fingers finding my pulse. "What has you so unnerved, sweet pet?" he asked, bending to run his nose across my cheek in a decidedly animalistic manner.

Because he's not human.

"You smell distraught," he murmured. "Is it your arm? Does it hurt?"

"No, it's… you healed me…" I trailed off, having said the first thing that came to my mind, then didn't know how to finish it.

He lifted just enough to stare down at me, his proximity a hot caress against my senses. "Yes. Are you wanting to thank me?"

The way he said it had goose bumps pebbling down my arms. I could only guess what he wanted me to do to show my gratitude.

His hand traveled from my neck up to my face, where he cupped my cheek. "Are you still in pain?"

I slowly shook my head.

"Good," he whispered. "And how are your memories?"

His minty breath clouded the air between us, seducing my senses. It would be so easy to taste him, his lips only a few inches from mine.

Stop it, I told myself. *He's dangerous.*

I recalled the way he killed those two vampires in his living area, how brutal and precise his actions were in destroying their lives. He hadn't even blinked, so lost to his rage that he exterminated them without a second thought.

It was exactly what he would do to me when he grew tired of my presence.

No, my death would be worse. He'd drain me with a bite, take back all the blood he'd fed me and then some.

I trembled at the notion.

"Are they still foggy?" Ryder asked, drawing me back to his questions regarding my memory.

"Yes," I admitted. "Like I dreamt my entire life before waking up in your basement."

"Hmm." He brushed his thumb across my cheekbone, then lowered his grip to my throat again. "You seem to have an adverse reaction to my blood, or perhaps it's something with the drugs you were given at the breeding camp. Maybe a combination of both." His gaze fell to my lips. "I'll look into it for you next week."

I blinked at him. "Why would you do that?" *Why do you care?* was what I really wanted to know.

"Because I can," he replied. "And you're my pet. I'd like to know what happened to you to make you forget. It's a sign of a programming failure, something I imagine society would find fascinating."

I'm sorry I asked, I thought, swallowing roughly.

"Don't worry, sweet Willow. I won't let them touch you. You're mine." He brushed a kiss against my mouth, similar to the one he'd gifted me in his sparring room. Quick. Warm. Underlined in promise.

"What am I to you?" I asked, my eyes searching his. "What classification is my role in your world?"

"You're my pet," he said, his lips curling at the sides. "Mine to play with and stroke as I please, and in exchange, I'll keep you safe."

"Why?" The university hadn't discussed the classification of a *pet*, and something told me Ryder had just made it up. Like everything else. *Is he even a royal?* I wondered again, confused by his antics.

His mouth met mine again, this time lingering for a heartbeat before he repeated, "Because I can." Those three words scattered heat throughout my body, awakening a forbidden emotion I didn't know how to handle.

For twenty-two years, I refused to allow myself even an ounce of hope. Until Blood Day, when I thought for sure I would become a Vigil. When the Magistrate had announced my fate, my heart had shattered into pieces, the stark disappointment a nightmarish cloud in my mind.

I remembered it plainly, even though it felt like a lifetime ago.

Hope was a dangerous emotion. *Happiness* was even more lethal. And I refused to allow myself to feel that way now.

Ryder didn't intend to keep me. He didn't intend to

protect me. He wanted to play with me for a few minutes, then discard me for his next fresh piece of meat.

"Why are there eleven headless bodies in your driveway?" a deep voice interjected, causing Ryder to smile against my mouth. He gifted me another kiss before sitting up to face the dark-haired male walking into the living area in an all-black suit.

Damien.

But that wasn't what grabbed my attention. My focus was drawn to the spot where one of the vampires had died. Specifically, to the pristine white carpet that was as spotless as the rest of the room.

Not only had Ryder cleaned himself up, but he'd also taken care of the blood and gore on the floor.

"Because the twelfth intruder still has his head in my basement," Ryder drawled, replying to the inquiry about the bodies outside. I quivered, both at the mental image his words created and from his palm claiming my side. His thumb slipped along my rib cage to rest just beneath the swell of my breast.

"I see." Damien slid his hands into the pockets of his slacks as he approached the couch to stand right beside us. "Did I interrupt mealtime?"

"No, I just finished a bag of O-positive about ten minutes ago." Ryder continued to stroke along my rib cage, his touch possessive and confusing. It made me want to arch into him and run away at the same time. My heart sped up at the conflicting response, my body turning into liquid fire beneath his hand.

I didn't know how to handle the flame burning inside me.

I didn't know how to handle *him*.

"Why are you denying yourself fresh A-negative?" Damien asked, the reminder of his presence helping to douse the flames only slightly.

A-negative was my blood type. While it was part of my records, I suspected that wasn't how he knew.

"Because she's recovering," Ryder murmured, his attention shifting to me once more as he drew his touch down my side to my hip. Both his touch and his gaze felt like a brand. And the implication in his tone suggested he intended to bite me… and soon.

I shivered, both enthralled and terrified by the prospect.

Damien snorted. "You said that the last time we spoke about it."

"Yes, she's recovering again," Ryder replied, his eyes lifting to meet Damien's stare. "Is there something you want to say to me, old friend?"

His friend didn't even flinch. "She's a problem."

"Because I won't eat her?"

"No. Because she doesn't have a designation and the others won't appreciate that. She's also not your toy to keep."

Ryder cocked a brow. "I'm a royal now. Doesn't that mean I can break certain rules?"

"You're a temporary royal, and you know what Lilith will do when she finds out."

So he is a royal, I thought. *A very strange royal.*

"Lilith can suck my cock," Ryder retorted, causing my eyes to widen.

No one ever spoke about the Goddess that way. Yet Ryder did it without care, his tone suggesting that he despised the queen of our society. A human would be killed for saying such a thing.

"I don't give a fuck about this new world rule or their maliciously contrived edicts," he continued, his grasp tightening on my hip. "And there is nothing temporary about my new position. So either get with the program or piss off."

Damien sighed. "You asked me to advise you. I'm just doing my job."

"Consider myself advised, and consider your advice ignored."

"Fine."

"Fine." The two vampires glowered at each other for another beat, then Ryder's grip loosened, his posture relaxing once more. "Want to meet Intruder Number Twelve?"

"What's his name?"

"I didn't ask. But he was the only one who tried to flee after setting foot on my property, which is why I kept him alive. Originally, I intended to play with one of the older vampires, but I changed my mind after observing Number Twelve's reasoning skills."

Damien arched a brow. "Of course you did. So does he still have a tongue?"

Ryder snorted. "Come on. I'm not a complete monster."

"The mess on your driveway says otherwise."

"I consider that more of a favor than a monstrous deed. They obviously weren't adding much intellect to the new world, what with trying to attack me and all." Ryder lifted a shoulder. "I strongly doubt they'll be missed."

"Whoever hired them may feel otherwise," Damien pointed out.

"You mean Janet? Yes, she may be upset, but I'll be putting her out of her misery soon."

"Janet sent them?"

"That's what our friend in the basement said, yes. He also gave me three other names of vampires who supported her assignment."

"So he's chatty," Damien mused.

"Very." Ryder smiled. "Feel free to run down and meet him. Then we need to discuss next steps. I'm thinking a lesson on hierarchy etiquette is required in the to-be-renamed Silvano City."

"Seems needed, yes," Damien agreed.

"Then you'll help me plan the arrival?"

"Of course."

Ryder smiled. "Excellent. Have fun with Number Twelve in the basement."

"Is that your chosen name for him?"

"It's the abbreviated version," Ryder explained.

Damien smirked. "Then I'll let you know if *Number Twelve* sings anything else useful."

"Brilliant. Just don't kill him."

"Using him to set an example?"

"It's like you know me," Ryder drawled.

"Some days," Damien said, glancing at me. "Is she coming to Silvano City with us?"

Ryder looked at me, his dark eyes flaring with black flames. My skin heated as he caressed me with that searing gaze.

I felt owned under that stare. Possessed. *His.*

My thighs clenched at the thought, my stomach flickering with a forbidden fire. Logically, I knew craving him was a death sentence. But my body refused to adhere to reasonable thought. I reacted to him because I was trained to react to him. It suited the supernatural chain of life.

Ryder was the hunter.

And I was his prey.

"Yes," he murmured after a long, hot beat. "Watch the living room footage from a little over six hours ago, and you'll understand why. She's quite gifted with knives." His eyes left me for his friend. "Everyone will expect her to be weak as a human. I can use that."

"She'll be even more underestimated if she's perceived as a member of your harem," Damien said, sending a chill down my spine. He spoke about me as if I were an object to be reassigned and used where needed—a startlingly accurate summary of my life.

"My harem?" Amusement flirted with Ryder's features. "Ah, right. I suppose I've inherited Silvano's toys."

"You have."

"And who's protecting them at the moment?"

"Garland," Damien replied.

Ryder grunted. "So you mean he's fucking them."

"Likely."

"Great." Ryder returned his attention to me, his pupils dilating as his gaze dropped to my chest, then gradually rose to my face. "Hmm, Willow would make a delectable addition to my harem."

"She would. But she's going to need a wardrobe to match."

Ryder nodded slowly. "Yes. Arrange it." The dark flames in his eyes glowed brighter, revealing a hungry vampire behind his handsome mask.

I swallowed.

Joining a vampire's harem had been near the bottom of my desire list, just a few steps above the breeding camp.

Yet the idea of being in Ryder's bed didn't turn me off. Which was exactly why I needed to fight it. His interest in me would be temporary, and when he finished, I'd be handed off to another.

And then to another.

Living out the rest of my days in sexual servitude, just waiting for one of the vampires to accidentally—or purposely—kill me.

His touch ventured up my side to my face, where his knuckles kissed my cheek in a tender caress. "Don't look so frightened, pet," he whispered. "I'll make sure you enjoy it."

Damien grunted. "Don't say that in front of the others. She's a toy, Ryder. Remember that."

He was right. Vampires didn't see humans as equals. They didn't care if we were hurt or frightened or dying. We were food. Fuck toys. Beings they enslaved to meet their needs.

Yet Ryder hadn't treated me that way, and even now, he continued to glide his fingers across my skin to my throat. "You probably want to take a shower. Then you need to eat."

Damien sighed loudly. "Fine, do it your way. I'll be with Number Twelve in the basement."

Ryder continued to ignore him, his eyes holding mine. "Tomorrow, I'm teaching you how to shoot a gun."

"That'll go over well," I heard Damien mutter from farther away.

"Then we'll work on improving some of your sparring techniques," Ryder continued, disregarding Damien's side commentary. "You fought well, but all of your instruction has been in regard to taking down humans. As I showed you earlier, my kind is different. We're stronger and faster. But all vampires have weaknesses. I'll teach you how to exploit those."

"Wh-why?" I asked, my throat dry. None of this made any sense. He wanted me to teach him about my courses—something he should already have had access to—and now he planned to add me to his harem and teach me defensive strategies reserved for Vigils.

"Because you're going to be my little secret warrior," he replied, his eyes twinkling. "You'll be the ally no one will anticipate."

"Ally?"

"My ascension won't be easy." He drew his fingers through my hair, his eyes following the movement. "There are those who want to kill me, as you've just experienced. And you, my sweet pet, are going to help me slay them all."

The prey becomes the hunter, I thought, mulling over the concept.

How had this become my life? My fate? How long would he keep me? Would I die at his side? Die because of him?

Would I die even faster without him?

My stomach twisted at the notion. He wanted to train me how to kill others. Perhaps I could use the knowledge to defend myself instead. To escape. To finally be free.

And go where? I wondered.

I couldn't answer that.

Ryder stood and held out his hand. "Now come, it's time for you to shower. I'll make you some plain chicken to eat afterward since I know my other food has been hard on you. We'll work up to it."

This vampire baffled my mind, yet I found my palm

rising to meet his. Warmth spread up my arm at the touch, the fire reigniting inside me. He tugged me up to my feet, his opposite hand finding my hip to steady me.

"You took sexual arts classes, yes?" he asked, his palm leaving my hip to press into my lower back. My chest met his bare torso, his heat a welcome blanket to my senses.

"Yes," I whispered, my throat suddenly tight.

"Good," he replied, releasing my hand to cup my cheek. "You're going to need that training in Silvano City. Because I intend to take full advantage of it." He pressed his lips to the edge of my mouth before gliding along my skin to my ear. "Try to use this week to prepare yourself properly, Willow. I'm not an easy lover, and I will be grading you on your technique."

My stomach flipped, his words showering me in a sea of warmth and fury.

I wanted to argue and fall to my knees at the same time.

It was a perplexing reaction that rendered me speechless, something he translated as acquiescence.

He led me upstairs without another word, his palm a fiery reminder against my lower back.

I had a week to figure this out.

A week before he expected me to perform.

And if he was like all the other royals, he didn't just mean with him, but with others. They notoriously shared their harems with higher-ranking officials of society.

Could I handle that?

Was I prepared?

Would my training kick in properly?

My knees shook as we entered my room. One glance at the bed had my thighs clenching, and not from fear but from the prospect of what Ryder intended to do to me.

This isn't what I want, I told myself. Yet that voice sounded weak. Unprepared. Terrified.

Because some part of me deep down did want this, and that was the part that scared me the most.

"Strip," Ryder said as he escorted me into the bathroom.

Rather than watch me comply, he focused on the shower.

It gave me a moment to catch my breath.

Then I remembered his demand, and heat suffused my skin once more.

I had no choice but to obey, which wasn't my problem. Naked, I could handle. It was the evidence of my arousal that I wanted to hide.

He already knows, I whispered to myself, recalling his superior senses. *He can smell it.*

That thought made my mouth go dry.

Rather than overthink it, I pulled off my shorts and shirt, refusing to acknowledge my shame at reacting to him. It was just another way for him to win, and I refused to give him that victory. Although, I really wasn't sure what game we were playing here, or if it was a game at all.

He placed his hand under the spray and nodded. "It's ready for you." Then he turned and ran his eyes over my body, his heated gaze falling to my mound. "You'll need to shave before we leave. I'll find you a razor."

"And if I don't?" I asked him, feeling the need to stand my ground for reasons I couldn't identify. It just seemed natural to fight him. At least a little.

His lips curled as he stepped into my personal space, his strides forcing me to back up into the counter with dual sinks behind me. He gripped the marble on either side of my hips, his body crowding mine.

"If you don't, then I'll shave it for you, Willow." He drew his nose across my cheekbone to my ear. "I dare you to defy me, pet. Because I'll very much enjoy punishing you for it." He nipped my earlobe sharply before adding, "Now be a good girl and take a shower. I'll bring you up some food after you're done."

Ryder pushed away from me with a smirk, picked up my clothes, and made a show of smelling them. "Mmm," he murmured in approval, his eyes running over me for the thousandth time since we met. "I look forward to tasting you later, Willow." He turned for the door, then paused with a single reminder tossed over his shoulder: "One week, pet. One week."

My knees buckled as he left, my heart racing in my chest. *One week*, I repeated to myself. *Fuck*.

Chapter Nine

Ryder

One Week Later

"Do I need to tell you what will happen if you try to run in the soon-to-be-renamed Silvano City?" I asked Willow after buckling her into the seat beside me on the jet.

I'd seen the glint of a plan flashing in her gaze all week while we'd trained. She was a natural with a gun, quickly picked up the sparring moves I'd taught her, and proved to have decent stamina in terms of running.

But besting me would never happen.

And I needed her to acknowledge that now.

I could see the wheels turning behind her eyes, mulling over my question. Finally, she conceded with a short "No." Because she knew what I'd do to her if she tried to run, and it wouldn't be enjoyable for either of us.

"Good," I replied, settling into my seat and meeting Damien's gaze across from me. He held a newspaper in his lap, his suit an exact replica of the one I'd chosen to wear today. Only, he'd paired his with a tie and I'd left my neck exposed.

"I like her dress," I informed him, which was my version of a thank-you since he'd selected the wardrobe.

"I know." He picked up the glass of whiskey beside him that the flight attendant had just dropped off, and took a long sip. "But she still doesn't look the part."

My brow furrowed. "She's in a translucent black gown. Her hair is styled. She has on fuck-me heels. What more can we do?" My cock had saluted her the second she stepped out of her room thirty minutes ago, and it still lay semi-hard for her in my trousers. Because Willow in that dress was a damn tease. That I'd craved her all damn week hadn't helped the issue.

However, I was sort of enjoying this drawn-out game between us. There were several times I'd scented her interest during our lessons, particularly when I had her pinned down on the ground after a sparring move.

She wanted me—of that, I had no doubt. I could take her right now and she'd submit, but I rather enjoyed the prospect of her begging me for it. And she wasn't there yet.

"She's too uptight," Damien pointed out as the jet began to move. The pilot was an old friend—one of the few I trusted to transport me. He came over the intercom with an expected arrival time, then navigated us into position for takeoff.

I studied Willow as we began to ascend, noting her stiff shoulders and throbbing pulse. "Is this your first flight?" I asked her.

She nodded, her nails digging into the armrest.

I nodded. "See, she's just nervous about traveling," I told Damien, not worried. "She'll calm down once we land."

He gave me a look. "No, I mean she's too uptight in

general. Harem members fawn over their royals, all pleading for another taste. She barely touches you. The others will notice and wonder why, which is the exact opposite of what you want if she's to be your little secret. Hell, you haven't even marked her, Ryder."

My jaw ticked as his statements registered. I didn't have a lot of experience with the harem mentality, as that all came about during the political reformation of our society. But he had a point in terms of her reactions to me.

Despite Willow's clear interest, I also sensed many moments of fear, which I thought might be brought on by her experience in the breeding camp. Except she told me she still couldn't remember what happened during her time there. I suspected she never would with whatever drugs they'd forced upon her.

I picked up my own drink, took a long swallow, and considered how to handle this.

Willow required an introduction.

And we were running out of time to facilitate the lesson.

It would also give me a reason to check her grooming habits. I could tell through the gown that she'd shaved just as I'd asked, but I wondered how thorough she was with it.

"All right." I set my glass down and looked at Willow. "Come with me, pet." We were at a safe enough altitude to move around.

I unbuckled myself and reached over to do the same for her, but she didn't move, her terror permeating the air.

"See?" Damien muttered.

"Yes." This wasn't going to work at all. "I'll fix it."

Damien dipped his chin in acknowledgment, saying nothing more as my focus returned to Willow.

"I need you to stand up and follow me," I told her. "Or we can do this here. With Damien."

Her blue eyes shot up to mine, her lips parting at the threat I didn't bother to hide. If she didn't want to comply, I'd punish her. And I'd use Damien to do it.

"I told you my intentions last week," I reminded her,

referring to our conversation where I warned her that I expected to take full advantage of her sexual training in Silvano City. "It's time to put your skills to the test. So choose, Willow. Are we doing this here or in the privacy of the back bedroom?"

I needed her on her game and ready when we landed, which gave us less than four hours to rectify this.

"You have three seconds to decide, pet."

When I reached one on my countdown, she forced herself out of her chair, causing Damien to smirk from his chair. "Pity."

I ignored his side commentary, my focus on Willow. "Good choice," I said softly, standing and leading the way to the back of the jet's cabin. Damien might be disappointed, but I didn't really want him involved in this. Willow was my pet to train, not his.

The scent of her fear followed me all the way to the open door near the rear of the plane and increased to a dangerous level when she saw the sizable bed waiting for us beyond the threshold. It took up the majority of the space, with a pair of nightstands on either side. And a single interior door led to a bathroom with a stall shower.

I turned and noted the tremor in Willow's limbs, her balance uneasy on her four-inch heels. The rumble and movement of the jet probably didn't help matters, but she remained on her feet.

"Close the door," I told her as I removed my jacket and set it on the bed.

She complied, her gaze lowering to the floor in a perfect display of submission. Her training was kicking in, chasing away her warrior side and replacing it with a meek female.

I moved toward her, walking her into the back of the door, and placed my palms on the wood on either side of her head. It left minimal space between us, forcing her to acknowledge my presence.

"Willow," I murmured. "Look at me."

Her throat worked to swallow, her pulse a raging

invitation that taunted my vampiric instincts. But I allowed her a moment to collect herself, then smiled internally when her blue eyes lifted to meet my gaze.

There's my little warrior, I thought, catching the glimmer of anger flickering deep in her irises. She hated what society had turned her into. That alone was a fracture in her programming, one I intended to wholeheartedly exploit.

I slid my knee between her thighs. The slits of her gown went all the way up to her hips, making it simple to part her legs without any hindrance from the fabric. It was meant to provide easy access, and oh, did it deliver.

Her nipples beaded beneath the fabric, the little rosy buds a beacon for my tongue.

But it was her mouth that fascinated me most, the way her lips parted in delicious surprise as I pressed into her personal space.

"Have you ever been with one of my kind, sweet pet?" I asked her softly, bending to run my nose across the flush of her cheeks. She smelled amazing, her blood tempting my inner beast to steal a taste.

"No." It came out as a whisper that would have been lost to most beneath the rumble of the jet, but I heard her just fine.

I pressed my lips to her ear and replied, "Then consider this your introduction to playing with vampires." I would go easy on her, give her just enough to addict her to my methods, and draw out the introduction between us.

She shivered as my mouth skimmed her throat, her pulse beating a mile a minute beneath the skin. I hummed against her, taunting her flesh, while my thigh flexed between her legs, applying pressure to the place I desired to seek out with my tongue.

"If I push you too far, tell me," I said against her ear. "Just say, 'My Prince,' and it ends. Unless we're in public—then I want you to call me Ryder."

Damien said the other day that humans were never allowed to address their superiors by their given names, which provided the perfect cover for me to escort Willow out of a room should I need to.

"What ends?" Willow asked, her hands forming fists at her sides.

"Everything," I promised, drawing my nose along the column of her neck in a warm taunt to both of our senses. "I'm not human, Willow. My proclivities are dark. I like blood. But it's not my wish to damage you. So if I'm really hurting you, I want to know. All right?" Some pain could be mingled with pleasure, something we would explore once I understood her true limits.

"By saying your name."

"When we're in public, yes. And call me *My Prince* when we're in private." My teeth skimmed her raging pulse, my incisors aching to pierce the thin membrane to reach the ambrosia beneath. But I needed this from her first. "Do you understand?"

"Yes." A note of hesitation lurked in her tone, telling me she didn't fully grasp the concept yet. Probably because she'd been trained to never say no. We'd fix that together.

"Do you want to call me Ryder or My Prince right now?" I asked her, testing her limit.

Her nostrils flared. "Ryder."

I smiled. "Are you sure? We're locked in a room and have a few hours. The things I could do to you are endless, sweetheart."

"You'll do them with or without my consent," she replied with a slight bite in her tone, one that made me even harder for her.

"Oh, Willow. You don't have to verbally consent to give me permission," I informed her softly.

She narrowed her gaze. "Is that your excuse?"

"No, darling. It's my explanation. Allow me to demonstrate." I placed an open-mouthed kiss on her neck, eliciting a quiver from her. Rather than bite her, I put my hands on hips to pull her with me as I walked backward to the bed. She followed on unsteady legs, her eyes on me the whole time.

Such a good little pet, I thought, pleased with her. "I'm going to sit down, and you're going to straddle me."

While I enjoyed having her pressed up against the door, I suspected her legs wouldn't be able to support her throughout our introduction. Sitting would be easier for us both.

I slid onto the bed until the mattress hit the back of my knees, and kept my feet planted on the ground. Then I pulled Willow between my spread thighs, her tremble at my nearness proving Damien's point from the jet's lounge area.

I'd been so consumed with the notion of teaching her how to protect herself that I'd completely missed the importance of preparing her sexually.

If she acted like this in front of the others, they'd consider her to be nothing more than food. And while being a member of my harem wasn't all that much better, she'd at least be marked as my personal property. And no one touched a royal vampire's property without permission.

Moving one hand down her hip to her thigh, I gave the muscle a squeeze. "Lift your leg onto the bed."

She did as I requested, her cheeks darkening to a redder shade as the lace of her gown split to reveal her creamy flesh to my view. It served as a decadent tease, the fabric still covering the part of her that I wished to devour. Mmm, the thought of spreading her wide had me eagerly reaching for her other leg.

"Now this one," I told her. I helped lift her off the ground as she complied with my demand, then I guided her to the place I desired, with her hot cunt pressed right against my zipper. "Bunch up your skirt, Willow. I want to feel you up against my cock."

Defiance flickered in her gaze, there and gone in the skip of a heartbeat. I secretly hoped she'd fight me, but resolve steadied her features instead as her fingers gingerly pulled the lace upward to sit around her hips.

"Higher," I said, wanting to see if she was as wet as I

suspected.

Willow shuddered, her eyes briefly leaving mine as she brought the fabric up to her stomach. I placed a palm against her lower spine to hold her steady as I leaned back just enough to see her pretty pink flesh.

Mmm, yes, she was very thorough with that razor. I was almost jealous. Next time I'd groom her myself and taste her afterward. Because the sight of all that glistening interest made my mouth water. Alas, we didn't have enough time for me to properly enjoy her now. So we would do this introduction a different way.

"This is why I don't need your verbal cue," I told her. "You're wet for me, Willow. But I dare you to call me My Prince right now and tell me to stop."

Her blush darkened, her lips parting on soundless words.

"Your submission is beautiful," I whispered, pulling her forward once more to press her slick heat against my aching groin. Just enough to taunt her with a hint of the pleasure to come. "And now, I'm about to make you burn so much hotter."

Willow's pupils dilated. However, I caught the challenge in her gaze. She wanted me to prove it. Or perhaps that was her way of attempting disobedience—a promise not to react.

Poor sweet pet had no idea what I could do to her. But she was about to find out.

I pressed my lips to her ear again and lowered my voice. "You're going to soak my trousers all the way through, and I'll wear your scent for the rest of the night. Everyone will know I played with you before arriving. They'll crave a taste, but I'll forbid them. Because you're my pet, and I'm not fond of sharing."

This new society might try to require it, but I refused to comply.

Because fuck Lilith's rules.

Willow's thighs tightened around mine, her arousal increasing from my words alone.

I smiled against her neck, pleased with her reaction.

"Mmm, we haven't even properly started yet," I murmured, running my nose along her sensitive skin to her pulse once more. I inhaled deeply, her attraction a heady scent in the air, coupled with the seductive taunt of her blood. My tongue traced her thrumming pulse, causing my dick to throb in my pants.

Fuck, it'd been a long time since I indulged in a woman, and having this one under my roof for two weeks hadn't helped matters.

I pressed my palm into her lower back, forcing her hips to grind against mine, the friction an addictive tease I wanted more of. "Ride me," I whispered. "Chase your pleasure, Willow."

She clutched my shoulders, the dress falling to pool between us and stealing my view. But I didn't care. I wanted her to lose herself, to drive herself into an oblivion by using me for her pleasure.

I sucked and nipped her throat, her neck, her collarbone, then returned to the place I needed to bite. There was no sense in drawing it out. I could feel her readiness through my trousers, and I could hear her soft intake of breath that told me she was losing herself to the moment.

She just needed a push, and I provided that with my mouth.

My incisors bit into her flesh, straight to her vein, causing her to scream in surprise. But the second her euphoric receptors kicked in, she began to moan.

It was all give-and-take between us—her blood in exchange for pure rapture.

She came apart on my lap, her body unaccustomed to my vampiric kiss. Something incoherent left her mouth, the sound one of surprise, which told me she'd never experienced an orgasm of this nature before.

I merely smiled in response, but her essence on my tongue kept me focused on the task of devouring her.

Willow's flavor was wickedly unique.

Potent.

Almost supernatural in nature.

However, I sensed her humanity, too. Taking too much would weaken her, and as an older vampire, I didn't need much to survive.

But fuck, she really did taste amazing. And if I wasn't mistaken, a hint of lycan lurked in her veins.

How riveting.

I licked at her wound, forcing my teeth to subside. Then I kissed a path down to her breasts, desiring to mark her there for everyone to see. She gasped as I tugged the neckline of her dress down to sink my fangs into her tit, just above her erect nipple.

Willow immediately convulsed again, a second orgasm ripping through her and soaking my pants in kind.

Oh, how I ached to free my cock and sink into all that delicious heat. She was so ready for me. Maybe tight, too.

Damn, I couldn't wait to take her. She was mine. My pet. My gift. I'd fuck every hole, fill her with my essence to the point where she'd drown in it. Only to revive her and do it all over again.

She'd beg me to do it.

Plead with me to take her over the edge into an oblivion unlike any she'd ever experienced.

Then she'd cry for more.

My strong warrior Willow. I meant what I said. I enjoyed blood. I enjoyed pain. If she didn't stop me, I'd likely destroy us both. But at least we'd die satisfied.

She whimpered above me, her nails digging into my dress shirt.

I released her breast to meet her gaze, noting the haze of desire clouding her features. She was on the precipice of another orgasm, her body moving against mine in short bursts. Yet she groaned as if it weren't enough, her cheeks reddening with exertion.

"Touch yourself," I demanded. "Show me how you like to be stroked."

She quivered, her head dipping back as her eyes closed. Her blush spread down her neck to her cleavage and disappeared into the black translucent material covering her breasts. I gripped the straps holding up the fabric and pushed them off her shoulders to reveal her gorgeous little nipples.

"Willow," I murmured. "Pet your pretty pussy for me. Make yourself come again." I shifted her on my lap, pulling her away from my groin and the friction she'd been using.

A small sound of protest parted her lips, then her hand fell between her legs to do exactly as I demanded. Leaving one hand on her hip, I used the other to lift her dress and watch her work.

Her tentative strokes told me this was new for her, that she hadn't been properly instructed on how to pleasure herself. Yet she quickly figured it out, her body trembling violently every time she brushed her clit.

Then she pressed her thumb to the little button and began to circle it, the movement hypnotic and sexy as hell. I wanted to flip her onto her back and replace her touch with my mouth.

But that wasn't the point of this exercise. I wanted to observe, and observe I did.

"Keep going," I encouraged her. "I want you soaked and sated, Willow. And I want you to scream my name when you come this time. As loud as you fucking can."

She resembled utter perfection in this state, her mind quieting as the needs of her body took over.

"This is what being with a vampire feels like," I told her as I palmed one of her breasts. My other hand remained on her hip to provide stability, ready to catch her if this next orgasm threw her into a state of unconsciousness. "You need to remember this when we're together, Willow. Remember how you feel right now, and know that this was only a brief introduction to what I can do to you."

I tweaked her nipple, hard enough to burn, then soothed it with my tongue. She groaned in response, her fingers moving faster now, her pace a chaotic mixture of passion and lust.

"I can fuck you so hard you'll forget your own name."

My words elicited a deep moan from her, followed by a tear down her cheek. She was overstimulated, her body breaking beneath the onslaught of too much ecstasy. But she could take it.

"You're almost there, sweetheart," I said, my lips going to her throat to lap at the wound I left against her neck.

Her resulting groan went straight to my cock. It took serious effort not to rip off my pants and sink balls-deep into her, but this wasn't so much about me as it was her. I needed her to understand what it would be like between us, to leave her craving more.

Willow's legs began to shake, her flush a permanent fixture against her skin.

"There it is," I murmured. "Come for me, Willow. Come hard." I bit her again, this time on her opposite breast, and growled as her world fell apart.

She screamed my name, her beautiful body mine to command in all ways. Rather than take more of her blood, I moved my mouth to hers and kissed the hell out of her while she cried from the insanity I'd forced upon her.

Her body spasmed violently, to the point where I suspected the pleasure had become painful. I held her through it, my lips praising hers every step of the way, until finally her emotions subsided and she began to relax against me.

I ran my fingers through her hair, not caring at all that I'd messed up her previously styled locks. Her dress would need to be fixed as well, or perhaps swapped for a new one.

When her breathing evened out, I pulled back a little to meet her drowsy gaze. "Show me your fingers, Willow."

She swallowed, then slowly removed the hand from between her legs. Her skin glittered with evidence of her arousal, and I practically salivated for a taste.

Instead, I told her to lick herself clean, and I watched as

she obeyed. Then I took her mouth in another kiss and groaned at the taste coating her tongue. It was perfect and everything I craved, but I wouldn't allow myself a proper taste yet. Delayed gratification would give me something to look forward to later, after I finished playing my part of royal vampire in Silvano City.

Willow panted against me, her blue eyes shining with heated confusion.

Rather than explain myself, I indulged her in another kiss. However, this one was laced with a hint of blood from my tongue.

She jolted at the contact, her taste buds aware of that flavor, and her eyes flew open with a dozen questions. Again I didn't explain myself, mostly because I couldn't. I just knew she needed more of my essence as a protective coating should tonight's events not go the way I intended.

Once I was satisfied that she'd imbibed enough, I pulled away from her and studied her flushed features. She appeared freshly fucked, just as I'd desired. Hmm, and while my blood would assist in her healing, she'd still have my bite engraved in her flesh long enough for others to know whom she belonged to.

Perfection.

"I think you're ready now," I informed her softly before kissing her again because I could. She returned my embrace, her movements lazy and sated.

Yes, I really did enjoy her in this state.

Maybe I'd keep her in it for the rest of the night. For fun.

Chapter Ten

Willow

My university experience had not prepared me for Ryder's bite.

I'd expected harsh touches and savage fucking and to pass out from his violent thirst for my blood. Yet all he'd done was make me come.

Three. Times.

I took a course during my nineteenth year on how to fake pleasure through pain. Nothing about my reaction to Ryder had required that developed skill set. My screams were natural and loud and bordering on insane.

My limbs continued to shake even now as I sat beside him in the car on our way to the heart of the city. Part of it was a result of my building anxiety, but most of it was from the rapture that had exploded through my system from his antics on the plane.

He'd held me afterward, his lips whisper-soft against my ear as he praised me for how I reacted to his bite. Then he'd uttered sinful promises, telling me just how he intended to fuck me, the types of positions he preferred, and how he couldn't wait to see my lips wrapped around his cock.

Each statement served as a warning of what was to come, preparing me to accept him mentally. Never once did he discuss sharing me, apart from claiming he wasn't fond of sharing with others. It went against everything I'd been taught yet seemed appropriate for Ryder because his behavior never matched society standards.

I glanced up at him, taking in his stoic features. His focus was on the front window as he scanned the buildings around us.

Darkness blanketed the night sky, and there was only a handful of lights on the street to illuminate our way. As vampires possessed enhanced eyesight, they wouldn't need much more than a few lamps here or there. Oddly, I found it to be adequate enough for me to see as well, something I attributed to drinking Ryder's blood on the plane.

My thighs clenched at the thought, my mouth salivating for more. He'd turned me into an addict, his essence my new favorite cuisine.

He leaned into me and brushed his lips against my temple. "Ready for another orgasm already?" he asked softly, causing my cheeks to heat.

Damien grunted from the front passenger seat. "While I'm glad you tamed your pet, her scent is making my jaw ache."

"Mmm, I'm rather fond of it," Ryder murmured, his nose skimming my neck as he inhaled. My heart skipped a beat in response, my body reacting to his lips caressing my pulse point.

Part of me wanted to beg for another bite.

Part of me wanted to run.

It was an intoxicating mix of desire and fear, making it difficult for me to breathe.

I'd gone into that bedroom with the expectation of being used like a toy, but I should have known better. Ryder never did what I anticipated. He was the opposite of what my experience told me to expect.

If he kept this up, I might start to *like* him.

Which made him the most dangerous being I'd ever met.

His teeth skimmed my throat as he reached up to tug on the strap of my dress. It wasn't the same one I'd worn on the plane but a sapphire gown with a similar translucent material that left me mostly on display.

Ryder drew the thin strap over my shoulder to my upper arm, his action revealing my breast to everyone in the car. I swallowed, uncertain of what he intended to do until he lowered his lips to my nipple and sucked it into his mouth.

I fought a groan, my lower abdomen clenching with raw need.

Fuck, this male was going to be the literal death of me. Something he drove home by sliding his sharp teeth into my skin just above my nipple.

This time I couldn't hold back my moan, his bite a euphoric hit to my senses—one he took away only a second later, leaving me panting in need beside him.

A growl from the front seat had me meeting Damien's hungry stare, his pupils blown wide at the display behind him. "You've made your point, Ryder."

"Have I?" he asked, his tongue dabbing at the marks he'd left in my skin. "I'm not so sure." He trailed his lips up to my throat, his fangs piercing my skin once more and driving me closer to the edge of ecstasy. Only, he pulled back before I could fall into oblivion.

"Your claim is clear," Damien said, facing forward again.

"You sound disappointed," Ryder replied softly, his minty breath warm against my cheek.

"It's not going to be well received by the others."

"You say that as though I should care," Ryder drawled as he slid a hand through the slit of my dress to palm my upper thigh.

His opposite hand went to my strap to draw the fabric up to my shoulder once more. Then he drew his touch downward slowly to fix my neckline and traced his bite mark with his fingertips.

"Everyone will know you're mine, Willow. To touch you without permission would be a grave offense, one worthy of death." He grazed my collarbone with his thumb, then gripped my chin to pull my gaze to his. "You are to remain by my side all night unless I instruct you otherwise. Understand?"

"Yes." My voice came out hoarse, his proximity and touch doing things to me I couldn't seem to fight. He was supposed to use me. Drain me. Kill me. Not ignite my veins on fire like this.

He pressed his lips to mine, the kiss both a threat and a promise. "Good girl," he said softly, then redirected his focus toward the front of the car. "Don't worry, Damien. You can sate your hunger with my inherited harem."

"Garland will be thrilled," Damien drawled.

Ryder snorted. "Garland can fuck off."

Damien didn't reply, but amusement flirted with the edge of his mouth—a smirk I caught in the reflection of the mirror.

The driver didn't say a word, his stoicism reminding me of my professors at the university. He'd met us at the airfield. *Rick*, Ryder had called him. They'd exchanged some words in a language I didn't recognize, their history evident in the way Ryder had addressed the other man.

I wondered how they met or how long they'd known each other, but I knew better than to ask. Just as I knew better than to request information on what to expect as we pulled into a circular drive in front of a tall glass building. Or it appeared to be glass, anyway, with all its long windows reaching into the sky.

I looked up at it as we exited the car, noting that it stood taller than all the surrounding structures. The moon reflected off the endless windows, illuminating the premises in a nightly glow that appeared almost mystical in its appeal.

Ryder fixed the collar of his white dress shirt and ran his hand over his jacket to check the button just below his sternum. He definitely looked the part of a royal now with his regal stance, ageless face, and confident gaze. Damien stood beside him, hands in his pockets, tie immaculate, and glanced sideways at his royal friend.

"Ready to make some heads roll?" he asked.

"I intend to do a lot more than that," Ryder replied, pressing his palm to my lower back. "Remember what I said, Willow. Stay by my side."

"Yes, My Prince," I told him, the formal address sounding wrong to my ears. However, there were others present now, thus requiring my submission. And while it should have come to me naturally, it didn't.

Ryder stroked his thumb along my exposed spine, my blue gown lacking a back. It was a small touch, but one that seemed to radiate protection. I found myself wanting to believe in that unspoken promise, to rely on him for my safety.

My lips threatened to curl down at the notion, my mind rebelling against the concept of trusting anyone other than myself. His kindness—if it could be called that—was temporary. It had to be. He'd show his true self soon enough.

Shoving my thoughts from my head, I focused on our surroundings, curious. The university had been located near a desert, the heat unbearable and dry and very unlike the humidity kissing my skin now.

A variety of greenery decorated the grounds, flowers of tropical shades framing the entrance to the building. I wanted to touch the fuchsia leaves and lean down to smell the aromatic perfume of the purple petals. However, I kept my hands to myself and followed Ryder's lead as he escorted me past the alluring landscaping to a set of doors that opened automatically to allow us entry.

Damien followed right behind us, his lethal presence a threat against my back.

I shivered as the cold air hit me across the face, the atmosphere starkly different from the balmy weather outside. Ryder propelled me forward, his steps certain as he entered the reception area with a royal flair.

Two vampires stood behind a desk, their attention on a set of screens, not us. I lowered my gaze to the marble floor in a necessary show of subservience while moving alongside Ryder. When we reached the two females, he cleared his throat.

An audible gasp sounded from one as the other stammered out an "Oh, Your Highness. I-I'm s-sorry. We weren't ex-expecting you."

"I didn't realize I needed to be expected," Ryder replied. "Were we supposed to call ahead, Damien?"

"No. It's your territory. You move through it as you see fit," Damien drawled as he stepped up to my opposite side, his arm brushing mine. "But I have it on good authority that the guest suite upstairs has already been prepared for your arrival. I believe Benita was handling the arrangements."

"I did." The feminine voice came from behind us, followed by a series of clicks that echoed through the lobby.

Ryder turned, pulling me with him. "Ah, Benita, darling. It's been a few decades."

"Yes, My Prince." Her long, bare legs came into my view, her heels a deep red that contrasted against the white flooring. Ryder reached for her, embracing her with a kiss that sent heat crawling up my neck. It was just a peck to her cheek, but their easy camaraderie painted a history that made my stomach clench.

Why do I care? I'm just his pet. Nothing more.

What I needed to do was allow this to be a reminder of my place. He had an entire harem waiting for him, at least from what I understood. Why would I be anything more than a quick bite to him?

This was the reason I considered his behavior to be dangerous. It encouraged false expectations underlined in naive hope.

"I've arranged one of Silvano's former guest suites for you. His penthouse still requires renovation, as do the harem quarters and anything else you'd like changed." Benita didn't back away from him, instead allowing her dark red nails to trail up his sternum.

His palm branded my lower back, holding me beside him as if I were an ornament. Which, I supposed, I resembled in this translucent gown.

"I see you brought a snack with you," Benita mused.

"My pet," Ryder corrected her, his thumb drawing a circle against my skin. I didn't understand what it meant or why he did it.

"I see." Benita cleared her throat and removed her hand from his chest. "Well, we have several options tonight for dining, if you're hungry. Otherwise, I can show you up to your suite. Which do you prefer, Your Highness?"

"I'm familiar with the guest areas," Damien cut in. "If you provide us with the codes, I'll see to it that everything is taken care of for our stay. Just as I will be overseeing the overhaul of the penthouse."

"Of course," Benita replied. "Then dinner first?"

Ryder shifted slightly as Damien moved closer to my opposite side. I didn't dare look up but suspected they were communicating silently through their eyes. The two of them were obviously old friends. I could feel the loyalty between them, their silence seeming to speak volumes about whatever they were planning.

"Yes," Damien said slowly. "Dinner first."

"I agree," Ryder replied. "But we can show ourselves in, Benita. You've done enough for us, and your assistance will not be forgotten."

The female curtsied in response, a platitude falling from her lips before she handed an electronic device over to Damien. "Everything you requested is on this tablet."

"Excellent," he murmured. "We'll take it from here, Benita."

"Of course," she repeated, her voice no longer holding the chipper note she'd displayed upon arrival. She curtsied once more, then walked away with a sway to her curvy hips.

I chanced a glance at the rest of her, noting her hourglass shape and reddish-brown hair. She wore a very short dress that revealed almost as much as my gown, except her fabric was opaque, while mine showcased every detail beneath the lace.

"Remember the rules," Damien breathed against my ear, causing goose bumps to pebble down my neck.

Ryder kissed my temple. "Maybe she wants to be punished."

I swallowed and immediately dropped my gaze again.

"Come, pet," Ryder whispered. "The fun part is about to begin."

Chapter Eleven

Ryder

Oh, how I adored silence.

Particularly, the kind of silence that followed a shocking event.

Such as my unexpected arrival in Silvano's notorious dining hall.

Human bodies littered the tables, each surrounded by vampires enjoying their chosen vein. Most of the mortals were on their last threads of life, their eyes holding a glassy gleam that my kind often ignored in this reformed society.

In my day, we used to leave our victims alive, not wanting word of vampires to spread. But that all changed after the revolution.

While I understood the need for evolving humankind, I didn't quite respect how it all had come about. We required blood to survive. Somewhere along the way, vampires had become gluttonous and forgotten that fact.

I paused just over the threshold of the room, taking in the scene of gawking patrons.

They'd all expected me to arrive next week, thanks to Damien's well-placed whispers. Even Benita had helped spread the rumors, making everyone here feel safe under the assumption that I wasn't scheduled to appear for several more days.

That'd been the point—I wanted them comfortable. It made it so much easier to encourage their congregation tonight. Particularly when I'd provoked the need for this meeting.

Number Twelve, whom I now knew as Julian, had delivered a very specific message on my behalf yesterday. From what I could see of the attendees now, he'd done exactly as I'd requested.

Seems the kid will live after all, I thought, pleased.

I stepped farther into the room with Willow beside me and Damien at my back. That seemed to be the motion that caused everyone to react, sending several vampires to their feet as they prepared themselves to greet me formally.

I played along, wandering from table to table, shaking hands, exchanging cheek kisses, and generally acting as though I didn't have any other agenda than to be social.

Willow remained by my side, her obedience resolute as I paraded her around the dining hall. Several eyed her with interest, their hungry gleams rivaling my own.

No one touched her, but I sensed their interest in enjoying my pet. Two even mentioned it after complimenting her assets. I neither confirmed nor denied their request, mostly because I didn't expect them to stay alive very long.

When we reached the final table—the one I desired to reach all along—I smiled. "Mind if I join you, Janet?"

"Of course not, Your Highness," she replied, doing an admirable job of appearing honored to accept my request.

That served as another indicator that Julian had done his job. If she knew I was aware of her recent assassination attempt, she would have tried to run upon my arrival rather than wait patiently for me to approach her table.

I pulled out one of two available chairs and sat down while Damien took the other seat. Willow went to her knees between us with her head bowed. I ran my fingers through her hair, wanting her to feel safe and protected. Her chosen position seemed to be one of mental programming, telling me that much more about the university's training.

Janet snapped her fingers to grab the attention of a nearby staff member. "Your temporary royal is here. Either bring him fresh blood or offer your own vein," she snapped.

The female human paled, her lower lip quivering just a little. "I will bring a selection for his choosing," she replied, her head bowed. Then she scurried away like a frightened little mouse.

"Is that attire normal?" I asked Damien, noting that the servant wore nothing else apart from the metallic piercings and their dangling chains.

"Yes. The more piercings they wear, the longer they've been serving," Damien replied as he picked up the limb lying lifelessly on the table and moving it onto the abdomen of the dying male. Janet had been feeding near his femoral artery. The teeth marks on his flaccid cock indicated she'd enjoyed that extremity as well.

"I see" was all I could manage to say. Similar sights around the room made my stomach roll. Everyone had returned to their meals, the sounds of whimpering a background noise everyone seemed to ignore.

It made my jaw tick.

Where was the excitement of the hunt? A predator seeking his prey? What enjoyment did easy acquisitions truly inspire?

I found it boring.

Irritating.

Disenchanting.

Willow's moans on the plane were so much more gratifying than the cries humming through the air now. She submitted to me because she relished the sensation. The mortals in this room were weeping over their loss of life, which was a very different sound indeed.

"So, how long do you intend to stay, My Prince?" Janet asked, her hazel irises flickering with hidden emotions. What she failed to realize was that I already knew her secrets.

Alas, I had a game to play.

And so I did.

"However long it takes," I replied vaguely. "There's so much I need to learn about Silvano's former territory."

"As well as our society," she added, her gaze flicking to the top of Willow's head before glancing at one of the staff members.

"Do you not feel my pet is dressed appropriately?" I asked her, not following the insinuation of her gesture.

"Oh, no. She looks quite edible in that gown. I'm just surprised you haven't offered to share her yet."

"As I just sat down, I've not had the opportunity to decide on such a cause yet." Willow trembled slightly at my statement, suggesting she hadn't believed my commentary on the plane about not sharing her. We would rectify that later, or perhaps my actions tonight would prove to her that I'd meant it.

Word games often required extensions of the truth. This dance with Janet would be no different.

The vampire to her left cleared his throat. "Silvano was fond of sharing his harem members with elite members of society." A slight Spanish accent smoothed his tone.

"Was he?" I asked, eyeing the now dead male on the table. "And he enjoyed sharing his servants as well?"

Janet laughed, the sound more condescending than humorous. "Oh, Ryder, how your reclusive ways have dated you." She gestured to the diners all around us. "These bodies are fresh from the blood farms. You know, where they breed and raise humans for our tables."

The male to her opposite side nodded. "Unfortunately, we're a bit short on adults at the moment, as there have been some issues down south at one of the farms. Silvano and Arrick were supposedly addressing it."

"Yeah, and where's the proof of that?" another asked.

Of the six other vampires at this table, I only recognized three of them—Janet, Tandem, and Dom. The other three weren't young, but they weren't old either.

Tandem was the one who'd questioned the proof, his tone underlined in that usual sardonic note he favored. According to Julian, Tandem had approved of Janet's plan. So had Jorge, who sat at the table beside us, his forehead dotted with perspiration. I caught his gaze as he glanced our way for the thousandth time, and arched a brow at him. "Is there a problem?" I asked him, not holding back the irritation in my voice.

"N-no, Your Highness. No problem."

Ah, he thought he spoke the truth. Unfortunately for him, he didn't. Because there was absolutely a problem—one I intended to solve soon.

I gave the poor excuse for a male a short smile before refocusing on Janet and did my best to feign disinterest.

This was the part of the game where I made her feel comfortable and didn't give away anything. Her punishment would be so much sweeter as a result.

I remained quiet while the vampires at the table complained about the lack of food in this region. Dom commented on the diversity issue, stating most of the humans were O-positive and he longed for a good A-negative.

Willow shivered at the mention of her blood type. I attempted to soothe her by shifting my touch to her tense neck, my fingers gently massaging the muscles.

The pointed conversation shifted to my pet, Dom's pupils dilating at the scent of her delectable blood. I almost dared him to ask for a taste. They were walking a thin rope as it was, treating me as an equal and not their better. It would provide me with the perfect opportunity to put him—and everyone else—in his place.

However, the female with the piercings returned before he could comment. A muscular male with similar metal ornaments accompanied her, his purpose immediately evident as he removed the dead human from the table. He didn't flinch or whisper a quick prayer. He just hefted the corpse over his shoulder and disappeared through a pair of swinging doors that led to what I assumed was the kitchen.

I noticed several other tables being cleared in a similar fashion, all by mortal males like the one who'd just serviced our area.

The female servant quickly took our soiled tablecloth and replaced it with another one, her movements agitated. Janet fondled her openly, tugging on the piercings and laughing when the girl squeaked. Tandem slapped the slave on the ass, telling her to behave.

Willow began to vibrate beneath my palm, her escalating pulse drawing my attention to her. But just as I was about to pull her up and into my lap, the muscular male returned with seven naked humans trailing behind him.

My eyebrows lifted at the parade, mostly because of the varying ages among them. The youngest couldn't have been more than ten years old.

"May I present our menu," the male said, his tone flat and void of emotion. His presentation reminded me of a maître d' informing me of tonight's wine selection as he went through each option, providing me with the slave's blood type and age.

I was wrong—the youngest was eleven. And the oldest was just nineteen.

Everyone fell quiet as they waited for me to make my decision. "Will you be distributing the rest to the other tables?" I asked, genuinely curious.

"Yes, My Prince," the male servant replied without looking at me.

"And this is the practice in most restaurants?" I pressed, this time glancing at Damien.

"Yes," my oldest friend confirmed. "In fine-dining restaurants, at least."

"I see." I made a mental note to ask him later about quick dining and what that entailed. "Well." I pretended to peruse the menu, not at all interested in the offerings.

"My Prince." The soft feminine voice came from the servant who had replaced our tablecloth. "We also have a menu of organs prepared, if you prefer to order off the list."

"Organs?" I repeated.

"Yes," Janet interjected, staring at the girl. "Fresh heart was a favorite of Silvano's. He perfected the art of extraction at the table. Perhaps you'd like to give it a try?"

The female servant trembled visibly, causing Janet to growl at the show of a reaction. But I suddenly realized what the poor girl was offering me. *Her* organs.

Fuck. Damien had never mentioned this practice to me, something I accused him of with a glance. His gaze was on the girl, a note of irritation in his depths. That little tell informed me that he didn't actually know and he was just as repulsed by the idea as I was.

"Who's in charge of this dining hall?" I tried to phrase it as a polite question, but it left my mouth as a demand, and it truly silenced the room. Even the humans stopped breathing.

"That would be me, Your Prince."

I had to rotate in my chair to find the one who spoke, placing my knee beside Willow's head.

A svelte female stood, her spine erect despite the clear nervous energy pouring off her.

"And you are?" I didn't recognize her, and she struck me as quite young.

"Meghan," she replied.

"Meghan," I repeated, arching a brow at her. "Your menu includes organs and children?" I phrased it as a question because I needed an explanation. Preferably a good one.

"Y-yes, Your Highness," she stammered, clearing her throat. "They were Silvano's preferred cuisine, so our restaurant is well stocked with those items."

I clenched my teeth, my blood heating with fury. Willow flinched against me, reminding me that I held her fragile neck in my palm, and I immediately eased my grip. I brushed my thumb over her raging pulse in a stroke of apology before focusing on Meghan once more.

"You'll be closing your menu early tonight," I informed her.

She frowned. "O-of course, Your Highness."

"You can't do that," Dom protested. "I've barely had my fill."

Congratulations, Dom. You've just been added to my show list for tonight. Rather than say that out loud, I turned back around to face him and said, "Don't worry. I've brought something else for everyone to enjoy."

Willow stopped breathing, her body freezing beside mine.

I nearly growled at her, irritated that she hadn't heard a damn thing I'd said on the plane. What part of my not wanting to share her didn't she get?

"Well, now I'm interested," Dom said, his lascivious tone directed at my pet.

Not going to happen.

Ignoring him and the trembling female beside me, I focused on Damien. "If you wouldn't mind retrieving our bags, I think it's time to share the gifts I brought for the elite members of Silvano's society."

Chapter Twelve

Willow

I couldn't breathe.

Ryder's anger suffocated me. This entire room threatened to drown me. And his commentary about bringing something to share had my heart literally stopping in my chest.

I'd been the only edible item on the plane.

He might have promised not to share me, but I knew better than to believe him. Tonight proved that.

A slight tug on my hair had me flinching out of my thoughts, my pulse kick-starting as I realized I'd missed something Ryder had just said. Was I supposed to move? To climb onto the table to be devoured?

Oh, Goddess, those poor humans. They were all dead. Drained. *Gone.* Soon I would join them, a soul in the afterlife. I just hoped I wouldn't be reborn.

Another yank on my hair had me wincing.

Ryder wrapped his palm around the back of my neck, his grip unyielding. I'd clearly missed something, because Damien was no longer seated beside me.

I tried to listen for a command, to understand what Ryder wanted, but a rushing sound overwhelmed my ears, making it impossible to hear. My throat worked to swallow while my lungs burned with the need for air.

This is it. This is how I die. He's going to force me onto that table and allow his friends to feast on—

A door slammed somewhere behind me, the vibration against the ground stealing me from my thoughts. Only then did I register that Ryder had released me. He still sat beside me, but he had a gun in his hand.

I blinked. *Is he going to shoot me first?* He held it low against his thigh, just under the tablecloth. I could see it from my angle, but it appeared hidden from the rest of the room.

"Here's your bag." The deep voice penetrated the bubble around my head, allowing me to hear once more. I jumped as something thumped right behind me.

"Perfect," Ryder replied.

"What's that smell?" one of the males at the table demanded. His voice held a nasally hint to it that made my skin crawl. He was the same one who complained about there not being enough A-negative in stock. Of all the vampires in this room, he unnerved me the most. I really hoped Ryder wouldn't share me with him.

"I think some of my gifts have spoiled," Ryder informed him as he pushed back his chair.

If anyone noticed the gun in his hand, they didn't comment. I remained in my submissive pose, uncertain of what he intended to do next. Both men were behind me now, the sound of a zipper echoing through the too-silent room.

My nose twitched at the acrid stench that followed.

"You see, about a week ago, I had a few visitors," Ryder

began, his tone conversational. "I brought them here with me to see if anyone recognizes their heads."

Gasps littered the air as he began tossing items from the bag onto the nearby tables. It took me a minute to realize *what* he was throwing around, and it happened right around the time one of the "gifts" rolled off the table to land on the ground by my knees.

My stomach heaved on impulse, the rotting flesh producing a smell I couldn't handle. Damien placed a hand on my shoulder and leaned over me to retrieve the head by the hair and more carefully set it on the table again. Rather than remove his palm, it remained there, his fingers giving me a slight squeeze of warning.

I swallowed the bile in my throat and parted my mouth for my next inhale, unable to handle the grotesque aroma in the air.

"What the hell is this?" the nasally voiced vampire demanded, the sound of a chair scraping following his words. "How dare you come in—"

Ryder silenced him with a bullet from his gun, the *boom* causing the entire room to stop breathing again.

A thud followed the gunshot.

"Apparently, my ascension wasn't clear," Ryder said after a beat, his voice underlined in power. "For those who need this stated in blunt terms, allow me to explain—I'm in charge. My word is law. I will be making changes around here, and you will abide by those changes or get the fuck out of my territory. Any questions?"

Silence.

Damien tightened his grip on my shoulder once more. I didn't understand why. I was still sitting on my heels, my hands loose on my thighs. Was it my pulse? Could he hear my quickening heartbeat? I couldn't control that, not with Ryder's dominance flaring at my back.

"Now, some of you might be thinking this is temporary and believe that you don't need to listen to me. So allow me to disabuse you of those illusions—I have every intention of staying. And as I'm one of the oldest of our kind, Lilith won't be able to refuse me. So I suggest you attempt to ally with me rather than against me. Which brings me to my gifts."

Ryder's thigh brushed my arm as he stepped forward to push his chair beneath the table. Then he bent to retrieve something from the tabletop. While I couldn't see it, I suspected it was the head that had fallen onto the floor before.

"Does anyone recognize this former immortal?" Ryder asked. "Or any of the others on the tables before you?"

Several comments followed his question, all voiced by different vampires around the room.

"Karim lived in the condo a few doors down from mine."

"Alfonzo worked security for Silvano's building."

"Stiles was in charge of human transport from the farm down in Hugo's area."

Additional details continued to float around the room, the vampires seeming eager to appease Ryder's request for information.

When the voices began to die down, he tossed the head back onto the table with a thunk. "Well. It seems we are all starting to understand each other. But there's one piece of the puzzle not yet discussed, which is the fact that someone sent twelve vampires to assassinate me."

Electricity hummed through the air on the heels of his statement, the tension pulling at my senses and making my heart race faster in my chest. Damien's hand was beginning to feel like a brand, his presence a fixture at my back that refused to budge.

Something was coming.

Something bad.

"So now for my next gift," Ryder continued, his hand appearing in my peripheral vision as he pulled a device out of his pocket.

What happened to his gun? Perhaps he'd set it on the table, or maybe Damien had it. The room had gone still, which could have been a result of Ryder's domineering presence. However, I sensed more was going on than I could see from my subservient position on the floor.

"Who sent you?" His voice sounded through the room again, but this time from the item in his hand.

The question was followed by a grunt of pain and then another male saying, "Fuck, man. I said I'd talk."

"Then talk. And I also suggest you remember who you're speaking to," Ryder replied through the recording, his tone implying dissatisfaction.

"There's a group of older vamps who don't want you in power." The male cleared his throat. "I didn't want to go along with this, I swear. But my maker made me."

"Who's your maker?"

Ryder stopped the recording there and asked, "Any guesses on what he said?" He paused before adding, "I'll give you a hint. She's in this room."

A hiss broke through the air, sending a chill down my spine.

Damien's grip on my shoulder shifted as he forced me to the ground, my nose hitting the marble below. Shouts and curses littered the air, as did an array of gunshots, each one making me flinch against the ground.

Screams followed.

Then a harsh gurgling sound.

Thuds against the floor.

General chaos.

And Ryder's angry tones.

Rather than remain on the floor, I curled my legs beneath me and crawled quickly toward the table with the desire to hide beneath it, only to have my ankle caught in a savage grip. My gown slid across the marble as the culprit yanked me toward him.

I struck out with my heel, landing a kick against my opponent's sternum. His grunt turned to a snarl as he wrenched me backward with his cement-like grasp on my ankle.

Just moments ago, I thought I was going to die at Ryder's hands and become a meal for his friends to enjoy.

Now, I saw my death reflected in a pair of evil blue eyes framed by a handsome face and underlined by a cruelly curved mouth.

His hunger hit me like a heat wave, his hands reminding me of lycan claws as he tried to pull me beneath him.

No.

No.

No!

I refused to play the victim card, all those days in a cell raped repeatedly while drugged. Glimmers of the memories flashed behind my eyes, reminding me of the pain and torment I'd experienced. Just enough to kick-start my heart and my survival instinct.

My training took over, my arms and legs moving with a precision I'd honed over the years.

This had happened at the breeding camps, too. I had a vague memory of making a lycan bleed. He paid me back in kind by slashing his claws across my stomach.

There and gone in a second, my mind protecting me from whatever vicious act came next.

Not this time, I thought, blindly fighting for my life. The vampire crawled over me, his strength insurmountable and resolute. I tried to knee him, to kick him, to scratch out his eyes. But he caught my wrists and forced them over my head, his lower body landing against mine.

And in the next moment, he disappeared.

A roar came from nearby, followed by my perpetrator's head landing on the floor beside me.

I gaped at it, then looked up to find Ryder standing above me in his immaculate suit.

He holstered his gun against his belt—a wardrobe attribute I'd missed in my earlier perusal of his outfit—and then he held out his hand for me.

I pressed my palm to his, my mind lost to a series of

questions. My world shifted as he pulled me upward. His lips brushed my forehead before he tucked me behind him in a protective gesture.

I clung to his jacket, confused and overwhelmed. My lungs ached, demanding more air. I inhaled Ryder's minty scent, his presence immediately calming my nerves. It was wrong, and frightening, but I needed it right then, and so I allowed it. I'd evaluate the reasons behind the comfort later.

As my pulse began to slow, I made the mistake of looking around the room.

My heart promptly jumped back into a chaotic rhythm, but for an entirely different reason.

Headless bodies decorated the tables, and blood dotted the clothes, chairs, and floors.

He massacred them... But how? He only held a gun.

The answer lurked in Damien's hand as he sauntered toward us. "Done" was all he said as he set a wicked dagger on a nearby table.

I peeked out from behind Ryder to find a handful of vampires standing in the corner of the room, the majority of them gaping at the scene. Two, however, wore smiles of approval.

Rather than drop my gaze the way I should, I studied them and the scene, both mortified and enthralled by everything at the same time.

It was so thorough and efficient—two adjectives I associated with Ryder. Powerful, too, which was evidenced by the blue-eyed vampire's headless body a few feet away from me. Another blade stuck out of his chest. That one must have belonged to Ryder.

Had the knives been in the bag of heads? They were too big for him to have concealed beneath his jacket. However he'd done it, I was impressed. Not only had he taken down over a dozen vampires in the blink of an eye, but he'd done so without getting a speck of blood on his suit. Even his hands were clean.

Ryder redefined the term *monster*. And rather than terrify

me, I felt… *hot*.

He'd just slain an entire room of evil in a way I could only dream of accomplishing.

Who are you? I marveled, studying his broad shoulders.

His claims to be a royal were real, but he was unlike any I'd ever studied. He was ruthless and harsh, two traits known for his kind, yet he'd acted out against his fellow vampires, not the humans. That alone made him unique. The events of tonight, coupled with everything else, and I just didn't know where to even begin with him.

"Consider yourselves warned," Ryder said, addressing the huddled group in the corner of the room. "I will not tolerate disobedience. I will not tolerate assassination attempts. And I will not tolerate disrespect. I am not Silvano, but I am your new royal. It's now your duty to inform the others."

A chorus of "Yes, My Prince" and "Yes, Your Highness" sounded from the group.

"Good. And to ensure you all truly understand who I am and what I can do, I expect you to work together to clean up this mess. The bodies are to be burned, and human help is not allowed. Why? Because my message is for you and you alone." He glanced at Damien. "Are there cameras in this room?"

"Yes," his friend replied. "Security footage covers all common areas of this building, including the kitchens, servant areas, and the incinerators out back that are commonly used to dispose of remains."

"Brilliant. Then I can use those feeds to verify that my orders are being executed properly." He returned his attention to the others. "Should any of you decide not to assist in cleaning up this mess, I'll visit you personally to ascertain why. My guess is, you won't like my response."

No one protested or dared to utter a word.

Perhaps they were as stunned as I was at his edict.

"Also, going forward, there will be no children on the menu," he continued. "There will be no organs on the menu or otherwise, either. Do I make myself clear, Meghan?"

"Y-yes, Your Highness."

"Should I find you incapable of following such a direct order, you will be replaced," he added, his tone severe. "And the children you've already procured are to be sent up to Silvano's former penthouse. I will find a use for them there. Also, the female human who tried to offer me her organs will be my personal server going forward. She will not interact with any other customers. Only me."

"Yes, My Prince. I'll see that it's arranged."

"See that you do," he replied, then looked to his friend. "Shall we?"

Damien nodded. "I believe your message came through loud and clear."

"Let's hope," Ryder drawled as he faced me.

His gaze registered surprise, confusing me for a moment before I realized what I'd done.

Shit.

I immediately lowered my head, taking on a submissive stance. But it was already too late, the tension in him palpable as he pressed his palm to my lower back.

He led me to the door and out into the lobby. I remained silent with each step, my heart racing in my chest.

Yet it wasn't driven by fear but by rebelliousness.

I'd broken a society rule.

Several, in fact.

That vampire who attacked me had every right to put his fangs in my body—at least according to the hierarchy of our world—and I'd fought him. Then I'd studied the room and met Ryder's gaze head-on. It made me feel powerful. Alive. *Indestructible.* Which was a ridiculous reaction because Ryder could snap my neck with a flick of his wrist.

However, some broken part of me didn't care.

I could make my own choices. If they earned me a death sentence, at least I'd go to the afterlife with my soul intact.

"You need a card," Damien said as he approached us. I dared a glance at him and found him holding a bag. Did it contain more heads? Weapons? Dangerous items?

Rather than ask, I lowered my gaze again and contemplated this newfound power in my spirit. I didn't want to bow or submit. I wanted to rise and fight. I wanted to do what Ryder had just done to that room of monsters.

He was like a god among vampires, old and powerful.

I peeked up at him, noting the handsome cheekbones and square jawline of his profile. Typical vampiric traits, yet they appeared even more masculine and lethal now. Because I knew what he could do.

His gaze slid to mine, his lips curling up at one corner. He should be reprimanding me for daring to look at him. Punishing me for fighting that vampire. Slaughtering me for breaking the molds of my society programming.

However, he did none of those things.

He just… smiled.

A ding sounded, alerting us that the elevator had arrived. He guided me inside with his palm against my back. Damien followed and dropped his bag on the floor.

"This is where you need the first code," Damien explained, uttering the numbers. He began to type them as the doors closed. "That's the one for the floor the guest suite is on. There's a second set for the penthouse."

"And how do you pause the elevator?" Ryder asked.

"Pause it?" Damien replied, glancing back at him. "Why?"

"Because I have one more lesson to dispense tonight." His eyes went to mine. "Willow misbehaved, and I want to ensure that never happens again."

Chapter Thirteen

Willow

My heart stopped.

What?

But he had grinned when I met his gaze, almost as if he were proud of me for disobeying the society rules. He'd also asked me to do that when we were alone. Yet now he wanted to punish me for it?

Were we not alone when I met his gaze?

Did he know I scanned the room when I should have been submitting?

Had I completely misread his cues?

The elevator car came to a halt, scattering goose bumps along my exposed arms. *What's he going to do to me?*

I didn't dare meet his gaze now, my shoulders caving in a way that made me feel small. A memory began to surface, something involving claws and tee—

"Willow." Ryder grabbed my chin and tilted my head to the side, forcing me to look at him. His dark eyes searched mine. "What do you call me if I push too far?"

My brow furrowed. "What?"

"Were you not paying attention on the plane?" he asked, tsking. "Then I guess we'll review it thoroughly now."

His palm drifted from my lower back to my hip as he stepped in front of me with his back facing the elevator door. He kept his other hand on my chin, forcing me to maintain eye contact with him.

"You call me by my given name when we're around others. You call me by my title when it's just you and me. Damien doesn't count as 'others.' Nod so I know you understand."

Was he implying that I could stop whatever was about to happen by uttering his name? Wait, no, it was his title in private that would cause him to stop. But would he really? It seemed unlikely considering he wanted to punish me for defying him.

"Hmm. That's not a nod." He started walking me backward until my shoulder blades hit a hard chest behind me. *Damien.* I hadn't even felt him move, my attention on Ryder.

"Perhaps she doesn't understand the purpose of a safe word," Damien suggested.

"Yes, nor does she appear to believe me when I say I don't share." His hand on my hip drifted to the slit in my gown, thus allowing his fingertips to brush my skin. Goose bumps cascaded down my limbs from his teasing touch.

What is this man doing to me?

His nearness stirred an intoxicating mix of hot and cold sensations deep inside me. How did he plan to punish me? What had I done wrong? Why does he smell so damn good?

I inhaled his minty essence, my tongue parched for a taste. His scent, combined with the cinnamon and spice of the male behind me, and I forgot how to utter my own name.

Two powerful vampires, caging me between their hard, lethal bodies.

Oh, Goddess…

"Your heart's racing, Willow," Ryder murmured, his nose going to my neck. "I can practically feel it in my mouth, pulsing madly. Are you afraid? Or is it something else?"

I couldn't answer him because I didn't know. My legs began to shake, my chest throbbing from the impulse of an unknown desire laced with darkness and intrigue.

His presence was hypnotizing me.

No, *their* presence was the cause. Two deadly vampires, trapping their prey and using their alluring wills to lull me into a pliant state.

There was no fighting this.

They were too masculine, too predatory, for me to resist.

Ryder hummed against my throat as his fingers drifted across my thigh to find the damp apex between my legs. He drew a finger through my slit, his touch like liquid fire. I jolted against him, then gasped as Damien captured my hips with his palms to hold me in place.

"I don't share, Willow," Ryder whispered, his lips tracing a path up the column of my neck to my ear. "I told you that on the plane, yet your reactions tonight suggested you don't believe me. So I'm going to teach you a lesson, sweet pet. Ready?"

No, I wanted to say. But I found myself nodding, almost as if he were my master and pulling my puppet strings. Perhaps he was. Vampires could control minds to an extent. Was he in mine right now? Conducting my actions?

His fingertip brushed my clit, causing me to groan and forget my own thoughts.

Ryder chuckled against my ear. "I'm accepting that sound as an affirmative." His teeth skimmed my jaw, stirring a tingling sensation inside, then his mouth captured mine in a kiss that was borderline harsh. I panted against him, my lungs burning for a deeper breath. But I couldn't pull in enough oxygen, my mind lost to his claim.

He consumed me.

Devoured me.

Owned me.

Each stroke of his finger drew me closer to a fire I would never escape from.

Each brush of his tongue erased my will to fight.

And each growl of approval melted another of my defenses.

I was lost to him, utterly and completely.

Then Damien joined the game, his lips a foreign caress against my neck. His hands on my hips burned through the thin fabric, his erection a prominent hardness against my backside.

I wanted to scream, to run, and to fall between them and beg.

Confusion and fear rioted inside me, chased away by a raging lust that erased the need for logic.

Ryder pinched my clit, the shock of pain shooting through my veins and forcing a gasp from me. He smiled in response, his lips sinister and sweet.

A part of me began to weep, the overwhelming power of the two men drowning me in a sea of insanity and sensual torment.

"Bite her," Ryder said as he dropped to his knees. "Make her remember you."

My eyes flew open, shock coursing through me. *He can't mean that.* He just said he didn't share. That was the point of this lesson, right?

I didn't understand the intent.

Couldn't figure out what to say.

Then Damien growled, the harsh vibration both a threat and a promise wrapped up in aggressive male intent.

My Prince…

The words taunted my tongue, a plea ready to escape my lips, only to be swallowed as Damien pierced my neck in a bite that I felt through every nerve ending.

Electricity thrummed to life in my veins, my heart shifting into overdrive, only to lose myself in a cloud of toxicity and rapture.

My thighs clenched, reminding me of Ryder's position between them. *What is he—*

Oh.

Ohhhh.

I cried out as his teeth teased my sensitive flesh, his hungry rumble fracturing any complaints I intended to utter.

Yes, yes, I thought. *More…*

He caught my swollen bud between his lips and taunted me with his tongue. Damien's arms came around me at the same time, securing me against him as he fed from my vein.

I was trapped.

Possessed.

Enraptured by them both.

One mouth at my throat, the other between my legs, driving me onward and higher, demanding my body cooperate and bend beneath their will.

I was theirs in the moment, floating in a sensation of dark bliss with rapture waiting for me on the horizon.

A pinch sent me flying, the sharp sensation from Ryder's bite below in a place I never expected to desire a vampire's mouth.

It shot me into another world of existence, blanketing me in fierce oblivion.

Screams left my mouth, my body shaking so violently I couldn't stand. Damien kept me safe, his mouth working at my throat in tandem with Ryder between my thighs.

He bit my clit, I thought, bewildered and aroused at the same time.

Spasms rocketed through me, my orgasm continuing long past the time it should have subsided. It bordered on pain, the feelings so intense I could hardly remember how to breathe.

If I died right now, I wouldn't mind. This sort of ecstasy was reserved for the afterlife, not the present. And yet, I felt my reality slowly beginning to awaken around me, the world shifting as sights changed.

We were no longer in a metal box, but in a hallway, and then a suite. And the hard male body behind me slowly morphed into a soft mattress.

Words were exchanged.

Something about children and visiting the harem.

I sensed Damien leaving and Ryder returning, his hands tracing my body as he leaned down to kiss me thoroughly. His tongue introduced me to a unique flavor, one I suspected belonged to me and the intimate bite he'd given me below.

I clung to him, afraid and confused by the fog clouding my judgment.

"You're okay," he promised me.

But I didn't believe him.

This wasn't okay at all.

He'd just ripped apart my world, captivated my mind, and brought me to heel with a few skilled bites.

Why was I here? How long would he keep me? What happened next?

I couldn't depend on him.

I couldn't trust him.

I needed to run, but I had nowhere to go.

"Shh," he whispered, his lips against my temple. "You'll learn to trust me, Willow."

Trust him? Never.

"You sent me to the breeding camp," I accused, lost to my delirious state. "I was supposed to be a Vigil. Go to the Immortal Cup. Now I'm a snack. A fuck toy. A pet." And it was potentially the best thing that had ever happened to me. How screwed up was that? I started to laugh, the sound hysterical in my ears.

This wasn't funny.

It wasn't even amusing.

Yet I had tears in my eyes that I didn't understand.

This was all so temporary.

The moment he grew tired of me, I'd become a meal. And wasn't that hilarious? I'd survived all these years, learned so many things, just to become dinner.

Another laugh left my lips, but it sounded wrong. Broken. Soul-destroying.

"At least as a Vigil, I would have been worth something," I whispered to myself, forgetting about Ryder.

Except he was still here, listening to every word I'd just said. How much of it was out loud? I couldn't say. I almost didn't care. He knew all of this anyway. It was his kind that demeaned mine, sentencing us to a fate of servitude.

"Yes, hunting other humans is a fantastic life for a mortal," Ryder drawled, his tone grating against my nerves.

"Beats being hunted and preyed upon by monsters," I replied, shocked by the words leaving my mouth. What had their bites done to me? All my inhibitions were gone, my mind exploding into the open without a filter.

I nearly attempted to apologize, but he was already replying.

"You think those Vigils never become a snack?" he asked, arching a brow. "Come now, Willow. I sense you're more intelligent than that."

That should have been a compliment, yet it didn't sound like one.

"This entire society is driven by a need to please your superiors," he continued. "Vampires and lycans choose what they want to do, whenever they want to do it. I could fuck you against the wall right now, and there isn't a damn thing you could do about it. I could take you against the balcony outside, then snap your neck while I come, and vampires would salivate over your remains. It's a cruel, unjust world, but it is what it is. Your species is weak. Mine is not. Therefore, you kneel. I don't."

I gaped at him, my senses starting to return beneath the cruelty of his words. He sat beside me on the bed, his dark eyes smoldering. I couldn't tell if he was mad at me for speaking out or angry about the world we resided in.

Perhaps both.

How had this evening taken such a sharp turn? My bliss had melted into a puddle of confusion and pain, my future incomprehensible. I no longer knew what to expect, and that terrified me.

Ryder wanted me to trust him.

He promised not to share.

And yet, Damien had just drunk from my vein.

"Do you like this world?" Ryder asked me softly, his palm coming to rest on my cheek. He'd tucked me under the covers at some point. Why couldn't I remember? Had I fallen into a state of unconsciousness after they fed? All I could remember was the pleasure, some hints of their conversation, and coming to in this bed.

Yet I still wasn't quite right, the haze of my pleasure still smothering me in a mist of chaos.

"Willow," Ryder said, his thumb tracing my bottom lip. "I asked if you like this world. Answer me."

"No," I admitted on a whisper. It was the wrong answer, yet an honest one. And if he wanted to punish me for it, I wouldn't fight him.

"And how do you feel about me?"

I frowned, my eyes trying and failing to study his expression. What did he want me to say? The truth? A lie? Alas, my mind couldn't create a tale. All I could utter was "I don't know."

His lips curled. "Then we're getting somewhere."

I didn't understand. Did he want me to hate him or to worship him?

"I'm not like other royals, Willow," he murmured, his gaze falling to my mouth. "You'll understand that soon enough." He leaned down to kiss me soundly, his touch an imprint on my very soul. "Sleep well, my Willow."

Something about that statement unnerved me, but I couldn't for the life of me determine why.

Instead, my eyes slid closed, drowning me in an ocean of thick ink, leaving me to rest on a cloud that was far too soft.

Mint tickled my senses.

Warmth enveloped me from behind.

Protection layered every inch of my body.

Some part of me realized it was Ryder, holding me while he lulled me into a state of comfort.

I swore I even heard him hum a melody, one that followed me into my dreams. But that couldn't have been real. My life revolved around nightmares, not fantasy.

However, for tonight alone, I allowed it to be real. My future heartbreak over the false hope would be worth the temporary reprieve.

We all had a price to pay in this life. Blood and tears would be mine.

Chapter Fourteen

Ryder

I combed my fingers through Willow's white-blonde hair. Her strands were so soft, like silk. I could pet her like this all night, the activity oddly relaxing.

My lesson hadn't gone as planned. I'd wanted to express that Damien biting her was the only kind of sharing I'd ever allow, but she'd lost herself to the pleasure before I could explain that part. Then she'd gone off on a fascinating rant about what her life should have been.

It demonstrated a significant flaw in her programming, one that would have earned her an execution in this world. But I found the fracture oddly endearing. I wanted to exploit it, draw that hidden part of her out into the open and seduce her.

I knew there was something special about her. A fire that

shouldn't exist but did. I wanted to bask and burn in her flames, to experience every part of her on the way to hell and back.

My sweet, darling Willow.

She had no idea what I wanted to do to her.

Her admissions tonight were just the tip of the iceberg. I was curious as to whether she'd remember all that she had said or if she would think that some of it had been in her head.

She wondered what I would do with her when I was done playing with her. It was a valid concern, one I couldn't address because I didn't know. I wouldn't send her back to the breeding camps, nor would I make her a meal. Both ideas repulsed me. And I certainly wouldn't give her to another vampire. She was mine.

A buzzing sounded from the monitor near the bed. I frowned at it as a sultry feminine voice said, "You have an incoming call from Silvano."

"Do I?" I asked, arching a brow. "That's odd considering he's dead."

"Command unrecognized. Would you like to answer, decline, or—"

"Answer," I cut in, irritated by the insufficient programming. What was the point of artificial intelligence if they couldn't pick up on a hint of humor?

"Answering now," the female said.

I rolled my eyes. "Thanks for the play-by-play."

"But I haven't even started yet," Damien replied.

I snorted. "The AI needs to be updated."

"I know."

"Tell Benita to take care of it."

"Already done," Damien replied. "But that's not why I'm calling."

I continued combing through Willow's strands, her mind quiet with sleep. "Has someone died?" Because that would be the only reason for his intrusion this late into the night. The sun would be rising soon, and while it didn't really impact me, the brightness made my kind uncomfortable. Our sensitive senses preferred the darkness.

"Yes." Damien cleared his throat. "Garland."

My eyebrows lifted. "How?"

"I killed him."

"Ah." I never much cared for the old vampire. Hell, I didn't really like any of my kind. Damien was the exception, probably because I'd created him. His sister also qualified as an exception, mostly because she wasn't actually one of us.

Her mate, however, was a different story entirely.

Ignoring my walk down memory lane, I focused on the reason for Damien's call. "Why?"

"I walked in to find him entertaining some of his friends in the penthouse. They'd already gone through six of your harem members before I arrived."

"How many are left?"

"Of his friends, or your harem?"

"The harem." I'd trained Damien myself. He would have killed all of Garland's friends, minus maybe one whom he would use to send a message. No need to go into the details, as it was exactly what I would have done in his situation.

"Eight," he replied. "They're scared shitless, too."

In other words, not my type. I preferred to play with fire, not mingle with mice. "I trust you'll take care of them."

He grunted. "You could use a fuck more than me. I've been regularly active. Meanwhile, you're playing with a pet that you've barely touched after how many years of inane celibacy?"

"Aww, I didn't realize you cared," I drawled. "Will you be grading me on my technique next?"

"Do you even know how to fuck in your old age?" he tossed back.

"Have you forgotten that I had nearly four thousand years of experience before I turned you?" I asked him.

"Yes, yes, I know, you find this all boring and dull. You miss the fight." I could hear him rolling his eyes.

"You're only a thousand years old, Damien. Give it

another millennium or two and you'll understand." There was an art to devouring prey—an art my kind seemed to have forgotten.

"I'll never understand turning down available pussy," he replied.

"Is it available or coerced?" I asked him.

"Asks the male who just consumed his pet in an elevator like a man starved for a good meal," Damien returned. "I never heard her consent."

"It was implied when she came." I brushed my knuckles across her cheek. "Besides, you're the one who suggested I work on her sexual reactions. I feel she's coming along quite nicely, don't you?"

"Hmm," he hummed, not sounding all that confident in my reply. "Well, as entertaining as this conversation is, I didn't call to discuss your lack of a sex life or the status of your harem. I have the situation handled, but another has arisen that requires your attention."

"Oh? Do tell."

"Lilith called here for you. She wants you to phone her back immediately."

My lips curled. "Does she?"

"Yes. So shall I detail the murder scene for you next while you stall? Or did our side conversation provide a sufficient waiting time for you?"

"This is why I keep you around," I informed him. "You know exactly how I'll handle each and every situation."

"Not every situation," he replied. I didn't need to ask to know what he meant—he was referring to Willow.

I'd caught the surprise in his gaze when I tucked her gently into the bed. It rivaled his expression when I advised him to stop feeding in the elevator before lifting her into my arms to carry her to my new suite.

Willow served as an anomaly.

A different kind of experience.

A challenge I didn't fully understand.

I had never treated females poorly in the past, but I also

never provided care in the way I had with Willow. He hadn't asked me why, which was good because I didn't have a ready response for him.

"I suppose I should return Lilith's call. Care to place wagers on what she wants?"

"My guess is she found out about your culling from earlier this evening," Damien replied.

"Likely." I frowned. "But that would mean someone fed her the information."

"You're surprised?"

"No, I'm curious. It would be in our best interest to determine who spoke to her. Then we can use the communication channel to our advantage." It would allow us to ensure the information flowing to Lilith was the information we wanted her to receive.

"True. I'll look into it."

"Good." I stared at the panel on the wall. "How do I hang up?"

Damien laughed. "I'll provide you with a tutorial later. After I disconnect, tell the AI you want to call Lilith. Her number is already programmed."

"You're a good friend," I told him.

"Which is why you're giving me exclusive access to your harem," he replied.

"Call disconnected," the AI chimed in.

Apparently, Damien had hung up before I could say another word. Not that I had one for him. If he wanted to play with the brainwashed members of society, I wasn't going to stop him. The only one off-limits to him was Willow.

Blowing out my breath, I focused on the screen above the nightstand. "Call Lilith," I said.

I waited for a response.

Nothing happened.

"Yeah, just tell the AI to call Lilith," I muttered, rolling off the bed to more closely study the panel. "Activate," I said, reading the button at the top right. "Sure, let's go with that." I pressed it and half expected something to explode, but no, that sultry voice just started talking again.

"Hello. How can I help you?"

"You could reprogram yourself for me and save me a lot of time," I suggested.

"I'm sorry. *You could reprogram yourself for me and save me a lot of time* is not a command I recognized."

"Of course it's not." *Fucking AI.* "Just call Lilith."

"Calling Lilith," she replied immediately, sounding quite pleased with her ability.

I was in the middle of rolling my eyes when Lilith answered, "What took you so long? I phoned your progeny over an hour ago, and why the hell don't you have your own phone?"

"Which question would you like me to address first?" I asked her, my lips twitching in amusement. Not only had Damien waited to get to the point, but he'd also stalled a bit before calling me.

Good man, I thought. Not that he could hear me. My immortality gave him eternal life, not telepathy.

"I want you to start by explaining what happened tonight. I've received a report of more than a dozen unsanctioned vampire deaths."

"Unsanctioned?" I repeated, scratching my jaw. "That can't be right, as I'm pretty sure I sanctioned them all."

"*Ryder.*"

"Yes? Am I cutting out?" I asked, looking at the screen. "This AI isn't working for me. Perhaps I should call you back later from a better line?"

Her growl echoed through the room from the speakers strategically placed along the ceiling. "Cut the shit, Ryder. If you can't handle your job, I'll come down there and handle it for you."

"Who said I can't handle it?" I countered.

"You just killed over a dozen vampires!" she shouted.

I arched a brow at the screen, not that she could see me. Or maybe she could. Who the fuck knew how this technology worked? "Yes, and?"

I could almost picture her pinching the bridge of her nose, her annoyance palpable even over the phone line. "Did you give them a trial?"

"Is a trial needed?" I asked her, feigning innocence. Oh, I knew the new society laws required paperwork and proper reasoning to sanction a death, but I couldn't give two fucks about Lilith's whole law-and-order charade. "I mean, they tried to kill me. I merely returned the favor by demonstrating how it should be done."

"What do you mean, they tried to kill you?"

"I mean, Janet sent a pack of vampire children to my estate in Texas to assassinate me. I killed them all, by the way. So there's actually over two dozen bodies on my scorecard at present." And I intended to add several more over the next few months.

Silence met my explanation.

I gave her five seconds before saying, "Lilith? Did my AI hang up on you? Silvano's technology truly is dated. As is his entire regime. Hello? Are you there?"

"I'm digesting your statement," she replied through her teeth.

"Ah. Well, do you require five days to ponder and deliver a verdict later?" I couldn't help the taunt.

Lilith had recently forced me to endure a five-day stay in Clemente Clan territory while she decided how to handle an issue with leadership replacement. After all that, she still hadn't delivered a true verdict, instead promising to apprise all the royals and alphas at her next council meeting.

Which was scheduled to take place roughly six weeks from now.

I supposed that meant I would have to attend.

Ugh. Fucking Chicago. It was so much better before Lilith redecorated the city to suit her vampiric bloodlust.

"Are you even listening to me?" Lilith snapped.

"I'm sorry. You cut out," I informed her. Technically true, except I'd really just tuned her out. Oops.

"No more killing," she demanded. "Vampire lives are sacred. Trials are required for offenses, and rehabilitation is used to correct misbehavior. Stop fucking around or I'll remove you from your *temporary* role."

I'd love to see you try, sweetheart, I thought at her. "Of course, *Your Highness*. Any other edicts you wish to bestow upon me?"

"Yes. Call me daily. I want updates."

I was about to counter that request when the AI said, "Call disconnected."

"Bitch," I muttered, both at the AI and Lilith. I ran my fingers through my hair and blew out a breath. "Fuck."

I had no intention of listening to Lilith or following her asinine rules. This was my territory now, and there was nothing temporary about it.

A sweet scent tickled my nose, reminding me of Willow's presence. I inhaled deeply, allowing the perfume to calm my nerves, then glanced down to find her looking up at me.

I frowned. "You should be asleep." I'd compelled her to dream.

Was I so distracted by Lilith that I released the compulsion? I searched my mind for the link and found it missing. *Huh. Well, that's new.*

"How much of that conversation did you hear?" I wondered out loud.

"Enough," Willow replied, sounding very much awake and not the least bit tired.

I considered her for a long moment. "Do you need food?" I hadn't fed her since we left the house earlier. Humans usually needed several meals. I'd been caught up in our arrival and had forgotten that fact. Rather than give her a chance to reply, I said, "Come on. We'll raid the kitchen together."

I pulled the blankets off of her, indicating it wasn't a request but a demand.

She slid out of the bed, her exposed legs drawing my gaze.

I'd ripped the lace off her earlier when she was lost in her pleasure state, then re-dressed her in a white shirt from my bag. It hit her midthigh, leaving her delicately exposed beneath the fabric. All I had to do was inch the fabric upward to bare her sweet pussy to my view.

Mmm.

The taste of her still taunted my tongue, and I was eager for another bite.

But first, I needed to feed her.

Chapter Fifteen

Ryder

Rather than speak, I turned toward the door and led her into the living area just off the bedroom, then to the kitchen and dining table beyond. It wasn't a large suite, but it worked as a temporary residence. There was even a balcony outside that overlooked the city. Not that I cared enough to catch the view, but Willow might enjoy it.

I rummaged through the pantry and fridge and found it mostly stocked in blood. No human food.

Because of course they wouldn't consider mortals in their preparation of a suite.

I tapped the screen on the fridge and grumbled when it revealed a similar layout to the one above the nightstand. Selecting the Activate button brought about the same response. After she finished her greeting, I said, "I want food."

"Please say what food you desire."

I arched a brow at the screen. "I want two filet mignons, a bowl of mashed potatoes, extra butter, and some plain green beans." I hadn't enjoyed a meal like that in ages; why not ask for the whole shebang?

"When would you like it delivered?" the AI asked.

"Now."

"Order submitted. Is there anything else I can help you with?"

"Yeah, I want you to add vanilla ice cream, hot fudge, sprinkles, and whipped cream to the order."

"When would you like that delivered?"

"Now," I repeated.

"Order submitted. Is there anything else I can help you with?"

"You could vary your statements," I suggested. "Repetition is boring."

"I'm sorry. *You could vary your—*"

I hit the Deactivate button before she could repeat all my words back to me. "Fucking AI."

A strange sound came from Willow, causing me to look at her. She had her hand over her mouth, her eyes wide.

"Did you just… giggle?" I asked her.

She started shaking her head vigorously.

"Why are you lying?" I demanded. "You giggled." And it was a sweet little sound. I kind of wanted to make her do it again.

She just kept staring at me with that deer-in-the-headlights look.

"Do you think I'm going to punish you for showing amusement at my expense?" I asked her.

No reply.

"I'm not sure what's more irritating: your silence or the AI's inability to carry on a normal conversation." I palmed the back of my neck and sighed loudly. "We're alone here, Willow. What are my rules?"

She visibly swallowed, her hand slowly falling from her mouth. "No rules," she whispered.

"Right. So if you want to giggle, then fucking do it."

"Okay." Her tone indicated it wasn't "okay" at all, but I let it slide.

We stared at each other for a long moment, her blue eyes firing with a thousand questions. "Ask me," I dared her. "What do you want to know?"

Her lips parted, then closed, and then parted again. "I…" She cleared her throat. "That was the Goddess on the phone, yes?"

I snorted. "Lilith. Yeah. Not a Goddess, though. She's just a vampire, and a young one at that."

Willow frowned. "Young?"

"Compared to me and a few others, yeah. Why? How old does she claim to be in this world?"

"She's ageless," Willow said. "And revered."

"By humans, yes. Not by my kind. She's just a vampire with a penchant for power." I folded my arms on the island and leaned against it while Willow stood on the other side. "I'm nearly five thousand years old. Lilith is maybe twenty-five hundred? I think a little less. She's powerful, but not an almighty being."

Willow gaped at me. "You're almost five thousand years old?"

I lifted a shoulder. "I've been around awhile."

"And you're a temporary royal?" Confusion marred her brow. "Are you not old enough to be official?"

I snorted. "I'm one of the oldest vampires in existence, pet. Only Kylan and Cam are older than me. And there's nothing temporary about my title. Lilith seems to think this is a trial run, but I outrank her in power and age. She can kiss my fine ass, as far as I'm concerned." Issuing those fucking edicts. As though I'd ever listen to her.

"Cam…" Something flickered in her blue eyes. "He challenged the Goddess and died."

"Is that the story she's created for the young minds of

this generation?" I asked, amused. "How wrong she is. Cam is very much alive."

"There was a public execution." Willow blinked as though picturing the image behind her eyes. "I've seen it in history books."

"Photos can be deceiving, as can stories." I pushed away from the counter, my dress shirt suddenly feeling a little tight.

I hadn't changed out of my clothes when I put Willow to bed, mostly because I preferred to sleep naked and hadn't decided where I would stay tonight. The couch didn't appear all that inviting, and I definitely wasn't making a bed on the floor.

Without saying a word to Willow, I left her in the kitchen while I went to the bedroom to change into something more comfortable—sleep pants. No shoes, socks, or shirt. Much better.

I found her sitting at the counter when I returned, her eyes going to my inked arm before trailing over the rest of me. She'd studied my tattoos during our sparring lessons, too, but never asked me about them.

"They're tribal designs from my human years," I told her now, feeling the need to share. They were nothing like the ones mortals had painted their bodies with in the last few centuries before the revolution. For one, I had no color, just black ink. And the symbols could only be read by the oldest of my kind.

Willow traced the art with her eyes as I stopped to stand beside her. "Did it hurt?"

"If it did, I don't remember." Mortal memories came and went, their histories so old I rarely ever thought of them.

Her blue irises flickered up to meet my gaze, a look of awe passing through her features. "We're taught that royals are lethal, demanding superiors. Not kind, or compassionate. And they obey and adore the Goddess. You're... not like them."

I scoffed at that. "Sweetheart, none of us are like that. Your mind has been filled with bullshit meant to tame you and keep you in line."

She said nothing, her gaze incredulous.

So I opted for a better explanation.

"Why do you think Vigils are humans?" I asked her.

"They're the elite of the mortal class, meant to protect those they serve."

"Why?" I pressed. "Why would I need a human to protect me?" I didn't mean it as a rude inquiry, just a straight one. "I could rip your head off in less than a second. Hell, you saw what I did in that room tonight. So why would I require a human army?"

She frowned. "I... I don't know." At least she was honest.

"Their primary job is to keep other humans in line," I informed her. "This world has trained you all to fight against yourselves, thus creating a perfect society of oppression. You're all taught at a young age to compete against each other for a slim chance at immortality. There's no unity or loyalty among humans now because that would be a threat to the society Lilith and her cronies created. It's utter bullshit."

I'd probably said too much, but who the fuck cared? I sure as hell didn't. And what would Lilith do, come in here and demand I put down my pet for providing her with a kernel of truth? Fuck that. I answered to no one, and least of all that bitch who fancied herself superior to me.

"You're not what I expected," Willow finally said.

"Good. I like being different." I winked at her, then took the stool beside her. "Maybe next time you'll believe me when I say I have no intention of sharing you."

"You shared me with Damien," she pointed out.

"Did I? He only drank from you. I didn't even allow him a kiss." I arched a brow. "Is that the sharing you expected?"

She fell silent for a moment, her expression contemplative. "No. I expected... more."

Because the university had taught her to bend over and take whatever her superiors required.

So boring.

What didn't bore me, however, was the curious glint in her pretty eyes.

"Do you want more, Willow?" My voice had fallen to a lower octave, my hunger rising to the surface.

"More sharing?" she asked.

"More in general," I corrected.

"With you?"

"Yes." I held her gaze.

"Do I have a choice?" It came out a little saucy on her part, but I allowed it. Inch by inch, I would peel all the programming layers off of her until I found the gem lurking beneath the stone exterior. Because that was what it was— a harsh coating that society applied to all humans, making them boring and lackluster.

But somehow Willow had cracked just enough to let her light shine.

And I wanted to see more of it.

"I haven't forced you to please me," I murmured. "Instead, I've only offered you pleasure. Perhaps you didn't have a choice in that, but we both know you enjoyed it." I dared her with a look to deny it.

She didn't.

"You confuse me," she said instead.

"I confuse a lot of people." It was a character trait of mine that I held in high regard. "Maybe you'll figure me out someday."

"I doubt it."

My lips curled. "We'll see."

A comfortable silence fell between us, only to be disturbed minutes later by the sound of a buzzer. "Your food has arrived, sir," the AI announced.

"You really do enjoy narrating the obvious, don't you?"

"I'm sorry. *You really do—*"

I leapt over the counter to reach the refrigerator screen

139

and slammed my finger against the Deactivate button.

This time, Willow's giggle registered as a complete sound and she didn't cover her mouth, but she did try to give me her best straight face when I glanced at her. It made me wonder what she looked like when she smiled.

I added it to my mental task list of things I wanted to accomplish with her.

Leaving her in the kitchen, I walked to the door and opened it to find the female server from earlier standing outside with a tray in her hand. "I see Meghan already delivered my message," I murmured, pleased. I hadn't expressed the need for her to be the one to serve me during non-dining-hall hours, but I wasn't going to complain.

The girl didn't say anything, just stood there.

"Do you want to hand the tray to me or come in?" I asked her.

She blinked as though confused. "I…" The tray began to rattle on her palm, her body beginning to shake.

"Here, give it to me," I said, reaching for the tray just before her arm gave out. I caught it in time to stabilize it, only then realizing how heavy it was for her frail body to carry up here. She fell to the ground in a bow, apologies running from her lips in rapid formation.

What. The. Fuck?

"Come inside. Now," I demanded, stepping backward with the tray. The poor girl began to crawl, making it the slowest trip over the threshold I'd ever seen. "Walk."

She pushed up off the floor, her white uniform stretching across her shoulders as she moved. I caught a red flare, then the hint of iron touched my senses.

She was bleeding.

I moved swiftly into the dining area to set the tray on the table. Willow stood waiting by the counter bar that separated the dining room from the kitchen. When she saw the server enter, her cheeks flushed a pretty pink color, and a new scent entered the air, this one primal in nature.

Territorial, I recognized. Willow didn't like having

another woman in the suite. Interesting.

I'd address it later.

Instead, I focused on the server. "Take off your shirt."

That scent from Willow grew, distracting me again.

Definitely jealous, I thought.

Whatever intrigue I found in that revelation was lost as the server removed her shirt, exposing a series of cuts across her creamy flesh. "Show me your back," I demanded.

She caught her lip between her teeth and turned, revealing the abused flesh between her shoulder blades. "Who the hell did this to you? And why?"

The girl shivered violently. "I… I did not please you and I was punished."

"By whom?" I snapped, livid.

"Madame Meghan," she whispered. "I'm sorry, My Prince. I promise to be better. I won't disappoint you again. I—"

"*Stop.*" The word came out harsher than I intended and sent the poor girl to the floor again. This was exactly what I despised about this reprogramming. There was no backbone, no fight, just a bunch of mousy mortals bending over backward to appease their masters at the expense of their personalities.

They were all walking doormats.

I stalked over to the fridge to activate the AI again. I didn't even give it a chance to speak; I just said, "Call Silvano's Penthouse. Now."

"Calling Silvano's Penthouse."

A beat passed before Damien answered, "I see you figured out your AI."

"Get the fuck down here. Now." I hit the Deactivate button, expecting it to hang up, but it didn't. Gutting the damn AI and transporting my own equipment down here had just become my first priority for the week.

"What's happened?" Damien asked.

"Just get down here and hang up the phone."

He didn't comment, just did as I requested, and I

immediately hit Deactivate before the AI could start speaking again.

This time, Willow didn't giggle. Her gaze was on the girl, and that perfume of jealousy had disappeared, replaced by acute concern.

My jaw ticked.

Comforting humans wasn't in my repertoire. Minus Willow. She was… different.

I met her gaze, then gestured with my chin toward the girl. "Help her."

Willow didn't ask how or why; she just left.

Frowning, I stepped out of the kitchen to find her disappearing into the bedroom. "What the hell are you doing?" I called after her.

"Helping!" she yelled back.

I couldn't decide if she was being serious or clever, but when she returned with several towels, I had my answer. She stuck a few under the sink in the kitchen, dampening them, then went to the girl on the floor to begin washing her wounds.

"Did Meghan whip you?" I asked, studying the markings along her creamy skin.

"Yes, My Prince," the girl said, her voice hoarse. "I promise not to—"

"Stop with the vows. I'm not displeased with you." Meghan, however, would need to take a few notes on pleading, because I was definitely going to slaughter her when I saw her again.

The next several minutes passed in tense silence. Willow tended to the girl while I watched the sun rise over the city outside.

My first night in Silvano City had me wishing it could be my last.

Unfortunately, this was just the beginning.

Chapter Sixteen

Willow

I washed the towels in the sink, watching numbly as the red water swirled around the drain.

The vampires had *whipped* that poor girl.

Fourteen marks, some deeper than the rest.

She'd vibrated with fear the entire time I tended to her, refusing to say a word even when I spoke to her. It was as if the lights had gone out in her eyes, chased away by years of oppression.

I understood that all too well. Without Rae and Silas, I never would have survived the university. They grounded me, befriended me, and kept me sane, even through our harshest hours.

Until the breeding camp.

I'd gone there alone, while they'd been sent to the

Immortal Cup to fight for a chance at immortality. Had they won? Were they still there now?

Part of me wanted to ask Ryder, to see if he knew. But he'd admitted to being a recluse and not well versed in recent events, so he probably didn't know.

Perhaps I could find out from someone else here?

No. That would be dangerous. And if the female I'd just finished cleaning up was any indication, they wouldn't be all that chatty, either.

A light touch to my lower back had me jumping away from the sink, only to find Ryder beside me, observing me with those piercing dark eyes. The man moved on silent feet, reminding me of a stealthy animal seeking out his prey.

"You're distraught," he said, studying my features. "Because of the girl?"

"I…" I swallowed. "No. I've seen worse." A memory of an assembly passed through my mind, a young male screaming for his life as the vampires lashed him from every angle before devouring his body.

We'd all been forced to watch.

Those who cried were punished.

It was a lesson on stoicism and acceptance and served as a warning of our fate should we choose to disobey.

I shivered at the gruesome imagery, then refocused on the towels. They were still pink, the white fabric forever tarnished by blood. When I reached for them to try again, Ryder captured my wrists beneath one palm and pulled me away.

"Leave them," he said softly, studying me once more. "Are you hungry?"

I should have been starving, as I'd gone most of the night without food, but my stomach protested at the notion of eating. So I shook my head. "No."

He drew me toward him, then released my wrists to cup my face between his palms. "Damien will take care of her. She's not going back to the kitchens."

I'd overheard that part of their conversation, as well as

the subsequent discussion about Ryder's penchant for saving humans.

"You can't save them all," Damien had told him. "They're cattle, Ryder."

"There's nothing wrong with respecting our food. Yet everyone in this new world seems to take immense enjoyment in cruelty, as though we have some sort of statement to make. Our kind won the war. Wasn't that enough?"

Damien had replied in a different language after that, one I didn't understand, but it sounded guttural and angry. It had made the girl with me shiver in fear, which had drawn his predatory gaze toward her. Then he'd sighed and muttered, "I'll take care of it."

"He won't harm her," Ryder said now, bringing me back into the present. "Just like he didn't harm you."

I stared at him—this vampire I didn't understand—and had no idea what to say to him. He was trying to make me feel better, and I had no idea why. That didn't happen in this world. Yet Ryder continued to defy every expectation, his words and actions making me see the man beneath his vampire veneer.

And what I found there scared me.

Because I *liked* that man.

"Your pupils are dilating," Ryder murmured, his gaze dancing across my features. "You're no longer distraught, but I don't know how to discern this look. What are you thinking, pet?"

"That I'm glad I can confuse you as much as you confuse me," I admitted out loud, giving him my current thought rather than the previous one.

"I think we should skip right to dessert, then." He stepped into me, causing me to back up against the counter behind me. He pressed his body to mine, his palms still cradling my face. "Have you ever had a sundae?"

"Like the day of the week?" Or was it a euphemism for something?

He chuckled. "No." He closed the gap between our mouths to brush a soft kiss against my lips, one that was almost tender in its sweetness.

I went to return the embrace, but he was already backing away toward the refrigerator.

"I know you said you weren't hungry, but a treat doesn't count as real food. And I think you've earned a sundae after the long night we've just endured together." He nodded toward the windows in the living area as if to highlight the early morning hour.

The sun spilling over Silvano City reflected off the other buildings, creating an array of color unlike anything I'd ever seen. The university ran on a night schedule because our vampire professors preferred darker skies. I never knew why, nor had I ever been in a situation where I could ask.

"You're deep in thought again," Ryder noted as he set two bowls on the counter adjacent to me. It was the one with stools on the dining room side.

"I was thinking about the sun." It sounded ridiculous out loud, but it was the truth.

"What about it?" he asked before returning to the refrigerator to open the bottom drawer. Icy air escaped the compartment, causing me to shiver as it reached my exposed legs.

"Vampires prefer night, so we rarely experienced the sun at the university," I explained, taking a step to the side to avoid more of the chilly wave.

Ryder closed the drawer after retrieving a carton, then he opened the doors above it to grab a few other items.

Once he had everything he needed laid out on the counter, he pointed at the stool side and told me, "Sit."

He certainly was a man of eloquent terms.

I obeyed him anyway, curious as to what kind of "treat" he intended to make. The ingredients came from whatever the girl had brought up on the tray.

Ryder had busied himself with storing the food in various places while waiting for Damien to arrive. It had struck me as a busy habit to avoid the wounded female. Another strange trait because most of his kind would have pounced on the injured human and finished her off.

"It's our senses," he said suddenly.

I frowned. "Senses?"

"Yes." He glanced up from his task of scooping white balls out of the container. "That's why we don't like the sun. It's too bright for our eyes."

"Oh." Why was he explaining this to me?

"We're bred for the night," he added, returning to his task. "Lycans are bred for the day. Although, I think many of them keep night hours now to stay in tune with vampires. But it wasn't always like that."

"You frequently speak as though this world is new," I said slowly. "Is it because of how much it's evolved in your existence?" He'd claimed to be close to five thousand years old. From what I knew of the world, we were only in year one hundred and seventeen.

"Would you believe me if I told you there was a time when humans ruled over everything?"

I scoffed at that. "That'd never happen."

"Not now, no. But for the majority of my very long life, mortals ran the world." He left to drop the carton in the drawer again before continuing. "It all changed when humans spotted lycans for the first time. They wanted to use them for super soldiers in their mortal wars. As you can guess, that didn't go over well. We were forced to put humans in their place as a result."

"As cattle," I muttered, referring to Damien's term. He wasn't the first to use that sort of commentary in my presence.

"It's true that humans are food. But we wouldn't exist without your kind, which is something my brethren continue to forget." Ryder picked up a brown bottle and snorted at the label before uncapping it and squeezing a liquid-like substance out of it over the bowls.

I wasn't sure why he considered this a treat. It didn't

appear all that edible.

When he finished, he sprayed another mound of white fluff on top, then sprinkled a colorful array of flakes across the creamy creation. He finished his masterpiece by adding a spoon to each bowl, then pushed one toward me. "Try it."

I studied the dessert, noting the way everything seemed to melt into each other. "What are the ingredients?" He'd ordered several things earlier, some I recognized, some I didn't. This was definitely not green beans.

"Try it and I'll tell you." He demonstrated by scooping his own bite and groaning as it hit his tongue. The sound, coupled with his expression of pleasure, had me clenching my thighs. It was oddly erotic, and extremely tempting. "Keep looking at me like that and I'll make you my personal treat."

I shivered at the sensuality in his tone. Because I believed him. And I wasn't sure my body could handle more of his bites right now.

He arched a brow at me. "Am I going to need to feed you, pet? Because I will, but it won't be a sundae that I put in your mouth." His dark eyes smoldered with intent, making his insinuation clear.

A dark part of me wanted to take him up on that offer. *What would he taste like?* I wondered, my thighs tensing at the thought.

This man had gotten under my skin with his eccentric behavior and addictive touch. He almost made me want to go to my knees and beg him for a taste, something I never thought I'd do around a superior being.

"Are you craving me for dessert instead?" he asked, his lips curling dangerously. He slowly moved around the counter, his approach quiet and purposeful. Then he took the spoon from my dish and brought it to my lips. "Open."

My lips parted automatically, his command a warm caress to my senses. He studied my mouth, watching as the contents hit my tongue.

I winced in response to the taste.

Too sweet.

It was like eating pure sugar.

I gagged, but I managed to force the contents down my throat, which seemed to amuse him immensely.

Ryder chuckled, the spoon just outside my mouth. "You took an entire course on deep-throating, and you gag on ice cream? I thought you said you passed?"

The mention of my university experience had me wincing again.

"My studies didn't involve sugary substances," I replied. "And I did pass. You can check my records."

"Oh, I intend to," he drawled. "I'm particularly curious about your performance evaluations. I mean, how does one get graded on anal? Do they time you to see how fast you can make a man come? And is it a mortal? Because that seems like unfair preparation, if you ask me. Humans are easy. I excite you with a few nibbles. Hell, I don't even need to touch your clit to make you shatter."

Heat crept up my spine to my nape, his proximity and commentary unraveling some hidden thread in my mind— one that coerced me into saying the first thing I could think of as a response. "We were graded on technique and accuracy."

"Were you?" he asked, setting the spoon down slowly beside my bowl. "Maybe I want to test you myself, see if you're up for the challenge of handling what I have to give."

I met and held his gaze, a strange sort of boldness sweeping over me.

Uncertainty swirled in his eyes—a look that said he thought I wouldn't be able to meet his sexual needs.

Perhaps he was right. Maybe he was too much for me. But if that happened, he'd push me to the side and find another pet. And I didn't want that to happen.

When he'd invited the other human into the suite, a part of my soul had fractured, unleashing some bizarre territorial instinct. I'd claimed him in that moment. It was an asinine reaction, one that would never last, but right now, I didn't want to share him.

This animalistic need to make him mine flourished inside me from an unknown entity, one that admired the beast inside him, noting his characteristics as an ideal mate. He was an enigmatic old vampire who never did what I expected, and I *liked* that.

It could have been the months in captivity that curved my instincts in this direction. Maybe something had happened in that breeding camp that broke some fundamental part of my psyche. I might never know, as I still couldn't remember much about my time there.

And right now, I didn't care to know.

What concerned me in this moment was that look of hesitancy in Ryder's gaze, the one that said he wasn't sure I could meet his needs.

I wanted to prove him wrong, to show him what I could do, to make him understand my training, and to demonstrate the skills I'd honed at the university.

Which was what prompted me to slide off the stool into his personal space before going to my knees before him. "Test me, Ryder," I said, inviting him to act. "Let me show you what I can do."

Chapter Seventeen

Ryder

Fuck.

I'd only meant to tease her, but my humor died the moment she dropped to her knees.

She was stunningly beautiful in this pose with her blue eyes radiating challenge and conviction—the perfect combination for a lethal allure.

How could I say no to such perfection? Such intrigue? My stomach tightened in anticipation, my cock throbbing with the need to comply with her request.

How long had it been since I experienced the pleasure of a woman's mouth? I couldn't really remember, my interest in such things having waned over the last century. But Willow had reawakened my *need*, her presence a provocation to a part of me I buried long ago.

What was it about her that enamored me so completely? Was it just a result of spending too many years alone? Or maybe this connection was a result of a simple desire to feel human touch again.

I reached for her and ran my fingers through her silky hair, marveling at her wondrous courage in what I deemed a cruel world.

If she wanted me to test her, I wouldn't say no.

"Are you sure you're ready for me, pet?" I asked her as I drew my thumb along her jaw to her chin. "I'm not easy like your mortals at the university."

Blue fire burned in her irises, her inner flame blazing to life inside her. "I'm ready."

So confident and poised.

Mmm. Yes, this would be fun.

"All right. Follow me." I walked backward toward the living area. When she started to stand, I tsked at her. "Oh, no, pet. I want you to crawl. Prove to me you want this."

Her pupils dilated in response, her resolve palpable.

And then she began to move, her limbs carrying her across the floor with a fluid grace that reminded me of a wildcat. How appropriate, considering her notable ferocity. This woman had survived hell, but rather than lose herself to her scars, she allowed them to strengthen and embolden her. Her experience gave her life, and that was one hell of a turn-on.

I settled into the room's only chair, the couch adjacent to my left. My position allowed me to watch Willow's every move, our eyes locked together in a dangerous dance of expectation. I could smell her arousal, the aroma a taunt in the air that intensified my interest. But it was her expression that truly held me captive.

She boldly held my gaze, the defiant look a startling contrast to her submissive crawl, and it set my blood on fire for her.

This female spoke to me on a level I didn't quite understand, yet she hadn't said a single word.

When she reached my sprawled legs, she slid her palms up my calves to my thighs without asking for permission. Instead, she conveyed her intent with her eyes, taking rather than giving, and silently promising me that I would enjoy whatever she intended to do. It created an intoxicating environment of push and pull.

Willow knew I possessed superior genetics, that I could snap her pretty little neck in a heartbeat. Yet in this moment, she demanded control. And so I temporarily allowed it, curious to see what she would do next.

Her fingertips trailed upward to the band of my black sleep pants. No hesitation. Just pure seductive female.

"Take off your shirt." Technically, it was my shirt. But she could keep it. The thin white fabric looked better on her than it did on me.

She paused to comply in a sultry display of eroticism. Her perky tits made my mouth water, her rosy nipples erect and begging for my bite. I nearly groaned at the sight, my stomach burning with an intense need to pull her into this chair to straddle my aching cock. Only, her palms returned to my pants, her fingers hooking beneath the fabric to draw them down.

I was momentarily paralyzed and lost to her ministrations.

She could ask for anything she wanted and I'd give it to her, so long as she continued to stare at me like that.

I lifted my hips to allow her to tug the fabric down my legs, leaving us both without clothes.

It was an odd experience because I typically didn't allow myself to be this vulnerable around anyone. However, it felt right with Willow, like I needed to put myself in a similarly weakened state to comfort her.

I widened my legs in unspoken invitation, studying her every reaction as she admired me from her knees. Her blue eyes focused on my groin, her tongue sneaking out to dampen her lips.

"You certainly look hungry now," I informed her softly.

She lifted her gaze to mine, saying nothing as she leaned in to give my dick a tentative lick.

"*Damn*," I breathed, that minor touch stirring a pit of molten heat in my abdomen. The caress of her tongue, coupled with her knowing look, and I was fucking gone for her.

Who is this magical little human? I wondered, in complete awe of her ability to consume me so utterly.

Her hand wrapped around my shaft, angling me to her desired position while she continued to hold me captive with her stare. Then she parted those pretty lips and took my head deep into her mouth.

I was one hundred percent corrected on her gag reflex. Because *fuck*. She was practically swallowing me, her throat working around me in a way that hindered my ability to think.

She took me all the way to her hand, blowing my fucking mind and enchanting me in a whole new manner.

She owned me in this moment, and her eyes said she knew it.

I threaded my fingers through her hair, needing to take back at least some semblance of control. She was pushing me into uncharted territory, forcing me to concede in a way I didn't understand.

But damn, it was worth every second of confusion. Because this woman was a goddess on her knees.

She knew exactly how hard to suck, when to nibble, where to lick, and hell, the way she worked her throat around me was pure magic. I wondered if she could even breathe, the tears in her eyes telling me perhaps she couldn't, but she forced herself through it anyway, determined to give me the best orgasm of my life.

I fell a little harder for her in that moment, her attention and commitment to the cause insanely admirable.

Tightening my grasp in her thick blonde strands, I urged her to move faster, pushing myself just a little farther into her, needing that extra semblance of power to take me closer to the edge.

She allowed it, her mouth working me over with a skill I intended to experience over and over again. Because one time wouldn't be enough. I needed everything Willow had to offer. She was about to become well and truly mine.

While I hadn't wanted to share her before, I definitely wouldn't now. That mouth belonged to me. Her pussy was mine to take. Her ass, too. I craved it all.

"You're going to swallow," I told her, not giving her a moment to disagree. I had to be inside her. I had to be part of her. I had to *own* her as much as she owned me in this moment. "Fuck, Willow."

My abdomen rippled with pressure, my balls tightening in anticipation. I was going to explode down her sweet little throat, coat her insides with my essence, and then devour her slick cunt until she passed out.

Just the thought of tasting her brought me that much closer to release, my veins burning with the desire to claim and mark and *fuck*.

Willow's tongue swirled along my head as she cupped my balls with her hot palm. I jolted at the contact, her precise movements sending me sailing into a cataclysmic oblivion that erupted across my senses.

My grip turned to cement in her hair as I forced myself to the back of her throat, my spasms shooting off deep into the cavern of her precious mortal body. On and on it went until I could hardly breathe. Willow's nails bit into my thigh, her expression a blur through my eyes, but I caught her panic in her scent and immediately released my hold. She gasped in response, my cock falling from her swollen lips as she panted violently with her need for air.

Poor little pet didn't care for breath play. I noted that as a medium to hard limit, not wanting to push her to a point of no return.

Yet I needed to repay the favor of what she'd just done for me. She could have no idea how long it'd been since I shattered so completely. However, it went deeper than that.

She'd just awakened a beast inside me that required so much more.

I scooped her up off the ground and carried her to the bedroom. Her wide eyes suggested a mix of confusion and fear, perhaps because her last experience with sex had been with the lycans. We'd work up to that. For now, I'd content myself with devouring her and showing her what sex should be.

Her back hit the mattress, her golden hair splayed across the pillows. "Grab the headboard," I told her. "And spread your legs. It's my turn for dessert."

My body still shook from the aftermath of my release, but I owed it to my pet to take her to the same heights. She'd already come several times in the last twenty-four hours. If I had my way, she'd come several more times before she slept, but the way her thighs tensed as I settled between them told me I'd be lucky to force one more out of her.

"Ryder…"

"That's not your safe word," I murmured against her clit. "Which is good because I know you can handle this, pet."

Her arousal heightened, dampening her slick folds even more. I hummed in approval as I dove into her tight little entrance with my tongue, tasting her unique flavor. It was fucking heaven, her flavor my new addiction.

I devoured her, licking every inch of her pussy before returning to the place I knew she desired me most. Her chest rose and fell, goose bumps sprouting along her body as her head moved back and forth on the pillows.

But she never once told me to stop.

Instead, her fingers wove into my hair, urging me onward.

She had come apart completely, all the rules and requirements of society long gone as she took from me what she needed. So I gave it to her in kind, reveling in this relaxed part of her and pushing her to the point of no return.

My name fell off her tongue as a sweet prayer, causing me to smile against her swollen little nub before taking it deep into my mouth. She screamed for me, her body coming unglued with the slightest amount of pressure.

And my little pet thought she couldn't come again.

I smiled before laving her through the pleasure-pain her rapture created.

She spasmed around me, her limbs locked tight, and her grasp in my hair became a harsher hold as I continued to lick her.

One wasn't enough.

I required more.

And I could do this all day, if she allowed me to.

I skimmed her sensitive folds with my fangs, teasing her flesh, threatening her with a potential bite. She groaned in response, her acceptance the most beautiful gift of my existence.

But I withheld from taking more of her blood, knowing I'd already imbibed more than enough of her essence today to last a while.

She moaned as I suckled her clit again, then jolted as I slid a finger inside her tight sheath. When I added a second, her body began to convulse. I curved my touch upward at an angle I knew would inspire her onward in her quest for pleasure. Her resulting groan confirmed I'd hit the right spot, then her walls began to squeeze, her legs shaking on either side of me.

Her responses to my touch couldn't be forced. This was all her and our chemistry driving her into a state of bliss she would forever remember.

"Come for me, Willow," I demanded, wanting to hear her fall into a delirious state once more. "Now." I bit her, not to drink blood but to unleash my endorphins into her system, and my sweet little pet's reaction didn't disappoint.

She cried out so loudly the entire city probably awoke to the scream. It was a gorgeous sound, one I intended to hear again and again. But the tears streaming down her face told me this was the last orgasm she could give me right now, her body beyond replete and bordering on pain.

Some of my kind enjoyed pushing humans to the brink of their sanity by biting them endlessly, but I preferred Willow to remain coherent and alive.

I slowly withdrew my fangs from the apex between her thighs, then licked up the droplets of blood that appeared on the marks.

"No more," she breathed. "Please… no more."

"Shh," I hushed her, kissing a path up her body until my mouth reached hers. I sliced my tongue open with my fang before capturing her lips and delving inside to offer her my essence for healing.

She vibrated beneath me, her body overloaded from the sensations, her mind caught between a state of euphoria and pain. But my kiss eased her back into our reality, my blood calming and curing her.

Willow's breathing began to even out, her heartbeat slowing to a more reasonable pace, and when I opened my eyes, I found her watching me with an expression I couldn't read. Rather than ask her what it meant, I opted to tell her what was on my mind.

"You've just initiated a dangerous game," I informed her softly. "Because now I want to know everything the university taught you, and more." I nuzzled her nose. "So I hope you're prepared, sweet Willow. You've awoken my inner beast, and it's going to take a lot to sate him."

If that's even possible, I thought, enthralled once more by the beauty beneath me.

However, one thing was astutely clear to me—Willow was my new outlet. She'd provide the escape I would so desperately need during this transition period. And afterward, I might just honor her with a new way of life.

"Get some sleep, pet," I whispered, brushing my lips against hers. "You're going to need it."

Chapter Eighteen

Ryder

Two weeks of meetings had me reconsidering all this royal bullshit.

Yavi—one of Silvano's pet sovereigns—sat across from me, droning on and on about his human shortage up in Mexico. He wanted permission to purchase more mortals for breeding. It was a ludicrous request with about a dozen flaws.

"Breeding," I repeated. "So do you have all the necessary lodging requirements and supplies in place to raise humans for eighteen or nineteen years each?"

"Well, no. But there's a sufficient market for infant blood, as well as that of small children. So the eighteen-year span isn't required."

Damien arched a brow from the corner of my new

office—I'd destroyed Silvano's space—and waited for my impending reaction. Only, Yavi wasn't done, his lack of awareness marking him as an insufficient leader in my book.

"If I bleed the lot I currently have, I can create available space for breeding. But I'll need at least three hundred females and maybe a dozen males to make it work." His beady black eyes met mine. "Some of the women won't make it to birth, but I've accounted for that in my request. There are also drugs that encourage twin or triplet litters, so I'd be requesting that as well."

"So you can breed an army of humans to bleed dry," I summarized.

"Exactly," he said, sounding as though he was relieved that I understood his request.

I looked at Damien. "When's my next call with Lilith?"

"In about two hours," he drawled.

I nodded, considering my options. Meanwhile, Yavi radiated excitement. He thought I meant to talk to Lilith about the resources. *Imbecile.*

"You mentioned a popularity for infant and child blood. I assume that means you have clients requesting this service?" I asked.

"I do."

"And do you have a list of those clients?"

He dipped his chin in the affirmative. "They pay top dollar as well. I always gave Silvano ten percent of the proceeds, so I'll be happy to do the same for you."

Liar, I thought. I'd already reviewed all of Silvano's books and knew this sniveling little twit had given Silvano a hell of a lot more than a measly ten percent.

Damien gave me a look, but I gave him a subtle shake of my head. *Not yet*, I was telling him.

"I need you to share that list with me," I informed Yavi.

He frowned. "Well, it's a personal client list, so I would need to—

"No, Yavi," I interjected. "You misunderstand. I'm telling you to give me the list, not asking."

"I… It'll take some time."

Another lie. I leaned forward with my elbows on the massive oak desk and dropped my laid-back act so he could feel the power beneath my facade. "You'll do it right now."

"I don't have that information with me."

I nearly growled at the third lie he'd uttered in less than five minutes.

"Careful," Damien warned, his focus on Yavi. "Ryder can smell untruths from a mile away, and if I can tell you're full of shit, he definitely knows."

Yavi gulped. "I… I…"

I cocked an eyebrow. "You what?"

He opened the binder he'd placed on my desk when he entered and began shuffling through papers.

I looked at Damien. "This is the guy on Lilith's list?" She'd sent over several names of candidates she was considering for the royal position in Silvano Region. I'd reviewed it out of curiosity—mostly so I knew whom to kill if she decided to take her threat any further—but now I was just amused by it.

No one in this territory posed a single threat to me. Lilith just hadn't acknowledged that fact yet, but she would soon when I informed her that I had no intention of stepping down.

The meetings might be tedious, and I hated the political games, but it was quite clear this world could use my expertise. This new society hadn't just gone to hell; they'd taken up residence somewhere beneath the devil's ass. I really needed them to resurface somewhere closer to humanity to save our kind from a serious blood shortage in the future.

And this idiot across from me only added to that problem.

He'd gone through thousands of humans in the last six months by allowing his "clients" to overindulge on the product. It was grossly inadequate and fucking unacceptable. Blood camps required sufficient handlers, not gluttonous fools.

"You could try writing the names," Damien suggested before glancing at me. "And yeah, he's on the list."

I shook my head. "She's lost her fucking mind."

"She wants a puppet," Damien corrected. "Which you are not."

I snorted. "I'll give her a puppet." Preferably with his head on a silver platter, delivered to her posh Chicago suite.

Oh, sorry. *Lilith City* suite.

I nearly rolled my eyes, but it felt too juvenile for the situation. Why the council chose her to lead them, I'd never understand. Several of them were too old to play into her scheming. Perhaps they were just bored and wanted to see how far she'd take it. As it turned out, she'd gone well into the deep end with all this reformation, destroying what used to be a rather intriguing world to live in. And none of them had done a damn thing to stop her.

Hence, my new role.

Someone needed to correct this shit, and apparently, that someone was me.

Yavi started scribbling on paper using one of my pens—which he didn't ask to borrow—while Damien supervised. I didn't bother to look, fully confident in Damien's abilities to memorize the names and handle them appropriately. Any vampire who chose to live on infant or child blood didn't belong in my territory. They can suck on rocks at the bottom of the ocean instead.

While Yavi worked, I used my monitor to flip on a visual of my suite. I'd left Willow fully sated in bed, her blood still a taunt on my tongue. She was an addiction I couldn't quit, not that I wanted to.

I found her still lying in the bed, her blonde hair fanning across both our pillows. The sheets were tangled with her legs, leaving her upper body exposed. Seeing her all soft and sleepy made me want to ditch this meeting and go back to my suite, but I had a full night of this shit to get through first.

She stretched as though she knew I was watching, her tits beckoning for my mouth.

Soon, pet, I thought at her, wishing she could hear me.

It'd been hard not to fuck her these last two weeks. However, a lot could be said for delaying the inevitable. It intensified my yearning and added a strange challenge to the mix. I wanted her to choose me. To beg me. To demand it.

Only then would I give in to the desire to truly claim her.

Yavi finally finished his list, his expression bordering on irritated as he slid it across my desk. I didn't even look at it, instead giving it to Damien. He folded it and slid it into the pocket of his black trousers, then went back to his corner again.

"Great." I leaned forward with my arms on my desk and my hands clasped together. "So here's the thing—I'm mandating a policy in my territory that forbids the purchase and consumption of blood from any human under the age of twenty. They're not mature enough until they reach adulthood, which is why they are typically not sent to the blood camps until that age." I glanced at Damien. "Right?"

"Yes," he confirmed.

"Fantastic." I refocused on Yavi. "So I believe our work here is done. Consider your request denied."

He gaped at me. "Excuse me?"

"Yes, you're excused," I agreed, falling back into my chair. "Damien, if you schedule another meeting of this nature, I'll kill you."

"You can try," Damien returned, smirking.

Fair. He wouldn't be all that easy a mark because he knew me too well. And he'd learned from the best—me.

"I'm sorry, but I don't understand," Yavi said. "You can't just deny my request. There's not enough blood to feed those living in Yavi City."

"Then perhaps you shouldn't have been so gluttonous," I suggested.

"Gluttonous," he repeated. "Blood is our right. We need more."

"Blood is a privilege," I corrected. "And you're not getting any more."

"You can't do this," he snapped, his personality finally shining through. I knew the sniveling bit had to be an act, and now the predator in him had come out to play.

Welcome to the game, I mused. *What's your next move?*

He slammed his fist on the desk. "Lilith will hear about this! You're not even a real royal. You're only temporary. Just wait until you're replaced. You'll be finished."

"Hmm," I hummed to myself. "Not the best move. Groveling might have worked in your favor. Of course, then I would have found you weak and unworthy, so perhaps not. But threatening me, well, that's definitely not a wise decision."

"You think you're so powerful; wait until Lilith strings you up by your balls," he seethed, standing abruptly.

"That would be a kinky sight indeed," I replied, not at all fazed by his little tantrum. "Unfortunately, the femme fatale scenario has never appealed to me. So I'll have to pass."

"No one wants you here, Ryder. I'd watch your back if I were you," he warned, turning on his heel.

An interesting phrase of words, I thought as I pulled a gun from one of the holsters I'd affixed to the underside of my desk. "Yavi," I said softly, causing him to pause in the doorway. "It's not me who should be watching my back." I pulled the trigger, releasing a bullet right into the rear of his head.

Damien sighed in the corner. "I knew you were going to do that the second you asked me about your call with Lilith."

"I needed to know how long I had to stage a scene," I replied, referring to our goal of catching the tattletale among us. We had a pretty good idea after these last two weeks of who might be passing intelligence on to Lilith. "The list is down to five, so I figure we'll provide another test."

He nodded. "Who should I call for cleanup?"

"How about Benita?" I suggested. "I'd like to clear her name sooner rather than later since we've confided so much in her already."

"A fair choice," he agreed. "Are you doing the honors, or am I?"

"I'll take this one since you have a list of animals to catch and all," I said, referring to the vampires who preyed upon children in this region. "You can offer them a chance to leave. If they don't comply, then exterminate them." What was a few more bodies to add to my growing death rate?

"Lilith will be thrilled," Damien deadpanned.

"Won't she?" I mused, standing up. "Now how long do I have before my next call?"

"An hour, why?"

I found an ax on my wall, weighing it in my hand. "I'm thirsty," I replied, wandering over to Yavi's prone form and calculating the appropriate arc with my gaze. I hefted it over my head and made a clean hit, dislocating his head in one strike.

"You're getting better at that," Damien noted.

I glanced at him. "I missed one time four hundred years ago."

He lifted a shoulder. "It's a fond memory of mine."

That explained why he brought it up all the damn time. I dropped the ax beside Yavi's corpse. "Ask Benita to clean that for me. I'll be upstairs playing with my pet."

* * *

I found Willow right where I left her, sleepy and satisfied among the black silk sheets. Her mouth opened to mine the moment I went in for a kiss, her supple form bending in approval as I slid into the bed beside her.

She didn't ask what I wanted or needed; she just let me take my fill and cooperated beautifully with each stroke and touch.

It was as though our bodies had learned to communicate

without words, which was astounding considering we hadn't even fucked yet.

I nibbled her pert tits on my way down to the deliciousness between her thighs. She moaned a tiny disapproval, her body still sore from my earlier feeding. However, her pained groans soon turned to satisfied sighs as I licked her to completion.

Her fingers slid into my hair, holding me in place as she wantonly rode out her pleasure without ever opening her eyes.

I adored her in this state—compliant and eager and mine.

As the last of her spasms abated, I slid up her gorgeous curves and kissed the hell out of her. My cock ached in my slacks, begging me to free him for a ride, but I didn't have time to do this properly. So I contented myself with this sensual moment, knowing I would wear her scent for the rest of my meetings.

"You're beautiful," I whispered. "And my favorite distraction."

She mumbled something in reply, her pleasure high consuming her. It was also probably the early hour. My meeting with Yavi had taken place first thing this evening, which explained my craving to return to Willow so soon.

"He wanted to talk about a food shortage," I told her. "Can you believe that?"

More mumbling came from her, causing me to smile.

"I wish we had time to shower, but I need to get back for another meeting." I didn't mention Lilith's name, because it sometimes seemed to upset Willow—another fault of her society programming.

She didn't reply, just sighed in contentment beneath me.

"I'll be back soon, pet," I promised, kissing her again. "Dream of me." I compelled her to dream just a little while longer and grinned when I heard her moaning in my wake.

Yes, I truly did enjoy her in this blissed-out state, and I couldn't wait to take her there again later tonight.

Chapter Nineteen

Willow

My body vibrated beneath Ryder's tongue. He'd spent the last two weeks waking me up in a similar fashion, calling me his "favorite kind of breakfast" each time.

I screamed as I came undone for the third time, my muscles tight and strained from the forced release. But then his mouth claimed mine, filling me with the delicious flavor of our mingled lust and blood.

He left me boneless on the bed as he rolled off of it to go take a shower. Sometimes he pulled me in there with him and coaxed me to my knees, but today he mentioned having an early meeting with one of the region's sovereigns. Something about a food shortage, which, I suspected, translated to insufficient blood reserves.

Or had that meeting already occurred?

I couldn't remember, my mind a bit fuzzier than this morning. I didn't ask questions, instead choosing to revel in the rapture coursing through my system.

Ryder had remained true to his word about not sharing me. I'd been nervous last week when he took me to a social affair in the city, but he hadn't allowed anyone to touch me, let alone snack on my vein.

Life with Ryder was borderline enjoyable, something I never could have anticipated. But I also knew better than to lose myself in the false hope of a future. While Ryder didn't seem to be tiring of me yet, I knew it was only a matter of time.

Perhaps it would happen after sex. So far, we'd only engaged in oral and hand-driven pleasure. Just last night, Ryder had come all over my chest and rubbed his seed into my skin before demanding I sleep in that state. I'd been too exhausted to argue, just as I was too tired to leave the bed now to wash his cum off of me.

I studied the moon outside, noting its full shape.

How many lycans are roaming around in wolf form right now? I wondered. *Are they hunting down humans, or was the moon chase held at a different time of year?* I pitied the humans who were sent to the holding pens for that purpose, just as I used to feel for those relegated to the breeding camps.

I still couldn't fully remember what happened to me with the lycans. Every night I dreamt of something important, but I seemed to forget the second I woke. I just kept visualizing dark green irises smoldering with sadistic intent. They were particularly bright in my mind now, staring back at me each time I shut my eyes.

I shivered, not wanting to know what it meant. Yet the moon outside didn't make me feel any better. If anything, the pale white rays coming from it left me even more uneasy.

Something isn't right, I realized, taking stock of my quivering limbs. Ryder had left me in this state before, but not quite like this.

My stomach clenched, shooting an odd sort of agony through my senses. I gasped and curled into a ball, fighting the shock of pain.

Maybe I hadn't woken up yet. This reminded me of my nightmares, the searing torment I felt all too often from my time in captivity.

I blinked, confused. *What's happening?*

This all had to be in my head. I was fine moments ago, reveling in the afterglow of pleasure. Then I went wrong somewhere. I tried to recall what happened, where I'd gone, but the seconds began to blend together into a fuzzy ball of uncertainty.

Had I fallen back to sleep?

Yes. That had to be it.

I reached down to pinch my thigh, needing to wake myself up, and shot upward in the bed with the sheets twisted around me.

What the hell?

I took in my naked form, noted my need for a shower, and listened for Ryder. The suite was silent.

How much time had passed? The moon appeared a little higher now, the midnight hour fast approaching.

Frowning, I slid from the bed and went into the empty bathroom to turn on the shower. When had Ryder left? Why couldn't I remember?

Shaking my head, I stepped beneath the hot spray and allowed it to wash away my nightmares. Maybe I'd dreamt of him between my legs this morning. That wouldn't surprise me with how intimate we'd been lately.

I thought of him as I cleansed my breasts, my nipples hardening as though begging for his mouth. He'd bitten me there a few days ago. It'd stirred a fire inside me that he'd stoked with a second bite to my femoral artery. Then he'd devoured me once more, shooting me to the stars with ecstasy.

Being kept as a harem member had its benefits. Yet today I felt a little caged, like I wanted to be outside in the fresh air. An odd desire, considering I spent most of my life inside.

After completing my shower ritual, I wrapped myself in a towel and ventured through the suite to the balcony doors. The moon taunted my senses again, making me tremble with a foreign energy I didn't understand. My knees nearly gave out, my limbs shaking so violently I had to step back inside.

I swallowed.

Maybe Ryder had taken too much blood.

Deciding that had to be it, I wandered into the kitchen to find a hot plate waiting for me with eggs and some sort of meat beside it, as well as a healthy portion of greens. The note beside it read, *See you soon, pet.*

The first time Ryder left me a message, I'd wondered at the purpose. Why would he bother to tell me anything? I still didn't quite understand, but every time he did, a warm and fuzzy sensation tickled my insides.

I rather liked that he communicated with me.

Another dangerous activity that left me bemused by our situation.

In fact, everything Ryder did bewildered me.

I removed the covering over my food and used a pair of oven mitts to carry the plate over to the counter with the stools. This kind of food suited my taste buds, yet the first bite didn't quite satisfy me the way it should. It actually came across rather dull. I tried another, my lips curling down at the odd quality of my meal.

My third bite barely went down my throat, my gag reflex kicking into high gear and refusing to allow me to eat any more.

I slid off the stool, feeling increasingly nauseated with each passing second. I barely made it to the toilet before puking everything up, including food from last night.

"Ugh," I muttered, curling into a ball on the floor, the cool tile beneath my cheek my only reprieve. *I'm just going to lie here for a minute*, I thought, my eyes drooping closed.

Only, those green irises flared to life once more, causing me to hurl all over again.

Fuck, I felt like I was dying.

A clammy sheen covered my hands and arms, my stomach rioting against every minor movement.

Tears blurred my vision, my lungs seizing in a tormented wave of discomfort.

What's happening to me?

I was lost between a heat wave and an iceberg, my senses either blazing hot or dangerously cold.

A memory of laughing hit me in the gut, the sound astoundingly cruel. *Please don't. Please!* my mental voice begged, but I didn't understand the purpose or whom I was talking to.

Until those eyes came back to haunt me once more.

They were framed by tan skin and long dark hair. Evil personified. A grin stretching over feral teeth.

I shook my head back and forth, begging him not to penetrate me again, too exhausted and sore from hours of his relentless torture.

Except he had something new in mind. I could see it in the malicious intent darkening his eyes. He revealed his razor-sharp teeth, drawing them down my body to my abdomen. I writhed beneath him, crying, imploring him not to do it.

But it was too late.

His jaw elongated in a partial shift, lowering over my belly, and slicing into—

"*Willow!*" My name vibrated through my thoughts, my world dancing in a hypnotic wave of insanity.

So much color.

I glanced up, then down, enthralled by the rainbow of lights.

Then a deep voice penetrated through my dizzying cloud, drawing me into the whiteness of the bathroom.

I'd fallen asleep on the tiled floor. Ryder crouched over me, his expression lined with a fury I didn't understand. Had

I done something wrong? Perhaps I'd ignored him too long. *Sorry*, I tried to say, but my throat was too dry to form anything more than a croak.

Whoa, I thought as my world began to spin, his arms suddenly a brand against my bare skin. *What happened to my towel?* Oh, who cared? We were spinning, and I was going to be sick again if he didn't stop.

My stomach heaved, only I had nothing left inside me to expel.

How long had I lain on the floor? I tried to squint toward the window, to search for the moon, but I couldn't find it. *Where am I now?*

A grungy cell appeared around me, one I knew well.

The mattress on the floor wasn't meant for sleeping.

I glanced around, listening as women wept while males grunted.

This was a horror show and my new life.

A chill swept down my spine at the reality of it all. Why had the Magistrate sent me here? I had excelled in all my courses. I was meant to be a Vigil!

Oh, no...

I backed up, terrified as a green-eyed beast appeared outside my cage, his lips curled into a snarl.

A lycan.

Naked.

Ready to fuck.

No, no, no!

I squeezed my eyes closed, refusing to accept it, only to have warm hands on my face forcing me to refocus. *Ryder.*

What's going on? I asked, tears tracking down my face as I wondered why he'd sent me to that awful place. Was I not good enough? Had I not pleased him correctly?

I wanted to sob.

And I wanted to kill.

It was a fascinating contradiction, my mind fracturing between defeat and vengeance. I'd given the university everything, and they sent me to hell. It was so damn wrong.

I should have gone with Rae and Silas to the Immortal Cup! I wanted to shout. And maybe I did.

Everything was so hazy now, my reality slipping away, down, down, down the drain.

I whirled with it, a circular motion of madness.

My name followed me along the way, as did those creepy green eyes, until everything around me disappeared beneath ripples of black.

Cold. Stark. Black.

Chapter Twenty

Ryder

Twenty Minutes Earlier

Screaming came through the phone line, the words a jumbled mix of curses and threats. I yawned as I allowed Lilith to continue her tirade. She'd just found out about Yavi's demotion, two hours after our first call earlier this evening.

Unfortunately, that left Benita on the suspect list as someone who might be informing on me to Lilith. That part disturbed me more than Lilith's hissy fit.

Damien walked in and paused at finding me with my feet kicked up on my desk and my hands tucked behind my head. Then he glanced at the phone vibrating against the wood from Lilith's tantrum. His lips quirked up in amusement before he sat in one of the two chairs across from my desk. He probably had an update for me but would wait until my phone call ended.

I started counting, wondering how long it would take for her to hang up on me.

When I reached thirty, I grew bored and decided to pull up my computer monitor instead to spy on Willow. It probably made me a bit of a creep, but I liked to check in on her throughout the evening. Mostly to satisfy myself that she still existed.

Only, when I pulled up the footage of the suite, I couldn't find her anywhere. The only areas without cameras were the bathrooms.

My brow furrowed and I left the footage up, waiting for her to reappear again.

That was when I realized Lilith had gone silent.

I picked up the phone to find the call disconnected.

"I don't think she approves of Yavi's death," I told Damien.

"No kidding," he drawled. "And here I thought she'd roll out the red carpet and throw a party."

"How long until she decides to surprise me with a visit?" I asked him. "Any guesses?"

"I give it a week, maybe two."

"Then that's our deadline for finding the leak." I really hoped it wasn't Benita, but I learned long ago never to trust anyone. And she'd seemed almost a little too eager to assist me lately. "I don't want anyone in this tower that I can't trust."

"So we'll be living here alone, then." He sounded amused. "Can I keep the penthouse full of willing females?"

I grinned and glanced at my screen again to search for Willow. "I'm quite happy with my pet right now."

Except she still hadn't appeared, which took away some of my humor. She'd already showered, something I knew because the last time I checked on her, she'd been in the kitchen. I pulled up that screen now, noting her mostly untouched plate on the counter.

Odd. The food had to be cold by now.

I half-heartedly listened while Damien brought me up to speed on his research of those on the list. He'd confirmed over half of them to be known for their proclivities in imbibing young blood, but some of the others weren't as well documented.

I gave him permission to question them a little more liberally to determine whether or not Yavi's information proved true. I wouldn't put it past the former sovereign to provide a few false names in an effort to hide others on his client list.

Ten minutes later, no Willow. I pushed away from my desk, my instincts firing red. "I need to check on my pet."

"You just went up there a few hours ago," Damien reminded me.

"I'm aware, but something's wrong." I could feel it in a weird sort of nagging sense. "I'll be back."

"I'll come with you," he said instead, following me out the door.

I didn't argue. We'd been through enough over his lifetime to know when to trust the other, and my gut was rarely—if ever—wrong.

Damien grabbed his tablet on our way. "No one has accessed or left the suite," he said as we entered the elevator. "However, Benita left early today, which I find interesting."

"Do you think she's our leak?" I asked him, dialing the code for the guest suite.

"It's hard to say. I'll keep tabs on her, as well as the other four." He tucked his tablet beneath his arm. "She's always been power hungry. The behavior fits the mold, particularly if she anticipates your downfall."

"Makes me wonder what she thinks she knows," I replied. "I'm the oldest in this region by several thousand years. Who could she expect to surpass me?"

"Perhaps someone not from this region," Damien suggested.

Yes, that was another route I'd considered, too. "Darius would be next in line for royalty."

"And he recently took a sovereign position under Jace," Damien added. "I'll reach out to our mutual contact. I know they're friends."

"He was one of Cam's progeny, so that makes sense." I stepped off the elevator onto the guest suite floor. "Let me know what she says."

"Always," he agreed, walking beside me down the hallway. I paused only to type in the external code, then stepped inside to scent the air. The kitchen was to my left, the food on the counter cold to the touch.

I called for Willow as I made my way through the large living area to the back hall, which led to the bedroom. "Check the other bathroom," I told Damien over my shoulder. I doubted she was there, but it would expedite the search to have him check the half bath off the living area.

The bedroom was empty, the bedsheets still rumpled from earlier.

"Willow?" I tried again, entering the bathroom.

The dual-headed shower was empty and mostly dry, and she wasn't by the double sinks. Which left the walk-in closet and—

"*Fuck.*" The tips of her small heels were peeking out from the water-closet entry.

I walked in to find her cheek pressed to the marble floor, her eyes half-mast. Kneeling beside her, I pressed my palm to her clammy forehead. "Willow?"

Her pupils dilated, but her mouth didn't move. So she was semi-aware, but not quite.

"She's burning up," I said as Damien entered.

I scooped her up into my arms, her towel remaining on the floor and leaving her naked. She shivered in response as if she were cold, but her skin temperature told a different story.

"Can you get me a cool washcloth?" I asked as I carried her to the bed and laid her down to check her vitals.

I frowned at what I found; her pulse had slowed to a dangerous pace. No wonder she was hardly awake.

"What the fuck?" I demanded, searching her for signs of injury and finding none.

She muttered something unintelligible that sounded like an apology.

"Did you do this to yourself?" I asked her, unable to find evidence of self-harm. Then I shook my head, because, no, Willow was a warrior. She wouldn't hurt herself in this manner.

So what was causing it?

I bit into my wrist and put it to her mouth. Her lips parted automatically, her body craving the immortal essence running through my veins. Yet somehow it didn't seem to be enough, the scent of deterioration thick in the air. I recognized it because I'd smelled it so many times throughout the millennia, that sickly sweet aroma of a human on the precipice of death.

It didn't make any sense.

Damien returned with the towels, laying one over her forehead and the other across her neck. His expression remained stoic, but I caught a flicker of concern in his gaze. He smelled her imminent death just as I did.

"I've given her blood every damn day," I told him. "She should be closer to immortal than mortal."

"Perhaps you gave her too much," he suggested.

"Too much?" I repeated. There was no such thing as "too much." "That's impossible."

"Mortals are fragile," he added. "Their reactions vary. The only foolproof method is to turn one immortal entirely."

His words rolled around in my head, the truth unraveling behind my eyes.

The only foolproof method is to turn one immortal entirely.

In any other situation, I wouldn't even consider that alternative. But Willow didn't fit the definition of ordinary circumstances. She was spectacular. Unique. *Mine.*

"You're right," I realized out loud. "There's only one method to ensure she survives."

"Oh, no," Damien said. "That's not what I meant. I mean, fuck, Ryder. You're the one who taught me that mortals are meant to die. It's why we don't get attached, remember?"

I did. And I still agreed with that sentiment. However… "This one is different for me."

"I said the same thing about Izzy."

"And she's still alive," I pointed out. Most thought she was dead, but that was another conversation entirely. "Willow can't be an *Erosita*, Damien." Her body had been defiled by the lycans, and even before that at the university. Only virgins could be a vampire's life-mate.

"I know. I get that. However, turning her goes against the Blood Alliance. Lilith might be able to look the other way in how you rule the territory, but this will cross the line."

"I couldn't give two fucks about Lilith's edicts." She could kick rocks, for all I cared. "This isn't about her. This is about Willow."

"A human you've known for a handful of weeks," he snapped. "Do you even hear yourself? This is insane, even for you." He began to pace, his shoulders tight with disapproval.

I considered Willow once more, found her glassy blue eyes staring up at me as if I existed in a dream, not reality. Her lips only half-heartedly worked over my wrist, her body shutting down with each passing second. Soon she would resemble a corpse, the warrior inside her gone forever. I tried to visualize it, to make myself see what needed to happen.

Damien was right.

This was the reason we didn't get attached.

Yet somewhere along the way, this female had seduced a foreign part of me. It might only be temporary, but even a few passing moments of the sensations she awoke within me were worth breaking a couple more rules.

I'd lived too long to deny myself something so precious.

"I need more time with her," I whispered, holding her dying gaze. "I don't accept that this is her fate."

"What is it with this girl?" Damien demanded, drawing my attention to him. "She's beautiful, yes. But why her? There are almost a dozen willing females upstairs waiting for a chance to warm your bed. Why this one?"

"She makes me feel alive," I told him, my voice hardening. "And I'm not done with her yet." I probably sounded like a petulant child whose toy had just been yanked away, but I didn't give a fuck. What was the point of having the ability to save someone if I refused to use it?

"Okay, and what happens when you are?" he pressed.

I couldn't answer that. It also wasn't important right now.

"I want to save her," I said instead, my decision made. It really wasn't up to him whether I did so or not. Willow was my pet, not his. And I had the ability to cure her, so I would. What happened after that would be discussed at a later point when our current situation was fixed.

"She's really gotten under your skin," Damien marveled, studying me intently. "I've never seen you so enamored with a human before."

"I need a place to take her to perform the change," I informed him, ignoring his side commentary. Maybe I had lost my head over the female on the bed. I'd evaluate it later, *after* I fixed Willow.

Damien remained silent for another beat, his expression giving nothing away. Then he conceded with a sigh. Because he knew better than anyone that once I made up my mind, I wouldn't change it.

"All right," he said. "We need to work quickly." He turned without another word, his loyalty resolute.

I didn't waste time thanking him or commenting further. I picked Willow up and adjusted her carefully in my arms. Her body temperature was rapidly decreasing, so I wrapped her in a blanket from the bed, then followed Damien into the living area, toward the foyer.

The sight of her breakfast on the counter gave me temporary pause. Her fork was lying at an angle that suggested she'd taken a few bites. "I want her plate checked for poison," I said.

"Your blood would be able to cure poison," he pointed out as he held open the door to the hallway. "But I'll have it checked."

I nodded, then passed through the threshold and led the way.

Damien called the elevator to take us to the ground floor. "We can't afford for anyone to know what you're about to do," he said as we stepped inside. "If it gets back to Lilith, she'll bring the council down on you, and while you may survive that, Willow will not."

I dipped my chin again in agreement. "Call for a car."

"Already done," he replied, lifting his tablet. "I know a place in the city where no one will go looking."

Of course he did. Damien had a lot more experience with this new world than I did. He'd been my only connection to society for the last one hundred years since my other lived in hiding as well.

Willow groaned in my arms, her eyelids fluttering closed. "Don't you dare die on me, pet," I told her.

"You'll need to initiate the transfer in the car," Damien said just before the doors opened.

I didn't so much verbally agree as I did mentally. He was right. We didn't have time to do this properly.

Several servants went to the floor in an immediate bow upon seeing us exit the elevator into the main lobby of the building. I ignored the receptionist who asked how she could help us, and immediately stepped out into the balmy humidity of San José.

No one asked any questions about the dying female in my arms. They probably assumed she was my late-evening snack.

Damien took the keys from the valet as soon as he exited the sedan. It was one of the many cars in Silvano's garage, all of which were now mine. I didn't bother to look at the make or model, just slid into the backseat with Willow on my lap and shut the door before the valet could reach it.

"Go" was all I said, not wasting time with the seat belt.

Damien practically floored it out of the lot, his penchant for driving quickly coming in handy right now.

Willow shivered, a soundless plea leaving her lips. "You'll be okay," I promised her.

She didn't reply, but her eyes flickered a strange yellowish tint in the dark, similar to a lycan's. I frowned at the startling change, then glanced out the window to take in the scene.

"It's a full moon," I said slowly.

"Yes," Damien confirmed, not that it was necessary. Now that I'd realized our current phase, I could feel the energy humming in the air despite the nearest lycan clan being hundreds of miles away.

I took in Willow's shivering form, the hairs dancing along her exposed neck, and that glimmer of yellow sheening in her irises.

Was this related to her captivity? She'd been in my care for roughly four weeks now, her initial escape taking place only a few nights after the last full moon.

Had the wolves done something to her? Something that had caused her current state of living in limbo? Because that was what this reminded me of—the limbo between life and death.

"Can you access her records from the breeding camp?" I wondered out loud. "Find out if they did anything specific to her?"

"Do you think it's related to her current state?"

"I think it's possible."

He navigated onto one of the city's highways—or I assumed it was one, with how fast we were going. "I'll find out everything I can."

"It would make sense," I continued thoughtfully, not acknowledging his vow because I had every expectation that he would see it through. "She's been unique from the moment I saw her. And her fighting skills are almost too good for a human." I'd sparred with her several times over the last few weeks. While I bested her each time, she more than held her own, which was why I enjoyed training with her.

"She's skilled," he agreed. "But the university excels in training."

I couldn't argue that point, even if I wanted to scoff at it.

Willow's shiver turned into a violent tremor, her teeth chattering as though she were standing in the Arctic. Damien turned up the heat without my having to ask.

"I'm going to start the process," I told him.

"We'll reach a reasonable burial site in about ten minutes," he replied, providing the necessary timetable.

I moved her into a better position for what I had to do, essentially laying her out along the backseat with only her upper body in my lap. Her head rested on my arm, which I lifted to bring her neck closer to my mouth. "She'll be ready in fifteen."

"There are shovels in the trunk," he added.

This must have been the car he planned to use to deliver messages to those on my list from earlier. He'd probably intended to kill a few of them to make his statement clear— leave or die. It was exactly how I'd handle it.

Willow sputtered, her lungs beginning to fail.

"I'm going to need you to stay with me just a few more minutes," I informed her softly.

Her expression didn't change, that yellow tint blinking in and out of her dying gaze. I ignored it and went for her neck, my incisors piercing the tender skin of her vein to begin the task of absorbing the entirety of her life essence.

She tasted as she always did, with no signs of any altered chemistry in her body. I evaluated each pull into my mouth, cataloging the flavors and searching for any sign of foul play.

Nothing.

No hints.

No drugs.

No poisons.

Just my sweet, alluring Willow.

I closed my eyes and consumed her, wishing for an entirely different experience. One where she writhed in pleasure, not death. She should be moaning, my bite engaging all her erotic receptors, but her trembles weren't born of ecstasy. They were savage tremors indicating her end of days.

Not on my watch, I vowed, quickening my pace and forcing her to yield her life to me. It'd been a long time since I'd done this—Damien being my one and only progeny—but the art of turning another into a vampire was ingrained in my being. I sensed the moment where I needed to pull back and open a vein for her, the magic of my existence pulsing to life inside me.

I ripped apart my wrist in my hurry for her to drink, then pressed it to her mouth, watching as precious fluid streamed passed her lips and also down the sides of her cheeks. I didn't care. I'd feed later to replenish myself. Now was about reviving my Willow, providing her with the energy she required to survive the change.

She didn't move, apart from her throat swallowing.

I sensed no emotions from her. No confusion. No sadness. No joy. It was as though I were feeding a corpse.

It felt wrong, yet I simultaneously sensed the process beginning to work. My head fell back against the seat, my vision spinning just a little from the onslaught of mixed signals.

She's not responding.

The bond is snapping into place.

This isn't right.

My progeny is being reborn.

I didn't even notice that the car had stopped or that

Damien wasn't with me anymore until he knocked on the window beside my head. I felt groggy, depleted, *hazy*. He frowned at me and opened the door, his words slurring through my ears. Then he looked at my lap, and his eyebrows shot up. I looked down to find the problem and realized Willow had lost consciousness at some point, but my wound remained open.

How much blood did she imbibe? Was it enough? Why was I so weak?

"She bit you," I heard Damien say, an emotional note underlining his tone. Awe? Fear? Anger? I couldn't decipher it over the roaring in my thoughts.

But I knew one thing that needed to be said. "Bury her. Us. Bury us." I didn't want to leave her alone in an unknown area throughout the day. She needed her Sire by her side to prosper.

"Hell no," Damien snapped, lifting his phone to his ear. I couldn't hear what he was saying. I kept repeating my command, but it lacked punch.

I shook my head to clear it, but that only made me dizzier.

"I don't fucking care. Track him down." Damien's words were clear until they weren't. Something about the triad. Ascension.

Fuck, I was a mess. I hadn't felt like this in… ever. Yeah, never. This didn't happen to me. And why the hell was I still bleeding?

I tried to focus on my wrist, my eyes widening, then narrowing at the jagged teeth marks. Huh. Willow really had bitten me. Why hadn't I felt it?

"Fine." Damien's voice came to me again. "Four hours." I scowled. "Bury us."

"We'll be there," Damien said, hanging up. He approached again, his expression hard. "I'd apologize for this, but I think you kind of deserve it."

I frowned at him. "What?" This wasn't the plan. We were supposed to—

Damien's fist flew at my face, meeting my jaw in an astonishingly accurate punch. I should have been able to duck, but I didn't even see it coming, nor did I have anywhere to go.

I also should have been prepared for the second one.

Only, I wasn't in the right frame of mind to comprehend his actions.

And it fucking hurt.

We're going to have a very serious talk in a few minutes, I thought at him, woozy and spinning in a world of darkness.

The third punch did me in.

I swore I heard him chuckle.

Or maybe that was me.

Because all I could think about was how I intended to kill him the second I woke up.

With at least three bullets.

One for each hit.

Dick.

Chapter Twenty-One

Ryder

My head fucking hurt.

What the hell did I do last night? It reminded me of that time Damien and I had indulged in six bottles of tequila just to see what it would do.

Answer: severe dehydration.

And it had sucked.

I'd refused to touch the shit ever since, which was a damn shame since I lived in Texas. Or did I?

My fingers flexed as I tried to lift them to my head, only to find them handcuffed behind my back. I frowned. *What the fuck?*

It took significant effort to open my eyes, almost as though I'd been severely drugged. My dry mouth added to the effect, as did my general dizziness.

"I need you to hear me out before you try to kill me," a familiar voice said, causing me to frown.

Why the hell would I want to kill Damien? He was my best friend. My progeny. One of the only beings in this world I could trust.

Only, a memory started to resurface that had me thinking otherwise. Something about my pet...

My eyes flew open as I realized what it was, then I winced at the intense light coming in from my living room windows. I looked around quickly, realizing where we were.

Back in Texas.

What the fuck?

I found the source of my confusion standing a few feet away with his arms folded across his plain white shirt, looking only slightly contrite.

"You fucking punched me." And, ugh, did we have to do this in daylight? It made the entire room so damn bright.

"I did a lot more than punch you," he admitted. "But hear me out."

"Get these handcuffs off of me." They were the ones I used to hold vampires in my basement. I could tell by the way they refused to bend.

"I will once I'm confident you won't try to shoot me."

"Oh, I'm absolutely going to shoot you," I promised. "Where the hell is Willow?"

"She's alive." The way he said it had me narrowing my eyes.

"You don't sound very sure about that."

"She nearly killed you, Ryder," he replied on a growl.

My eyebrows shot up, a humorless laugh leaving my lips. "Pretty sure I'd remember that."

He scrubbed his hand over his face, allowing me to see his exhaustion. "Something's wrong with her."

"No shit," I deadpanned.

"No, you don't understand. She *bit* you." He started to pace. "She took a chunk out of your damn wrist."

"I did that when I was trying to feed her," I snapped.

Although, I did vaguely recall jagged teeth marks on my wrist, the memory somewhat clear.

He shook his head. "No. I mean, yes, you did, but then she bit you, Ryder. Like, really bit you." He stopped in front of me. "She bit you like a fucking lycan."

I tried to recall exactly what had happened after I opened my vein for her, but it was a blur. However, I did remember feeling strange and knowing the process had taken on a unique twist.

Rather than comment on it, I glanced around again. Damien must have knocked me out with drugs afterward to get me on a plane back to Texas. I could only assume he had a logical reason for it. "Why are we here?"

"I called Izzy because I wanted to talk to Luka, but she insisted on sending me to Jace. So I spoke to him based on her recommendation. Then I found out he was currently in Clemente Clan territory, and, well, I arranged a meeting. Edon's on his way here. With Jace. They'll be here any minute now."

"You invited a royal vampire into my private home." I uttered the words slowly, unable to comprehend why my progeny would make such a decision.

I didn't enjoy entertaining company of any type, let alone a damn royal. There were sixteen others in existence, seventeen if I included myself, and eighteen if I counted Lilith. They were the oldest and most powerful of my kind, and I liked exactly one of them—myself.

Well, I could tolerate Kylan on a good day.

And maybe Jace.

But today was not a good day.

Which was why I demanded to know: "Have you lost your fucking mind?" Because my progeny knew how I felt about the pretentious members of the council. Inviting one into my sanctuary ranked somewhere around eating cow shit. Hence the reason I'd gone after Silvano when he trotted an army of unwanted company through my lands.

"I could ask you the same thing," he muttered,

collapsing into my favorite recliner chair as though he owned it. "Izzy swore to me that Jace won't take advantage of the situation. He's only coming to help."

I'd known Izzy for the same length of time as I'd known Damien. They were twins, after all. But Damien had been my confidant and best friend, while Izzy had been more akin to a little sister to me. Which was why it had infuriated me when Cam took her as his *Erosita*.

A thousand years later and it still made my blood boil.

She was too good for him.

At least the bastard knew it.

Except he'd left her alone for over a century now with Majestic Clan. Oh, it wasn't by choice—that much I understood—but he was doing one hell of a job finding his way back to her.

I shook my head, not wanting to go down that land mine of a thought trail right now and instead focused on the present situation.

"Where's Willow?" I asked again.

Damien sighed and pushed away from the chair, leaving me handcuffed on the couch. We were going to need to discuss this behavior at length later. After I shot him a few times.

I carefully twisted my hands as far as the metal allowed to begin working on the release mechanism I'd built into these. Every gadget I owned was one I knew how to manipulate. It was Survival Instinct 101 to program in failsafes only I could figure out.

Damien knew this about me, which meant he also knew it was only a matter of time before I freed myself and kicked his ass.

He returned a minute later with an unconscious Willow in his arms. I frowned as he laid her down beside me. "She's missing a vital trait to indicate life," I told him, a snarl underlining my tone. She didn't have a damn heartbeat, nor was she breathing. When I finished breaking out of these cuffs, he was a dead man.

"I realize that," he muttered. "She's in some sort of limbo state, and she's been there for hours."

I paused at that. "Hours?" A mortal couldn't remain in limbo for *hours* without a heartbeat. But as I looked at her again, I noticed the lack of rigor mortis setting in. "How many hours?"

"Seven," he replied. "She took her last breath before we boarded the plane. I tried to resuscitate her, but she fell into this state… and hasn't come back."

"Because you didn't bury her."

He shook his head. "She wasn't transitioning, Ryder. You couldn't see it through your delirium, but your blood didn't take."

"How is that possible?" In all my very long life, I had never heard of a human rejecting the transformation into the undead life.

"I don't know. That's why I called Izzy," Damien said. "It's like Willow's trapped in the lycan conversion phase, not a vampire one."

I stopped messing with the handcuffs and studied Willow, a memory nagging at me. "Her injuries that day by the river…" I trailed off, picturing them. "It looked like she'd been ripped open by a wolf." I'd thought they were claw marks, but… "What if those wounds had been created by teeth?"

"Then she would have begun the transition while waiting for the follow-up bite," Damien said, his tone indicating he'd already considered this avenue of thought. "She should be dead."

"Yes," I agreed.

The lycan transition required a sequence of two bites. If the mortal didn't receive the requisite follow-up bite, the human would die an excruciatingly painful death.

I gaped at my darling pet, her warrior strength taking on a whole new meaning. "If she was bitten at the camp, then she ran all the way here while fighting the transition."

"And then you gave her your blood," Damien put in,

drawing my gaze back to his, another piece of the puzzle sliding into place.

"Effectively curing her," I whispered. "At least temporarily."

"And you continued to give her blood over the last month."

"So my essence kept her alive and in limbo this entire time," I breathed, awed. "That would explain her sudden catatonic state. The moon energy would have encouraged her to shift last night." While lycans could control when they took on their wolf forms, a young changeling like Willow who hadn't indulged in her animal side might not be able to so easily fight it. "Except she couldn't shift."

"Because she's missing the second bite. And you couldn't turn her because she was already in lycan limbo," Damien said. "That's my theory."

"Which is why you wanted to talk to Luka."

"Which is why I wanted to talk to Luka," he agreed. "But we're getting the new alpha next door instead."

Edon.

I'd met him briefly last month during the whole Silvano fiasco. My predecessor had orchestrated some sort of game with the old alpha of Clemente Clan—Walter. It hadn't gone according to plan for either of them, as they'd died. Hence my newly appointed position and Edon's ascension. Which reminded me… "Did I hear you mention a triad at one point?"

"Yeah, he completed it last night before his ascension. Jace was in the middle of the post-celebratory festivities when I called."

I could only imagine what that meant. Jace had a notorious fetish for lycans. "I see."

Damien cleared his throat. "That's not all. I was able to download Willow's file on the flight here. It reflects a history of noncompliance at the breeding camps. There are videos of her fighting them while they rutted. The footage is… graphic."

We'd lived through countless acts of violence. As such, not much fazed me and Damien, but I caught the glimmer of remorse in his gaze. That alone implied whatever Willow had experienced was the epitome of vile.

He cleared his throat again. "They marked her for termination, determining she wasn't suitable to carry a child due to her inability to comply."

Damien stared at me, his look telling me he had more to say and I wasn't going to like it. I dipped my chin in a subtle way to encourage him to continue.

"Willow was marked for termination after her third week at the camp, yet Blood Day was several months ago. That means there are at least two months of data missing from her record. I've heard rumors of what lycans do when playing with humans. None of them are good."

"Then I suppose it's a good thing Edon is coming over. I have a few questions for him."

"I imagine you do, yes," Damien agreed.

We fell into a comfortable silence while I finished unlatching the cuffs at my back. I brought them around to lie on the coffee table before me. Damien didn't even flinch. He knew I'd free myself and had banked on providing enough information up front that I wouldn't lunge at him.

"I'm still going to shoot you," I promised. "But as we're expecting company, I'd prefer my only ally to be healthy and aware for the meeting."

He lifted a shoulder, uncaring. "I'll take a bullet."

"Three," I corrected. "One for each hit."

"Then, technically, you owe me four," he drawled. "I had to make sure you were really unconscious."

My jaw ticked as I studied my wrists. The only evidence of a wound was the dried blood on my sleeve, which could have been from me slicing open my own vein. Except I felt the lethargy in my body, an odd sort of sensation I hadn't experienced since my youth. It indicated I'd gone too long without blood. As I could survive on very little in my old age, the hunger rioting inside me was telling.

I'd lost a lot of my essence, and somehow, I hadn't felt it until it was too late.

"There's another bag of O-negative in the warmer," Damien said. "You've already gone through three. It's how I revived you."

My eyebrows shot up. "Three bags?"

"Plus two on the plane to keep you alive," Damien replied. "Your wound was healing at an almost mortal rate. I've never seen anything like it."

I glanced at it again, then down at Willow. "Only lycan bites can slow a vampire's healing."

"Thus adding credence to the theory," Damien murmured. "She's clearly not your average mortal."

"What the hell did they do to her?" I wondered, awed and sickened at the same time.

"A question we should have an answer to momentarily," my progeny said as my alarms began to blare with an intruder warning. We both looked at the screen to see a car coming our way with four individuals inside.

Damien stood and walked over to zoom in on the panel to reveal Edon behind the wheel. The body thermal image beside it indicated two more lycans sat in the back, and a vampire in the trunk. Jace was obviously the latter—he would have chosen to hide from the sun to conserve his senses—but I wasn't expecting the former. "Did Edon mention bringing company?"

"Silas and Luna," Damien replied. "His mates."

Yeah, I knew who they were. I'd met them briefly last month. "Okay."

"I'll stall them while you shower and change," Damien said.

I shook my head. "No. We've already spent time we didn't have to waste. Let them in now."

While it went against my instincts to grant entry to a royal and an alpha while in a weakened state, I knew my house better than they did. If they chose to fight me on my turf, they'd pay a hefty price.

Damien seemed ready to argue but smartly chose not to. "At least drink some blood while I go greet them."

I only partially conceded on that point. "Do they know about Willow?" I asked as I went to retrieve the blood from the warmer in the kitchen.

Each step hurt more than it should, further confirming I'd been in a bad spot when Willow drank from me.

I frowned, concerned by my temporary loss of focus during her transformation. That never should have happened because I should have felt the depletion long before it became a reality.

Had I just been so lost to the sensation and desire to help her that I'd ignored all the signs in my body? If so, that made her far more dangerous than I ever could have anticipated. Because she'd truly brought me to my knees.

Hell, had Damien not been there, she might have even killed me.

I picked up the blood bag as he joined me in the kitchen.

"No. Izzy told Jace we had a problem involving a lycan, and that's all I allowed him to know as well," he said, answering my question about what Jace and Edon knew. "I also phrased it in a way that insinuated urgency."

That was one of his talents—communicating in a manner that stressed importance without giving away the key points.

The sound of a car door slamming out front had me saying, "Then let's go bring them up to speed."

Chapter Twenty-Two

Ryder

I leaned against the frame of my front door, watching as Edon and Jace walked up the path with Luna and Silas behind them. Jace glanced at the blood bag in my hand and arched a brow as I brought it to my mouth to take a long pull from the contents.

"I've had one hell of a night," I said by way of explanation.

He took in the blood on my sleeve and my rumpled suit. "Looks like it."

I grunted and pushed off the frame, not allowing them entry yet. The second they were inside, they'd be able to smell Willow—if they couldn't already—and I wanted answers first.

"Tell me about your breeding camps, Alpha," I said,

addressing Edon. "What happens when you mark a human for termination?"

His obsidian eyes met mine, his dominance palpable as he took my measure. He had a few inches over my six-foot height, and his shoulders were slightly bulkier than mine, but I suspected I'd still best him in a fight, even in my current state. Mostly because I could use his two weaknesses against him—the pair of pups at his back.

"You brought us here to talk about the breeding camps?" He sounded incredulous. "I thought you had a lycan problem."

"I do, and that might turn to plural—*lycans*—depending on how you answer my question. So I'll ask again: What do you do with humans marked for termination?"

"We kill them," he answered immediately.

"Do you?" I countered, glancing at Damien.

"Is that an immediate sort of thing or a gradual process?" my progeny asked, arching a dark brow.

"How about we not dance around the issue and get straight to the point," Jace interjected, stepping forward. "Ismerelda doesn't make a habit of calling me for unnecessary chitchat."

A fair point well made. Every time she picked up a phone, she risked her life. It was why I usually texted with her in code, but Damien had felt the situation warranted a voice discussion. Which meant he took my and Willow's situation seriously.

Maybe I would only shoot him once instead of four times. He really was a loyal friend, as was Izzy. And if she trusted Jace, then I could temporarily extend him the same courtesy.

I finished my blood bag and folded it in my hands before saying, "One of your terminated humans recently ventured onto my property. She was in bad shape and dying, but I cured her with my blood."

Jace's dark eyebrows shot up into his hairline. "You saved a human?"

I nearly smiled. "Does my temporary humanity shock you?"

"Yes."

At least he didn't feel the need to lie. "Is it because you wouldn't do the same?" I wondered out loud.

"No, because we live very different lives," he replied.

That was fair and true. "I don't care for this new world or the penchant for treating humans like cattle. Honestly, it would have been kinder of me to let her die, but she tried to attack me, and I found that rather amusing. So I've kept her. She's mine. And now she's dying again." I looked at Edon. "Which brings me to what I need to know—what really happens when a human is marked for termination?"

"They're supposed to be killed immediately," Edon informed me, his dark eyes holding no signs of emotion. "But I'll admit that I haven't ventured to that part of my territory for some time. I've only recently ascended."

Fair enough. "Well, this human was marked for termination three weeks after her Blood Day assignment, yet she stumbled onto my property just over four weeks ago. And even more important, we believe she was bitten."

That evoked a reaction from the alpha's dark eyes. He shared a look with Luna and then Silas, a slight hum of energy coming off the three of them. I suspected they were mentally communicating, something that happened with lycan mates. It also occurred between vampires and their *Erositas*, but not between Sire and progeny.

From what I learned during my time in Clemente Clan territory, Edon had turned Silas into a wolf. He'd won the last Immortal Cup, which earned him the gift of eternal life. And in this case, it appeared he'd won the heart of his alpha, too.

Luna gave a slight nod, confirming one of my observations from last month.

Edon considered her an equal.

That was a rare trait in alphas these days.

Making a quick judgment call, I opted to lay all my cards

on the table. They'd figure this out anyway, so I might as well ensure they had all the pieces of this puzzle. "I also tried to turn Willow last night, and it did—"

"Willow?" Silas repeated, his blue eyes widening.

I frowned at him. "Yes, that's her chosen name. I prefer it to the serial number of her birth. Anyway, as I was—"

"I need to see her," he interjected again, causing me to question his survival instinct. That question turned into a raging red flag as he moved around Edon and attempted to enter my home without an invitation.

I caught his shoulder and shoved him back, which stirred a growl from the ballsy pup. Edon stepped up to his side in a show of solidarity, just as Damien moved to my side.

Jace sighed audibly. "Honestly, children, can we play nice for five more minutes and discuss this like adults?"

"I need to see her," Silas stated again as if it were his God-given right to make demands on my land.

Luna moved forward and put her hand on his arm as she softly explained, "He had a friend at the university named Willow. She went to the breeding camp, and he learned from Kylan last night that her location is currently unknown because she escaped."

"Kylan? What the fuck does Kylan have to do with this?"

"His *Erosita* also went to the university with them," Luna replied. "Kylan tracked down her location as a favor for Rae, and passed on the information to Silas via Jace."

I wasn't even sure where to begin with all of that, the information startling and revealing a whole new level to the game that I hadn't even begun to explore. Perhaps I wasn't the only one who disliked this new way of existence. Izzy had always claimed there were others, but I hadn't cared enough to ask. Now I wondered if I was looking at the *others* she'd mentioned in passing.

With a shake of my head, I stepped backward into my house.

Worst case, it wasn't the Willow they knew, and we could

continue our conversation appropriately.

Best case, Silas knew her and Edon would be encouraged to help her. Not that I needed the added motivation. He'd be assisting my pet whether he wanted to or not.

I led the way without a word, Damien a solid presence at my back. He stepped up to my side to take the blood bag from my hand when we reached the juncture between the kitchen area and the living room. I went left while he turned right. Then I moved to Willow on the couch and crouched before her to ensure nothing had changed.

She still had no heartbeat but otherwise appeared alive.

Silas cursed, confirming he knew her even before he tried to elbow me out of the way to reach her. I immediately shoved him back and growled menacingly. "Hurt her and I will kill you."

He postured right back at me. "She's not on my couch dying."

"I tried to turn her to save her, mutt. *Your* kind did this to her."

Luna squeezed her way between us, placing her palm on my chest and not so gently pushing me away from her mate. I stared down at the fiery little female, momentarily impressed by her might. "He's not trying to hurt her, Ryder. She's one of his best friends."

Silas wrapped his arms around Luna, pulling her back into him as though to claim her, but I caught the hint of need in his gaze—a need for comfort. She spoke the truth about his connection to my Willow. They truly were friends. How fascinating that my pet never mentioned him or Kylan's *Erosita*. Was that because she didn't trust me enough to comment on her previous life?

I made a mental note to ask her once she woke up.

Because she was going to wake up.

I refused to accept the alternative.

"May I?" Edon asked, gesturing to Willow.

I dipped my chin, only because I needed his opinion on her state. As Silas seemed content with holding his female mate, I went to sit beside my pet, leaving everyone in the room within my peripheral view while I focused on Willow.

"You failed to mention that he tried to turn her," Jace said conversationally, standing near the entrance of the room. His words were directed at Damien as he rejoined us.

My progeny chose to stand beside Jace, which served as a purposeful position that would aid in a swift defensive strategy should it become necessary. There were weapons hidden in every room for this very reason. I never left anything to chance, and neither did Damien.

"It wasn't relevant to the conversation," my progeny replied.

"That your maker attempted to illegally turn a human into a vampire?" Jace reiterated. "You're right. Not relevant at all."

"It wouldn't have been required had she not randomly fallen ill," I put in. "She's been drinking my blood regularly, yet something about the moon last night forced her into this limbo state. My guess is, one of Edon's lycans bit her. *Illegally.*" I added that last word for Jace's benefit.

"If his lycan meant to kill her, it technically wouldn't be illegal, just cruel," Jace replied. "It takes two bites to turn a wolf."

"Which is why I need to bite her now to complete the transition," Edon interjected, looking at Silas, not me. That strange hum of electricity followed, the two males engaging in a conversation within their minds once more. Hell, they'd probably been talking this entire time.

"Speak out loud," I demanded. "You're saying our theory was right, that she's mid-transition. So complete it. Now."

"It's not that simple." Edon shook his head, making me want to throttle him. "How long has she been in limbo?"

"Roughly seven hours," Damien told him.

"In addition to how many days, twenty-eight or twenty-nine? Perhaps longer?" Edon ran his fingers through his dark hair and blew out a breath. "She's only alive because of

Ryder's blood, which, I imagine, is quite old. I have no idea how that will have impacted her transition."

"It kept her alive," I said. "That's how it impacted her. Now bite her and fix it."

"Even if I do, she'll be killed for being turned illegally." Edon glanced at Silas again, not me.

Right. I'd had enough of puppy playtime. "You're acting as though I brought you here for a debate. I didn't. You'll bite her, or I'll find a lycan who will."

"Technically, Damien invited us," Jace said, his tone conversational again. "And you also failed to mention he'd fallen off the deep end over a human."

"It's a fairly recent development," my progeny muttered. "I'm still working on a solution."

"Is it a result of royal stress, perhaps? From what I understand, Silvano's former region is quite a mess. No one wants to inherit it, even with Lilith actively searching for a replacement."

"He's handling it," Damien replied.

"I am," I agreed. "And I would handle this, but I'm not a fucking wolf. Your lycans started this, Alpha. Fucking fix it."

Edon sighed. "And I imagine you want us to protect her as well? In case you've forgotten, we're currently under scrutiny because of your predecessor igniting a war."

"Protecting her won't be your concern," I said, exhausted from this discussion. Every moment we wasted debating her fate brought her a second closer to death, and that was unacceptable.

"Then whose concern will it be?" he tossed back.

"*Mine.*" I allowed him to hear the power in my voice, underlined with my age and superiority. "Willow is mine."

A ripple of shock went through the room, my proclamation having the desired impact.

"I tried and failed to turn her because of something your mutts did to her. Now either you can fix it for me or I'll take her to your breeding camp and find someone else who will.

And trust me, Edon, you don't want me anywhere near that compound right now, not after what Damien found in her files."

His pupils flared at my threat, the alpha in him not taking kindly to my aggression.

"You think I've lost my mind," I continued. "Wait until you see what I'll do to bring her back."

Damien cleared his throat. "I suggest you bite her. Ryder's not one to issue idle threats."

"Why are you doing this?" Silas asked, a note of confusion in his tone. It took me a moment to realize he was addressing me, not his mate—who, in my opinion, needed to hear the same damn question because he was continuing to stall despite my threats.

Regardless, I focused on the young wolf and replied, "Because she's mine." I'd already said that, but if he needed to hear it again for it to register, then so be it.

Maybe his hearing had been impaired during his own transition. I truly hoped that didn't happen to Willow, but we'd cross that bridge when we came to it.

"What does that mean, exactly?" he pressed. "How is she yours?"

"Ask her what it means when she wakes up," I countered. She probably wouldn't have an answer, but he didn't need to know that. "Unless you want her to die?" I added. In which case, I'd note him as a horrible friend and ally.

Silas remained silent for so long I thought he wasn't going to respond. I was about to pick up Willow and leave when he quietly said, "My heart broke when the Magistrate sent her to the breeding camps. She deserved better." Emotion darkened his tone, his expression taking on a stern edge. "There's no positive path in this world. However, Willow deserves the right to choose, and she can't do that while in limbo."

"She would never choose death," I said, certain.

Apparently, that was the right thing to say, because Silas

gave me a look of esteemed approval in response. "I agree. But there's only one way for her to tell everyone else that." He looked at Edon. "You have my vote, Alpha."

"And mine," Luna said.

Edon considered them both, then nodded. "All right. We face the consequences together."

"Always," Luna murmured, a hint of emotion in her voice. Then she placed her palm on his shoulder while he picked up Willow's arm.

"This may not even work," he warned me. "The energy around her is unique, but my only experience has been turning Silas. I'm going to try, but I can't promise anything."

He didn't wait for me to acknowledge his comment; he merely turned his head and sank his teeth into her forearm.

Silas winced as though reliving a memory of the pain of transition. Then he watched Willow with the predator in his gaze, his nose twitching as the scents in the air began to change. Luna's lip curled into a slight snarl, the three wolves reacting to the magic.

I glanced at Damien. He remained stoic, while Jace leaned against the wall, hands tucked into the pockets of his trousers. We'd need to have a long conversation after this if Edon succeeded. Because Jace would be required to report this to Lilith and I couldn't allow that to happen.

He met my gaze, a hint of knowledge passing between us.

We would either come to a mutual agreement or we wouldn't. The latter would be a shame, as it would necessitate his death and I'd always been rather fond of the easygoing immortal. He knew when to turn on the mediator role and when to flick it off. I'd witnessed that just last month after Silvano had lost his head.

There was something brewing in the background; I could almost taste it. He'd met with Darius and Kylan several times while in Clemente Clan territory. I'd also seen him with Luka.

Part of me had wondered what they were all up to, but I

hadn't cared enough to ask. Now I felt like asking and would once Willow was tended to.

I returned my gaze to her, my fingers automatically combing through her hair.

Edon had released her arm, his palm now on her abdomen. He seemed to be trying to find her soul, power pouring off him in waves. I'd misjudged his strength before. This male, despite his young age, was a force to be reckoned with. I could taste his primal energy in the air, witnessed the impact it had on his mates, and nearly felt the need to bow before him as a result.

He'd just earned my respect in a matter of seconds, a fact very few in my history could claim.

The hairs along my arms rose as he growled, the command in that sound one that caused Luna and Silas to tremble in response. The vibration grew, his chest emanating a command—one he directed at Willow.

Then Silas added to it, his own growl bolstering that of his alpha, the rumble intensifying by the second.

Luna joined just as suddenly, the three of them matching in tempo and stirring electricity in the air. It hummed along my skin and shimmered off of Willow, her body beginning to quiver despite her missing heartbeat.

My eyes widened as she began to shift, her bones breaking with a sickening crunch that had my pulse thrumming in my ears.

Breathe, I begged her. *Breathe, damn it.*

The growls only grew louder, the energy a rampant spiral of unseen forces swimming around us as Willow continued to change. I didn't release her, not even when her head morphed beneath my palm to properly form a snout. Her hair went next, seeming to melt into her new form to change to a pretty white fur coat.

And still she didn't breathe.

I swallowed. *Come on, Willow. You're stronger than this.*

But what if she wasn't? What if I'd missed all the obvious signs of this and had reacted too late?

She might be gone forever.

Because I hadn't paid attention.

Because I'd treated her as a pet, not a person.

I'd considered her memory loss a blessing, but what if that had been the key all along? One I'd overlooked in my eagerness to play with her.

My chest physically hurt from the thought, the sensation foreign.

I'd been so sure this would work that I hadn't considered the alternative, that I might never hear her sweet voice again. Might never witness that fighter inside flaring in her eyes. Might never have another chance to tease her, worship her, *taste* her.

My jaw clenched with the possibility, my mind reliving every moment I'd spent with her in rapid succession.

From the moment with the hammer, to her gagging on ice cream, to the way she crawled across the carpet.

I'd been enamored with her from the start.

It wasn't supposed to end like this. We needed more time. We weren't done. I required more from her, just as she required more from me.

I refused to accept this.

"Come on, Willow. Breathe," I growled, the rumble adding to the cacophony around me. "*Breathe.*"

She was fully transformed now, her wolf form absolutely stunning save for the lack of a heartbeat in her chest.

I moved my hand from her head to her rib cage, my fingers threading through her fur.

"*Breathe.*" It came out as a plea-mingled demand, a complete oddity and not at all spoken in my usual voice. I could feel myself breaking inside at the realization that this might be my last moment with her.

How had she gotten under my skin so completely? Four weeks of knowing her and I felt as though half of my soul was leaving me for another realm.

It was insanity.

I'd lived for nearly five thousand years. I never got

attached. Yet at some point, Willow had become more than just my pet. She'd become a constant in my life that I intended to keep. I just hadn't acknowledged that until now.

Until it was too late.

Because she still wasn't breathing or moving.

I didn't understand it.

Was it a result of my blood impacting her transformation? Did she need more?

I shook my head, agonized over the insanity of this entire situation. And I did the only thing I could—I bit my wrist and placed it in front of her snout. It was all I could offer her. I'd tried to change her, I'd tried to cure her, and now I was going to force her to die with my blood on her lips.

Because she was mine to protect and I'd failed her.

I leaned in to press my face to her neck, my wrist against her snout, and I forgot about everyone in the room, the growls, the watching vampires, the waiting lycans, and focused only on Willow.

You weren't supposed to leave me yet, I told her. *I wasn't done.* We *weren't done.*

She, of course, didn't reply, but that wasn't the point. I had to say these things, to make her understand, even in the afterlife, that she was cared for by at least me. As short as our time together was, I'd tried.

The world dealt her a cruel hand.

It wasn't deserved.

The Blood Alliance had created this depraved, cold existence. It had to end. There had to be another way to coexist, one where we respected our food and didn't torment them in this nature.

I vowed to her silently that I would avenge her, that I would find the wolves who did this and end them.

Then I would dismantle the alliance.

Those assholes allowed this debauchery to exist. They thrived on it. And I was done playing their fucked-up game. Lilith wanted me to behave. Well, I would show her a behavior that made my previous actions appear angelic.

I growled with the need for vengeance, my hands tightening into fists. I wanted to rant and rage and destroy.

This fucking world would go down in—

Everything stopped, my senses going on high alert. I'd heard the faintest hint of something. Had I imagined it? Was I losing my mind?

I waited.

And waited.

And then I froze all over again at the subtle beat.

I lifted to stare down at Willow, my wrist still by her snout.

Another minute passed.

Then I jolted as her tongue snaked out to lick my skin. The touch was followed by a wheeze as her lungs filled again, her immortality kicking in to repair any internal damage.

"Willow," I whispered.

She didn't reply, but her heart kicked off with another beat, and then another, and then more.

"She's alive," I marveled, stroking my fingers through her fur. Only then did I realize the room had gone silent around me, everyone having taken a few steps back to observe. I didn't bother to ask why. I didn't care. "She's alive," I repeated, my soul feeling whole once more.

How someone could impact me so strongly in so little time, I would never understand. Perhaps she just arrived at the right time, providing me with the mental outlet I didn't know I needed.

However, now we would have time to figure it out. To move forward.

I won't let anyone hurt you, I vowed, my desire to destroy the alliance still standing stern in my mind. *You're mine, sweet pet. My Willow.*

She licked my wrist as though she heard me, and I chose to think of it as her claiming me in return.

"Do you realize what she is?" Jace asked, breaking the

silence and drawing me out of my relieved state.

Rather than answer, I just looked at him, uncertain why he chose now to speak up. I arched a brow, the only indication he was going to receive that I'd heard him and that I was waiting for a follow-up comment.

"Ryder, you and Edon just created a fucking hybrid."

"Well, Lilith's going to love this," Damien muttered.

I ignored him in favor of Jace. "A hybrid," I repeated. "That's… what?"

How could he tell that?

Willow wasn't even awake yet.

Except, as I studied her now, I realized that I could smell it—the vampire and lycan mix inside her. "Oh, shit…"

Chapter Twenty-Three

Ryder

A hybrid.

We'd created a fucking hybrid.

I ran my palm over my face, then gripped the back of my neck. "She's been living off my blood," I said, pacing the length of my office. "I had no idea. I gave it to her to ensure her strength, wanting her to be as protected as possible. But I never could have guessed it was the reason she's survived this long."

Fuck.

Edon and Jace stood just inside the door, their expressions unreadable. I'd run upstairs to shower and change into a pair of jeans and a T-shirt, needing to get rid of my suit. Silas and Luna had agreed to watch Willow. Damien was supervising.

"The full moon last night would have triggered her need to shift." Edon sounded thoughtful. "Or it could have been linked to my ascension. There was a lot of lunar energy in Clemente Clan as a result, and obviously one of my wolves initiated her change at the camp."

Yeah, that was a conversation we still needed to have. "You realize I want those lycans slaughtered, yes?"

"You might have to fight Silas for the opportunity," Edon replied. "Damien just showed him the files he found on Willow, and my Enforcer is demanding retribution in my head as we speak."

"Good." Not the fighting part, but the retribution part. "He can help."

Edon grunted. "You underestimate his need for vengeance."

"And you underestimate mine," I countered, stopping in front of him. "One of your lycans bit her for sport, probably to leave her in torment to die. I intend to return the favor. Then I'm going to castrate every single lycan who touched her. And if I'm not satisfied with the results, I'll burn the fucking building to the ground with all your mutts inside." I'd remove the humans first, of course.

A muscle ticked in Edon's jaw as he squared off with me. "You don't have jurisdiction in my territory, *Your Highness*."

"I wasn't asking, *Alpha*."

"Gentlemen, we'll determine the proper recourse for punishment once we've resolved the more pressing issue, which is the hybrid sleeping in the living room," Jace interjected. "The council will expect her to be terminated." He held up a hand as I growled. "I'm not saying I agree. I'm saying we have a problem."

"Lilith will insist on Willow's execution," Edon agreed, his wide shoulders visibly relaxing as he took a less defensive posture. "She'll make it public, too."

"Yes. But you both already knew that was a possibility before turning her." Jace's silver-blue eyes locked on me.

"So what was your plan for hiding her?"

"There was no plan, as I never intended to hide her," I admitted flatly. "You may be comfortable living beneath the council's authority, but I find the activity rather tedious. I haven't survived this long by being told what to do and how to do it."

Jace's lips twitched. "I've always admired your fuck-all attitude, Ryder. However, in this case, I don't think it'll be enough. Unless you're okay with the council voting to exterminate your new creation?"

I lifted a shoulder. "They're welcome to try. That doesn't mean they'll succeed." I'd train Willow myself, and given her combined traits of lycan and vampire, I suspected she wouldn't be all that easy to kill. They'd have me to contend with as well. Damien, too, if he chose to help.

"You can't take on the entire council by yourself," Jace pointed out.

"You assume the council will all eagerly jump to do Lilith's bidding," I returned. "I'm confident they won't. You're proof of that."

"And what do you mean by that?"

"Isn't there an edict against consorting with the opposite species?" I arched a brow, fully aware that, yes, such an edict existed. "Yet your penchant for lycans is well known."

"Relationships are forbidden. I just fuck."

"Perhaps," I conceded. "But you're also standing in my office having a willing conversation about how to hide my precious pet rather than reporting my actions to Lilith."

"I could have sent her a message while you were changing. Perhaps I'm just stalling you."

I smiled. "You didn't."

"How are you so certain?"

"Because my system network won't allow any electronic communication to leave this property without my permission." I walked around my desk to click a few letters and numbers on my keyboard, then spun the screen around. "The only message you sent was to Darius telling him you've been delayed by an intriguing situation."

Jace gaped at the monitor, his calm exterior allowing the first fracture of surprise to filter through. "That's impressive."

"You don't know the half of it," I replied, shutting off the screen with another keystroke. "But that's not the topic for consideration at the moment. The more pressing item is the fact you've not reported a single damn thing to Lilith. And neither has Edon."

I allowed those two facts to sink in and reveled a bit in their silence. It showed just how little those in charge knew about me and my abilities. I meant it when I said I hadn't survived this long by adhering to the requirements of others.

Society had evolved over my lifetime, and I'd evolved right along with it.

I didn't do archaic methods. The technology era was one of my favorites, and I'd done my due diligence in learning everything I could about the capabilities. Then I'd built and created my own survival network.

The screen before them was only the cusp of my abilities. The council thought they had the market on technical surveillance. What they didn't realize was that I'd tapped into it a century ago and had piggybacked off their infrastructure to create my own safe haven.

This new world didn't scare me. It only pissed me off.

"So while the three of us only make up a small section of the council, I'm willing to bet there are more who are not pleased with the current dynamic," I continued, confident in my assertion. "Some members may opt to hunt me and Willow down, but I can handle a few irate lycans and vampires with one hand tied behind my back. Which leads me to my next statement—I see no reason for Willow to hide."

Jace's calm exterior had returned, his age and superiority a mask he often hid behind. I understood because I wore a similar expression when thinking through my options.

Edon was less skilled in hiding his emotions, but that

went with traditional lycan culture. His brethren operated purely on animal instinct in this transformed generation. Yet Edon had proved himself different purely by taking two mates and allowing them to stand equally at his side.

Many alpha males commanded submission, even from their alpha females, which had fundamentally broken key points of lycan culture. However, Edon's actions suggested he wanted to repair those fractures. It had fascinated me last month and intrigued me even more now.

"Not hiding Willow will come with consequences not just to you but to me and my clan as well," the lycan said slowly. "And given that the next council meeting was scheduled as a result of the actions of Clemente Clan and Silvano Region, I'd say we're in for one hell of a discussion."

I snorted. "By 'discussion,' you mean a tantrum thrown by the Goddess herself." I couldn't stop myself from rolling my eyes. "I've been subjected to daily tantrums for two weeks now. I think I can survive another."

"So what do you plan to do?" Jace asked. "Walk into the council meeting a few weeks from now and just tell Lilith no?"

"Actually, I haven't decided if I plan to show up yet or not. It's on my calendar, but I may schedule something over it." I canted my head to the side. "Why do you allow her to lead? Is it because adhering to her edicts is easier than arguing?"

"She's created an order in society that I haven't felt the need to break yet," he replied.

"Yet," I repeated. "That's an interesting term."

His stoic features gave nothing away. "Let's just say I know how to play the game. That doesn't mean I enjoy it."

"So don't play."

"And then what?" he pressed. "If we all go rogue, as you're suggesting, what happens? The human population is down to ten percent of what it was a hundred and fifty years ago. Without regulations, we risk our primary food source. We both know our brethren require rules for a reason. They can't be trusted to control themselves."

"The fact that you're saying all this tells me you've been contemplating another way to rule," I inferred. "Rather than ask for my opinion, tell me your ideas. What do you propose, Jace?" He ruled as a British monarch in a past life, his penchant for politics and governing well known.

"That will make for a much longer conversation."

"And a far more interesting one," I added. "Hiding Willow would be a short-term solution at best, one we both know won't work in this society. So rather than banter about what I would deem an inconsequential item, let's discuss a more long-term solution. Tell me about your vision. Then I'll tell you if I agree with it or if I have some suggestions."

"What makes you think I have a proper plan?" Jace countered.

"Because you just told me you did." I gave him a look. "If I wanted to play games, I would call Lilith. Don't waste my time and I won't waste yours."

Jace studied me for a long moment, then conceded with a nod. "Fair enough. You obviously know Cam is alive. I'm guessing you were also informed of his intentions prior to the reformation."

I dipped my chin in confirmation. Izzy's survival as Cam's *Erosita* had required assistance from several key players, myself included. But I'd helped from the shadows, Damien serving as the face of the operation. My name had been left out of it, mostly because I wanted to remain hidden indefinitely. But Silvano's latest antics had forced my hand, and now I was too curious to return to my reclusive shell.

It'd be easier if I just took Willow and remained here for eternity, but after everything I'd witnessed in Silvano's former region, I couldn't just sit by idly and allow the situation to worsen.

The council had gone too far.

It was time for another change.

And as Jace detailed his ideas, I realized he had more

than a proper plan in place; he had a full-on strategy for what was needed.

Edon remained quiet while Jace spoke, confirming he already knew about the revolution. I suspected he found out recently, given the events in his clan.

I sat in my executive chair while Edon and Jace took the two lounge chairs across from my desk, Jace speaking the whole time.

Thirty minutes later, I had a newfound respect for the male.

There was only one problem with his grand design.

"A decade is too long to wait," I said at the end. "It needs to happen now."

"We're not ready yet."

"By the time you're ready, it'll be too late," I informed him. "One thing I've learned over the last four weeks as a royal is that vampires are being too gluttonous. There are not enough humans to satisfy our immortality. They're being killed left and right, allowing precious blood to go to waste in the process."

I turned on my computer again to show him the report Damien had been working on for me in regard to my newly inherited region.

"Look at these trends." I swiveled the monitor toward him, ensuring he could read it. Then I switched the diagram to show him the progression. "And that's ten years from now."

The numbers were telling because they were all negative.

"I estimate your ten percent value to be around five right now, assuming this behavior is similar throughout the world. Your region may be governed differently, but can you tell me Ankit, Lajos, Sofia, and, hell, even Helias are running their regions similarly?" I scoffed at the very notion. "Those sadistic assholes were some of Silvano's best friends. And don't even get me started on Ayaz and Aika."

Cormac was perhaps one of the few vampires in the world not killing humans aimlessly. Naomi, too, maybe.

"I would have said the same about Kylan, but he's proven surprising," Jace murmured.

"Maybe to you. But I've known him for a long time. He's bored, not sadistic." I didn't particularly like the royal jackass, but I tolerated him far better than I did those in Silvano's circle.

"He was suspected of killing his entire harem." Jace pointed out.

"*Suspected* being the operative word in that sentence," I returned. "And I've heard my fair share of rumors on your cruelty as well, but that doesn't mean I believe them."

"You should."

"I don't," I countered, leaning forward. "Justice isn't cruel; it's a necessity. Some just choose to view it differently."

He considered me for a long moment before conceding with a slight nod. "True."

"A decade is too long," I stressed again. "You can't wait that long. It'll be too late to revive the human race." I looked at Edon. "And I haven't even begun looking into what your kind is up to, but the moon chase pretty much says it all, in my opinion."

"I've outlawed that in our clan," he said.

"Good."

"The breeding camps are next," he added. "We don't need humans to create lycans. We can do that among ourselves. Breeding with a mortal should be rare and done in situations where it's a guaranteed success, not as a series of experiments."

"I'm sure Willow will approve." I sure as hell did.

His dark eyes hardened. "Good. But on the subject of Willow, I have a requirement."

"A requirement?" I repeated, arching a brow at the young alpha. That took some serious confidence to say to one as old as me. "Which is?"

"I agree that hiding her isn't really an option," he said slowly. "That said, she's partially mine and therefore my responsibility. If she wants to remain with Clemente Clan, I'll accept and protect her. And if she opts to stay with you, I'll expect you to do the same. But that's my requirement— she gets to choose where she goes."

Chapter Twenty-Four

Willow

Mint. My nose twitched. *Mmm, Ryder.* His scent was strong, which meant he was nearby. I rolled onto my side to reach for him, only to hit air. No mattress. No pillows. Just air. Frowning, I rotated to my opposite side and found a solid block of fluffed leather instead.

I peeled one eye open to see the back of a couch.

That would have been fine had I not seen my *paw* against the black leather. I shrieked, and it came out as a wolfish whine that had me scrambling off the couch and onto the ground. *On four legs.*

Fuck!

I started to spin, bumping into the coffee table with my rump, my snout hitting the end table, and my nails clawing at the white carpet. *The same color as my fur.*

Oh, Goddess. Oh, Goddess!

This had to be a nightmare. Some sort of cognizance designed to help me get over my trauma from the breeding camp.

Which I could fully remember now.

My heart began to race with the onslaught of horrors, the growls, the mid-shift rutting. *Oh, oh, oh,* I didn't want to go there. *No, no, no!*

I released another of those shriek-whines and began to run, only my legs didn't know how to work. They spun beneath me, and I went face-first into the floor.

A male voice told me to stop. I snapped in response, trying futilely to escape the cage of my mind. I needed to wake up. This couldn't be happening. I didn't want to walk down memory lane again!

"*Willow.*"

Ryder's voice. I jumped up, searching for him, begging him to release me from this insanity. *Wake me up! Wake me up!* I begged him. *I don't want to be here. I don't want to know this. I don't want to remember. Please!*

The bellows and commands continued to riot in my mind, the door wide open on a series of events I never wanted to live through again. I shook my head, refusing to let them take me.

Oh, but the one with green eyes, he always haunted me.

He visited me daily.

My punisher.

My captor.

My aggressor.

I hated him, loathed him, wanted to attack him, to bite him, to slaughter him, to hurt him like he did me. The coward used restraints. How sad for him that a poor, defenseless, little human female could put up such a fight that he needed to *chain me* to the wall to fuck me.

I laughed at him.

He hated that.

He wanted me to fight.

Fuck you, I thought. *You pansy-ass mother—*

"Willow." Ryder was closer now, his minty aftershave heaven to my senses.

Yes, yes, I thought, scrambling to my feet again. *Wake me up. Please wake me up.*

I could see him now, approaching me slowly from around the sofa. He had a hand out as if to calm me. I cocked my head to the side, confused. Why had he entered this strange dream?

Then I realized he wasn't alone. Another vampire stood with him. One with icy blue eyes and a jawline that struck me as severely acute. I sniffed at him, noting his woodsy aftershave.

Then another approached.

A lycan.

Bulky.

Dark hair, dark eyes, dominant and terrifying.

I backed up at his presence, not wanting to play with his kind. He was too masculine. Too predatory. Too alarmingly beautiful and cruelly so.

"Willow," another voice said, drawing my gaze right to a blond male I never thought I'd see again. Except he was all wrong. Not human like I remembered him, but lycan, too. And alpha. Strong. Just like the other.

I whimpered again, confused. That wasn't my Silas.

Wake me up, I begged, looking at Ryder again. *Wake me up.*

He began to murmur words in a foreign language, one I didn't understand, but the melody struck me as familiar. He'd sung this to me once before, after the elevator incident. It was soothing and warm, making me feel safe.

I started toward him, only to notice yet another lycan in the room. This one female. Alpha, too.

It caused my fur to twitch, my instincts flaring to life. I snarled at her, keeping her away from Ryder as I approached him. Dream or no, this bitch was not touching him.

"Did she just snarl at me?" the female demanded.

"She's territorial when it comes to me," Ryder explained, his tone amused. I glanced at him, and he began to hum again, luring me closer until my head met his palm. He sat in his chair, bringing us closer, and drew his fingers through my fur. It felt oddly good, allowing me to relax a little more, content.

Each stroke seemed to chase away my nightmares, returning them to a foggy state in my mind that I firmly preferred in the past. All that needed to happen now was for me to wake up.

I closed my eyes, hoping to expedite the process.

But movement had my lids springing back open.

Silas had stepped forward to crouch near the chair. Not within touching distance, but close. *Too close.*

Part of me wanted to growl. *You're not real.*

"Her connection to the pack psyche is unique," the alpha said from the other side of the room, causing my hackles to rise again. "I can't hear her as I do the others, but I can sense her denial."

"No idea why she'd be in denial," a familiar voice drawled. *Damien.* I hadn't sensed him, his presence hidden behind the alpha. Perhaps because I was lower to the ground and unable to see much over the couch and chair. "She went to bed human and woke up a hybrid. I'd be in denial, too."

I blinked. *What?*

"Your bedside manner is fantastic," Silas said, sarcasm evident.

"I have no bedside manner," Damien replied.

"No shit," my best friend snapped before looking down at me with his bright blue eyes. "Willow, sweetheart, can you shift back into your human form?"

I stared at him, uncertain of what he meant. *I'd prefer to wake up.*

Except I was starting to fear this might not be a dream.

"She went to bed human and woke up a hybrid."

What the heck is a hybrid? I wondered, shivering.

222

Ryder slid his touch to my nape, giving it a little tug. My attention immediately returned to him as though we were somehow connected. And maybe we were. I'd imbibed a lot of his blood. "It's okay," he whispered, coaxing me to lay my cheek against his thigh while he continued to pet me.

"Can you help her transition back?" I heard him ask.

"Yes," the alpha replied. "But it may hurt her."

"Then that's a no," Ryder corrected.

"I have a suggestion," the icy-eyed vampire announced, pushing away from the wall. "How about we give Ryder and Willow some privacy to discuss what's happened. Perhaps she'll turn back on her own as a result. And in the interim, I'm going to take a nap. The daylight drive was rather draining, and Ryder's penchant for skylights isn't helping matters."

"Damien knows his way around my guest wing and can provide you with appropriate accommodations." Ryder's palm paused on my head. "Do you want to go up to our suite, little wolf?"

Only if you agree to tell me this is all some sort of messed-up dream, I wanted to say. Instead, I just leaned into him more, feeling oddly safe beside him. Which was strange because I knew Silas better. We'd spent most of our adolescent and teenage years together.

You're a lycan now? I asked, looking at him again. *An alpha lycan? Does that mean you won the Immortal Cup?*

My heart fractured a little with the thought.

Silas had gone on to win his immortality, while the Magistrate had sent me to the breeding camps to die.

Except I'd escaped. I'd fought. Just to fall into Ryder's hands.

My attention returned to the royal vampire, his dark gaze unreadable as I stared up at him. I beseeched him to explain to me how this all had happened, to tell me what *hybrid* meant.

"Damien, show everyone to the guest quarters." It wasn't a request but a demand. Ryder released me and stood, saying, "And, you, follow me."

I couldn't say no even if I wanted to, which I didn't.

He stepped around his chair, moving with his usual authority. I glanced at Silas, momentarily uncertain, but he gestured for me to go with a nod of his chin. "I trust him not to hurt you," he said softly.

Ryder snorted. "How endearing."

"Would you rather me say something else?" Silas countered. "Perhaps that I'm baffled as to why my two best friends ended up with ancient royal vampires as mates?"

"Who said I'm her mate?" Ryder asked, arching a brow.

"I can smell it," Silas muttered. "And you look at her the same way Kylan looks at Rae."

Rae's with Kylan? I thought, my eyebrows going up. *Wait, do wolves have eyebrows?* Then I shook my head, going back to the important thought again. *How did Rae end up with Kylan?*

He was a sadistic royal known for slaughtering his harem.

Oh, Goddess. Is Rae okay? I demanded, a snorty sound coming from my muzzle as I focused on Silas.

"Now she's snarling at my mate," the female alpha muttered.

"Willow," Ryder said. "I'll explain everything if you follow me."

Yes, please. I turned away from Silas and his… I stopped, glancing at him. *Wait, did she just say you're her mate?*

"Willow," Ryder repeated, a hint of command in his tone.

Right. Follow him for answers. Okay. One step after another, I made my way to the bottom of the stairs, then looked up with a huff. I could barely operate my four legs on a flat surface. How the hell was I going to maneuver upward?

Ryder didn't seem to notice, his feet already carrying him up the steps.

I tried to follow and stumbled, yelping in annoyance.

He paused then to look at me, his eyebrow arched

haughtily. Then he narrowed his gaze and returned to the first floor to really study me. "Where's my little warrior? Did she perish during the transition to hybrid? Because I could swear she knew how to crawl quite well on four limbs back in San José."

I growled, annoyed. *Yeah, she did. In human form!*

"You're really going to let a few steps defeat you?" He yawned as though bored. "And I thought you were here to intrigue me. Maybe I will go see if the other female wolf knows how to go up stairs."

That caused my hackles to rise. He did *not* just bring that other bitch into this.

"This behavior is tedious," he continued. "Stop feeling sorry for yourself and figure it out."

Figure what out?! I wanted to rage. *What the hell is a hybrid? Why do I have four legs? Who are all those people? What are we doing here?*

"Your growl is an improvement, I guess," he said flatly.

Oh, I'd show him an improvement. I lunged for him, my instinct to bite taking over.

He rapped me on the nose with two fingers in response, tsking. "No. Biting."

"Two words I will never say to a woman," Damien put in as he started up the stairs with the others trailing behind him.

"You would if her bite nearly killed you," Ryder tossed back.

"I wouldn't say 'nearly,'" Damien replied.

Ryder grunted. "You did say 'nearly.'"

"Did I?" Damien was at the top of the stairs now. "Hmm, maybe I overexaggerated."

"I'm shooting you five times now."

Damien sighed loudly. "Fine."

I glanced between them both, confused as to what the hell they were talking about. Then a hand smacked my rump, one that didn't belong to Ryder. I spun on my heels to face the alpha male with dark eyes and hair. "Ryder's right. Stop feeling sorry for yourself. Being a lycan is a gift. Now stop spoiling it and *move*."

Silas came to stand beside him. "I forgot how much I loathed you in the beginning of my transition."

"You took your transformation like a proper alpha. She's over here pouting."

"She's not an alpha," the female said conversationally. "More like a beta."

"Still strong for a human turned lycan," the male alpha replied. "And she's a hybrid on top of it. Time she acts like the powerful product she is and stops moping around."

Maybe if someone told me what the hell is going on, I wouldn't be moping, I thought at him, a growl coming from my throat.

He growled back, the sound powerful and domineering, sending me several steps back into Ryder's legs. "Some advice, little one," the male said, that rumble still evident in his tone. "Never challenge an alpha. You'll lose every time." He stared me down, his dark irises whirling with power, demanding I yield.

Some part of me knew to look away, an inner voice that was new to me, telling me naturally that to submit was part of life. Yet another part of me demanded I remain standing, questioning this wolf's right to dominate me.

I felt split in two, divided between a hierarchal world and a predatory existence.

"Well, that's impressive," the alpha mused. "How about you lean on that stronger side and shift back, then we can test that challenge." He squared off with me, his strength an intoxicating presence that threatened to swallow me and force me to my knees.

Yet that other half of me glared back, incapable of bending.

I don't answer to you. Energy hummed through me at the conviction in my internal tone, my vision blurring with a shimmering haze that reminded me of that moment between sleep and reality, right before a dream ended.

Yes, yes. I closed my eyes, welcoming the sensation and

allowing it to swallow me whole as my universe turned right-side up again. Only, the hard surface below me reminded me of cold concrete, not the warmth of Ryder's bed.

For one heart-wrenching moment, I wondered if my time with him had been a fantasy. One contrived by my mind to save me from the horrors of my true existence. But I could smell his minty aftershave, the familiarity a balm to my raging senses as I stretched to loosen stiff joints.

"Ryder?" I whispered, my voice hoarse as though I'd slept for too long. And perhaps I had. That'd been a messed-up cycle of dreams. I vividly remembered it all as if it'd been real, the dual worlds still very much alive within me. The scents were with me, too. Alpha lycans and an ancient vampire.

My nose twitched, and I slowly opened my eyes to find myself at the bottom of the stairs in Ryder's house, curled in a ball.

I blinked and glanced up to see the alpha male from my dreams smirking at me. Ryder stood a few feet away, his shoulder braced against the wall. "I thought you said your method would hurt," he drawled.

"It would have had I forced her to shift. But she did that on her own," the male replied, still staring at me. "All because her inner vampire wanted to challenge my wolf." His eyes ran over me with interest. "I'm ready to dance when you are, sweetheart."

"She's not yours to play with," Ryder informed him.

"I didn't say I wanted to play," the alpha returned.

Silas wrapped his arm around the other male's waist and leaned in to nip the man's neck sharply, eliciting a growl from the alpha. "That's a challenge, Alpha," Silas said.

"Protecting your friend, Enforcer?" the alpha asked.

Silas nipped him again. "Just providing you with a better match."

The sweet scent of oranges tickled my nose, making me sneeze. It was coming from one of the lycans. The female, maybe?

Why can I smell that?

"If you're preparing to frolic on my lands, then ask Damien to turn off the security," Ryder said. He bent down to scoop me up into his arms. "I'll be upstairs having a long talk with my pet."

Chapter Twenty-Five

Willow

Of course, *now* Ryder decided to carry me.

Not when I couldn't figure out how to use four legs and needed help, but when I had two legs again and could walk just fine.

As much as I wanted to say something, I couldn't, because the thought of *four legs* evaporated whatever amusement I had at the situation.

"I'm a wolf," I whispered, more to myself than to Ryder.

"Are you?" Ryder asked. "I hadn't noticed."

I glared at him.

He smirked back.

And somehow that lightened the situation again just a little. He carried me into his room and kicked the door closed with his heel before setting me on his bed. Then he leaned down to place his hands on either side of my hips, causing me to fall backward into the mattress. He hummed in approval as he lowered himself over me to touch his mouth to mine.

"In fact, you feel very human to me, Willow," he said softly, nibbling my lower lip. He winked and rolled off me to lie on his back beside me with both of our legs dangling off the bed. It was an almost playful position and so very Ryder-like to me.

"Tell me what happened."

"A demand?" he asked, shifting again up the bed to rest on his side with his head propped up by his hand. "How very wolfish of you."

I crawled backward to join him, then moved into a similar position. His gaze dropped to my breasts, only then causing me to realize my nudity. "You've seen it before," I said. "Now tell me what happened."

"Hmm," he hummed. "Perhaps I'm still intrigued after all."

"Ryder."

"Willow."

Ugh, this man! "Tell me what happened."

He sighed as if it were some big deal to inform me how I'd become a wolf. Or a hybrid. Or whatever the hell I was.

"What's the last thing you remember?" he asked softly, reaching across the small space between us to tuck a stray strand of hair behind my ear. His touch relaxed me almost instantly, his power over me lost somewhere between enthralling and terrifying. He'd become my lifeline these last few weeks, a beacon of light in a sea of darkness.

Nothing he did matched what I expected, including now as he traced a line down my neck to my collarbone, his dark eyes hypnotically beautiful.

"I remember being in bed with you," I whispered. "I think I fell asleep while you were in the shower. Or perhaps you'd already taken one. It's foggy. But I recall feeling ill. I think I took a shower, too. There was a towel. And food.

But it made me sick." I shook my head. "I don't know what happened after that. Except, you were angry. I think I tried to apologize."

"You did, and I wasn't angry with you." He cupped my cheek again and leaned in to kiss me softly, his lips plump and promising against mine. "I couldn't figure out what was hurting you. That was when Damien mentioned the fragility of mortals. So I tried to turn you."

My heart sped up with his words. *He tried to turn me?* "Into a vampire?"

"No, into a bat," he drawled, nipping my lower lip before pulling back to give me a look. "Yes, into a vampire, pet. But apparently, you tried to bite me during the transformation instead. In all my millennia, I've never been bitten by a lycan. Or, I suppose, in your case, a partially turned lycan. However, it carried the same impact. I was high from blood loss, and my wound wouldn't close. So Damien knocked me out and brought us both here."

"I… I bit you?" That was what he'd said to Damien. Along with the tidbit about how I nearly killed him.

"I guess you were hungry," he murmured, not sounding upset about it. "I'd almost depleted your blood supply for the transition, so you merely returned the favor. Unfortunately, it didn't work out well for either of us." He continued into a recollection of what happened once he woke up again, telling me the theory about how I'd been bitten the night we met, how his blood temporarily cured me with his immortality, and how the full-moon energy had demanded a shift my body couldn't handle. Which had led to Edon's arrival and his subsequent bite.

"Edon's the dark-haired alpha?" I guessed.

"Yes, he ascended last night. Luna and Silas are his mates." Ryder focused on me for a moment, his eyebrows dipping down. "You've never mentioned Silas before."

It wasn't a question, but I sensed his unease. "Does that upset you?"

"He claims to be one of your best friends," Ryder

replied, avoiding my question.

"He is. And Rae."

"Why didn't you tell me about them?"

"I…" I trailed off. "I didn't know how to mention them."

He fell silent, studying me. "Am I difficult to speak to?" he finally asked, his hand roaming down my side to my hip. "Do I frighten you, Willow?"

The question caused my heart to skip a beat. Did he frighten me? Sometimes. But a dark part of me enjoyed that fear. It could be sensual. Provoking. Invigorating.

Because while he held all the cards, his age and experience severely superior to my own, I felt connected to him in a manner that allowed me to trust him.

Perhaps it didn't make sense.

Maybe it implied a fracture in my mental state.

But Ryder had shown me an odd sort of kindness in a world overrun by cruelty.

He tried to turn me, I marveled again. "Why?" I asked him, taking our conversation in a new direction. "Why did you try to turn me?"

"Because we're not done yet," he replied, his voice just as soft as mine.

"And what happens when we're done?"

He stared into my eyes, his dark irises glittering with an emotion I could almost taste. Only, I didn't have a name for it. Something dark and possessive. "Edon wants you to have a choice. We were in the middle of discussing it when you woke up."

Another shift of topic, but that was Ryder's way. Always unpredictable. Always thinking. "A choice of what?"

"Clemente Clan or Ryder Region," he mused, closing the distance between us. I fell to my back as he moved on top of me, his thigh parting my own. "He wants you to choose an alliance. Remain with the lycans or play with me."

His elbows settled onto the mattress on either side of my head, basking me in the warmth of his body and sending a shiver down my spine. He leaned down to skim his nose across my cheekbone to my ear.

"Do you want to choose, pet?" His teeth grazed my earlobe. "Should I agree to the new alpha's demand?"

I shivered again. "Would that mean we're done?"

"Mmm," he hummed, sliding his lips to my throat. "We're not done." He kissed a path back up my neck to my jaw, then gently nibbled my chin before hovering his mouth over mine. "And we may never be done, Willow. My immortality lives inside you now. Forever."

"So I'm part vampire, part lycan."

"You are," he agreed.

"Is that…? Has that ever happened before? Is that allowed?" My stomach flipped with the question, understanding slowly seeping into my mind. "You broke the rules when you tried to turn me…" *Oh, Goddess. What did that mean for me?*

He grinned, his dark eyes radiating amusement. "And I'd do it again," he admitted. "As to your former question, I don't know. Jace seemed familiar with hybrids, as he was the one to point out what you'd become. I'll have to ask if he knows any others."

"Jace?" I repeated. "Like the royal?"

"Did you miss him standing in the living room?"

My heart stopped. *Jace* was the icy-eyed vampire. "He's… he's a royal."

"I'm aware."

Why didn't he seem concerned about this? "They're going to kill me, aren't they?" I asked, my pulse slamming back to life with a vengeance. "W-why would you do this to me? Offer me life just to… just to…?" I couldn't finish.

He said something I couldn't hear, my head spinning with visuals of my impending demise. And words. So many words.

We're not done yet played on repeat.

No wonder he wouldn't tell me what happened when we were done. *My death* was the answer. I grabbed his shoulders to shove him away, but he didn't budge, his dark eyes studying me in that frustratingly curious way. As if I were an object that amused him.

Which was exactly what he thought of me.

A pet.

A thing.

A life to play with and toss away.

"*Get. Off. Of. Me.*" The words came out clipped and underlined in a strange sort of commanding tone. Yet I could hear the hysteria in it, too.

Oh, but he wouldn't budge.

If anything, he just appeared bemused.

How could he be so cruel?

He'd saved me to kill me.

All to what? Fuck me first? Enjoy me as a passing amusement until he grew bored?

That was the plan, wasn't it? To keep me around until I no longer *intrigued* him.

I tried to shove him away again, but he was too damn heavy. *Ugh!*

"You're quite angry," he mused, his words cutting through the chaos of my mind. "Why? Most mortals crave immortality. Should I have let you die?"

"I *am* going to die," I snapped. And yeah, my voice sounded a bit more hysterical now.

His brow furrowed. "I don't understand. You seem very much alive to me."

"Because you turned me into a hybrid!"

"Exactly. So what's the problem?"

Was he messing with me? Was this some cruel immortal mindfuck? "Did you have permission to turn me?" I demanded.

"Permission from whom?"

"The council. The Goddess. I don't know. Whoever makes those allowances." If there even was such a thing. "Only two humans are gifted immortality every year after earning it in the Immortal Cup."

He scoffed at that. "What a ridiculous rule. I turn who I want to turn, Willow."

"At what expense? My life? Yours?" I nearly laughed. "Oh, but they won't kill you. You're a royal. That's against the Blood Alliance." Or it required a trial or something. Regardless, he'd be fine. I would not.

"Is it?" he asked, considering for a moment. "Interesting. But no, I turned you because I wanted you to live. It had nothing to do with permission or edicts."

"Do you understand what they will do to me?"

"I understand what they may try to do, yes. But you seem to be under the misconception that I'll allow it, which I won't. You're mine, Willow. They'll have to get through me to touch you, and I assure you, that won't be an easy feat."

I blinked, his words a splash of cold water to my senses. "You...?" I wasn't sure what I wanted to ask. It didn't make sense.

He arched a brow. "What about me? Are you questioning my ability to keep you safe? Is that because you nearly died last night?" He frowned. "I... I suppose I did fail you to an extent. I should have noticed the signs. And I was admittedly careless when I initially healed you as well. Had I evaluated your wounds more extensively, I might have noticed the bite mark."

His gaze turned inward, his expression less confident.

"Do you feel I can't adequately protect you now as a result of my carelessness?" He seemed to be asking himself more than me. "I... I can still train you and improve your current techniques. If you trust me to do so. Unless... do you prefer the lycans? Would you rather learn more about your animal nature and how to fight as a wolf?"

I gaped at him.

This wasn't a mindfuck at all, just Ryder yet again doing exactly what I didn't expect.

He had no ulterior motive.

He'd saved me to do just that—*save* me.

And now he had every intention of ensuring I survived.

He even wanted to continue to train me.

A rule breaker until the end.

A royal who did the opposite of what society told him to do.

A man who did what he wanted, however he wanted it.

"You're looking at me strangely," he observed, his tone holding a touch of uncertainty. "I don't handle displays of emotion well, Willow. If you're about to cry, please don't. I won't be able to fix it."

No, I imagined he wouldn't. Because he thought with logic and resolve. His way of showing he cared was through pragmatic behavior, such as by sparring with me.

That hadn't been for him, my mortal form too slow to keep up with his immortal strength and experience.

It had been for me.

To teach me how to protect myself.

To give me a fighting chance in this life.

That was how Ryder showed emotion. Just like when he tried to turn me. It served as a practical response to a problem, one he only wanted to fix because of how he felt about me.

"You wanted me to live."

"Yes, I've already said that." He frowned. "Lycans are supposed to have decent hearing. Perhaps being a hybrid is negatively impacting your senses."

He worded it too seriously to be a joke, but I couldn't help my resulting smile. "I heard you."

"Did you? Because I had to repeat the bit about not allowing others to kill you as well."

Okay, maybe I hadn't heard that part originally over my initial freak-out. Although, now I understood. He just didn't care about the rules. He never had. I should have realized that before losing my head, but it was all a lot to take in.

I'm a hybrid.

Immortal.

Half vampire, half lycan.

And according to Ryder, he didn't know of any others in

existence.

"Now what?" I asked him. "Do I hide?"

"From?"

"The council."

He grunted. "No. Fuck them and their rules."

"But Jace is here… and Edon…" I trailed off. "I don't… I don't know how to interpret all this, Ryder. I need to understand what to expect." Ryder said he could protect me, and I believed him, but I'd also witnessed their reach and control. This world was not kind to those who broke the rules. I'd observed countless incidents over the years to know what they would do to me if they caught me.

"What you can expect is that I will not hide you, nor will I put up with anyone telling me who I can and cannot turn. Just like I've ignored Lilith's demands regarding my leadership. She feels it's her right to dictate to me. I feel otherwise." He cupped my cheek, his lower body settling more firmly over mine. "You're mine, Willow. The others can fuck off."

"It's not that easy."

"But it is," he countered, leaning down to press his lips to mine. "What's done is done. I won't be changing it, and I certainly won't allow them to kill my progeny."

"Progeny," I repeated, tasting the word.

"That's what you are now, Willow," he murmured. "Nearly five thousand years of life and I've only made two—Damien and now you. Do you really think I'm going to allow a council full of pompous pricks to dictate my decisions?"

"No."

"Good," he murmured. "We're getting somewhere."

He said something similar to that the night he asked how I felt about him. I told him I didn't know at the time. I lifted my hand to his face, my gaze dropping to his mouth as I considered the question again.

And how do you feel about me?

"Ryder?" I whispered. "I think I know how I feel about

you now." But I didn't want to explain it with words. Ryder preferred and understood actions. So rather than elaborate, I threaded my fingers through his hair and pulled his head down to mine.

I craved him like I'd never craved anyone else in my existence.

I wanted to experience him.

Devour him.

Claim him.

The latter was a foreign concept, one driven to the forefront of my thoughts by a new desire inside me. *My wolf*, I realized with an inhale doused in Ryder's minty essence.

Mmm, more, my wolf demanded, her presence loud in my mind. She was half of me now, motivated purely by animalistic *need*. While my vampire side reminded me of Ryder, pragmatic and focused.

Yet both halves of me were ready for this now.

Ryder had possessed me from the very moment we met, his essence a lifeline that thrived inside me. However, it went deeper than that. We were bonded on a level of existence I might never understand. It was more than the Sire link. He'd tapped into my heart. My being. My *soul*.

He'd become the enigma in my world. He overrode all the bad, replacing it with his version of good. And I wanted him to do that now, to erase the horrors of my past and give me a memory to rely on when the nightmares threatened to take over.

Because I remembered everything now.

Every brutal moment of the camps.

Their utter savagery.

I'd fought them every step of the way, even while drugged. I'd hated them. Begged them to stop. Screamed at them in hatred. Broke every rule of decorum imaginable. They'd turned me into a beast hell-bent on surviving. I'd forgotten that, Ryder's blood an odd sort of antidote that allowed my mind a moment to heal and seal off the pain.

But my reawakening had brought it all back.

Except, at some point, I'd realized how to shut it off.

Ryder.

He'd become a hero, only to me. His presence the balm I required to heal wounds created by others. It was a dangerous reliance, an addiction that would harm me in the end, but for the moment, I allowed it. And I showed him my gratitude with my mouth and tongue.

Ryder had healed me in so many ways yet had broken me in others. He'd shattered my expectations, reprogrammed my views of society, and possessed my very spirit.

Our relationship wasn't conventional. Hell, it wasn't even a relationship.

And I accepted that.

I accepted *him*—this old vampire and his eccentric ways.

My Ryder.

Chapter Twenty-Six

Ryder

The female beneath me vibrated with a myriad of emotions. I could taste each of them on my tongue as she worshiped me with a kiss that captivated each of my senses.

Willow spoke to me in a way no one else ever had. Not with her mouth, but with her body and mind. I sensed her inside me, possessing me in a manner I had no desire to fight.

My sweet little pet had evolved into an enchantress, seducing me without trying and drawing me into a dangerous web of passion. It ensnared us both, weaving our lives together to create a destiny underlined in temptation and rightness.

I took charge of her kiss almost as soon as it began, testing her limits and desire with the intensity and force of my mouth. She met me back with equal ferocity, her teeth dragging along my lower lip and biting down in silent demand.

"You're tempting my inner beast," I warned her. "He doesn't know how to play nicely, pet."

"I don't want to play nicely," she returned. "I want to fuck. I want you to remove *their* touch. *Their* hands. *Their* mouths. I want it to be erased, gone, replaced by you."

I didn't need to ask whom she meant. *The lycans.* I growled in response, not liking their presence between us.

"Oh, I'll erase them," I promised her. "And when we're done, you won't be able to even think about fucking another immortal without remembering what I've done to you."

"Prove it," she dared, arching up into me.

"A dangerous provocation."

"Stop talking and fuck me, *Sire*."

"Fuck, Willow," I breathed. "Where has this side of you been hiding?"

She growled in response, the reverberation from her chest making me growl back at her. My pet had blossomed into a hybrid with *teeth*. Mmm, I approved. Yes, I very much approved indeed.

I drew my own teeth along her jaw, going to her ear. "I'm not going to go easy on you, Willow. Remember your safe word."

"I don't need it," she vowed.

No, she wouldn't. Because I knew her limits now. I'd never push her past them. Never share her. Never allow another to so much as *touch* her. She belonged to me and only me. And by the time we finished, she wouldn't want another either.

I sank my teeth into her throat, needing to taste her. She cried out, her nails scraping down my back through my shirt. Then she began to claw at the fabric as though it deeply offended her that I still wore a shirt. I chuckled against her neck, amused that my fiery little wildcat was thoroughly living up to my expectations.

"Ryder," she growled.

I palmed her breast and squeezed, then released her from my bite just long enough to say, "Patience."

She didn't agree, her fingers yanking at my shirt as I returned my teeth to her neck, taking a deep pull from her vein. "Mmm." I'd never tasted a hybrid before, and I found the flavor to my liking.

Her moan encouraged me to drink a little more, her body writhing beneath mine as a result of the endorphins overwhelming her system. "At least we know you still enjoy my bite."

"More," she demanded, arching into me again. I still had my thigh lodged between hers, allowing my wanton little vixen to press her cunt against my leg.

A crueler master would have shifted to keep her from riding me, but I rather enjoyed the feel of all that heat radiating from her core.

I returned to her neck, allowing her to feel the pleasure of my vampiric kiss once more. She screamed in response, her nails digging into my shoulders as she forgot about her quest to disrobe me. She rocked against me, her orgasm a sensual caress to my senses.

"Oh, oh, oh," she chanted, her lithe form quivering violently.

I released her neck, my lips returning to her ear. "Did I mention how intense orgasms can be for an immortal?" I traced my nose along her cheekbone, inhaling her aroused scent. She reminded me of cherries—sweet and tart and begging to be bitten.

I nibbled her lower lip, her breath a pant against my mouth. She seemed incapable of speech, her body still humming with pleasure below mine.

"It can make you feel as though you're living in a fire," I added softly, smiling as she shuddered. "Burned alive by the passionate intensity of the release."

I went to my knees, still straddling her thigh, and removed my shirt. Her blue eyes sharpened, the animal lurking behind her gaze admiring me with open approval. She dampened her lips with her tongue, her pupils dilating.

Hmm, I suddenly had an entirely new appreciation for Jace's lycan preference. It had never been on my desire list, but seeing the female wolf come to life beneath me awakened a whole new world of possibilities.

Willow was durable.

Feisty.

Immortal.

And *hungry*.

Her nipples hardened to little points, begging for my tongue. I bent to lick one, then caught the other in my mouth, sucking deep and stirring a mewl of pleasure from Willow's plump lips.

She combed her fingers through my hair, holding me to her as she wantonly took what she desired. Then her opposite hand went to my pants, her thumb deftly popping the button of my jeans.

I bit her in response, punishing her for trying to set the pace.

My name left her mouth on a cry of protest that ended in a groan. I'd meant to distract her from her goal, but my clever little pet was focused. She yanked down my zipper, freeing me to her palm. I rarely wore undergarments, something she'd learned during our time together.

She stroked me harshly, perhaps to return the favor of my bite. I growled against her tit, moving to the other to give it the same attention. She jolted beneath my fangs, her head tossed back in a display of glorious rapture.

Three bites would send a human to the moon and back.

But my Willow was no longer human.

Instead, it only heightened her arousal, driving her toward another cataclysmic release that I intended to feel with my cock.

I pushed her right to the edge, her pulse an erotic beat against my tongue. Then I released her and backed off the bed. Her snarl went straight to my balls, tightening them in anticipation of the fucking to come.

Because that was what this would be.

I needed to own her tight little hole and stake a claim so deep that no one else could ever fucking touch her there again.

"Present yourself to me, Willow. Let me see how badly you want me."

She gave me a come-hither glance in response, then spread her legs in blatant invitation.

"That's not what I meant," I murmured, removing my pants. I hadn't bothered with shoes or socks earlier, leaving me barefoot and naked before her now. Her eyes dipped down my torso to my groin, her legs widening even more. "Mmm, but I won't deny that's a delectable view." I crawled back onto the bed, dying for a taste of her.

She groaned as my tongue parted her slick folds, her earlier orgasm leaving a sweetness behind that I reveled in now. But I refused to touch her where she wanted me most, desiring to prolong the moment and intensify her need even more.

I wanted her to shatter for me.

To reach for the stars and barely come back.

For that, she needed a little push. Just enough to taunt and tease without giving her the end result she craved until I decided it was time.

I settled between her thighs, thoroughly tasting her and barely grazing her clit with my teeth. Her fingers found my hair again as she tried to dictate my position, but she soon found I was in charge. I nipped her—not where she wanted—and licked the wound closed. Then I drew my nose down to her femoral artery, just to inhale the sweet scent of her blood and the need coursing through her veins.

She was a writhing mess on the bed, a slight sheen of sweat coating her soft skin.

Perfection.

I drew my nose along the crease of her thigh, inhaling her addictive perfume. It was quickly becoming my favorite aroma.

Placing a kiss on her hip, I began a seductive path up her body, alternating between nibbles, licks, and the gentle press of my lips against her over-sensitized skin. She had tears in her eyes—the good kind—when I finally reached her mouth. Then she attacked me with her tongue, her nails biting into the back of my neck as she devoured me.

It served as a subtle claim for control, one I allowed her because it was hot as fuck. I balanced on my elbows on either side of her head and gave her the access to my body that she craved. She wasn't shy about what she wanted, her legs wrapping around my hips to draw me closer to her needy little pussy.

I drew out the moment, sliding my dick along her damp seam rather than entering her. It wasn't the position I had in mind, but I couldn't deny the intimacy of taking her this way for our first time. It would absolutely not be our last. I had too many ideas of what I wanted to do to her, enough to last an eternity at this rate.

I felt starved for this female.

Insatiable.

Obsessed.

I grabbed her hips, angling her where I wanted, and slid partially inside. Just enough to give her a taste, to allow her to begin to acclimate, and to feel her need clench down around me.

She was immortal now, could take the thrusts I longed to give, but there was something so gratifying about prolonging this moment—our initial joining.

I pulled my mouth away from hers, demanding her attention.

I wanted to watch her expression as I slid home, observe her mounting excitement, see the flicker of uncertainty and pain, and swallow the cry she would eventually release as I began to really move.

She didn't disappoint, her pupils blown wide with yearning and trust. The nightmares of her past were nowhere near her here. I wouldn't have been surprised if she'd forgotten them completely, her focus solely on me.

Her hunger was a palpable presence that forced me to drive into her a fraction of a second faster than I'd originally intended. And yet, it was infallible and precise and everything we needed.

"Ryder," she breathed, her hips rising to meet mine.

I looked down between us to see where our bodies joined, drawing my shaft out of her to the tip before plunging back in and smiling at her hiss of surprised pain.

"More," she demanded.

"You really are the perfect pet," I praised her, doing exactly as she requested and bending to take her mouth as she cried out from my harsher thrust. I'd held back in our sparring lessons, not wanting to hurt her. But my sweet Willow was no longer breakable. At least not in that sense.

However, she would shatter for me now.

Completely.

I kept one of my hands on her hip, teaching her the angle I desired, while my opposite palm went to her throat, claiming her.

She panted against my mouth, my name a whisper between us on repeat as I dictated our brutal pace, pushing her toward that unavoidable edge.

Her nails ripped through my skin, dragging a jagged line down my back as she bowed off the bed, her body on the cusp of ecstasy. I could taste it, feel her walls clenching in undeniable tension as she fought to find her release, to leap into the oblivion awaiting her. She began to quiver, goose bumps dotting her skin, but the inevitable orgasm didn't come.

Not yet.

Because I controlled it now.

She'd been trained to respond to my bite without realizing it.

And I taunted her with it, nibbling her lip, drawing out her pleasure-pain, waiting… thrusting… taking her to the brink of insanity… *there*.

I bit down, just enough to release the endorphins into her blood, then smiled as she screamed.

Fuck, that had been worth the buildup because she was squeezing the hell out of my dick now, forcing me to follow her into rapturous bliss.

It was like a damn eruption as pleasure rippled through me and shot off an explosion deep inside her in a searing display of possession.

But it wasn't me who owned her. *She* owned *me*.

Milking me.

Drawing out the best fucking orgasm of my very long existence.

I thought her mouth had undone me. I was wrong. *This* undid me.

"Fuck, Willow," I managed to say on an exhale. "*Fuck*."

"Yes," she replied. "Again."

I half laughed, my face buried in the crook of her neck as I tried to regain some semblance of control. Somehow, after all that, she'd managed to top from the bottom. And she didn't even seem to notice.

I would have been impressed if I wasn't so shocked by it.

This woman consumed me entirely. And I couldn't even be upset. Not after *that*.

I rolled slightly, pulling her on top of me, then gave her ass a smack. "Start riding. I'll catch up in a minute."

She sat up, her tits swaying as she complied.

That she moved so easily told me I had a lot more work to do because she should be just as depleted as I was right now.

All right, pet. I accepted the challenge with a subtle thrust upward. *Prepare to shatter… again.*

This was going to take all day. Perhaps all week. Good thing we had time. The others would just have to wait.

Chapter Twenty-Seven

Willow

I bent over the bed, my legs spread, as Ryder entered me from behind. "Oh," I groaned, sore from the last few days in bed. Or had it been a week now? I really didn't know. We'd only left a handful of times to grab food and water from the kitchen.

The others had left us alone.

Or that was what Ryder had said. Something about them coming back later. Maybe today.

His teeth grazed my shoulder, drawing me back to him. "Arch more."

I leaned back to wrap my arm around his neck, curving my body up off the bed. He groaned in response, one of his hands leaving my hip to palm my breast. Then he began to pound into me, causing my world to shake from the force of his thrusts.

It hurt in the best way, leaving him imprinted inside me and burning away the presence of all those who came before him.

This was exactly what I'd needed to heal.

Every time I closed my eyes now, I saw dark, midnight eyes, not green irises.

My nightmares had been chased away by very real dreams of Ryder between my legs, driving me toward rapturous oblivion. Some of those dreams weren't dreams at all, but true events. Others I thought might be fantasies I longed for him to fulfill. Like this one. It almost felt too good to be real, but the growl against my ear told me otherwise.

"Push your hips backward, Willow," he demanded. "Yes. Just like that, sweet pet. Just. Like. That."

I cried out from the mounting pleasure, my body raging against me for putting it through this so soon after the last orgasm. But Ryder was a demanding lover. And I wouldn't have him any other way.

He pumped into me, his pace savage yet sweet, kissing that part deep inside me that only he seemed able to touch. I began to convulse, the pressure becoming too much. His palm left my breast, sliding down my torso to my clit. He pressed his thumb against me, rolling it in a way I couldn't ignore just as his fangs bit into my neck.

"Ryder!" I screamed, my universe collapsing beneath a tremor so violent that I lost my sight. I heard him groan behind me, his seed hot inside me, pushing me to the brink with his own pleasure and causing me to shudder through another round of orgasmic quakes. It was blissful delirium, an existence unlike any I'd ever known. All because of Ryder and his euphoric bites.

Oh, but it was more than that.

It was *him*. His skill. His determination. His strength. His domination. His everything. I was utterly lost to him. Claimed entirely. A true pet, longing to be stroked day and night and ridden to oblivion.

My chest burned, my breaths coming in pants as Ryder gathered me into his arms and carried me to his walk-in shower. He set me on the bench just inside, putting me at eye level with his still-hard cock. I leaned forward, taking him into my mouth and groaning at the taste of our mingled arousals. He cursed, then threaded his fingers in my hair and forced himself deeper.

"Don't stop doing that until I tell you to," he said.

I nearly laughed. As if I would stop on my own. I was addicted to the taste of him. *Our* taste. I just wanted to stay in bed with him forever. Or in this shower.

He reached over to turn on the water, the spray coming down like rainfall from above. It trickled over my head to my eyes, forcing me to close them as I hollowed my cheeks around him.

"Fuck, I love that," he said, weaving his fingers back into my hair to hold me to him as he curled around me from above. The water disappeared, his larger body blocking it and allowing me to open my eyes again.

I found him braced above me with his forearm against the wall, the rest of him a display of firm muscle and lean strength. It made me want to lick him—something I'd done several times over the last few days. He'd said it was the animal inside me, but I was pretty sure it had nothing to do with my wolf and everything to do with natural desire. Ryder had the kind of body that was meant to be worshiped, and worship him I did.

He growled as I took him deeper, his hand still in my hair while he remained braced on his other arm. I felt caged in by hot, sensual male. Surrounded by his heady scent. Claimed by his cock lodged deep in my throat.

I never wanted this to end, and I proceeded to show him that by unleashing every talent I'd ever learned and combining it with what I knew he enjoyed. I cupped his heavy balls, used my thumb to massage the base of his shaft, and established a rhythm meant to drive him mad.

It worked.

He muttered something about never getting enough of me, his body tense with a need that shouldn't have been possible given our last few hours in bed. But he was insatiable, his stamina resolute and finely primed.

"Damn it, Willow," he breathed, his head hitting the back of my throat. "You're going to make me come again down that pretty little throat."

I groaned in approval, working him over with my tongue and mouth.

It didn't matter how long this took, my goal to satisfy him unwavering.

Part of me realized I'd gone mad with lust for him, lost to this cocoon of sensual bliss he'd evoked around us. I refused to fight it. Because for the first time in my life, I was enjoying myself.

Ryder made me feel alive. Happy. Cherished.

Such a bizarre combination, especially as I sat in such an inferior position now, but I felt his reverence in the way his thumb stroked the sensitive space behind my ear. He had a death grip on my hair yet ensured I could sense his admiration.

His cock began to pulse in my mouth, his muscles tensing along his abdomen, telling me he was close to erupting. I sucked him through the initial tremors, coaxing him to give me everything and to lose his control just for a moment.

"Willow," he groaned, his body beginning to shake. And then I felt him on my tongue, his salty essence flowing into the back of my throat.

The tendons of his neck strained, his face a beautiful mask of furious rapture. Mmm, I loved this moment, his vulnerability and pleasure an intoxicating gift that I cherished.

He growled, delighting my inner wolf. It was followed by a curse, and eventually praise. Ryder called me his sweet pet, his fingers combing through my hair while he continued to shelter me from the water above.

"You've destroyed me," he marveled, a note of awe in his tone. "Come here." His touch drifted down to my chin, a slight pinch causing me to release him from my mouth, then he guided me upward to my feet. I moaned as he captured my lips, his tongue a whispering caress that opened me completely to him. He pulled me beneath the water, kissing me as the warm spray washed away the evidence of our time in bed. Yet I could still smell him, his minty essence forever embedded into my skin.

I still didn't understand everything about being a hybrid—hell, I barely understood how I'd become one—but all my concerns swirled down the drain as he held me.

He'd told me how the lycan transformation process usually worked. Just as he'd explained the vampire transition. I'd technically not undergone either in full, but rather, I'd experienced some convoluted marriage between them both.

However, I was definitely immortal. Yet Ryder claimed I was stronger than a newborn, his ancient bloodline working magic inside me that Edon's bite had brought to life.

"We'll figure it out together," Ryder had vowed.

I believed him.

We stroked each other and kissed throughout our shower. He lathered shampoo into my hair, then helped me rinse it. I tried to do the same for him, but his height proved superior to mine. He chuckled when I went to my tiptoes to try to check his dark strands for suds. Then he caught my hips and pulled me against him, his semi-hard erection a brand against my belly.

I was about to comment when I heard a deep voice nearby. My nose twitched, Damien's scent—cinnamon and spice, something my wolf recognized more than I did—swirling around me.

"What is it?" Ryder asked, his lips near mine.

"Damien," I whispered, my nose twitching again. "I

suddenly got a whiff of his cologne." There was another scent with him. I sniffed, trying to identify the source. *Woodsy with a hint of cinnamon,* I thought. *Rich. Masculine.* "He's with someone else."

"Jace," Ryder murmured. "Damien messaged early this evening that he and Jace were coming back tonight."

"Coming back?" I repeated. "When did they leave?"

Ryder smirked. "I'm taking your lack of awareness as a compliment, pet." He nipped my lower lip. "They left seven days ago. So did your wolf friend and his mates. They're all coming back today."

"Oh." No wonder the house had been so silent. I hadn't thought much about everyone else, too consumed by Ryder to really notice. But now I realized how careless I'd been. "I want to talk to Silas."

"I imagine you do," Ryder agreed softly, brushing a kiss over my lips. "You also need some blood." He palmed the back of my neck, his thumb brushing my pulse. "I've fed plenty this week. You haven't. I'll heat some up for you."

"Blood?" I repeated, my nose wrinkling.

His lips quirked up on one side. "You're half vampire now, pet. Hybrid or not, blood is a staple."

"I don't feel thirsty."

"You are," he promised. "You'll understand when you smell it."

I didn't agree but chose to follow along. He dried me off with a towel, then found me a pair of jeans and a tank top to wear while dressing himself in jeans and a T-shirt. We both remained barefoot, our hair still wet as we wandered downstairs to find Damien in the kitchen.

He held out a mug to Ryder, his lips curling into a taunting smile. "Admit it. You missed sex."

Ryder grunted and took the mug from him, then handed it to me. "Smell this," he told me. I frowned but inhaled the aroma coming from the inside and groaned with want. "Drink."

Blood. How had he known I was hungry when I didn't?

Rather than ask, I took a sip from the cup and moaned at the flavor on my tongue.

"Wait until you try it fresh from a vein," Damien said.

My brow furrowed, uncertain I liked the sound of that.

But he wasn't waiting for me to reply, his gaze on Ryder. "Was a week of fucking long enough to make up for a century of celibacy? Or do you require more time?"

"Your concern with my sex life is touching, Damien."

"A century of celibacy?" a deep voice asked from behind me. "Why the bloody hell would you indulge in such desolation?"

Ryder sighed. "You're both too young to comprehend the meaning of boredom."

"He blames his age," Damien put in.

Jace stepped to my side, his presence causing my heart to skip a beat in my chest. I'd seen photos of him at the university. Most of the females found him devastatingly beautiful, several longing to join his harem.

I never desired such a position, but I couldn't deny his handsome features. He had an aristocratic appeal that lent to his regal elegance, making his royal title all the more appropriate. And being this close to him now, I could *feel* the power and hot energy radiating off of him.

It made me less interested in my mug and more interested in stepping closer to Ryder. He pressed his palm to my lower back as I moved into him, his presence an immediate shield of protection that allowed me to feel at peace once more.

"She must be quite the female," Jace murmured. "To break your boredom streak, I mean."

"He doesn't share," Damien said conversationally. "It's why I have his harem."

"Ah, that makes more sense now," Jace replied. "And a pity regarding the lack of sharing. I've never tasted a hybrid before."

I shivered at the way he said it, his tone a sensual caress that felt foreign to my senses. Not wrong, just not right either. Ryder kissed my temple and took my mostly empty mug away from me.

"Here, make yourself more useful," he said to Damien, handing it to him. Then he cupped my cheek and pulled me into him, his mouth claiming mine in a show of domination that left me winded and dizzy against him. His opposite arm went around my waist to hold me upright, while the hand on my cheek moved into my hair to angle my head to his preference.

I shuddered, overwhelmed by his sudden display of possession. Yet I clung to him as if he were my lifeline, my fingers digging into his shirt as I fought to kiss him with the same ferocity as he did me.

A beep sounded, followed by Damien clearing his throat. "More blood, *Sire.*"

Ryder grinned against my mouth, his arm remaining around me as he released my hair to reach for the mug again. This time he sipped from it, his eyes on mine the whole time, ensnaring my focus. When he reached the bottom of the mug, he set it aside and kissed me again.

I sucked the blood from his tongue, my inner beast reveling in the flavor. He hummed in approval. "She tastes divine," Ryder said, his gaze holding mine. "And Damien's right. I don't share." He nipped my lower lip, then laved the wound, his mark clear.

My wolf perked up, her instincts taking over as I repeated his action, taking his lip between my teeth and biting down. It was so natural to me that I didn't think about the repercussions until Ryder growled.

My eyes flew upward, my heart in my throat.

Oops.

Chapter Twenty-Eight

Willow

"What did I say about biting?" Ryder asked, his dark eyes swirling with hot promise.

"My wolf, uh, reacted," I whispered.

"Hmm."

"Technically, it wasn't a rule," I added slowly, referring to his "No biting" comment from last week.

"It was implied."

"But there are no rules," I reminded him, feeling slightly bolder than I probably should.

He studied me while he licked the blood from his lip, the wound I'd created a pronounced mark on his mouth that made my inner wolf preen with satisfaction. I'd grown used to her presence this last week, something about the animal feeling right inside me, as though I were always destined to have her there.

The vampire was a little different, creating a war in my head. That part of me was mortified that I'd bitten him so blatantly, especially as the wound was clearly not healing the way it should. He'd told me how my bite had impacted him before, so I should have known better than to sink my teeth into him now.

Except he didn't seem upset with me for it.

And my wolf refused to apologize as well.

I licked my own lips, tasting my blood there. But the skin was already healing.

Damien snapped his fingers beside us, making me flinch. "Enough showing off. We gave you a week to fuck. Now I need your focus."

Ryder glanced at him slowly. "I needed more than a week."

Damien rolled his eyes. "You have eternity now, right?"

"Eternity with one woman," Jace mused. "I suppose if you were going to pick one, a hybrid is adequate."

Ryder finally released me to face the other royal. "Didn't your new sovereign recently take an *Erosita*?"

Jace grinned. "So you have been paying attention."

"I told you he has," Damien interjected. "Ryder likes to play recluse, but he watches everything."

"What else have you told him?" Ryder asked, his focus still on Jace.

"Enough," Damien admitted.

"He showed me the data you both collected these last few weeks on Silvano Region. You were right about the blood shortage."

"And?" Ryder pressed.

Silence fell.

I glanced around Ryder to see Jace staring at him with those chilly blue eyes that revealed nothing. It was a bit of a surreal experience to be able to study him in the flesh. The former human in me demanded I go to my knees in subservience, but my wolf refused. Meanwhile, my vampire was… conflicted.

I felt like I had three battling personalities inside me—my past self versus the two making up my present.

"You're right about our need to act sooner rather than later," Jace said after a tense beat. "Silvano wasn't the only royal with a penchant for gluttony. While my region is self-sustained, it won't remain that way if I'm required to start sharing my resources with others."

"Which is the way this will go," Ryder added.

"I agree. Lilith won't allow her favorites to starve." He slid his hands into the pockets of his black trousers, his suit as impeccable as the rest of him. "Speaking of, I had an interesting chat with her the other day. She wanted to know my thoughts on your reign."

"Did she?" Ryder asked, sounding amused. "And what did you tell her?"

"Well, first I inquired as to how she knew I was in your capital city."

"Did she tell you?"

"She evaded."

"Of course."

"I just found it a bit interesting since Damien did such a decent job keeping my presence hidden while we were there," Jace added conversationally. "But I'm sure you both can handle that issue."

"We can," Damien confirmed, glancing at Ryder. "I may have used his presence as a test."

Ryder nodded. "It's what I would have done."

"I know."

"Anyway," Jace continued. "I told Lilith I found your leadership to be unconventional. She took that to mean I disapproved."

"Naturally," Ryder drawled.

Jace smirked. "She asked if I would help her vote you down at the next council meeting."

Ryder stepped back, his shoulder bumping mine as he relaxed into the counter behind us. He mimicked Jace's pose by sliding his hands into his pockets. "I didn't realize my position was up for a vote."

"She seems to think it is," Jace replied.

"Fascinating." Ryder glanced at Damien. "Perhaps we should invite her in for a visit. It seems the *Goddess* requires a lesson on superiority."

"I'll work on arranging it," Damien agreed, causing me to tremble.

The Goddess was not an immortal I ever wanted to meet. I'd been taught to pray to her, to fear her, and to worship her, all in one breath. "Ryder," I whispered.

He slid his arm around my waist again, pulling me into him. "She won't touch you," he vowed, kissing my temple.

He spoke with such conviction that I wanted to believe him, but the former human in me didn't relax in the slightest.

He's inviting the Goddess to visit after illegally turning me. This can't go well...

But before I had a chance to voice my concern, the alarms on his system sprang to life. He released me to walk over to the panel beside the refrigerator—which happened to be behind Jace—and flicked through the screens with ease. Jace moved to stand beside me while Ryder entered a series of codes.

I shifted awkwardly to the side, which elicited an amused smile from Jace. "Don't worry, baby wolf. I won't bite you."

"She's not yours to flirt with," Ryder cut in, his back to us.

"That wasn't flirting," Jace replied, his icy eyes going to Damien. "He really is out of practice, isn't he?"

"And I suspect he'll remain that way since he seems to favor monogamy at the moment," Damien muttered, shuddering.

"The wolves are here," Ryder said, ignoring them both.

"Monogamy?" I repeated, my voice a soft whisper.

All three men looked at me, but it was Jace who said, "I suppose that would be a foreign concept to one raised in this environment."

"It's a foreign concept to me, and I've lived a millennium," Damien muttered.

"Truth," Jace agreed.

Ryder growled at them and moved to pull me into his arms again. "Ignore them. They're teasing me, not you."

I had already grasped that aspect of the conversation. I just didn't understand why. So I asked him, "Why?"

He just shook his head. "They think I've taken you as my mate."

"Think?" Damien scoffed. "You chose her a month ago. Or did you *think* that place I took you to in San José for the ritual was just a coincidence? I saw your decision from a mile away."

"We're not discussing this right now." A hint of demand underlined Ryder's tone, causing Damien to concede with a nod. "Let's go greet the wolves. I want to hear how Edon's inquisition went."

Ryder's hand found mine, his grip reassuring as he pulled me along with him toward the front door. Silas stood on the other side, his shoulder propped up against the brick siding of the house. Edon and Luna were beside him.

It was my first time really *seeing* my old friend and understanding what his presence meant. I didn't really think so much as act. "Silas," I said, releasing Ryder to reach for my old friend. He pushed off the house to wrap me up in a hug, his refreshing scent new and oddly reassuring. It reminded me of a new day. Which was fitting considering his new beginning. "You won the Cup."

"I did," he replied, his arms sturdy and strong around me. "Fuck, it's good to see you again. I know I just saw you a week ago, but it didn't feel real then. It does now."

"I know what you mean," I whispered.

We fell into a comfortable silence, holding on to each other as our history flourished between us, culminating in a beautiful moment of completion. "We're still alive, S."

"Yeah we are, W," he returned, knowing exactly what I

meant. "And so is Rae."

Tears prickled my eyes, and for once, they weren't born of sadness or pain. Except that wasn't true, either. Pain and sadness were what had brought us to this moment and allowed us to truly live.

We'd been through hell together.

And we'd survived.

Finally.

His grip tightened, his emotions rivaling mine. I buried my face in his neck, inhaling his scent, as he did the same to me, our wolves strangers to one another, and yet, my beast *knew* his. I felt it in my very soul. Perhaps because his mate had turned me. Or maybe because this was our destiny all along.

But we'd worked hard for this moment.

So many lives were lost.

So much blood spilled.

So. Much. *Pain.*

I shuddered against him, the moment more powerful than I could have imagined, and only when we pulled apart did I realize we stood outside alone. The others had given us this moment, allowing our hearts to break and heal without their intrusive gazes, and I felt more than a little grateful to them for recognizing that need.

Silas cupped my face, his forehead falling to mine. "You have no idea how agonized I was to watch them take you away that day. You should have been with us. Not at the camps. And after the footage… I…" He choked on a swallow, his guilt painted in every line of his face.

"You couldn't have done anything, Silas. You know that. *I* know that."

"But that doesn't make it any less true. Shit, Willow, what they did to you…" He trailed off again, his anger and grief vibrating through his features. "*Fuck.* I want to kill that bastard all over again."

I frowned at him. "What bastard?"

"The one who *bit* you," he said through his teeth. "I

ripped off his head."

Now I gaped at him. "*What?*"

"I spent twelve hours ensuring he felt every bit of the agony you expressed in those films before I ended him." His statement came out with a low growl in his voice, his wolf roaring behind his blue eyes and allowing me to see the alpha he'd become.

This man, the one I grew up training with, had become a lethal immortal. And that knowledge made me smile. Because it was so perfect for him.

"Lycan looks good on you," I admitted, shaking my head. "Goddess, can you believe this is our life?" I'd heard what he said about the lycan who bit me, understood that he was dead, but that truth paled in comparison to the joy thriving through me now at our *existence*. "We did it, Silas," I said, an emotional wreck all over again. "We… we did it…"

He pulled me into another hug, holding me while I cried, all the misery from my former life pouring out of me on a wave of agony that had built inside me for so many years.

All those tests.

All those courses.

All those fucking games.

To finally—*finally*—become a superior.

"I always said we could do it," Silas whispered.

"You did," I agreed. "And you were right."

I held him so tightly I swore I heard something wheeze inside him, but he never asked me to stop. Instead, he held me through it, my emotions spiraling in a chaotic rhythm I gave up on organizing.

Fury. Relief. Sadness. Loss. Joy.

"I'm a mess," I whispered, laughing a little.

"I get it," he promised.

And I knew he did.

Hours probably passed while we stood outside, hugging as though our lives depended on it. Making up for all the years we were forced to swallow our emotions, to stand up and fight, or die trying.

We'd never experienced peace. Until now. This moment. Just us, breathing in fresh air, our bodies more alive than they'd ever been.

"I love you," I whispered to him. "You know that, right?" I'd never been allowed to admit that out loud, but I felt it in my heart and knew it to be true. He was my oldest friend. My only family.

"I love you, too," he whispered back. "And Rae, too."

"And Rae, too," I agreed. They were my siblings. My lifelines. My world.

Until Ryder had slid in and created a new home inside me. A new safe place. A new state of being.

"But don't say it in front of Kylan," Silas added. "He's possessive of his *Raelyn*."

"Kylan," I repeated, recalling what he'd said the other day. "What did you mean about Rae being with him? And since when does she go by Raelyn?"

Silas chuckled. "Oh, it's quite a story," he said, shaking his head and lightening his grip.

"As good a story as you becoming a lycan and mating two alphas?" I asked him, arching a brow as he stepped back.

His cheeks reddened as he reached up to grab the back of his neck. "That, uh, well, they might be equally good."

"Then start talking," I told him. "I want to know everything."

He chuckled again and threw his arm around my shoulders. "All right, W. We'll start with Kylan and Rae." He began walking me back into the house. "It all started when Rae decided to bite a royal vampire."

"I might know a little something about that," I admitted, thinking back to Ryder's lip.

"Was it in front of the entire council and Lilith herself?"

I stopped walking. "She didn't…"

"Oh, she did," he assured me. "I thought for sure she was dead, but Kylan picked her for his harem instead."

I frowned. "After the Immortal Cup?"

"She never went to the Immortal Cup." He led me through the door. "I guess I should start at the beginning."

"That'd be helpful."

His lips twitched. "All right. Once upon a time…"

Chapter Twenty-Nine

Ryder

My lip still stung hours later, reminding me of Willow's presence even though she was in the other room with her old friend. "Is it normal for a lycan bite to take this long to heal?" I asked Jace. He sat in my study with his ankle crossed over his opposite knee.

He appeared amused by the question. "Longer, usually."

"Hmm." Well, at least I knew what to expect going forward. "This is why we're not supposed to play together."

"But the danger of it is intoxicating, isn't it?" His gaze was knowing. "Makes you feel alive."

He wasn't wrong. I did like knowing Willow could hold her own against me. At least subtly. We'd work on her skills to truly make her an opponent. Then I'd really enjoy playing with her.

"We're also harder to entice," Edon interjected, sounding bored. "Take this conversation, for example. I'm utterly bored by it, while you two seem rather ramped up with excitement."

I looked at the alpha, amused. "You'll do," I decided out loud. And not just because he'd brought me the head of the lycan who had tormented my Willow.

His dark irises danced over me, assessing. "Still to be determined."

My lips quirked, amused by his easy banter. The alpha certainly had balls challenging me like that. "You'll learn," I tossed back.

He lifted a shoulder, then looked at Jace. "We have less than three weeks until the next council meeting. I'm going under the assumption that Willow's nature won't remain a secret for much longer. So what's our plan?"

"Why is he the leader?" I interjected.

"Because he's the one I trust most in this room," Edon replied without looking at me.

It was a fair assessment, albeit a risky one. "And how well do you know Jace?" I wondered out loud.

"My reputation isn't the debate here," Jace murmured. "And I'm not the leader, Ryder. But Edon's right. We need to discuss our play for the council meeting."

"I vote we don't go," I suggested. "It's a waste of fucking time with a bunch of pompous pricks who just want to sit around and debate the best method for killing humanity. I'll pass."

"You have to attend if you want to solidify your royal seat."

"I've already taken it," I pointed out. "Lilith is welcome to appoint a new royal. I'll just kill the opponent and remain in charge." I looked at Jace. "Honestly, what's she going to do? She's a child compared to me."

"She subdued Cam," Jace said solemnly.

"Did she, though?" I countered. "Or did he willingly go underground to play the long game?" We both knew he was

266

still alive. And while I wasn't his biggest fan, I could admit his affinity for strategy was quite admirable.

"Darius believes he allowed himself to get caught." Jace's admission surprised me. It showed we'd moved forward in the game, his olive branch now tangible. "I'm inclined to agree because he left behind a road map that we've followed for the last century."

"A road map?" I repeated just as Damien joined us. He shut the door softly before walking over to sit in the chair beside me.

My study was similar in size to my office but set up differently. It resembled more of a library with my bookshelves covering three of the four walls. And a large sofa sat in the center—the same size as my executive desk in the other room—with recliner chairs situated across from it. I sat in one while Damien settled into the other. Edon and Jace shared the couch.

Luna had excused herself when Silas and Willow came inside. I suspected she and Willow would become fast friends now that the territorial lines were all drawn in the proverbial sand.

"Talk to me about this road map," I said when Jace didn't elaborate. "Damien's my progeny and best friend. I imagine he's showcased his loyalty over the last week to you, yes?"

"He has," Jace agreed, his eyes remaining on Damien for a moment before returning to me.

Hmm, that lingering look held a story. It hadn't been one of open consideration, rather a glance that held a secret. Interesting. Something had happened this week between them. Something that allowed Jace to feel he *knew* my progeny. And it went beyond the obvious events.

I made a mental note to follow up on it later.

"The theorized course I detailed the other day wasn't my grand design. Cam created it. I've merely been working with the pieces I can play while waiting for others to arise, but after seeing the reports on your region, I think a strategy is required. We need to find Cam."

"Chicago," I said. "Have you looked there?"

"It's not an easy city to navigate beneath Lilith's control. I also feel that's too obvious."

"Which is exactly why he's there," I drawled. "Lilith would send you on a merry goose chase while keeping him in the one place you'd never look because it's 'too obvious.' That fits her playbook to a T."

"At the very least, you'll find evidence there," Damien added. "She's not going to leave his fate to chance. Wherever he is, she keeps a close watch over him because he's the only one who poses a significant threat."

"So why hasn't she just killed him?" Edon asked.

"Power," I replied immediately. "She gets off on it."

Jace nodded. "Killing him is too easy. My guess is she visits him to lord her kingdom over him and his ideals."

"This has been our world for a hundred and seventeen years. Surely she's grown bored by now?"

I shook my head. "A century is nothing in his lifetime."

"And she believes his *Erosita* is dead, thereby forcing him to live in agony of losing his other half. She would adore throwing that in his face, as she despises the mating practice."

"Why?" Edon asked.

I looked at Jace, aware of the history, but not wanting to tell the story.

"She's broken," he said softly, his blue eyes taking on a gleam I understood far too well. *Fear.* It was the reason many of us didn't take mates. We knew what could happen if we lost our other half. Lycans could experience the same sense of loss, but there was a key difference between us— vampires were forced to live forever without their other half, while lycans eventually died.

I would argue the former was much, much worse.

"Humans killed her mate," Jace continued in that same tone. "It fractured her in a way few understand, mostly because she hides it very well. But I believe the fractures lie in her innate hatred for humanity. This all started as a punishment to avenge her lost love. However, it has evolved into so much more. She's married to the power now. Law and order are her mistresses. And any deviation from her intent results in chaos that she defuses through punishment."

"You almost sound sorry for her," I noted.

"I am to an extent," Jace admitted. "The pain of her loss debilitated her mind to a point where she cares nothing about the very species that created her lost love. And yet she craves their love as a form of penance."

"That's why she took on the Goddess role," Edon realized out loud. "She forces them to love and worship her, as her mate once did."

"To an extent, yes," Jace murmured. "And I find that very sad indeed."

"Well, I just find it insane," I said, shrugging. "She should have been put down a long time ago. It would have saved us all from this madness."

Jace shook his head. "There were too many of our kind and the lycans fighting for this path. She merely took advantage of an already available base and turned herself into their leader."

I conceded on that point with a nod. "True." Once the lycans were discovered by humans, the war became inevitable. And Lilith, as broken as she was, played every part appropriately. Cam had been her primary adversary. Taking him down placed her on top, and her ego was what kept him alive. "I still think he's in Chicago. She would want to speak to him regularly, if nothing else but to seek validation for her overwhelming victory."

"Then that would imply he's coherent, yet he's not spoken to his *Erosita* in over a century."

I nodded again, considering. "She must have him overpowered in some fashion."

"That's what concerns me," Jace admitted. "*How* is she keeping him prisoner?"

"You think she has a weapon of some kind."

"Yes," he confirmed. "It's the only thing that makes sense."

Damien scratched his jaw. "If that's the case, then we need to be prepared. She could use it against you."

"Unless it only exists in Chicago," I said slowly, thinking through every angle. "She's contesting my leadership at the next council… in Chicago."

"It's where she intends to discuss the Clemente Clan incident as well," Edon added, catching on quickly. "And she demanded Kylan attend, yet grounded him from all other functions."

"When was the last time she held a council meeting on her home turf?" I wondered out loud.

"The meetings are infrequent occurrences," Jace replied. "We meet at Blood Day annually. Otherwise, we only meet sporadically."

"But after the incident in my clan, she said we would be changing that," Edon replied. "That's the other purpose for the gathering in Chicago—to begin a quarterly cadence of meetings."

"Or to make one hell of a power play," Damien muttered, taking the words right out of my mouth.

"Well, fuck," Jace said, rubbing a hand over his face.

A hush fell through the room, the shock wave palpable.

Because Jace's words summed it all up nicely—*fuck*.

I had to hand it to the cunt; she'd played her cards well.

It was just too bad she had me as an opponent on the board now. Because I saw the flaw in her plan from a mile away, and I fully intended to exploit it.

"Do you think she knows about our plans?" Edon asked, breaking the silence.

"Not exactly, but I think there have been too many disobedient events for her liking and she intends to deliver a statement," Jace said. "Which means you and Kylan are in trouble. Ryder, too, since she's clearly baiting him. And my guess is she intended for me to tell you about the vote on your position, which also means I'm on her list, likely as a result of the recent power shifts in my region."

"With Darius becoming your sovereign," I ascertained. "He was a known recluse as well, but more so because of his ties to Cam."

"Yes. Their relationship was well known and would give Lilith cause not to trust him. The only reason she has any faith in me is because I've played along with her game for the last century. Yet her using me as a pawn suggests she's onto me, and perhaps has been for some time."

"Or she never trusted you," Damien said.

"Also likely," Jace agreed, shaking his head. "That fucking bitch."

"Still feel sorry for her now?" I asked, half joking.

Jace grunted. "What the fuck are we going to do?"

"Oh, that part's easy," I said, causing Damien to smirk beside me. He knew exactly what I planned to say. "We beat her at her own game."

Jace arched a brow. "Okay. How?"

"By not allowing her to host that council meeting in Chicago," I replied, looking at Damien. "It's Benita, isn't it?"

"Yep."

"Excellent. Can you let her know I'll be returning with my pet? Tell her we'll be needing extra blood."

"Consider it done."

I smiled. "You're so good to me, Damien."

"I try."

I started to return my focus to Jace when another thought struck me. "Oh, do you think we should host a barbecue as well? Perhaps in two weeks' time? There are a few clients from that list you could invite. The ones who like children."

Damien massaged his chin, considering. "Yes, that could make for quite a party. Maybe we should add the rest of the region's sovereigns to the invite list as well, just to ensure an explosive ending."

"I do enjoy a bloodbath," I mused, smiling.

When I finally looked at Jace, it was to find him smirking. "Sounds like bait."

"Doesn't it?" I replied. "I'd invite you to watch the fireworks, but that may make it too obvious."

"Yes, I think my role here is to continue functioning as her pawn."

"I agree." I met Edon's gaze. "And yours will be to continue reformation in your pack. I'm sure she's receiving updates from someone on the inside. Let her think you're reverting. It'll help her mental state along and hopefully coax her into coming out to play."

Edon nodded. "The breeding camp incident should have reached her by now."

Yes, I imagined killing three dozen of his lycans would cause quite a stir in her world. The fact that he chose to keep all the humans and try to rehab them into his society would only make matters worse for her.

"Can you get a message to Kylan?" I asked, bringing us to our final matter of business.

"Yes," Jace said.

"Tell him we need to go on a double date while in Chicago. It's become quite evident to me that my pet needs her friends." I glanced at Edon again. "Your Silas will continue to visit her. He seems to please her."

Edon snorted. "You can tell him that yourself. He doesn't take orders well. That's why he's my Enforcer."

"He'll obey mine," I said, certain. Finally, I addressed Damien. "I need another few days. Can you handle San José without me until our arrival next week?"

"I'll make all the arrangements. But I'm keeping your harem."

"I have no use for them."

"I know," he replied. "And I'm keeping Tracey."

"Who the hell is Tracey?" I asked.

"The servant girl Meghan whipped."

I growled at the memory. Meghan's resulting death had

been far too quick. "Be good to her."

"Oh, I've been very good to her," he replied, sharing a look with Jace.

Ah, I thought, catching on. *That* was the secret. They'd played together this week. Well, so long as all parties enjoyed themselves, I didn't need to know more.

"I'm going to find my pet," I told them all, standing. "We still have positions to try." One of which included anal. We hadn't explored that yet. It would be either this week or soon after because I intended to own all of her, just as she so completely appeared to own me.

"Don't forget to feed her," Damien reminded me. "Blood and food."

"Oh, she'll be well fed," I promised, walking to the door. Then I paused to look at Edon once more. "Do you still feel she requires a choice?"

"I think she made it last week," he replied.

"I think she did, too," I agreed.

"Her mark looks good on you, by the way," Edon said, his lips twitching.

I licked my bottom lip, noting the soreness. "I'm about to go repay the favor."

"Enjoy," Damien drawled.

I smiled. "I intend to." She was my reward, after all. My beautiful hybrid pet. My distraction. My new reason for living.

Chapter Thirty

Ryder

A few days turned into eleven before Damien called and said he needed me in San José.

Willow sat beside me in the car, her leg jumping against mine. Rick was driving. He'd also piloted the plane here. His loyalty remained resolute, which was evidenced by his lack of a comment upon seeing my upgraded pet.

Her scent noted her as part lycan, but her eyes swirled with the power of a vampire, making her hybrid uniqueness rather evident. Yet he'd remained as silent as ever, just as he did now behind the wheel.

"Pet." I placed my palm on her thigh, giving it a gentle squeeze to halt her fidgeting. "Stop."

We'd agreed to a charade of sorts where she continued to play the submissive human role in public. It would make everyone believe I'd created a hybrid for a pet—a passing amusement of sorts. Which would allow her worthiness to go undetected by the masses.

Everyone would underestimate her abilities and, even more importantly, my growing affection for her. The former served as an asset, while the latter qualified as a weakness.

"Sorry," she whispered.

"They won't touch you," I vowed. "Only I can pet you."

She wore one of the revealing gowns Damien had procured for her harem wardrobe. However, I'd added a leather collar to the mix. Overkill, perhaps, but I found it rather entertaining.

At least I hadn't affixed a leash to it.

Hmm, although, that gave me more ideas to play with in the bedroom later. Not that I needed additional scenarios. My list for her just continued to grow no matter how many items I'd crossed off of it. And we still hadn't indulged in anal yet.

I sighed. At this rate, we'd be fucking for the next century at a minimum. Wouldn't that amuse Damien?

While I'd become obsessed with bedding her, we'd also been productive during our alone time together and had spent ample hours testing her new speed and agility. She still had work to do as a baby immortal, but her aptitude for fighting showed in her ability to pick up new skills quickly and efficiently. She made a fine protégé indeed.

I removed my palm from her thigh and wrapped it around the back of her neck instead, pulling her in for a long, sensuous kiss. It'd become my indulgence. She ran her tongue along my bottom lip, smiling at the slight bump in my skin.

"No biting," I whispered. It'd become her favorite thing to do, but I couldn't afford to show the weakness today.

"That just makes me want to bite you more," she admitted.

"I'm still healing from the last one," I reminded her. It seemed to take about twelve to fourteen hours for her bite marks to fully disappear. The one on my lip now had been created during sex before we went to sleep. After receiving Damien's message upon awaking, I'd told her not—

"Sire," Rick said in Polish, drawing my attention to him. "We have company."

"Where?" I asked him, also in Polish. He spoke English but preferred his native tongue. My Polish wasn't great, but I understood it well enough.

He gestured with his chin to his mirror. "Behind us."

"How far are we from the tower?" I asked as I reached around Willow to grab her seat belt and buckle her in.

"A mile and a half," he said while checking his mirrors again.

I grabbed my belt just as he jerked the car to the side. "There's another!" he shouted, still in Polish.

Clicking myself in, I said, "Floor it."

His foot hit the gas, causing us to soar down the street as I pulled my phone from the pocket of my suit jacket. I selected Damien's name, hitting Dial.

Ring, ring.

"Ryder!" Willow shrieked.

I looked left just as a vehicle crashed into my side of the car. *Fuck!* The world spun around me, my equilibrium shifting violently. Another hit came from behind, the impact causing the belt to bite into my neck.

Another jolt sent us careening in the opposite direction, stirring a brutal wave of nausea inside me. Willow yelped, her soft cry lost to the echo of shattering glass and general chaos.

Blood rushed to my head, the metal buckle digging into my hip as the belt fought to keep me in my seat.

It took me a minute to realize we were upside down, my bag on the ceiling of the car. We'd finally stopped spinning, but the sound of nearby doors slamming told me we were about to experience a lot more than a car wreck.

I didn't think; I acted, unbuckling myself to reach my bag and yanking open the zipper. Damien's message today had arrived with a hint of urgency, making me wonder what chaos awaited me. So I'd packed appropriately.

"Rick," I said, voice low.

No reply.

He must have been knocked out by the impact, his air bags taking up most of the front two seats. Willow whimpered beside me, her fingers fumbling for the buckle.

"I've got you," I whispered, reaching up to help her down.

Settling her beside me, I pulled out two guns from the bag—I already had a third strapped in a holster at my side— and handed one to her. Then I went to my stomach to take in our situation outside.

Willow followed my lead, her dress doing nothing to save her from the glass. I at least had a suit on, but there was no time to try to shield her. We'd already used precious seconds just to get ourselves into this position and properly armed. The only item in our favor was the slow approach from our assailants. They weren't sure what sort of condition I was in, and they were being smart about not rushing over to check.

I glanced backward at my feet, noting the other side of the car. We were pinned up against metal siding, suggesting a building had stopped our roll.

Right. That left only one way to go.

"Stay here and shoot anyone who comes near you that isn't me," I instructed her in a hushed tone. Her lycan ears would allow her to hear just fine. The vampires outside, not so much.

I cracked my neck to the side, loosening my stiff muscles from the original impact, and mentally calculated the angles of each approaching assailant. I could see five from my current position but estimated at least three more based on the number of times we were struck and the manner by which they'd attacked.

Some of those doors had sounded damaged. Others had not.

Which meant a party had been sent after me.

The question was, did they want me alive or dead? Because that would play into what they did next.

Hmm, they hadn't opened fire on the gas tank yet, which was what I would have done if I wanted my victim dead. And their slow approach suggested they were instructed to take me, not kill me.

That gave me a slight advantage because I had no compunction about destroying them permanently.

The scuffles of shoes sounded, the assailants creeping closer.

I could still only see five sets, their approach suggesting their amateur training. They were extremely close together, making what I had to do next far too easy.

Five, I started counting down. *Four. Three. Two…*

I fired a bullet into the ankle of Idiot One, sent a second into the calf of Idiot Two, and shot a third into the shin of Idiot Three. Idiot Four and Idiot Five took off to the side, giving me the distraction I required to quickly crawl out from the rubble, my gun already aiming in the direction of their general trajectory.

Bam. Bam.

I rolled behind the front of the car, quickly checking my periphery and back. *Clear.*

Then I focused on the groans.

Their sounds told me where to fire next, making clean shots to their heads almost too simple.

Where are your buddies? I wondered, glancing around, searching for the rest of them. There was no way someone had been ballsy enough to send only five men after me.

Except, I found no one else. "You've got to be shitting me." Talk about insulting. Who the fuck had this brilliant idea? I stood up from my crouch, looking around. "Seriously, is there no one else?"

Aside from a few people peeking out their doors and windows at me, it appeared we were alone.

I stalked over to the men behind this shit show of an

operation and gaped. "*Vigils?*" I glanced around. "Someone sent *humans* to kill me?" *What the ever-loving-fuck is wrong with people?!*

This had to be a nightmare.

But no. Nope. They were all mortals.

I returned to the car, bending down. "Come out here," I told Willow, my tone underlined in an annoyance I couldn't hide. Because this was just fucking wrong. "Grab my bag."

She worked to obey, her hiss of pain reminding me that she was not properly dressed for this operation at all. "Shit." I squatted. "Hold on." I shrugged out of my suit jacket and handed it to her. "Lay that on the ground and crawl across it." I gentled my tone just enough for her to know I wasn't displeased with her but with our entire situation. "Rick?" I called to him.

Still no reply.

"Damn it," I muttered, standing again to go look at the cars that were used to ram us. Four total with two unconscious mortals inside the more damaged of the vehicles. They must have been knocked out on impact. What a ridiculous operation.

Willow yelped as she tripped over her heels, landing on the hard cement. I returned to her, noting her destroyed outfit and the blood coating her skin. It made me want to kill the mortals again. This time, slowly.

Fortunately, her immortal genetics were already working to heal the superficial scrapes.

"We need to find you something better to wear," I said just as a hum fell over the city. I blinked, looking around, trying to locate the source as everything went pitch black.

Willow jumped, the hairs along her arms standing on end as electricity sizzled through the air.

I narrowed my eyes. "This was all a distraction." One meant to keep me from reaching the tower before the real show began. I shook my head. "That wicked cunt."

"What is it?" Willow asked, her voice holding a slight

tremor. "Why…? Where did all the lights go?"

"She cut the power to San José," I said, a smile flirting with my lips because I couldn't help but be a little bit impressed. "She probably shut off power to my entire region, actually."

"I don't understand."

"Lilith," I explained. "She's showing me that she holds all the power—literally—by shutting off our access to her resources."

"She can do that?"

I snorted. "Apparently. See, the vampires and lycans used a similar tactic when fighting the humans during the reformation. They cut the mortals off at their knees by removing their access to their precious technology and then proceeded to show them why our kind is superior by forcing the humans to essentially fight with their hands alone."

However, the problem with employing this tactic now was that I didn't require Lilith's electricity or power to fight. I had my own.

"She assumes I require her resources," I added out loud. "Proving she knows nothing about me." I bent to evaluate Rick's position. He was in bad shape in there. Sighing, I opened my bag to retrieve a knife, then went to work on cutting him free from his belt and the bags around him.

"You're fucking heavy," I groused, yanking on him to pull him free. He wasn't breathing, his neck twisted at a bad angle from the accident. It was going to take him hours to recover, marking him as useless in our plight.

I stood and went to the closest establishment to bang on the door. A few of the patrons had peeked out through the windows during the whole situation, none of them trying to help. Further proof this region had gone to hell under Silvano's reign.

A short blonde human answered the door with her head bowed. "Yes, Sire?"

"Do you know who I am?" I asked her.

"My superior," she replied immediately.

"Your royal," I corrected her. "Look at me."

Her fear permeated the air, her limbs beginning to shake. "I-I'm sorry, My Prince. I didn't… I didn't know…"

"Look at me," I repeated.

Her tremor became a full-on quake of obvious nerves as she attempted to draw her focus up to me. She got as far as my mouth, her head seemingly unable to lift any higher.

I decided to let it go since I didn't have time to waste on this nonsense. "Where is your owner?" I asked her, hating the question but knowing it was one she would understand.

"Here, My Prince," a feminine voice replied from the stairs as a dark-haired vampire navigated the dark with flawless ease. "To what do we owe the honor?"

"A bunch of Vigils decided I needed to make a detour," I growled. "Or did you miss the chaos outside?"

"I heard it," she admitted, her cheeks blossoming with red splotches. "I… I didn't know how to react."

An honest answer rather than an excuse. That fact alone just saved the woman's life without her ever knowing it was at risk due to my growing wrath. "I need your help," I told her.

"Anything, My Prince," she said.

"I hope you mean that," I replied, taking in the rest of the room. There were five other humans, all appearing to be in relatively decent health. Another point in the female's favor. "What's your name?"

"Patricia," she replied.

"Patricia," I repeated, glancing around. "What kind of an establishment is this?"

"A hair salon and spa." She moved from her perch on the stairs, heading down the rest of the steps before turning left to go open a door toward the back of the lobby area. My night vision allowed me to see the series of chairs and supplies beyond.

"Your humans cut hair?"

"They do," she confirmed.

I glanced at them again. "They don't offer blood?"

Her eyes seemed to cloud over. "Only when a client demands it."

"Like Silvano?" I guessed. Several humans visibly trembled at the mention of his name.

"He was a former patron, yes."

My jaw clenched, aware of what he probably required during his visits. "I see. Well, I have a task for you. Come with me." I turned to find Willow kneeling beside Rick. She'd arranged him in a way to facilitate his healing. "I have two tasks, actually," I said as I walked toward her. "My pet needs functional clothes and tennis shoes, and I need someone to watch over Rick while he heals."

Patricia gasped upon seeing Willow, her eyes narrowing at what she would recognize as an illegal creation.

"Are we going to have a problem?" I asked her, arching a brow.

"N-no, My Prince. No problem."

"Good." I went to Rick and carefully picked him up so I wouldn't undo Willow's attempt to reset some of his disjointed bones. Yet after a few steps, I realized that was futile. He'd need to be completely realigned again.

"I'll find her some clothes," Patricia said, disappearing into her establishment again and up the stairs as I entered with Rick.

The humans inside quickly moved to the side, one going as far as to open the door at the end for me with his head bowed. "Is there a bed or something I can lay him on?" I asked the male.

"Yes, My Prince," he said, leading me to another room that appeared to be set up for massages. I sniffed the air for any signs of foul play in the room and only found the too-sweet aroma of fragrant oils.

The mortal pulled a handful of towels out from a cabinet and went to work on trying to pamper the table. I nearly told him to stop, but his tremors had me striving for patience. These humans were all terrified of me.

Fucking Silvano, I thought, angry all over again.

When the kid finished, I laid Rick down and nodded for Willow to come inside. She'd been observing from the threshold. "Can you help me?" I asked her softly.

She replied by joining me and running her hands over Rick in a similar manner to how she had the servant girl after she'd been whipped. "Where did you learn this?"

"University," she replied, focusing on his neck first.

"They have medical classes?"

"No." She looked up at me. "But I had a lot of exposure to broken bones throughout the years. Some of us chose to help."

I frowned, not liking the sound of that. However, now wasn't the time to press for more information. "I'll be right back," I promised her, leaving to go retrieve my bag from the street. I dug inside it to find a phone that wouldn't rely on Lilith's network to operate, then I dialed Damien again.

It rang twice before he picked up.

Only it wasn't him on the other line.

"Hello, Ryder," Lilith greeted. "How nice of you to call. It's been a few weeks since we last spoke."

Chapter Thirty-One

Willow

The polite clearing of a throat had me glancing at the doorway to find Patricia waiting with clothes. I finished setting Rick's leg, then turned toward her. "Thank you," I said softly, unsure of how to act around her. Ryder and I had agreed on me playing the submissive role in public, but that was before the attack on the street.

Rather than turn to leave, she joined me in the room and walked over to light a candle in the corner. I didn't need it to see, but the human in the room visibly relaxed. He had gone to stand by the wall, silently awaiting his next order.

"What's your name?" Patricia asked.

Apparently, we were going to have this conversation while I changed. All right, then. "Willow," I said as I set the clothes on a chair. My dress was glued to my skin by my

284

dried blood, making it a rather painful process to remove.

Patricia moved to a sink and dampened a towel with water before handing it to me. "Here."

"Thanks," I replied, wary.

"You must be new," she said after a beat. I glanced up at her, confused. "You remind me of myself when I first changed," she added. "Timid. Uncertain of how to address the beings who are no longer your superiors."

I swallowed, unsure of how to respond to that. So I focused on removing my dress instead.

"You didn't win the Immortal Cup this year," she murmured. Not an accusation, but more of an assessment. "And you smell like a lycan but have the grace of a vampire."

Since that wasn't a question, I continued minding my own business and sort of wished she would, too.

"Are you all right?" she asked softly, the concern in her voice giving me pause as I finished wiping the blood away from my legs. My dress was in tatters on the floor, the lace unsalvageable.

I looked up at her. "They were superficial scratches. I'm healed now."

"That's not what I meant." She bent to pick up the fabric and threw it in a nearby bin. Then she went to wash her hands. "The first twenty-two years, there was no Immortal Cup. It's something they don't tell you. But they had to go through an entire generation of brainwashing before they produced a prime crop for the fight. Six were actually chosen that year to win, not two. Lilith said it was to reward the first successful graduating class."

I watched her as I drew on a pair of stretchy black pants, curious to know where she was going with this.

"Jace was given first pick. Then Kylan. And finally, Silvano." Her eyes took on a faraway gleam. "I'd wanted to be a lycan, but Silvano felt otherwise. He dragged me back here…" She swallowed, blinking away the memory before locking gazes with me. "I'm just saying, if you need someone to talk to, I might understand more than you think."

"You were in the first Immortal Cup?" I asked, awed by that revelation.

"Yes. Year twenty-two." She straightened then, her face going blank. I understood why the moment Ryder's minty cologne touched my senses. He entered with a phone to his ear, his expression flat.

I pulled a shirt over my head, then frowned at the violent energy wafting off of him. His facial features indicated he was fine, while his body radiated a primal energy underlined in murderous intent.

He nodded toward the exit, indicating I should follow. Then he turned without a word.

"I should go," I said as I quickly put on the socks and shoes she'd brought me. They were a little snug, but they worked better than the heels I'd kicked off outside earlier.

Patricia caught my arm as I started to leave. "If you ever need help, let me know."

I looked at her—*really* looked at her—and noted the true concern in her gaze. "Ryder's not Silvano," I finally said. "Pay attention to him. He'll surprise you." It was all I could say without really knowing her. While I could sense her sincerity, it wasn't nearly enough to trust her.

I didn't need saving from Ryder.

But he'd made it clear that we couldn't allow others to know that. Not yet.

Patricia gave me a sad smile, one that seemed to say she worried about my mental state. Given how long it took me to see the real Ryder with continued exposure to his decisions, I understood her hesitancy.

She released me as I stepped away, then didn't try to stop me as I left.

Ryder stood outside, the phone still to his ear. "I said you have my attention," he said, his voice radiating a calm not reflected in his stance. Upon seeing me, he bent to lift his bag up over his shoulder, then he grabbed my hand and we started walking.

Apparently, his commentary to keep Rick safe went without further related tasks.

"I'm new to this, Lilith," he said a few minutes later. "You'll have to review the rules more clearly with me."

Just hearing her name sent a chill up my spine, but Ryder seemed focused on whatever she was saying. He also appeared to know where to go because he navigated the alleys with ease.

Vampires were outside, all glancing his way in shock at seeing him strolling down their streets.

Several had candles lit inside.

A few even dared to try to approach him, but one shake of his head sent them scampering backward.

His mood radiated off of him in an intoxicating cloud of danger and savagery. I felt dizzy from it, my feet moving quickly to keep up with his long strides.

"I see," he replied again. "I'll think on it during my walk over. Then we'll talk more." He ended the call and shoved the phone into his bag with a growl that stole the breath from my lungs.

This was Ryder angry.

I hadn't seen this side of him yet.

On the next block, he finally stopped walking and pushed me up against the side of a building, his mouth capturing mine in the next breath. I shook against him, shocked and dismayed by his sudden affection. Only, it didn't feel very affectionate. It felt furious. Threatening. Paralyzing.

My lungs stopped working.

Why did this feel so desperate?

A sensation of foreboding twisted in my stomach, causing my eyes to prickle with tears.

It seemed as though he was saying goodbye.

"Ryder," I whispered.

"Shh." His tongue entered my mouth, demanding my compliance and reciprocation. I responded because I didn't know what else to do. This male had come to mean something to me, and I showed him that with my body since I knew he preferred actions over words. Only, he didn't seem to return the sentiment.

Something was very wrong.

Fundamentally broken.

Missing.

I clung to him as though I could pull the man I knew back to the forefront and reclaim him with my wolf, but he wasn't there. This man kissing me now resembled a stranger, his emotions locked up tight.

He finally pulled away with a stoic expression. Not an ounce of feeling resided in his gaze. I searched for his inner beast, for the vampire I'd fallen helplessly for, and found a vacant shell of a male in his place.

It all happened so quickly, the reality of it a punch to the gut.

"Come, pet," he said, his tone holding an icy edge to it that resembled the kind of royal I'd originally expected him to be. "We have a meeting to attend."

I shivered, my heart in my throat. "Ryder..."

"It wasn't a request," he said, turning without grabbing my hand, his steps clipped as he expected me to follow.

I did only because I had nowhere else to go. He was my Sire. My lover. My hope. Where had the light gone? It'd flickered out almost as quickly as the electricity in the city, his presence replaced by a dark, ominous fog.

We have a meeting to attend. I didn't have to ask to understand whom we were about to meet with. *Lilith.*

My veins iced over, making my steps stiff.

He continued ahead of me in silence, his shoulders a line of tension.

"Don't do this," I said when we reached the next alley. "Don't shut me out."

"You were never in," he returned coldly.

"Lie," I accused, my feet freezing on the ground, my legs refusing to move. My wolf had come fighting to the front, her dissatisfaction driving my instincts. "You're mine."

He turned slowly, his expression eerily tolerant. "I belong to no one."

"My wolf says otherwise."

"Your wolf is a child," he returned. "An infant. *You* are an infant."

I narrowed my gaze. "You're against eating children, yet you ate me just fine when we woke up earlier."

His eyebrows shot upward.

There, my wolf said, noting the beast flickering in his dark eyes. My words had shocked him nearly as much as they'd shocked me, the sass something I'd internalized for so many years that it almost felt rejuvenating to release it now.

"I'm young," I continued, stepping toward him. "But that only means I have a lot to learn. You're going to teach me. You're going to keep me. And I'm keeping you." I stopped less than a foot away from him, then poked him in the chest as my wolf growled out, "You're *mine,* Ryder."

I took the last step to close the gap between us, very aware of the aggressive energy growing around him.

"Tell me what's happening," I demanded. "Talk to me like your equal. Not your pet. Not your fuck toy. But as your *mate.*"

"You're not my mate," he tossed back, the words so cold and heartless I nearly collapsed beneath the weight of his sharply phrased denial.

However, my wolf reacted differently, her fury a wave of fiery resolve that sent my palm upward to crack across his jaw. "*Lie.*"

His head swiveled with my slap, his anger mounting in response. But I'd take that reaction over this stoic asshole pretending to be my Ryder. "Willow." The warning in his voice only made me want to push him more, so push him I did—literally—with two hands against his chest.

"You don't get to do this," I told him. "Not after you've convinced me to trust you. To believe in you. To see this different side of you. To change every perception I've ever had of this world." I shoved him again. "You don't get to take that man away. He's *my* vampire. And I refuse to allow this emotionless asshole to taint what we have. So you turn him right off and come back. *Now*."

I went to jostle him a third time, only to find my wrists caught in his grip.

He dropped his bag on the ground and walked me backward into yet another wall, but this time when he took my mouth, there was a passion I recognized. A fire I longed to stoke. A flame I could happily die inside.

His fangs sank into my lip, my blood pooling between us as he deepened the kiss. He wove his fingers into my hair, tugging harshly, while his opposite palm went to my hip.

I returned his ferocity with my own, my anger and fear exploding through my tongue.

He'd betrayed me.

Tried to tune me out.

Had *hurt* me, not physically but emotionally. And I let him know with my teeth that he would not be doing that again.

He growled as I bit him in the same way he'd bitten me, my wolf staking her claim once again, reminding him I wasn't just a plaything or a pet. I was *his* pet. His progeny. His lover. His future.

We hadn't spoken about the next steps, and I no longer needed to because I was telling him now with my mouth exactly where we were headed.

He couldn't push me away.

He couldn't ignore me.

He couldn't claim I meant nothing.

Because I saw through that veil of emotionlessness.

His beast recognized mine. He might not be able to shift, but I'd awakened that part of him. I *felt* it in his touch, our souls dancing in a way no one else could understand.

"Fuck," he whispered, his hand going to my waist as he lifted me into the air. I wrapped my legs around him, devouring his mouth with my own, claiming him as if it were the first time.

And maybe it was.

I'd been living in this world of uncertainty.

Unsure of what happened next.

When all along I just needed to take it.

Our blood mingled in our mouths, his palms roaming over my body in a dark obsession, his arousal prominent between my thighs.

But this wasn't about sex.

It was about a vow, about fulfilling our destiny together.

"Don't you ever deny me again," I told him, panting against his mouth.

"She has Damien," he replied, his voice breaking. "She made me listen to his screams until there was silence."

I cupped the sides of his face, noting the emotions shattering through his gaze. "Oh, Ryder," I whispered, realizing what had set him off. He'd shut down because it was too much for him to accept, the pain of his progeny's agony ripping him apart.

I saw it then, the hopelessness of the male battling the rage of his inner beast.

He'd closed himself off to avoid processing it all.

But that wasn't the solution. Actually, after everything he'd told me the last few weeks, I suspected that was exactly what Lilith had wanted.

"Don't let her into your head," I said. "You're not like them, Ryder. And that's your biggest strength. At least to me."

His dark irises roamed over my features as though searching for the truth. I opened myself to him, allowing him to explore me without any barriers. Because there were none between us. He'd possessed me from the very beginning. He owned me. I still wore the collar around my neck to prove it.

He kissed me again, this time gentler, his mouth saying words only my heart could hear.

And then I felt his resolve snapping into place.

My Ryder never did what anyone expected. But for the first time, I had an inkling of what was to come. Only because I'd learned to anticipate his unprecedented reactions.

"Thank you," he whispered before slowly returning me to my feet. "Let's go."

This time I felt the warmth in his hand as he laced our fingers together, just as I noted the assuredness in his stance. He retrieved his bag once more and nodded, some sort of decision made.

Whatever it was, I hoped it involved blood. Because I was thirsty for it.

Chapter Thirty-Two

Ryder

Lilith had given me an ultimatum.

"Return to your reclusive property willingly, and I'll let you take Damien with you. Or you can try to fight for your royal position, in which case…"

That was when the screaming had started.

I never wanted to hear that sound from his mouth ever again.

He was in pain because of me. Because I'd asked him to help me bait Lilith, then I'd left him here to handle all my duties alone while I'd played with Willow.

Everything inside me had shut down in response, my guilt evoking emotions I'd thought were long dead.

Then Lilith had delivered her parting words. *"And, Ryder? I know all about your little hybrid. Kill her as a sign of good faith, and I'll allow you entry into the building to retrieve your progeny."*

She wanted me to choose between Damien and Willow.

She wanted me to choose between returning to my solitude and doing what was right.

Well, I refused both choices.

I'd decided on a third option.

One she wasn't going to like.

Willow had pulled me back from a decision I didn't know how to make. I'd turned off my emotions, preparing to offer myself in exchange for Damien's life, and she'd forced me to see the crucial flaw in my reasoning.

It'd all happened so quickly, my mind shutting down at the bizarre sense of failure overwhelming me.

I never lost.

I always won.

And for the first time in my very long existence, I felt as though I'd been defeated.

Then the little warrior beside me slapped common sense into me, reminding me that we were in the middle of a battle, not at the end of it. I couldn't give up before the game had been called.

Lilith had played me well, her continued mastery in this match impressive. She'd pitted us all against each other at some point, placing her pawns around the board in exactly the locations she desired.

Only, I'd brought her here through some plays of my own.

I'd removed the queen from the sanctity of her kingdom and brought her to my playground for a reason.

She might have arrived early and thrown me off-kilter with her underhanded moves, but I still had a few plays left in me.

Lilith had chosen the wrong vampire to fuck with.

She'd underestimated my skill and age from the beginning, just as I'd underappreciated her knack for deviousness.

But now I knew better.

And she did not.

Which I intended to use to my full advantage.

I paused a block away from the main building to gather my bearings. I'd checked the map on my phone before deciding on our route, and now I wanted to check it again. Dropping the bag, I opened it to retrieve the device, then clicked on the GPS I'd pulled up while talking to Lilith.

Willow glanced at it, her blue eyes glowing with intent. "What's the plan?" she asked, her faith in me resolute.

"Lilith wants your head," I said.

Her eyes flew upward. "What?"

"She said I have to kill you to be allowed entrance into the building. Which tells me she has guards in place. But I'm wondering if she's accounted for all entry points." Benita would have provided her with all the door locations. Just as I assumed Benita was to blame for Lilith being able to capture Damien. That was a decision she would soon regret.

I analyzed the roads leading up to the building, determining my preferred approach.

"The Vigils who attacked us probably belonged to Lilith," I said. "Which suggests she's using humans to guard the doors, too." Unless she'd found a few allies in my region through Benita, which was also entirely possible.

I started going through the bag again, pulling out items that would help us. I handed two grenades to Willow. "Don't pull those pins," I warned her.

I found the gun she'd originally had in the car—she must have put it back when I was talking to Patricia—and I evaluated the ammunition left in the bag.

"It's too bad I didn't bring a rifle." Then I could have gone up to the roof of a building and picked off her guards, only that would provide her with enough time to kill Damien. So never mind. A rifle would have been a bad play.

Calculations rolled through my head as I added up weapons and bullets, considered trajectory of entry, and speculated the number of guards she'd have queued up inside.

"She would've arrived by air," I said, more to myself than to Willow. "And she would have landed between the time I spoke to Damien earlier and our arrival. Rick would have noticed any nearby air traffic, so I'm guessing she only had one jet. A small one. Maybe ten passengers, max. She's also banking on her Damien card keeping me in check."

Which all added up to her being insufficiently guarded. At least in theory.

"All right, here's what I want you to do," I said, a strategy unfolding through my thoughts. "You're going to run like hell toward the entrance. Act as though you're terrified. Scream and beg for me not to do this. Put on one hell of a show. Then, when you're close enough to the front, I need you to pull the pins out of those grenades."

I paused to show her how they worked. Once I was satisfied that she understood, I continued.

"So you pull out the pins, then throw the grenades at the glass entrance and dive behind the palm tree planters outside for cover."

I dug back into the bag again to find some earplugs.

"You'll need these to protect your lycan senses," I added, handing them to her. Then I picked up the gun she hadn't used earlier. "Can you hide this somewhere?"

She looked at her shirt and pants before shaking her head. "Not if I'm carrying these." She held up the grenades.

Hmm, unfortunately, I hadn't brought additional holsters.

"The grenades will have to do. If they're like the Vigils, they won't even be armed anyway." My kind very rarely played with weapons now that humans were no longer a threat. Another miscalculation in Lilith's approach—she expected me to react like a vampire, not a mortal. She clearly didn't understand my appreciation for toys that killed.

"Where will you be?" she asked.

"I'm going in through the glass," I told her, checking the gun in my holster and reloading it appropriately. Then I picked up her discarded weapon, and a third one from the bag. These would have to be enough because I couldn't carry this bag with me into the building.

"Glass?" she repeated.

I stood, smirking. "You'll see." Then I stepped into her and pressed my mouth to hers. "Start running, little wolf. Act scared."

"That's it? No other pep talk? No further plan?"

"Trust me, it'll be enough. Now go be my distraction. I have some work to do."

"You going to tell me which way to go?" she demanded, sounding adorably annoyed by my lack of directions.

I kissed her again, just because. My lip was still bleeding from her earlier bite, reminding me of her yanking me back to a proper frame of mind.

She'd grounded me in a way no one ever had. And I was pretty sure I gave her my heart in that moment for safekeeping. Or perhaps she already owned it. I couldn't really say, but she absolutely had it now.

"It's one block down through there," I said softly, gesturing at the road. "You can just make out that hideous floral display Silvano installed as a driveway entrance."

She followed my gaze to see what I meant, her nose curling. "I can smell it."

"Yeah. It's awful."

Her eyes slowly returned to mine. "I'm glad you're you again. This Ryder I understand."

"Do you?" I asked, slightly amused. "Because I seem to recall you once saying you would never understand me."

"That was human Willow," she replied. "Wolf Willow understands you just fine."

My lips quirked. "Then it must have been your wolf I met that first day when you tried to fight me even while dying."

"Seems like something she would do," Willow admitted.

I smiled. "She's your warrior half."

"Then what does that make my vampire half?"

"Your logical side," I replied. "Which is why I'm speaking to that side now when I say move your sweet ass because I'm tired of Lilith's little game."

I intended to end it tonight.

Willow nodded. "You'd better know what you're doing." She took off before I could reply, forcing me into action. I went around the building beside me to the nearby alley, then ran down it to the end, beating her to the other side. With age came speed, and her human legs weren't nearly as fast as her lycan ones.

Well, they might be faster right now. She was still pretty clumsy on four legs.

I watched from the shadows as she did exactly what I told her, running across the road and screaming at me to reconsider.

While she made a scene, I observed the main entrance.

Several Vigils stood outside, all watching her. They held machine guns, thwarting my earlier expectations, but they didn't aim at her. Instead, they watched for me.

I leaned against the wall, observing their behaviors, noting their shifting positions. They were nervous, not because of Willow's approach but because of my inevitable one.

Well, they wouldn't have to worry about that much longer. The second Willow was within throwing range, she did exactly as I told her.

I pushed off the wall, slinking through the shadows created by the buildings. The Vigils didn't have supernatural eyesight, marking them as inferior. They needed the moon to illuminate me before they knew where to aim.

Three.

Two.

I stepped out from my hiding spot, the Vigils drawing their weapons, and smiled when the grenades went off just in time.

Then I did exactly what I told Willow I would do—I ran right for the glass windows of the front lobby.

Two bullets took out the windowpane, granting me entry with one leap over the flower bed.

Then I wasted no time taking out everyone who stood inside, raining down bullets on a series of unprepared vampires who had stupidly expected a row of Vigils to take me down.

I blamed Lilith for their ignorance as I dove behind the receptionist counter, just in case a Vigil had survived, then peeked out beside it to take down those who remained standing.

It happened in a few blinks, my vampiric age and speed aiding in my attempt. My experience with weapons helped, too.

When I finally came up for air, it was to find over a dozen bodies on the ground, some of whom had been taken out by the blast. The others all had one or two bullets in them. None of them were truly dead yet, just wounded enough to stay down.

I rolled my neck, looking for the source of my problems. No electricity meant no video footage, which meant she had to be nearby to witness my approach.

Had it been me, I wouldn't have cut the power and I'd have remained high up in the tower to watch the feeds below, thereby allowing myself enough time to plan a counterattack.

I also wouldn't have turned off the resource my human Vigils required to do their job.

No light equaled minimal sight clearance—a weakness I'd exploited beautifully with the help of my pet.

If I wasn't already pissed off by Lilith's antics with Damien, I would have been pissed off by the insult that she thought this would be enough to take me down.

"Oh, Lilith," I called, whistling as I began my search of the lower level.

I was banking on her penchant for entertainment. She'd want to punish me by making me watch Damien die rather than have me walk in to find him already dead. It was her fatal flaw—her need for attention.

"Come on, darling," I said, peeking into the administrative area behind the reception desks and finding it empty. "I thought we had a date?"

A muffled grunt met my commentary, causing me to grin. *Thanks, Damien*, I thought at him, following the sound. He always did find me amusing, or at least, that was how I interpreted his reaction.

"Why are you playing hard to get?" I asked, entering the restaurant. Lilith stood near the center of the room beneath the unlit chandelier. Damien sat in a chair beside her, bound and gagged and missing an eye.

They were otherwise alone, implying she thought this would be enough to bring me to my knees.

Or perhaps she had reinforcements coming.

That would explain her prolonged silence.

"Have you completely lost your mind?" she demanded, arching a perfect blonde brow. It sort of matched the rest of her—all glorious perfection in an exquisite white gown. She capped off the purity act with a battle-axe in her right hand, really driving home the whole avenging angel facade.

"I'm not sure it's wise for you to question the sanity of others, Lilith," I said conversationally. "I mean, you did lead a revolution to enslave the human race, all to what? Avenge your Michael?"

She growled. "Do not speak his name."

I looked around. "Oh, if I say it three times, will it make him appear?" I asked in a conspiratorial whisper. "Or is that another old wives' tale? I've mixed them up over the millennia. I think a mirror is required?"

"You dare make jokes about my loss?"

"Forgive me," I drawled. "I tend to make light of situations that piss me off. Such as you removing the eye from my progeny. Is that supposed to be a metaphor? An eye for an eye? Because I'll be needing your eye now as payment."

She tapped the battle-axe against her ankle, a sign her

patience was beginning to run out.

"You're stalling," I observed. "Are we expecting company?" I wasn't naive enough to think it would be this easy. While her ego served as a serious weakness in her decision-making, she wouldn't leave herself this vulnerable without a purpose.

Of course, I held two guns and had a third on a belt.

So maybe it was that easy.

All I had to do was lift and aim.

Which I did now. "Will they save you in time, Lilith?" I asked her, no longer smiling. Because unlike her, I didn't believe in long, drawn-out shows of amusement. I preferred action and death.

"You won't shoot me, Ryder," she said, sounding bored.

"I won't?"

"You can't."

Her tone implied such confidence that I almost wondered if she knew something I didn't about my weapons. Which was utter insanity. I'd just used them to take down her pitiful excuse for an army.

My mind whirred with quick math.

And yeah, I had plenty of ammunition left to send a few bullets into her skull.

"Pretty sure I can, Lilith," I informed her.

She shook her head as though sad. "I had no idea you'd grown so delusional over the years. I should have come to check on you. Old age can really alter the mind."

This nutcase was calling me delusional? I almost didn't even know what to say.

She pulled out her phone then and set the battle-axe against Damien's leg. Within seconds, the power returned, flickering to life and momentarily blinding my senses. But it wasn't enough to derail my focus. My aim didn't waver, my suspicion mounting.

"We'll need to record this for the trial," she explained conversationally.

"Trial?"

"Yes, your upcoming trial," she replied, her attention on her phone. "You're clearly unfit to lead, and after your display of disobedience tonight, I'll also be moving to have you terminated."

My eyebrows shot up, and a laugh left my throat. "Terminated?"

"You're a danger to our society, Ryder," she said, her tone severe. "You've slaughtered countless members of our kind over your very short tenure, and now you're pointing a gun at my head as though you have the authority to shoot me." She tsked sadly. "I take part of the responsibility for this. It's clear to me now that I never should have left you alone."

"Oh, you take responsibility?" I drawled. "Here I thought I was responsible for myself, but it's good to know you feel invested in my well-being. Truly, it's touching, Lilith."

She sighed again, returning her attention to her phone. "If you'll just provide me with another minute to pull up the proper application, I'll begin the recording."

I snorted. "So let me get this straight. You feel I'm a danger to society and want me terminated, yet you expect me to stand here and just… obey?"

She ignored me, thereby answering my question.

"I'm not sure what impresses me more—your ineptitude or your arrogance," I said, frowning. Something wasn't right. She'd shown true strategic genius in her previous plays. While she clearly underestimated me, I knew better than to misjudge the situation now. That'd been my mistake before.

What are you really up to? I wondered, narrowing my eyes.

I looked at Damien, noting the perspiration on his brow. That could have been brought about by pain, but his expression said something else entirely.

Concern.

Not for himself, but for me.

I frowned. *What am I missing?*

302

This was the woman who had publicly taken down Cam. Now she wanted to record us. That implied a hidden agenda, something I hadn't taken into consideration. We thought the threat resided in Chicago, but what if Lilith had mobilized it?

I slowly lowered my gun, my senses flaring, searching for a viable threat and coming up blank. Other than a few groans from the other room, nothing—

A blaring alarm shrieked through my skull, rendering my senses useless. *Fuck!* I pressed my palms to my ears, only slightly aware that I'd released my weapons. The ground bit into my knees as I collapsed, the echo roaring through my thoughts, paralyzing my every instinct.

"Finally," Lilith said, her voice far too loud and commanding in my head. "I just had to find the right frequency."

Right frequency? I repeated to myself, cringing as that scream continued to pulverize my mind. *What the fuck are you doing to me?!* Only, the words wouldn't leave my mouth. Or maybe they did. I couldn't hear a fucking thing beyond the screech drilling through my brain.

"Now that I have your attention," Lilith continued, her voice only slightly louder than the chaos roaring behind her. "I'm going to start by terminating your progeny. You'll be able to see again in a moment when I slightly lower the frequency, but you'll still be immobilized."

I swore I heard her heels clicking.

Felt her fingers combing through my hair.

Smelled her too-sweet perfume.

What the hell? How is this happening?

"Then I'll transport you back to Chicago to meet the others," she said, her voice almost soothing in comparison to the piercing sound debilitating my thoughts. "We'll stage your termination at a later date—likely during the council meeting. Of course, I may keep you. Your age and blood will prove quite fruitful."

Was her nail tracing my neck?

My shoulder?

Fuck, this was insane.

I could *feel* her inside me. Her voice a hypnotic caress I longed to hate, yet craved over the damn alert shredding my mind.

I began to shake, rage boiling inside me.

I should have shot her when I had the chance.

Why the fuck had I waited? I knew better, that this couldn't be *that* easy.

She cooed in my head. "There, there," she murmured, the sound akin to nails on a chalkboard.

I wanted to strangle her.

Destroy her.

Fucking rip her head from her neck.

And I wanted to shoot myself for not taking advantage of the moment I had to take her down. Goddamnit, I knew better.

"Yes, it's done," I heard her say, seemingly to someone else. "Did you find his hybrid?"

Willow.

Shit!

I tried to growl, to demand she leave her out of this, but that alarm only bellowed louder. Fuck, it hurt. Was I even breathing? Living? Had I died without realizing it? Was this hell? I'd never really believed in the afterlife or perpetual torment. But I did now.

This was agony.

Utter devastation.

Insanity.

I winced, only vaguely aware of the ground beneath me.

"Well, go find her," Lilith snapped. "Don't come back without her!"

Her voice offered me a moment of reprieve. *Willow's still safe.*

Run, little wolf. Run, I urged her, my mind fracturing from the sound. I blinked in and out. In and out. The word *run* playing over and over in my thoughts. To the point where I didn't know why I said it but vaguely remembered it was important.

Run.

Run.

Run.

Chapter Thirty-Three

Willow

Several Minutes Earlier

The buzzing in my head irritated me while I ran toward the building. Some sort of frequency that seemed to be tickling my eardrums through the plugs Ryder had given me.

It must be a lycan thing, I thought, pushing it away as soon as the line of Vigils and their guns came into view. *Shit...*

The hysteria in my voice as I screamed for Ryder not to kill me took on a very real tone, only I was directing it at the humans standing sentry outside the building.

Yet other than look at me, they did nothing, their focus intent on the area behind me.

Because those guns were for Ryder, not me.

They didn't see me as a threat, just as he'd predicted. Given the size of their weapons, I was okay with that. I wasn't ready to test the limits of my immortality yet.

Instead, I kept up my act and ran right for them while shooting panicked glances over my shoulder. Then I unpinned the grenades in my hands and threw them at the Vigils before diving behind the nearby planter. I crawled as far as I could, trying to get away from the inevitable blast, and collapsed beneath the violent vibration that rocked the front of the building.

Fuck! If it hurt that much *with* the earplugs, then I didn't want to know how that would have felt without them.

I curled into a ball, my ears ringing madly.

Come on, Willow, I coached myself, counting the seconds. *Come on. Come on. Come on.*

There wasn't a plan after this part, but lying on the ground outside the building didn't seem like the smartest place for me to hang out.

Gunfire startled me from my inner musings. Glass shattered and Ryder leapt through the air like a god, entering the building just as he said he would.

I blinked, stunned.

Then more shots rang out through the air, each one resembling thunder against my sore ears.

And that damn *buzzing* wasn't helping.

Where the heck was it coming from? Maybe it had something to do with the electricity being down?

I frowned, looking around, trying to find the source, when I heard Ryder calling for Lilith inside. *Did he just say something about a date?* I shook my head. Only he would issue taunts in this situation. I preferred it to his coldness. It helped me feel more at home. This was my Ryder, the confident vampire with millennia of experience.

Was I supposed to join him now? Or wait?

A soft shuffling noise drew my focus to the side of the building. It paused, followed by a soft curse that had my eyes widening.

I was a sitting duck right here without a weapon.

Shit.

A trio of bushes sat just off to my left, the greenery calling my name. I crawled over as quietly as possible, removed the plugs from my ears, and waited for the source of the sound to appear.

Ryder's deep tones graced my ears, his words indecipherable as a result of the distance between us. But my wolf relaxed, content with his status.

Meanwhile, the vampire in me strategized my next play.

I needed a knife or a gun, preferably the former. While Ryder had showed me how to fire a weapon, I wasn't nearly as comfortable with it as I was with a blade.

"Ugh," a female groaned. Then I heard her shake off debris as though she'd been knocked out or had fallen from my blast. The ground had rumbled pretty violently, and the side of the building her sounds were coming from was only a few feet away from where I hid now.

If I'd learned one thing as a new immortal, it was that my senses were much more heightened now. So the explosion would have impacted all the others nearby as well.

A female stepped into view, her shoes a deep red. One appeared to be missing a heel, which suggested I was right about her falling down.

I took in her bare legs and short black dress. Her face was hidden by the branches.

She sneezed, then cursed about dirt and started hobbling toward the entrance. My nose twitched at her ferrous scent. *Vampire*, I guessed. Because she didn't appear to be bleeding, just a little roughed up.

I winced as the irritating buzz intensified in my head. *What the heck?* I tried to shake it off, but the sensation only appeared to grow. It felt wrong. Foreign. *Invasive.*

The lights suddenly came roaring back to life, causing me to cringe at the abrupt brightness surrounding the streets and building. I blinked, my eyes watering from the unexpected change. It gave me a new appreciation for Ryder's dislike of the sun.

Fortunately, my senses almost immediately adjusted, the vivid scene taking on a new hue through my wolf's eyes. She started pacing inside me, her restlessness twisting my stomach with a sense of dread.

Instinct prickled down my arms.

Something's wrong.

Frowning, I slowly maneuvered away from the bushes and toward the front of the building, staying low in a crouch and silent on my feet. Blood and burn marks painted the ground, most of the mortals dead or on their way there.

I paused at one who was mostly intact, patting down his thigh for potential knives. Finding none, I moved to the next corpse and located a dagger in his boot. A third body gave me a second blade. And the fourth had a pistol that fit nicely in my hand.

Ryder had taught me how to shoot with a similarly sized gun back at his house. I checked the ammunition like he'd taught me and found it fully loaded.

Excellent.

I stole the belt and holster from the body and latched it around my hips. It wasn't a perfect fit, but it had a slot for one of my knives, which allowed me to keep at least one hand free.

A bellow of agony had my wolf growling in my head. *Ryder.* I nearly started running, my instinct to help taking over, but the colder part of my mind—the vampire in me—held me captive.

What would Ryder do? I asked myself, moving on to another body to search for more knives.

If he was in trouble, I needed daggers I could throw.

I found a few, their weight reasonable and precise.

Then I heard the sound of a heel on marble coming from inside.

Shit! There was no time to duck behind another bush, so I squirmed partly under a dead human, allowing his blood and stench of death to hide my scent.

It was instinctual and fucked up, but I didn't have time to evaluate the decision.

"Find the hybrid," a female voice muttered. "Grab Damien. Get Ryder. Anything else?"

My brow furrowed. *Who the hell is she talking to?*

"Oh, and if you could also do the entire job without so much as a 'thank you,' that'd be great," she continued. "Sure! I'd love to. Shall I eat you out as well?"

The female grunted, stepping right over me. It was the same one from earlier with the red shoes.

She sighed audibly. "Where the hell do I even start?" She pinched the bridge of her nose, stopping a foot away from me. "It reeks of death out here."

Yeah, it does, I agreed.

"Fuck," she muttered, then looked up and down the street. "Oh, Willow!" she called. "Ryder's looking for you!"

My brow furrowed. *You don't really think that's going to work, do you?*

She whistled next, then took a few more steps before yelling for me again, claiming Ryder had sent her.

Uh-huh, I thought at her. She continued on, varying her behavior between hobbling several steps and shouting lies. I waited until she was about twenty feet away before I started the process of worming my way out from beneath the dead body.

She was too busy whistling and calling for me to notice my slow progress. It took a few minutes, mostly because I didn't want to risk her seeing me, but I finally made it out and into a position where I could shoot her.

Only, I didn't want anyone to hear gunfire.

So I palmed a knife instead.

If I couldn't detect conversation inside, then the trouble was far enough away that I didn't need to worry about someone overhearing this bitch grunt.

I slowly rose to the balls of my feet, creeping forward in a squat.

The female cursed and kicked off her shoes, completely unaware of me approaching from behind. Considering she thought I was dumb enough to fall for her calling act, she absolutely didn't anticipate me sneaking up on her.

I weighed one of the daggers in my hand, contemplating the throwing velocity required, then released it when I was about five feet behind her. It hit her square between her shoulder blades, resulting in a shriek that turned into a grunt as I pounced on her from behind.

She went down with an "Oomph."

I took another knife and drove it into her skull with a force created by my lycan side.

Aside from a gurgle, she fell silent.

I quickly looked around to see if anyone else had noticed and found a few vampires peeking out of nearby buildings, most of them probably wondering what the hell this female had been yelling about.

When no one reacted other than to gape, I rolled off her and onto the balls of my feet.

She'd wake up eventually with a headache. While I suspected she might be Benita, I wasn't sure, as I'd never really seen her aside from her shoes when I first arrived with Ryder—and that felt like forever ago now. He'd only brought her up a few times with Damien, then mentioned to me that he thought she was passing information on to Lilith.

Which, if that was true, meant Lilith had somehow won inside.

Given the agony I'd heard from Ryder, that seemed unfortunately likely.

Swallowing, I began the process of creeping through the dead bodies again, this time with the aim of entering the building. My left hand still gripped several knives, leaving my right hand available for a potential throw or to grab my sidearm.

I moved silently—something that seemed to come naturally from my wolf side—and kept low. With all the lights on inside, it was easy to see the morbid scene in the lobby. The majority of the bodies were lifeless with only a few limbs twitching here and there. I stepped through the entrance Ryder had made rather than through the doors, then ducked behind the reception desk area. That was probably why he'd chosen this path—he knew a natural shield existed on the other side.

"…see yet?" I heard a female asking, the tone sending a chill down my spine.

Lilith.

How many films had I been forced to watch in school that featured her voice? How many tapes? How many recorded ceremonies of worship?

My throat went dry at the memories.

She presented herself as this benign, beautiful goddess. We prayed to her daily. Begged her for her precious gift of immortality. Longed for her to *choose us* for the Immortal Cup.

It was driven into our minds at a young age.

She haunted my dreams as a child, her voice one I both adored and feared.

And to hear her callous tone now further drove home the lies she'd fed us.

Such a small thing, but a defining trait she'd just shattered within seconds of hearing the *real* her.

Because that tone she'd used on Ryder a moment ago radiated malicious intent.

"Oh, Damien, how uncomfortable you must be," she continued. "Don't worry, sweet child. It'll all be over soon, just as soon as your Sire *opens his eyes*."

My skin rippled with electricity, that hum in my head intensifying once more and making me wince. *It's her*, I realized. Something she was doing. But I had no idea what.

I forced myself to swallow, then crept out from behind the desk to survey the room again for any signs of life.

Nothing.

"Come on, Ryder. I know it hurts, but I expected you to be stronger than this," she continued. "Where's that rebel I've come to loathe? The one who thinks he can just waltz in here and dismantle every law I've ever created?"

Her voice was coming from the dining area off the lobby. I hadn't been in that room since the first night Ryder and I had arrived when he killed all those vampires.

The memory warmed my blood—a reaction I very much needed with the ice flowing through my veins. It helped me tiptoe toward them.

"Do you have any idea how many centuries I've been planning this?" she asked conversationally. "Michael and I thought of *everything*. As I think you're now learning, hmm? As I recall, you're fond of technology, but I bet you never could have imagined *this*."

Ryder growled in response, which stirred a tinkling laugh from Lilith.

I paused outside the door, waiting to see if she could sense me. A lycan would be able to smell me. What about a vampire?

Although, I was covered in the blood of that human from the ground. Perhaps that would help mask my wolf half?

"It's based on the hive mind," she added. "A telepathic link that disables the mind and body. Fascinating, isn't it?"

I frowned. *A telepathic link?* I almost risked glancing around the corner but held myself back, not wanting to give myself away yet.

"I've used it to break so many of our kind." She sounded so proud. "Cam, of course, refuses to behave."

Her heels clicked against the floor.

"Perhaps you can share a cell with him," she mused.

"He's gone half-mad, so that should suit you just fine. At some point, I'll take his *Erosita* from Luka, merely to see what fun I can have with her to fracture him further. It's just been more amusing for now to hold it over his head and taunt him with *what-ifs* and *whens*. You should see him try to reach out to her. It's terribly sad."

This was what I expected from vampire kind.

Lilith resembled evil in its purest form.

And somehow she'd taken Ryder down.

"There you are," she said.

I froze, thinking for a second she'd found me, but her next words were still directed at Ryder.

"Look at those beautiful dark eyes spinning with rage," she cooed. "I love it. Let's make you really mad, shall we? Up you go."

A scuffling noise tickled my ears, and I imagined her trying to help him sit up. Which implied he was awake but paralyzed from whatever she'd done with her telepathic link.

If I could find the source, then perhaps I'd be able to wake him back up.

But the source had to be inside.

A gun skidded across the floor, narrowly hitting the edge of the door frame. "Won't be needing those, hmm?" Lilith said.

Did that mean she was unarmed?

Metal slid another way, suggesting she'd just kicked away another weapon.

I palmed the handle of the gun at my side, then glanced at the one a few feet away. It was the same one Ryder had handed me when the car flipped over.

Was it loaded or empty?

Did I want to risk it or go with the one at my side?

"There," she said, sounding pleased. "This presents a perfect angle, allowing you to see Damien's head roll."

My eyes widened. *What?!*

That would kill him.

Which was why she told him it'd all be over soon.

Fuck, I needed to act.

She was clearly alone in there. But she had some sort of weapon that had disabled Ryder. What chance did I have against *that?*

Does it matter? I asked myself. *Either I stay here and listen to him die or I try to stop her.*

There wasn't even a question.

I had to do something.

Ryder had nearly lost himself over Damien being hurt. If she killed his progeny…

No. Not happening.

I had weapons and surprise on my side. She'd also underestimate me just like everyone else had.

Do it, I coached myself. *Do it now!*

I stepped into the doorway to find her back to me as she bent to pick up a battle-axe. Ryder sat in a chair across from her, completely unmoving.

Stop staring and move! I shouted at myself, bending to pick up the gun she'd discarded.

Still silent. Still unseen.

Because she wasn't expecting me.

The hybrid.

Ryder's pet.

She began to speak, but I tuned her out, focusing on the gun and aiming it at her. I had one shot to get this right.

Ryder's instructions filtered through my mind, my breathing calming as I pretended he was right behind me, coaching me and telling me what to do.

When you first start, always aim for the torso, he'd told me. *It's a bigger target and easier for a newbie.*

Her white dress melted from my mind into the targets he'd lined up outside.

My wolf focused.

Seeing the dot in the middle.

Then my finger pulled the trigger.

The sound was deafening, the crack of the bullet making me wince.

Then beautiful red bled into my vision.

Lilith spun around, shock evident in her expression as she dropped the axe. "*How dare you,*" she sputtered.

The human in me fought not to bow.

But that human no longer told me how to move or how to react. My wolf had taken over now, her fury at the female for hurting her mate roaring to the forefront of my mind as I stepped forward and sent another bullet into her torso. And another. And another. Until all that was left were clicks without the subsequent crack.

I roared with a rage I didn't know I was capable of feeling and charged her with a knife, plunging it into her heart and sending her to the ground.

She glared up at me with cruel green eyes, her hands locking around my throat, squeezing.

So I stabbed her again. And again. Then drove a blade right through her fucking eye.

I put another in her neck. A third into her chest. Then patted my side, searching for more.

Only then did I realize she'd stopped moving. That I'd taken her down. And when I looked at Ryder, it was to see tears rolling down his cheeks, his dark eyes glistening with a pride I felt to my very soul.

Except he still wasn't moving.

"How do I fix it?" I asked him, spinning around and searching for whatever had caused him to sit there like that.

A growl drew my attention to Damien.

I gasped upon seeing his empty eye socket, his handsome face a battered mess. He growled again, this time in impatience. The ball in his mouth preventing him from speaking. I stood and moved to him with a tremble in my limbs but somehow managed to unfasten the leather strap behind his head. "Her phone," he said immediately. "Find her phone. It's in her dress."

I went back to her, searched the shredded fabric for a pocket, and finally found it near her thigh.

"Use her right index finger to activate it," Damien instructed.

I wasn't sure what he meant until the screen lit up, asking for identification. I did as Damien said, then gaped at the screen littered in codes and pictures.

"Bring it to me," he demanded.

I jumped back to my feet and held it before him to review. He had me select various icons, swiping this way and that, until finally I pulled up one that seemed to interest him. "There. Press the red button."

"Are you sure?"

"Do it," he snapped.

My finger shook as I followed his command.

Silence.

I swallowed. "Damien, are you—"

"That fucking cunt!" Ryder roared suddenly, causing me to jump so high I nearly lost the phone. He stalked forward, grabbed the axe, and sliced it through her neck so fast that I would have missed it had I blinked.

Then he began hacking into her chest, cursing at her with each swipe, his fury a palpable wave that had my wolf doing circles inside me in excitement.

What the hell?!

I gaped at him, confused by my inner reaction and subsequently terrified of the beast staring at me when he turned around.

He grabbed me in the next second, his palm a brand against the back of my neck as he pulled me in for a kiss that stole my very breath.

I melted into him on instinct, my tremors turning to full-on quakes of desire-filled violence.

A throat cleared behind me, but Ryder was too busy devouring me to pay it any mind. Then Damien said, "Could you at least untie me before you fuck her? I'm all for watching the show, but I'm in a little pain here."

Ryder ignored him for another beat before smiling against my mouth. "You are so fucking mine, Willow."

"I thought we established that outside," I replied, a little breathless.

He bit my lower lip hard enough to bleed. "Don't move. We're not done yet."

Chapter Thirty-Four

Ryder

Damien's screen flashed with data from Lilith's phone, the progress bar inching upward slowly as he downloaded everything from her device into our system.

I palmed the back of my neck and stretched the stiff muscles going down into my shoulders. Whatever the fuck Lilith had done to my head still remained in lingering pulses, shooting sporadic spasms down my spine.

Beating her with that axe had felt good, just as Damien had enjoyed chopping off the head of several immortals in the lobby, but the lasting impacts of her visit left me feeling weaker than I wanted to admit.

Lifting my arms over my head, I tried to loosen up my joints to rid myself of her lingering touch.

A telepathic link replicated through the use of technology, I marveled for the thousandth time. She'd somehow found a way to harness lycan hive-mind energy and apply it to her advantage.

I was both sickened and impressed.

No wonder she'd taken down Cam. I also had a new appreciation for why he hadn't reached out to Izzy. "She must be accessing the mind through the mating connection," I said, pacing. "That's the only telepathic link I'm aware of, except in the rare occasions where it's enabled during blood exchange."

Sadly, that wasn't an ability I possessed. Mmm, how I'd love to enter Willow's thoughts. Especially right now since she was napping downstairs. Leaving her in our suite to shower alone had been excruciating—seeing as all I wanted to do was fuck her up against a damn wall—but I couldn't leave Damien to clean all this up on his own.

It was my fault he'd been here alone when Lilith had arrived.

Just as it was my fault he'd been turned into a pawn in this dangerous game.

I wouldn't make that kind of a mistake again.

"Hmm, accessing our psyche via a door reserved for mates would explain the alarm sensation," Damien replied. "Your mind would fight the intrusion and blast signals of wrongness, which could be interpreted through sound."

"But how did she paralyze me?"

"Some sort of mental manipulation through the link?" he suggested. "Or it was your body's natural defense to shut down." He hit a few strokes to check the progress on our download. Only sixty percent and we'd been at it for almost ninety minutes. The bitch had a lot of data on her phone.

"Going through the mating link would also explain why Cam hasn't reached out to Iz." I had always assumed he was trying to protect her through some backward approach, and after feeling the pain of the mental intrusion, I fully understood that protection. However, my short-lived experience also indicated it might be literally impossible for him to contact her. "It felt as though my brain had been shut down. All I could do was focus on Lilith's voice."

"We'll have more information as soon as her phone finishes downloading," he said, leaning back in his chair. He'd changed into a black T-shirt and matching pants. Aside from the patch over his left eye—to protect the regeneration and healing process—he appeared as good as new. "Do you think Benita's awake yet?"

I considered the damage he'd done after finding her outside with a knife in her head. "If she is, she's in a great deal of pain," I drawled.

"So sad for her," he replied. "Somehow I don't think this was what she had in mind when she decided to betray us to Lilith."

"You don't think she enjoys waking up to an axe in her stomach?" I asked, feigning surprise.

"I really hope she heals around it."

"So you can you rip it back out of her?" I guessed.

"This is why we're friends," he said, gesturing between us. "You get me."

I stopped pacing to cock my head to the side. "Are we having a moment, Damien?"

"I believe we are."

"Do you require a hug?" I asked, arching a brow.

"I think I'm good."

"Then we are indeed friends," I replied, causing him to smirk. "Want me to go check your freezer for you?" He'd installed a walk-in freezer in the penthouse, equipped with a security panel that had made me drool a little. He really did know how to impress me sometimes.

He considered the offer. "No. I'll check on the contents in a few hours."

"You really do want the axe to adhere to her," I said, amused. He'd strapped Benita to a chair inside to ensure she wouldn't be able to remove the battle axe from her abdomen. That was after he'd handed Willow the knives she'd used to take the female down.

My pet hadn't understood the purpose until he referred to them as trophies with a wink. It'd served as a sign of affection from Damien—a rarity, but well earned.

"It'll make it so much more fun when I walk in to play with her later," Damien said, referring to Benita's positioning.

"How much do you think she knows?" I wondered out loud.

"Hopefully enough to satisfy my bloodlust." He scratched his jaw and shrugged. "Or I'll just keep her alive for fun and visit her whenever I need a workout."

I grunted. "She's in for a world of pain."

He glanced at the sleeping brunette on the couch in the corner, his eyes narrowing slightly. "The bitch deserves it after what she did to Tracey."

I studied the petite female. "You like her."

"She's under my protection," he corrected. "Benita had no right to touch her."

"She showed great loyalty by telling you about Benita's threat," I murmured, walking over to stand near the couch.

Benita had given Tracey the task of drugging Damien, stating that if she didn't comply, Benita would feed the poor girl to Lilith. Rather than buy into the threat, she'd informed Damien of the truth—an admirable and brave thing to do.

Her decision had allowed Damien an opportunity to shoot off a few messages before willingly imbibing the contents. Then he'd sent Tracey to inform Benita that the task was done, and Benita had rewarded the human by turning her into a snack before leaving her up here to die.

She seemed to be recovering now, thanks to a healthy dose of Damien's blood in her system. I'd offered mine, but he'd been adamant about it being his own.

"Do you intend to reward her beyond saving her mortal

life?" I asked him, referring to the option of turning her into an immortal.

"Would you support me if I did?"

I glanced at him. "I always support you."

He nodded but said nothing more. Which meant he was still debating his options. Fair enough.

I palmed the back of my neck again, pacing. The download bar inched ever so slowly, causing my jaw to tick. "How long until the others arrive?"

"They won't be here until later in the morning," Damien said, checking one of his monitors. "They're flying in from all over the world. Rick's helping direct the air traffic, since he insists on working through his recovery."

I smirked. "Typical Rick." He'd called as soon as he woke up, pissed that he'd missed the fight. "It's going to be one hell of a party tomorrow."

"Yep," Damien agreed. "You can go to her, Ryder," he added after another minute. "All the pressing details have been handled, and I'm well enough to monitor the download on my own."

While he was right, I couldn't seem to convince my feet to move toward the door. It felt imperative I remain by his side, not just because of the monumental discoveries lurking in Lilith's files but because I owed this man my time. "It's my duty to oversee this region, and I've not taken it seriously enough. Instead, I left you here to manage everything in my absence, and I nearly lost you as a result of my own selfish choices. It won't happen again."

He lifted his one working eye from the monitor, his expression holding a note of disbelief. "You're fucking with me, right?"

"This isn't something I would joke about."

He huffed out a laugh. "Seriously, this feeling shit isn't for us. You know that."

I didn't share in his humor. "Lilith nearly killed you."

"And she incapacitated you," he tossed back.

"She nearly killed you to hurt me," I rephrased.

"She nearly killed me because she was a psychotic bitch on a power trip," he drawled, pushing away from his desk to stand.

"Look, you put me in charge here because I'm good at it." He moved around his desk to walk toward me. "What's more, you know I enjoy it. If I didn't want to play strategist, I wouldn't. If I didn't want to kill vampires who prey upon children, I wouldn't. And if I didn't want to attend meetings and tell people to fuck off all day, I wouldn't."

He stopped right in front of me, daring me to argue.

"You like to issue edicts and demands, but we both know I only obey the ones I want to obey. I'll fight you when I disagree, just like I'll tell you when I need you. And I'm saying that, right now, I don't need you. So stop being a pansy ass and go fuck your wolf. Because after that display earlier, she's earned a few orgasms. Unless you're entering another century of celibacy? In which case, I'm happy to go take your place. Because that show earlier in the dining hall was hot as hell."

"I don't share," I growled.

"Then go do your damn job," he snapped. "And let me do mine."

I narrowed my eyes at him. "You seem pretty damn good at issuing edicts just fine without me."

"I learned from the best," he countered.

"Yeah. You did." I grabbed his shoulder and pulled him into a hug, which earned me an annoyed grunt from Damien. But I didn't care. "Don't ever let yourself get captured again," I told him, meaning it.

He relaxed slightly, just not enough to return the embrace. "Save the emotions for your pet."

I laughed and released him. "Get caught again and I'll kill you myself. Better?"

"Yep."

I shook my head. "Do you want me to check in on the

324

cleaners downstairs?"

He gave me a look like I'd lost my mind. "Are you playing a game of delayed gratification? Is that the purpose of this inane questioning?"

"I'm trying to help, jackass."

"You'll help me more by going back to Willow and letting me do my job without your mothering." He returned to his seat in a huff, his annoyance palpable. But I caught the hint of a smile on his lips as well. "If you need a task to feel useful, then go thank your wolf for me. Tell her I appreciate being alive so I can continue being your bitch for eternity."

"Funny," I said.

"Actually, I'm considering a new job as a comedian," he replied without missing a beat. "Will you serve as a reference?"

"Of course."

"Excellent." He refocused on his screen. "And don't ever hug me again."

"You enjoyed it."

He flashed me a look of mock concern. "If you consider that enjoyment, then perhaps I do need to go tend to Willow on your behalf. I'd hate for you to inflict the same mediocre level of enjoyment on her, especially after everything she accomplished tonight."

"Keep doubting my sex life and I'll make you watch."

"You say that like it would be a punishment," he drawled.

"It would if I didn't allow you to join in," I tossed back, heading for the door. "And for the record, you're not invited to join in. Ever."

"Ryder," he called as I stepped through the threshold.

I popped my head back in and cocked a brow. "Yes?"

"For the record," he repeated slowly, "I would have missed you, too."

I stared at him for a moment, seeing the absolute

sincerity in his features, and dipped my chin in acknowledgment.

There really wasn't anything more to say, so I left him to manage the rest of the download. We'd talk more about the assignments later. Regardless of his opinion, it had been wrong of me to leave him here to do this on his own.

I was the royal of this region now, and I needed to truly take charge.

Because the queen bitch was dead.

Now all hell was about to break loose.

And I couldn't fucking wait.

Chapter Thirty-Five

Willow

A jolt of heat spiked through my core, drawing me from the cocoon of blankets around me. My wolf prowled behind my senses, her growl a vibration in my chest that I couldn't contain.

Ryder.

His presence overwhelmed me, his minty essence infiltrating my every breath.

He's here.

But I couldn't see him, the cloud of silk around me disrupting my view.

"Did you just growl at me, pet?" he asked, his tone holding a dangerous edge that had my thighs clenching.

The mattress dipped to my left, followed by the sheets

softly drawing over my skin to reveal me to the predator looming over me. I inhaled his aroma, his fragrance giving me new life.

Shampoo.

Droplets of water.

And the heat of a very aroused male.

They all mingled together to create the most intoxicating cologne.

I reached for him, needing more, but he caught my wrists in his hand and pulled them over my head. "Stay," he said, continuing the process of removing the silky fabric to expose every inch of my naked skin. "Is this gift for me?" he asked, referring to my nudity.

"Yes," I whispered.

"Mmm, good girl," he praised, leaning down to kiss my mound.

I trembled at the touch, my body on fire from his mere existence. That he decided to lick a path to my hip only heightened my need.

"Ryder," I moaned, nearly reaching for him again. But his eyes glinted up at me in the dark, his inner beast issuing a challenge with that look. I almost wanted to test him, just to see what he would do.

"I wouldn't," he murmured, reading my intent.

"Why not?"

"I'll bite," he promised.

My nipples hardened at the prospect, my legs tensing. "Oh, that sounds like a reward, not a punishment," I pointed out.

He grazed my upper thigh with his teeth. "A reward?" he repeated, his mouth skimming my slick folds. "Do you deserve a reward, Willow?"

My heart began to pound. "Yes."

His smoldering irises grinned up at me. "I agree, pet."

I groaned as he pierced me with his tongue, his palms gliding up and down my legs as he settled between them.

There was something different about his touch. It was more potent than usual. More intense. More reverent.

I arched into him, his mouth an intimate kiss that shattered my thoughts, forcing me to focus completely on him.

He took me so entirely, his aura consuming me from the inside out.

I felt owned and protected, cherished and respected, devoured and *loved*.

My eyes flashed open—I couldn't even say when they had closed—my chest beating a chaotic rhythm.

That was the difference.

Emotion.

It had always been there before, underlying every touch and kiss, but now he was allowing me to truly experience it. Or perhaps he was finally allowing himself to feel it.

I stared down at him, mystified and enamored all at once, my pleasure exploding on a surge of rapture that left me panting and dizzy beneath him. My cheeks were damp from it, my lashes lined with unshed tears.

It all hit me so suddenly that I stopped functioning.

And then he was there, kissing me, his lips a gentle worship against my own, allowing me to taste the arousal on his tongue.

"Shh," he whispered, nuzzling me and adoring me and making me feel light-headed all over again.

What is this sensation? I wondered, floating in a cloud of erotic mist with Ryder as my only guide.

My wolf stretched inside me, content.

My vampire merely accepted what she considered to be obvious.

And my former human, who I realized was still very much a part of me, stared at the wondrous man caging me beneath his strong, very naked body.

"Mine," he said simply, drawing his teeth along my lower lip.

"Mine," I agreed, glancing between his dark eyes, still stunned by the emotions rolling off him.

He kissed me again, his cock nudging my entrance. "Wrap your legs around me," he demanded, pressing into me.

I squeezed him with my thighs, my ankles locking behind his back as he slammed home.

"Hold on," he said, his voice gruff.

I grabbed his shoulders, my nails piercing his skin as he slid out only to violently thrust back into me. "*Ryder.*"

"More," he returned, picking up his pace and taking me with a ferocity I had never seen in him before.

He pistoned into me, his need a darkness that threatened to consume us both. I encouraged it—*welcomed* it—and held him to me while lifting my hips to meet his.

It was savage, animalistic insanity.

I drew blood.

He bit my neck, nibbled my chin, and recaptured my mouth.

It was hard.

Fast.

Harsh.

And stunningly perfect.

His beast had taken over, forcing me to feel his yearning, his claim, his need to keep me.

"Forever," I heard Ryder whisper, the reverence in his tone a kiss to my senses. "*Mate.*"

My inner walls clamped around him, that word one I recognized to my very soul. "*Mate,*" I echoed, coming apart beneath him in a climax that blanketed my vision in shades of black. His teeth sealed around my shoulder, biting down in a way that made my wolf howl in approval.

I sank my teeth into his shoulder as well, moaning at the taste of his blood on my tongue. He growled my name, his orgasm erupting inside me in a pulsing wave of heat and bliss. His tremors rivaled mine, both of us breathing heavily.

And then we were kissing each other as though our lives depended on it.

His air became mine.

My air became his.

Our bodies were already moving again, his shaft still hard and virile inside. He rolled onto his back to let me ride him. Then later he rolled me beneath him again to plunge deep inside me. And eventually he sat up, forcing me to straddle him as he slowed the pace and stared into my eyes.

I vaguely noticed the sun, realizing we'd been doing this for hours and hours.

But I couldn't stop.

Nor did I even want to try.

I felt connected to him. Branded. Entirely possessed.

His arms came around me as I circled mine around his neck, our tongues dueling in a lazy kiss that matched our rhythm below. He'd come inside me countless times, just as I'd fallen into ecstasy over and over again.

But this pace had nothing to do with pleasure. We were merely existing together, our bodies marrying one another in a dance only known to mates.

I didn't fully understand it. However, my hybrid nature did.

We were creating an eternal vow to each other.

Born of an emotion I never truly understood until I met Ryder—*love*.

I loved Rae and Silas as my sister and brother.

But Ryder I loved as something *more*.

My other half.

My soul's ideal connection.

My wolf's beast.

He kissed me softly, his tongue whispering the words back to me as we came together in unison, our bodies exhausted and depleted yet renewed and full. I started to cry, the sensation almost too much. He drew his lips over my skin, absorbing each tear as though it were his due, then he eased us back onto the bed again with me beneath him once more.

"You know what this means, right?" he asked me, his voice a low, masculine purr to my senses.

"You're keeping me," I told him, palming his cheek.

"I am," he said, smiling down at me. "My forever pet."

"I'm not calling you my master," I murmured, yawning. It seemed like the right reply, mostly because my wolf refused to be completely tamed.

He chuckled. "You will if I tell you to."

"Mmm," I hummed, neither agreeing nor disagreeing.

"You're magnificent, Willow." He drew his lips across my cheek to my ear. "And I'm not just talking about the sex."

I smiled, my eyes falling closed. "You're magnificent, too." I yawned again. "And I am talking about the sex."

He laughed this time, the sound a rumble from his chest to mine, making my legs clench around him. "You intrigue me, pet," he said, playing on one of our first conversations.

"That's good," I whispered. "I rather like being alive."

His lips curled against my cheek. "I like you being alive, too."

"Then I guess I need another hammer."

"Going to try to hit me with it?" he mused.

Probably not. "Yes," I said instead.

"Good." His nose skimmed my jaw. "Try not to miss this time."

"I won't."

He rolled off of me to draw me into his side, my head using his shoulder as a pillow. My bite mark on the opposite side hadn't started to heal yet, pleasing me in the darkest sense. *Mine.*

"I love you, Willow," he whispered, his lips pressing into my forehead. "In case that wasn't clear."

"It was," I assured him, grinning. "I love you, too."

"Get some sleep," he added. "I have a surprise coming

for you tonight."

"A surprise?"

"You'll see, sweet pet," he promised. "Now dream of me."

"I don't need to dream," I told him. "Not anymore."

Because he was my dream. I just hadn't known it. And now that I had him, I'd never let him go.

He was the light at the edge of my dreams, that little glimmer of hope I was too scared to believe in. So I ran to the nightmares instead, hardening my heart to prepare for the world around me.

It was still a violent existence.

Monsters continued to lurk in the shadows.

And the world wouldn't brighten overnight.

But I had a beast in my corner now.

My royal. My prince. My Ryder.

My star in an otherwise dark night.

I would forever reach for him.

Just as I knew he would forever light my path.

My eyes fell closed.

No dreams.

Only my reality.

With my forever mate.

* * *

I woke sometime later to the sensation of a finger drifting across my jaw. My eyes blinked open to find Ryder standing above me, dressed in an all-black suit. "Your surprise is here," he whispered.

"What?" I asked, my mind fuzzy from sleeping for what felt like too long. A glance out the windows showcased a pitch-black night with the city lights gleaming all around. I much preferred the view from his house, something about the isolation calling to me.

"Go have a shower. Then you'll understand," he said

softly, his thumb tracing my lower lip.

"Are you joining me?"

"Mmm, an offer I'd love to accept, but I have company to attend to." He leaned down to kiss me softly before pressing his lips to my ear. "And so, my darling pet, do you."

I frowned, not understanding.

Then my nose twitched.

We had company in the suite.

"Silas," I recognized, smiling.

"Yes, he's here," he replied, a secret twinkling in his gaze. "Go shower, pet. You'll see."

I blamed a night of fucking and my groggy state for missing the obvious. Because it wasn't until I'd showered, changed, and walked into the living room that I finally caught on to the *surprise* he had in store.

She stood in the middle of the living room, her familiar red hair glistening beneath the lights, as she turned to greet me with a smile I felt to my very soul. "Rae!" I ran to her, throwing my arms around her neck and holding on for dear life. She broke the second we touched, her shoulders shaking as we embraced in a sea of silent tears, our misery turning to joyous disbelief.

Silas watched from the side of the room, his own eyes holding a glimmer that said he understood.

Because he did.

We all did.

It was that unspoken feeling between us, that knowledge that we would never see each other again after Blood Day. Yet we never actually said it. We refused to acknowledge it. But it was there, that dreaded feeling of our pending separation and subsequent deaths. And it came true the second they called my number, gave me a designation, and sent me off to the breeding camps to die.

We couldn't show our fear that day.

We were forced to hide our tears.

But we could shed them now.

And we did. For each other. For our past. For our future. We were alive.

Together.

And immortal.

It was the miracle we never could have anticipated, an impossibility that floored all of us now. Our tears turned to smiles, blossoming into laughs. And then the three of us were hugging, our trio flourishing with renewed friendship, underlined in *hope*.

"I can't believe you're here," Rae finally said, grabbing my cheeks as though to convince herself I was alive. "And a *hybrid*? What's that like?"

"Oh, no. I want to hear about being Kylan's *Erosita*," I said. Silas had told me all about Rae's relationship with the infamous royal, but now I wanted to hear it from her.

"I imagine it's similar to being Ryder's mate," she replied, arching a brow. "That's what he called you when I arrived this morning."

"Did he?" I asked, my cheeks warming. It was one thing for him to say it to me, another to refer to me in that manner to others.

"His exact words were, 'You. Upstairs. My mate wants to see you,'" Silas said, doing a horrible impersonation of Ryder's voice. "Apparently, I'm also mandated to be here. He informed me I am to visit monthly at a minimum."

My lips twitched. "That sounds like Ryder."

"Edon wasn't amused," Silas replied.

"Neither was Kylan," Rae agreed.

"'My Raelyn has a name,'" Silas said, deepening his voice and giving it a slight accent.

Rae frowned at him. "You do not have a future in impersonations."

He lifted a shoulder. "I'll just keep being an Enforcer, then."

Rae and I both nodded, agreeing that was a much better path for him.

"Oh, you need to meet Juliet," Rae said.

"Juliet?" I repeated.

"Darius's *Erosita*," she replied. "He's Jace's sovereign. Sort of a scary, broody vampire—"

"Says the female mated to Kylan," Silas drawled.

"But she's really sweet," Rae continued. "She's a blood virgin."

"What's a blood virgin?" I'd never heard of such a thing.

"A human with a unique blood type. They're raised at a completely separate school, then auctioned off to the wealthier vampires." She pinched her lips to the side. "She's a little different from us. Softer. More accepting?"

"She was raised to be a fuck toy for vampires," Silas muttered. "That had to be hell on her mind."

"We were raised to want to kill each other all in the name of immortality," Rae reminded him flatly. "That *was* hell on our minds."

I snorted in agreement.

Rae waved it off and began telling me more about Juliet—someone she'd apparently been spending a lot of time with—and her odd relationship with Darius. Unlike Ryder, Darius *did* share Juliet. At least her blood. Typically, with Jace.

Hearing his name brought up memories of my turning, so I told Rae about what had happened.

Then we lost ourselves in a conversation underlined in storytelling, all three of us bringing one another up to speed, sharing things we'd learned, and explaining how we'd ended up in certain places.

By the end, I felt almost human again.

Yet not.

Because unlike when I was human, I actually smiled now.

And laughed.

And genuinely enjoyed myself.

All because I tried to fight two vampires while dying

from a wolf bite.

Two vampires I ended up saving just last night.

By taking down the Goddess herself.

How's that for a twist of events? I mused. *So what the fuck comes next?*

Epilogue

Ryder

I glanced at my phone, checking on Willow again, and smiled as she chatted animatedly with her friends.

Kylan peered over my shoulder. "Stalker," he muttered. But I caught the happiness in his gaze at seeing Rae.

"Not all of us have telepathic links to our mates," I said, putting away my phone.

"Yes, it's quite strange to me that you can't speak to her. I was able to talk to Silas after giving him my blood nearly two months ago."

Edon growled at the mention of the incident, which I assumed was in relation to his mate being shot by a silver bullet and nearly dying as a result. Kylan's blood had saved him.

"I've never possessed telepathy as a gift," I admitted. "I

338

suppose the Almighty decided I was blessed enough in looks, skill, and other areas that I didn't require the additional compensation."

Kylan smirked. "I've always adored your wit, even when improperly applied."

"There was nothing improper about it." I lifted my ankle to place it over my opposite knee, then fixed my gaze on Jace, who sat at the head of the table. "I see you're in charge again."

"It appears to be my role of late." He didn't sound very pleased about it. "But as I'm the only one who seems keen on deciding a path forward, I'll be taking that job until someone else says otherwise."

I glanced at Kylan again. "You want to lead?"

"Nope." His lips popped on the *p* sound.

"Neither do I," I said conversationally. "That would leave Jace as next in line."

"It would," he agreed. "Everyone else is too young."

"Age isn't always the deciding factor in leadership," Darius piped up.

"Are you saying you want to lead, then?" I asked him.

"Absolutely not," he replied.

"Then your comment is invalid. Anyone else?" I asked, glancing around the group of vampires and lycans.

We had representation from all over the globe, our group barely fitting in this conference room meant for thirty.

I was actually impressed to realize Jace had so many immortals on his side for this rebellion. Together we represented three of the now seventeen vampire regions— I no longer counted Lilith's former territory—and three of the seventeen clan countries.

That might not have seemed like good odds, but the age and experience in this room said otherwise.

There were also several gray areas on the map of regions or clans Luka and Jace suspected might fall to our side in the case of an eventual war—one I'd accelerated by removing Lilith's head.

However, that had worked well in our favor because we were now in possession of every detail we could possibly desire about the existing council.

We'd spent two hours today going through all her notes on each leader, flagging the alphas and royals she held the biggest contentions with as ones for us to pursue for potential recruitment.

Now we all glanced around, agreeing without a vote on Jace's clear leadership role. While I wouldn't admit it out loud, I could quietly say, *He was born for this.*

Because he was.

He possessed an even-keeled approach, and his penchant for playing the political game was evident in how he'd handled himself the last century and a half. He was also genuinely well liked, even by those who were among Lilith's strongest allies.

"All right, leader," I said to him. "What do we do now?"

"We find that lab," he replied, referring to the one Lilith had clearly been running experiments out of. "And we find Cam."

"Does he come equipped with a wizard gown and a wand?" Kylan asked. "Because we'll need that for the next council meeting."

I smirked, amused. Because he had a point. All Jace kept harping on was finding Cam, as though he would magically appear with all the answers. And while I wanted to find him—especially after learning what Lilith had done to him—I didn't see how that would solve any of our problems.

"I was under her telepathic thrall for less than thirty minutes," I said. "It gave me a taste of what Cam's been going through. Trust me when I say he's not going to be of sound mind when you locate him."

It had taken me hours to get rid of that odd sensation in my head. I couldn't imagine what it would be like for someone suffering from that intrusion for over a century.

Jace nodded, confirming he'd heard both comments. "We have two options. We can either preemptively inform the world of Lilith's demise or we can wait until the council meeting. There are merits to both options. The former allows the others to come to grips with the reality before we see them. The latter gives us the element of surprise."

"Why are we even discussing attending?" I asked, slightly miffed by the very notion of giving in to Lilith's political bullshit for one more minute of my life. "Do we consider ourselves part of her council? Or is this our council?"

Jace's icy blue eyes met mine, a challenge in his depths. "Do you feel we have enough allies in this room to take them down and provoke change?"

"I think we have enough allies in this room to make them consider a discussion regarding change," I countered.

"It's a fair consideration," Ivan informed us. He sat beside Darius. We'd met briefly at the beginning of all this. Jace had introduced him as a political advisor of sorts. Apparently, he had a foreign policy background in the old world.

"Go on," Kylan said, clearly unconvinced. "Tell me how six leaders will fare against twenty-eight."

"That's twenty percent of their council. But more importantly, we have three of the oldest vampires on our side. And there's power in age, as I believe you're quite familiar with," Ivan returned.

Damien gave me a look from across the table, one that said, *I like him.*

I tilted my chin in agreement. The vampire had courage. I valued courage.

"On the lycan side, we're less top-heavy," Luka said. "Logan and Edon are new alphas. Jolene has been out of the game for several centuries. And my word may sway some, but not all of them." He steepled his long fingers together on the mahogany wood, leaning forward.

"However," he continued, "Lilith's telepathic technology indicates she used lycans to create it, something

I doubt my brethren will approve of. If we can find further proof of that, you'll win over the lycan vote."

"Which brings us back to finding the lab," Jace said. "And Cam."

Silence fell, everyone considering the next play.

"Can we keep her death a secret until the next council meeting?" Darius finally asked. "Is that even feasible?"

"We have her phone," Damien replied. "We can continue to communicate on her behalf. I can also build something to resemble her voice, should someone call."

"A Lilith AI," I said, shuddering.

Damien's lips twitched. "Is that the upgrade you had in mind?"

"Do you want me to burn the building down?" I asked him.

"You two should date," Kylan interjected.

"He's not my type," Damien said. "His pet, however…"

I growled at him. "Careful."

"Can we postpone the council meeting?" Edon asked suddenly. "To give us more time to find the lab? You have her phone. Couldn't you just send out a blast saying she needs to move it to next month? Say she's dealing with Ryder and his bullshit here, or cleaning up his mess and working with him. Whatever's believable."

"The two of us working together would not be believable," I put in.

"It would if Willow can play the role of Goddess," Luna said from beside Edon. She'd remained quiet for most of the discussion, but she was very much aware.

"Elaborate," Jace said.

"She's blonde. Tall for a female. Similar figure. Put her in the right clothes, only show her from behind, keep her away from the crowds, and you have a glimpse of a Goddess."

Several of us gaped at the woman, including myself. Then I laughed. Because it was fucking brilliant in the most immoral and depraved sense. Which, of course, made me love it. "I can almost feel Lilith rolling over in her… well… the freezer. No grave yet. Or coffin."

"That might actually work," Damien said, ignoring me. "I could capture some photos and leak them. We can have her in Ryder's office when he goes to meet with others in the conference room. He'd just need to shut the blinds as he leaves to give her privacy—something Lilith would demand. For a few weeks? We could totally pull this off."

"While Jace and I search for the labs in Chicago," Darius said.

"That also gives us time to reach out to a few of the members on Lilith's unhappy list," Jace added.

"Let me do that," Kylan said. "Everyone knows I'm dissatisfied with Lilith already. It won't come as a shock when I call and say vile things about her."

Jace nodded. "Meanwhile, Luka, Logan, and Edon can start working on the clans closest to home. Find out what their pain points are. And, Jolene, it's time to start reaching out to your older contacts who might be willing to help inspire a revolution within their clans earlier than expected."

"That's why you turned out halfway decent," I said, looking at Edon. "Jolene kept you in line."

Edon grunted at me, obviously still sour at my commanding his Enforcer up to my room earlier. Well, he'd just have to get over it. Willow needed her friends.

And I needed her.

I checked my phone again to find her no longer in the suite. Frowning, I searched the hallway to see it empty as well.

"Does she know you stalk her?" Kylan asked, looking over my shoulder again.

"Where'd they take her?" I demanded.

Kylan nodded toward the glass doors to where the three of them were approaching. "I told Raelyn they might want to venture upstairs so Willow could agree to the asinine plan of impersonating the Goddess."

"It's not asinine," Luna fired back.

"It's brilliant," Edon assured her.

"I didn't mean to imply it won't work; it's just a lot to ask of a recently turned hybrid who will have to mask her scent everywhere she goes in that stench Lilith referred to as a perfume."

"It really was horrible," I agreed.

"I know," Kylan replied. "You would think she'd have chosen a more attractive scent. I mean, particularly as she essentially conquered the world."

"There's just no accounting for taste," I told him.

"Sadly, true," he murmured as the doors opened. Rae entered first, walking straight to Kylan to sit in the empty seat on the other side of him.

Willow didn't appear as certain, her surprise at finding herself in a room full of vampires and lycans palpable. I stood to offer her my chair, as there weren't enough in the room, while Silas wandered over to stand behind Edon and Luna. His smirk told me he was communicating mentally with his triad, a trait I now envied.

"Come, mate," I said to Willow, holding my hand out for her.

Her eyes smiled at my chosen nickname. I still intended to call her my pet as well, but in this room right now, I needed her title known so they understood she was my partner and equal.

Rather than sit, she stood beside me, allowing me to wrap my arm around her lower back. "Rae mentioned you needed me." She spoke softly and only to me, not to the room.

"We want to dress you up as Lilith," Kylan drawled. "For some photo ops."

Her eyes grew. "What?" She looked at him, then back to me.

"Only from behind," I told her. Then I elaborated on Luna's plan—in a far better way than Kylan had—and included why we wanted her to pretend to be Lilith. By the end of my explanation, Willow seemed a little more comfortable.

"Oh. That makes sense," she agreed, nodding. "I can try, yes."

"Then we have the beginning of a plan," Jace announced, seemingly satisfied.

"There's one small issue to discuss," Damien interjected, his focus shifting to Luka. I knew what he was going to say because he'd given me the detail earlier. It hadn't surprised me, considering what Lilith had said last night. "You have a spy in your clan feeding information to Lilith. I have the name and information saved for your review. The culprit was feeding details to Lilith about my sister."

Luka's eyebrow shot up. "Lilith knew about Izzy?"

"Yes," I replied. "She told me last night that she uses the information to taunt Cam."

Silence fell again.

Darius and Jace shared a long look, their mutual concern evident.

"He won't be the same man you knew," I warned them. "I can't properly explain to you the sensation of having her in your head like that. Just… expect him to be violent when you release him from the technology."

They both nodded, saying nothing more.

"I think we're done for now," Kylan said.

"Yes," several others agreed.

"Walk with me to my office," Damien told Luka. "We'll talk."

I didn't recognize the name of the culprit in his clan, but I imagined it would be a difficult discussion. No one enjoyed identifying a traitor. Case in point, Benita. She was still very much alive in Damien's freezer, keeping Lilith's corpse company. Seemed appropriate enough to me.

"It wasn't Mikael, was it?" Kylan asked suddenly.

Damien frowned at him. "Who?"

"The traitor in Majestic Clan," Kylan clarified.

"Oh, no," Damien replied. "Why?"

"Just ensuring I didn't make a grievous error in

judgment," Kylan replied.

"He's acclimating quite well," Luka said, giving Kylan a gentle grin. "I'll update you on him later, if you like."

"I might, yes," Kylan said, his attention shifting to Rae. She smiled at him and reached out to squeeze his hand. They were talking to each other in their minds, making me envious all over again.

Yet as I looked down at Willow, I realized that it wasn't really needed at all. Because we read each other in different ways. Through our eyes and our bodies. Like now, I could tell she wanted me to pull her closer and kiss her, so I did. And her resulting sigh told me it was exactly the right thing to do.

"Thank you for my surprise," she murmured.

"You're welcome." I cupped her face between my palms, staring deep into her pretty blue gaze. "My shoulder still stings from your bite."

She grinned. "Good."

"I thought you might feel that way." My feisty little mate and her possessive wolf seemed to enjoy marking me. Fortunately, my inner beast liked it, too. "Did you find a hammer?" I asked her.

"Not yet."

"Hmm, that's too bad," I drawled. "I think I might be getting bored after all."

She narrowed her eyes. "Do I need to bite your other shoulder?"

"How about something a little lower? But not too harshly."

Blue fire danced in her gaze. "I might like that."

"Me, too."

The clearing of a throat reminded me that we had an audience. But I couldn't give two fucks that they'd overheard. We all had our kinks. Mine just happened to involve drawing blood.

"I told you the danger is intoxicating," Jace murmured, a wicked glint in his gaze.

"It certainly makes me feel alive," I returned, recalling his comment. "Come on, mate. I think we're done here for now."

We'd keep the charade alive for the time being. Allow the world to think Lilith still lived.

Then it would be on Jace to inform them all of the truth.

I paused at the door, glancing at him over my shoulder. "'King Jace' has a nice ring to it. Or will you prefer 'God' when you take over the council?"

"Don't even joke about that," he returned, not at all amused.

"Who said I was joking?"

He scowled.

I grinned.

King Jace.

Yeah, I could respect that.

"Good luck," I told him. "You're going to need it."

The Story Continues with Kingly Bitten...

KINGLY BITTEN

Once upon a time, humankind ruled the world while lycans and vampires lived in secret.

This is no longer that time.

Calina

I have thirty-six hours to live.
Thirty-six hours to find a solution.
Thirty-six hours to kill them all.

My friends. My family. My subjects.

It's a cruel fate, one my maker subjected me to over a century ago when she placed me in this hell. I learned then that freedom is a falsehood. Escape doesn't exist. I'm a ticking time bomb, slated to erupt.

Until *he* appears from above. A vampire. A walking god with icy blue eyes. He claims to be our salvation, but I see him for who he really is—the devil in disguise.

Jace

I don't want to be king, but I'll become one if it means I can have *her*—the gorgeous ice queen I found waiting for me inside Lilith's labs. She feigns indifference, claiming I do nothing for her, but I see the embers stirring in her stunning hazel eyes.

Only there's more to her than a pretty little face.
She's neither vampire nor lycan.
An immortal without a classification.
A secret I must now contain in a world collapsing in chaos.

Welcome to the new beginning.
My name's King Jace. Allow me to be your guide…

ACKNOWLEDGMENTS

Wow, where do I even start?

This book nearly killed me.

That sounds like a joke, but it's probably not.

In full disclosure, this was not an easy experience, but Ryder really pulled me through. His voice is probably one of my favorites. I just want to talk to him all day. Maybe that makes me a little crazy? Ryder says it's fine, though, and I tend to do whatever that man tells me.

I'll summarize with this: deadlines suck.

I would not have survived this one without the help of Katie and Jean and their alpha-reading eyes. They helped me keep Ryder in line—actually, that's a lie; there's no keeping that man in line—but they tried to help!

And then Bethany, my editor extraordinaire, helped edit this in pieces… again. Sorry. I firmly blame Ryder. Have I mentioned how chatty that man is? We tossed out whole pieces of his outline. There was an entire sequence I had to delete because he would not stop talking! And he still wants anal. The damn man. Maybe I'll write a bonus scene.

Ryder: Correction. You will write a bonus scene.
Me: Shh. This is quiet time now, Ryder. Your book is done.
Ryder: Oh, human. Have you learned nothing?

Do you see what I'm dealing with here? I mean, my God, that man is something else.

Anyway…

Thank you, Katie, Jean, and Bethany, for helping me pull this together. A special thank-you to Joy for beta-reading and helping me feel better about the content. A HUGE thank-you to Louise, Diane, Kathy, and Chas for keeping my brand and name alive while I disappeared for weeks on end.

Thank you to my readers for being there for me, sending me positive notes, reviewing, commenting, and providing me with daily encouragement to continue. I love you all and really enjoy chatting in Foss's Night Owls!

Thank you, Tracey, for letting me use your name. Jace sends his love. And apparently, so does Damien. Your friendship means the world to me. Sorry Meghan whipped you. Also sorry Benita tried to kill you. I'm starting to think I might not be a very good friend. Um, oops? Sorry!

Thank you to my ARC team for being patient with me and my last-minute ARCs.

And last, but certainly not least, thank you, Matt, for putting up with this crazy dream of mine. I love you. You're my forever mate. <3

Until next time, y'all…

Who's ready for Jace?

ABOUT THE AUTHOR

USA Today Bestselling Author Lexi C. Foss loves to play in dark worlds, especially the ones that bite. She lives in Atlanta, Georgia, with her husband and their furry children. When not writing, she's busy crossing items off her travel bucket list or chasing eclipses around the globe. She's quirky, consumes way too much coffee, and loves to swim.